THE BATHROOM

NEW AND EXPANDED EDITION

THE VIKING PRESS NEW YORK

THE BATHROOM

ALEXANDER KIRA

First published in 1976 in a hardbound and paperbound edition by The Viking Press, Inc.
625 Madison Avenue, New York, N.Y. 10022
Published simultaneously in Canada by
The Macmillan Company of Canada Limited
Published by arrangement with Bantam Books, Inc.

LIBRARY OF CONGRESS CATALOGING IN PUBLICATION DATA

Kira, Alexander.
The bathroom.
Includes index.
1. Bathrooms. 2. Plumbing—Equipment and supplies.
3. Human engineering. I. Title.
TH6488.K5 1976 747'.76 75-19052
ISBN 0-670-14897-0
ISBN 0-670-00612-2 pbk

Printed in U.S.A.

ACKNOWLEDGMENT
Little, Brown and Co.: From "Splash!" from *Verses from 1929* by Ogden Nash. Copyright 1935 by The Curtis Publishing Company. Reprinted by permission of Little, Brown and Co.

This book was composed at University Graphics, Inc., on the VIP, in 9-point Helvetica, with other sizes for display lines. It was printed at The Book Press.

TO PHILIP
AND HELEN

PREFACE TO THE NEW EDITION

The present volume, founded on the first edition of this work published in 1966, which reported on the seven-year research project carried out at what was then the Center for Housing and Environmental Studies at Cornell University, has been extensively revised and considerably enlarged in scope on the basis of almost a decade of continuing study. The original material has been reorganized, revised, and amplified. Two major new parts have been added: one that deals with the particular problems posed by public facilities and one that examines some of the unique personal hygiene problems faced by aged and disabled persons. In addition, completely new illustrations have been prepared which, it is hoped, are clearer, more thorough, and more natural than seemed possible a decade ago. A limited number of photographs of current products have also been included to illustrate the response the industry has begun to make over the past several years.

The focus of this second edition remains, as before, upon the examination of our personal hygiene needs from the following viewpoints: our attitudes toward personal hygiene activities and the facilities we use to accommodate them; our basic physiological requirements; our patterns of performing the necessary actions; and the development of design criteria to fulfill those needs. The emphasis remains essentially on "what" to provide; the consideration of such "how" problems as hydraulics, sanitary engineering, manufacturing technology, and building codes I leave to others far more competent in these areas than I am.

The likelihood of fully realizing the substantive improvements described and suggested in the following pages depends very much on the consumer's level of concern and willingness to demand and pay for more rational, more convenient, and safer solutions. As has been amply demonstrated time and time again, a society can have anything it cares enough about and is willing to pay for. I observed previously that the ultimate responsibility for a rational approach to personal hygiene rests not only with the producers but also with the architects, the builders, and consumers —in fact, with all of us. The producers must be willing to continue the development of sound and useful products and to promote their availability directly to the ultimate user—who, unfortunately, is most generally not the purchaser. Perhaps most important, the architects and builders—who actually are the purchasers and who actually are responsible for the design of our bathrooms—must begin to think of hygiene facilities as an important part of the home and as an important aspect of our daily lives rather than as a necessary evil to be accommodated according to the dictates of some obsolete handbook or drawing template in whatever space is left over with whatever part of the budget is minimally required to meet legal standards. The ultimate tragedy is that here, as in so many other aspects of human existence, all too many of us have allowed our taboos and guilts to interfere with the fullest development and realization of our physical and mental well-being.

Over the years that I have been studying the problems of personal hygiene and its accommodations, I have been privileged to receive invaluable help, advice, and encouragement from hundreds of persons the world over; persons who contributed richly of their time, of themselves, and of their institutional resources. It is impossible even to begin to identify them all, but to all I am profoundly grateful and deeply appreciative.

To Doris Schwartz and Ruth Stryker, however, I owe a particular debt of gratitude for their longstanding interest, their encouragement, and their very special determination and skill in educating me in some of the subtleties of the personal hygiene problems of the aged and the disabled.

I also want especially to thank those persons who directly assisted me in the preparation of this second edition and who made the task a pleasure instead of a burden: Julia M. Smyth for her dedication and her painstaking research, checking and rechecking of endless details, and her editorial judgment; Esther Dickson and Jean Warholic for their expert typing and willingness to work at all hours; my good friend Jan V. White for his enthusiasm and invaluable counsel on the design and preparation of the new illustrations; Gertrude and C. Hadley Smith for their professionalism and dedication in printing hundreds of photographs in the face of seemingly impossible deadlines; my colleague Richard H. Penner for his expert preparation of the drawings; my good friend Humen Tan for his professional renderings of the suggested approaches to fixtures; and my models for their patience, interest, trust, and unselfconscious performance of very personal activities.

I also wish to extend my especial thanks and appreciation to the following firms for graciously supplying me with photographs of some of their recent products and, in particular, for *making* products that reflect some of our shared concerns: Adamsez, Ltd., American Standard, Armitage Shanks, Ltd., Buderus'sche Eisenwerke, Butzke-Werke AG, Closomat Sanitär-Apparatebau, Jacob Delafon, Eljer Co., Hansa Metallwerke AG, Kohler Co., Olsonite Co., Röhm GmbH Chemische Fabrik, Villeroy-Boch Keramische Werke KG. In this regard, I also wish to express my very sincere apologies to those other manufacturers of sanitaryware around the world whose products equally merit inclusion but, unfortunately and sometimes painfully, could not be included, given the limitations of space and budget.

And, of course, I must thank once again all those persons and institutions who made the original study possible, without which foundation the present work could not have come into being.

Finally, I would like to recognize all those persons who wittingly or unwittingly contributed to my investigations. Some are anonymous to me; some prefer to remain anonymous to you. To all I would like to express my appreciation.

Alexander Kira

Ithaca, New York
May 1974

CONTENTS

LIST OF ILLUSTRATIONS

THE BATHROOM

PART ONE

PERSONAL HYGIENE FACILITIES

The development of design criteria for the major personal hygiene activities (body cleansing and elimination) must be based on the analysis of each of these activities in terms of the following: first, the complex cultural and psychological attitudes surrounding the subject—attitudes that influence our hygiene practices and our reactions to equipment; second, the basic physiological and anatomical considerations; and lastly, the physical or "human engineering" problems of performing the activity. As we are well aware, man may know what is good for him, but his response to this knowledge, more often than not, is determined by other, more subjective considerations—which tend to be variable, contradictory, and fleeting, but which are also potent forces in molding design decisions. Physical man, on the other hand, remains fairly constant; that is, his physical capabilities, limitations, and biological needs, though variable, are essentially the same the world over and essentially the same as they were thousands of years ago.

Thus, although this study has attempted to be scrupulously objective, on the one hand, in its explorations of physiological processes, anatomy, and anthropometry, it has, on the other hand, been quite deliberately conceived within the framework of contemporary Western culture. Consequently, the discussion that follows represents, to a certain extent, a compromise between realities as they exist and as they are defined with our time/place setting. Some of the personal hygiene practices of other places or times could seriously be recommended as being more desirable from the standpoint of either health or physiology—*if* our values, ideals, and way of life reflected the same cultural attitudes as those under which the practices evolved. As the discussion will show, however, there are almost as many psychological and cultural problems to be solved in developing design criteria as there are purely physiological or functional ones, and in some instances, it may almost be said that *the* problems to be solved are the psychological and cultural ones.

HISTORICAL ASPECTS OF PERSONAL HYGIENE FACILITIES

1

Man has always and everywhere been faced with the same fundamental problems of personal hygiene that concern us today. The ways in which he has coped with them have, however, varied enormously, not only from one culture to another but also from one era to another. While available technology has certainly played a role in this, by far the most important determinants have been our various philosophical, psychological, and religious attitudes regarding the human body and its processes and products. These attitudes are not only central to our conceptions of ourselves as human beings but are also held strongly and are often embodied in religious laws and enforced by legal sanctions. All the world's religions, in all their branchings and shadings, have had viewpoints and teachings on the body, sex, birth, death, illness, menstruation, elimination, and cleansing. As we shall see later, these have often been contradictory and have obviously been strongly influenced by the social climate of the period as well as by the then current medical knowledge and opinion. Virtually the only absolutes in this entire area of human existence have been those natural and involuntary bodily processes over which we have no control whether we like the facts or not.[1]

The availability of technology, as we are constantly being reminded, is essentially a question of sociopolitical demand. Technology per se has had relatively little life of its own. As our recent experiences with the space program, with pollution controls, and with consumer-product safety have amply demonstrated once again, technology is to a very large degree a variable that can be speeded or slowed according to the social and cultural demands of an era. While we can create new technologies to satisfy our demands, we can also ignore particular technologies and allow them to lie idle for years. Thus, on the one hand, we have the legacy of civilizations such as the Minoan and the Roman, which created stupendous feats of engineering and produced hygiene facilities with piped hot and cold running water, water-flushed sewage systems, and steam rooms, and, on the other hand, a notable lack of such facilities centuries later, when basic technology was considerably more advanced.

The other central issue that figures in our responses to personal hygiene is that of "community." If one asks, "Why do we care or bother about personal hygiene at all?", the only real answer has to be "Because of other people." In other words, because of other people, in large numbers living in close proximity in more or less permanent locations, our individual behavior becomes a matter of group concern and ultimately of group regulation. Obviously, if one lived out one's life in isolation in a thousand square miles of wilderness, one's personal hygiene habits, or lack of them, would be of little consequence to anyone but oneself. The tighter the density of our living arrangements, however, the more important our personal habits become to the group. Since man has been a social or tribal animal throughout most of his recorded history, the matter of body care and personal hygiene has, for all practical purposes, always been with us. Although the *need* for more or less sophistication in our hygiene facilities is based on numbers and propinquity, the *response* to that need is based on ideological considerations.

As we shall examine in further detail in the section on public facilities, the provisions for personal hygiene are also related to the wealth of society at any given time. As in many other areas, facilities are initially provided on some communal basis, and only when the resources permit do we find the inevitable shift to personal and private facilities. Thus, as a society grows, we find a pattern that begins with public baths, for example, and gradually shifts to neighborhood baths, to family baths once a week, and finally to private baths—all dependent on the availability of water, water transport, fuel, and other factors. Whereas we had some startlingly sophisticated facilities as far back as two thousand and more years, these were rarely private facilities except for the wealthy few. A personal bathroom as we know it today is a very recent development, one that is by no means universal even now and even in the most highly developed nations of the world.

Of particular consequence for our purposes, however, is that the concepts of personal privacy, which loom so large in our lives today, are also a relatively recent development and are directly related to the opportunities for privacy on the one hand and to the religious attitudes of the last two hundred years on the other. One obviously has to have the conditions that permit modesty before a society can make modesty into an operable virtue. Or, contrariwise, if you make modesty of sufficient concern, then you also develop the means to achieve it.

From the time of the Roman Empire on through the eighteenth century, bathing was a public activity, sometimes communal, sometimes familial. During the seventeenth century, ladies and gentlemen had private bathtubs (often designed for two), but they also entertained while bathing and frequently had their portraits painted while in their tubs. Japanese and Scandinavians still use female attendants in bathhouses for men as well as women, and in many parts of the world, whole families still bathe together as families have done for centuries.

A similar lack of modesty and guilt—and of privacy—has also existed with respect to the elimination processes. Not only was defecation simply not always private; it was also often an activity to socialize over:

> Kings, princes and even generals treated it as a throne at which audiences could be granted. Lord Portland, when Ambassador to the Court of Louis XIV, was deemed highly honoured to be so received, and it was from this throne that Louis announced *ex cathedra* his coming marriage to Mme. de Maintenon.[2]

The same thing is true of that modern unmentionable, the bidet, which was "first mentioned in 1710 when the Marquis d'Argenson was charmed to be granted audience by Mme. de Prie whilst she sat."[3]

On the other hand, even when privacy became

important, there was little that could be done to conceal the outdoor privy, though in the towns the walkway to it was sometimes trellised and made as attractive as possible. In rural areas, the inevitable sunflowers hid the building—but they also made it easy to recognize. The privy was also often used by more than one person at a time, and the goings and comings could scarcely be private. Similarly, the difficulties attendant upon providing the Saturday-night bath tended to make it a family affair, though presumably it was as modest as could be managed under the circumstances. During the great wave of urbanization of the last century, however, even such family privacy became difficult to achieve. When facilities first came to be permanently installed, and supplied and drained, they were to a large extent communal; that is, the single bath at the end of the hall served several families, or the water closet was tucked into a found space under the stairs and used by all the occupants. Overuse of facilities results, however, not only in irritations and delays but also, inevitably, in unsanitary conditions. It is easy to imagine how being transplanted into a crowded urban environment and sharing hygiene facilities with total strangers could cause one to be more particular about locking the door and so on. The many unpleasantnesses and traumas that likely occurred in such circumstances have undoubtedly played a part in establishing some of the attitudes we hold today. We thus came, in time, to hold that every family or household unit ought to have its own facilities and privacy. In a similar fashion, the irritations and overcrowding in today's average small house are leading us inevitably to demands for still further privacy and further individual facilities.

In its most basic form, hygiene facilities have always been more or less the same: a container for holding water for washing and a container for holding body wastes, which were ultimately disposed of in one of two ways—by return to the soil or by washing away with water. Depending on the spirit of the age, the accommodations were more or less sophisticated. At times the containers were permanently incorporated into the architecture and supplied with running water and water-flushed sewage systems, and at times containers were portable utensils; water was pumped or carried and wastes were simply dumped. The earliest known modern hygiene facilities are to be found in the Minoan palace at Knossos dating back to approximately 2000 B.C. Many of the early monasteries, which were the sole guardians of culture at the time, also had elaborate water and sewage systems and facilities. The tight, self-contained world of the medieval fortress developed its own unique solution to the problem of waste disposal—toilet facilities located up high in turrets and towers, to elevate one close to heaven in order to counteract the baseness of the act, with chutes built into the walls that emptied into the surrounding moat; apropos of which, it has been observed that it took more courage to swim a moat in real life than any Hollywood hero could imagine.[4] Obviously, the possibility of long sieges made it imperative to dispose of wastes outside the compound. It is also somewhat startling but comforting to note in *The Life of St. Gregory* that this isolated retreat is recommended for "uninterrupted reading." Until comparatively recent times, however, the most commonly found facilities were simply portable containers that came in a wide variety of shapes, sizes, and degrees of luxury, depending on the station of the user and the age in which he lived, from ancient Roman bathtubs carved out of solid blocks of marble to some of the finest furniture of Sheraton, Hepplewhyte, and others, which contained washbasins, bidets, chamber pots, traveling tubs, and so forth.

Essentially nomadic and rural peoples have almost invariably resorted to an earth system of waste disposal and have had to content themselves with locally available water supplies—which were frequently scarce and consequently treasured. The growth of permanent communities, however, ultimately necessitated centralized water supplies and a method of waste disposal more sanitary and efficient than simply dumping slop buckets out the window, though this was a common practice in cities for centuries. The continued growth of cities forced the development of a common water-borne sewage system, particularly after it was recognized that disease and epidemics could spread rapidly throughout an urban population so long as unsanitary conditions prevailed. It was also inevitable that the means would be devised to connect the containers in the households and buildings directly to the system and thus end the carrying of water and wastes to and from the outlets of the central systems.

Once the connections to a general system were made, it was possible to have permanent fixtures placed within houses and buildings. By the end of the nineteenth century, installed hygiene facilities, very much in the form that we know them today, began to be found in more and more middle-class homes, at least in the urban areas. Under the circumstances, it is not surprising that having a well-functioning plumbing system and fixtures placed in such a manner as to conserve costs took precedence over the human aspects related to the use of the fixtures themselves. In fact, the chief concern was to have the waste products disposed of in such a manner that the health of communities would be protected. This concern still poses some of the most pressing problems in many of the world's rapidly expanding urban concentrations. In a number of communities, the lack of water has also seriously limited the possibilities for growth. With the continuing expansion of population it may well be that the capacity of present systems will, in time, become self-limiting, and we may have to turn to some new technologies for the disposal of wastes.

Probably the next development of any importance in connection with the bathroom as we know it today was the standardization of its size and equipment. The three-fixture, five-by-seven-foot bathroom, which is still the norm in the United States, dates approximately from the building boom of the early 1920s, when, for the first time, virtually all new residential construction, at least in urban areas, was required by law to include at the minimum a private bath for each dwelling unit. The twenties were also a period in which a number of elegant, innovative, and lavishly equipped custom-designed bathrooms were produced for wealthy patrons.[5]

Regrettably, these have not survived as well as the famous and familiar furniture of the period. With the onset of the Depression we entered a period of some three decades or more when, because of economic conditions and wars, followed by frantic building booms, bathrooms remained essentially fixed at minimal levels. During the sixties there developed a trend toward providing several bathrooms, even for the average house in the United States, but these still tended to follow the standard minimal pattern. It has only been in the past several years that we seem to be moving toward a more adventuresome and liberal approach toward the bathroom. It has been suggested that, whereas the fifties and sixties were the era of the kitchen and family room, the seventies will be the era of the bathroom and body care. Certainly from a marketing viewpoint, there is every reason to suspect that this will prove to be the case, since the bathroom remains the single most underdeveloped area in the average house today.

In Europe, on the other hand, the past several decades have been concerned with the provision of central heating, followed by up-to-date kitchens. Ironically, while much of Europe today is still concerned with the provision of private bathroom facilities for each dwelling unit, the facilities being provided are in some ways more sophisticated than those found in the average dwelling in the United States. On the other hand, even as recently as 1970, some hotelmen in Europe were proposing to build hotels without a private bathroom for each room! As in so many instances, a late entry into a capital expenditure market means that you acquire the very latest in design and technology. Certainly in much of Europe and the rest of the world, the upgrading of housing accommodations remains a major challenge in the years ahead, and the provision of any kind of sanitary facilities remains a problem for many.

During the thirties, and particularly during and immediately after World War II, a number of ingenious improvements were proposed and even tried, mostly in terms of prefabrication. None, however, were successful, and few of the ideas ever found their way into practice. The actual significant progress that has been made in this period is quite small, so much so that the average bathroom today is barely distinguishable from one built forty years ago. To a large extent, the forces responsible for this are to be found, both in the United States and abroad, within the structuring of the plumbing industry, which has followed the pattern peculiar to the home-building industry: field erection and assembly of thousands of independently produced and often unrelated items. With few exceptions, the bathroom has rarely been conceived of as an entity, certainly not by the plumbing industry. But our attitudes toward personal hygiene have also kept us from giving the problem the attention it deserves, as we will examine in detail later. In a great many ways, the average bathroom supplied by the average builder and architect is still minimal in every respect—in terms not only of contemporary needs but also of contemporary technology, values, and attitudes.

SOCIAL AND PSYCHOLOGICAL ASPECTS OF BODY CLEANSING AND CARE

2

IMAGE AND APPEARANCE

Freud has remarked that "anatomy is destiny." As man has realized from the time of the Greek myth of Narcissus down to the present day, the human body and its image play fundamental and universal roles in his life. The way we look, or think we look, affects our lives and our accomplishments.[1] In his search for understanding of himself and of others, man has, in practically all ages, tended to equate physical appearance with personality, character, and intelligence. While few of us today would place much credence in the claims formerly made for physiognomy, phrenology, or somatotyping, almost all of us still react instinctively to people's physical appearance and form judgments that are sometimes difficult to change, even with evidence to the contrary. We can "tell" a person's race, religion, and place of origin by his appearance, and we can "fall in love at first sight." We believe in the notions that all beautiful people are desirable, fat people are jolly, small men are egomaniacs, high foreheads indicate intelligence, and large breasts signify a supremely desirable woman, and more. Most of us are, indeed, very much tempted to "judge the book by the cover" and are constantly being reinforced in this belief by advertising appeals and the hard evidence indicating that, while appearances may not solve all our problems, they certainly are a good beginning.

Reason aside, there is ample evidence that our appearance is certainly critical in the formation of first impressions at the very least. Experiments conducted with respect to the influence of height, clothing, and other aspects on perceptions leave no doubt that we respond to such visual cues and, indeed, seem to find reassurance in fast and easy identification. Recently, in fact, a "wardrobe engineering" consultant has set up shop to help businessmen dress consistently with the image they are trying to project.[2]

Certainly the phenomenon is not new; although canons of beauty have varied enormously from culture to culture, mankind has from time immemorial been preoccupied with his image and appearance and their enhancement. In our eternal search for approval, for love, for success, we have engaged in an extraordinary variety of dressing, grooming, and decorative mutilation practices.[3] We have also searched for the fountain of eternal youth from time immemorial, though the premium placed on youth by society has perhaps never been so strong or pervasive as it is today. This emphasis is, of course, tied to other profound changes in our social structure and our value system, and while it may be deplored, it is very much an operable fact of life leading many middle-aged persons to affect the hair and clothing styles of their children, to wear wigs, get hair transplants, undergo cosmetic surgery, get their teeth capped, diet, exercise, and so forth. Advocated at every turn, body and skin care and grooming have perhaps never played as big a role in society as they do today. Much of this, of course, also has a positive side with respect to health and general fitness. On the other hand, a great deal of this body care and personal hygiene is essentially cosmetic and superficial, as we shall examine in more detail later, and is a result of strong social pressures to appear young, thin, and beautiful. One observer has noted that one of the most persecuted minorities in the United States today are the fat people, who are discriminated against in endless subtle, and not so subtle, ways by a society that puts a premium on thinness. "Life-insurance companies, the cosmetic and clothing industries, and mass-media advertising are just a few sources which mark overweight as a central target for puritanical fervor and vindictiveness. . . . Based upon the Protestant-ethic value of ascetic impulse control, self-denial designates fatness as a self-indulgent immorality which induces retribution." And, of course, we must also remember that gluttony ranked as one of the original "seven deadly sins," so that our discrimination in employment and other matters on the basis of physical appearance can be amply justified on moral grounds. In many other societies, however, fatness is looked upon with great favor, and indeed, amplitude was considered a mark of beauty in the United States up until the first World War.[4]

One consequence of these attitudes is that more demands are being placed on our already generally inadequate bathroom facilities in terms of both sheer space and additional facilities. It also suggests that in some subtle respects the attitudes toward the bathroom as a space may also be undergoing some change.

THE IDEA OF CLEANLINESS

Body cleansing, like all universal and habitual activities, is subject to ritual uses and to a variety of philosophical and psychological meanings. Ritual cleansing is a practice that can be found in some form among all peoples and in almost all periods of history and still survives in many of the world's religions. Thus, circumcision, the washing of the hands at communion, washing of the feet, bathing in the holy Ganges, and other practices are all body-hygiene practices that have more symbolic than hygienic value. Most commonly purifying rituals such as these are performed after coming into contact with ritually contaminating things, persons, or acts; or before coming into contact with that which is holy—whether this be a person, place, or act to be performed. (This either/or ritual aspect is neatly exemplified in the delicious slander that holds that "The Frenchman washes his hands before urinating, the Englishman after.") Contaminants can range from death to menstruation, childbirth, murder, persons of inferior caste, and so on. Thus Pilate must actually, and symbolically, wash his hands as well as proclaim his innocence. Conversely, the traditional Saturday-night bath is a reflection not only of practical considerations having to do with the availability of hot water and other resources but also of preparation for the Sabbath. In a somewhat similar fashion, persons in many cultures bathe before embarking upon intercourse, which in itself is regarded as a sacred ritual. Lovemaking without careful washing and grooming has long tended to be regarded as profane. Today, the ritual also survives in the form of shared bathing and has become part of the erotic foreplay.

Whereas this ritual cleansing is universally practiced in some form or other, we can also find periods of significant exception in the history of Western civilization. Within our own culture we have tended, broadly speaking, to vacillate back and forth between materialism and sexuality and spiritualism and asceticism. On the one hand, we have regarded Man as some poor, base creature tempted by the Devil into the vilest habits, a creature who could only achieve grace by suffering and whose flesh and its demands were only at best to be tolerated. On the other hand, we have held that Man is the noblest of God's creatures, that the human body is a thing of beauty. Each point of view has had its champions and each has led to excesses—the first to the almost total neglect of the body and of personal hygiene, which neglect led in turn to widespread disease, not to mention personal discomfort, and the second to sensualism and sexuality. In a great many respects, the history of hygiene, like the history of sex, is directly related both to our religious beliefs and the power of the church at any given period, obviously for many of the same reasons.

In very broad terms, it may be said that those epochs which have been relatively pragmatic in their conceptions of mankind have generally had high standards of personal hygiene. The Greeks and Romans, most of the antecedent Mediterranean cultures, and many Oriental cultures all practiced a high level of hygiene and permitted man a high degree of acceptance of himself and his physical being. The sophisticated and elaborate bathing practices that developed in the Roman Empire and that were accommodated in public facilities of a scale and grandeur unequalled since were a natural outcome of an essentially hedonistic approach to life. It is regrettable perhaps, though hardly to be wondered at, that this approach—unchecked by countering forces—led to sensualism and vice, so much so that the term bath, or *bagnio,* ultimately became synonymous with brothel.

On the other hand, periods of intense preoccupation with sin, sex, guilt, and ultimate salvation in another world have always tended to denigrate life and the pleasures of living and have resulted in a denial and a suppression of the fundamental aspects of life and of the body. This is exemplified by the early Christian era, when dirt was considered a badge of holiness and when refraining from caring for one's body was a pious act of self-denial leading to ultimate salvation and when it could be said that "the purity of the body and its garments means the impurity of the soul." As Havelock Ellis has noted, "It required very little insight and sagacity for the Christians to see—though we are now apt to slur over the fact—that the cult of the bath was in very truth the cult of the flesh."[5] In short, what we find in such periods is not ritual cleansing but, rather, ritual filth and dirtiness.[6]

Our own, more recent heritage is different still and is summed up in the somewhat righteous Protestant dictum: "Cleanliness is, indeed, next to Godliness." Dirt and bodily filth are to be condemned; but while the way to salvation lies in personal cleanliness—it is not to be enjoyed; it is a duty. We have, therefore, either the best, or the worst, of both possible worlds, depending on one's viewpoint.

One inevitable corollary of this attitude is that "the lower classes smell," whether their skins be black, brown, or white. It has been observed that one of the bases of the class, or caste, system is that "we ostracize and despise those who do the most necessary and unpleasant tasks with the least opportunity to keep themselves clean; the provisions of sanitation being always found in greatest profusion where they are least needed, in proportion to means. Thus wealth and cleanliness are the marks of idleness (and superior virtue), dirt and poverty being the insignia of labour."[7] In Reginald Reynolds' book *Cleanliness and Godliness,* the author observes that the British learned to bathe from the Hindus and it took several generations before the daily bath was firmly established among the British upper classes. "As yet they deserved the title of 'The Great Unwashed' which their descendents were to confer in ridicule upon the poor; and deserved it better than those for whom the name was invented, because they were de facto both great and dirty."

This attitude is, of course, by no means confined to recent Western society. Evidence of it is as old as mankind and can be found in ancient China and elsewhere, with respect not only to attitudes but also to the physical trappings by which we proclaim our station—such as the long fingernails, which have been a badge of wealth and idleness from the times of the early Chinese emperors until the recent democratic advent of applied false fingernails, by which every typist could pretend to the station of her more elegant sisters. And indeed, the redoubtable Sherlock Holmes could instantly deduce a man's occupation and position simply by the evidence of his hands. It is only in relatively recent times that "a gentleman" would deign to sully his hands with "manual" labor and not be concerned.[8]

Our philosophical equation of cleanliness with Godliness or purity and goodness, and of dirt and filth with immorality is also abundantly clear in our use of language and in the way we have broadened the applicability of the concept. When, for example, we describe a person as being "clean-cut," we are not only referring to physical appearance but also are imputing a certain moral integrity as well. When a criminal suspect is called "clean," it denotes an innocence—at least this time. We also speak of, and occasionally practice, "washing one's mouth out with soap" as though this literal but essentially symbolic cleansing could actually expiate the moral or spiritual sin. Similarly, a "dirty" old man may be physically quite clean, and the term "the great unwashed," when used today, merely describes that segment of society which is deemed inferior in a multitude of ways having nothing necessarily to do with their actual physical cleanliness.

These symbolic associations also result, inevitably, in symbolic rejections. Speaking of the early radicals and socialists, Orwell remarks that many of them made it a point of honor never to appear clean or cleanly dressed, transforming the punishment of labor into a badge of defiance. In recent years many of the world's rebellious young have similarly adopted rags and personal filth as a highly effective, literal as well as symbolic, offense to the establishment and the values they reject. Indeed, many a person in the older generation has been heard to lament that they (and their ideas?) "wouldn't be so bad if they weren't *so dirty*!" Others of the young, in their zeal for a return to Nature and a more fundamental way of life, apparently view cleanliness and personal hygiene as "unnatural" and as still another artifice of civilization to be avoided. In this new constellation of views we find still a different equation. We appear now to have moved from cleanliness and sensuality, dirt and spiritual purity, and cleanliness and moral superiority to dirt and sensuality—the romantic return to the "natural man."

Interestingly, this symbolic rejection of cleanliness has been common on a smaller scale for years, even among the most respectable people. Perhaps the clearest example is the almost inevitable behavior of men off on a fishing or hunting trip when no one shaves or bathes until it is time to return to the expectations and responsibilities of civilization. Indeed, one is led to suspect that in many instances, the actual fishing or hunting is the least of the pleasures involved. Shaving and bathing are simply responsibilities to be abandoned, much like a return to the tradition of the little boy's resisting parental authority in taking a bath. Rejection of hygiene thus becomes a convenient, innocuous, and highly visible way to reject authority, even if briefly.

CLEANSING VERSUS APPEARANCES

The issue of responsibility, expectation, and implied authority also raises the very basic question of the degree to which we each practice personal hygiene because we enjoy it or believe in it, or both, and the degree to which we cheat but carefully maintain the expected facade of apparent cleanliness through grooming and clothing. There is little doubt that much of the grooming and body care practiced in the Western world today is essentially ritualistic insofar as it is chiefly practiced for display and sexual attraction rather than from any genuine concern for one's bodily well-being.

Our concern with apparent cosmetic cleanliness is not limited only to our person but applies to many other areas as well. One of the commonest objections voiced with respect to colored fixtures, for example, is that they show dirt more readily than white fixtures. Similarly, and curiously, if we examine common attitudes toward most household finishes and furnishings we find remarks like: "Oh, it's lovely but it will show every footprint or fingerprint." A careful examination of the kitchen carpeting on the market shows that it is invariably highly patterned and multicolored so as to disguise the spills and stains. In fact, the more deeply one delves into such cleanliness behavior the more apparent it becomes that our primary concern is with visual rather than actual cleanliness. Dirt and soiling exist only in the eye of the beholder.

A great deal of our hand washing, for example, is done to protect our clothing and the things we handle rather than to clean our hands. Similarly, a great deal of the perfunctory hand washing done after elimination in a public restroom is done simply from fear of embarrassment—because we have been taught that it is the proper thing to do. In one recent survey of a large public men's room only 60 per cent of the patrons bothered to wash, even under those circumstances.[9] It is probably a safe assumption that in private the figure drops considerably and that in the home it is the rare exception rather than the rule. The most compelling evidence, however, is found in the case of perineal hygiene, where even the most apparently elegant and fastidious are often to be found wearing underdrawers soaked in urine and smeared with fecal matter.

This question was brought sharply into focus in Germany a few years ago when it was reported in the public press that "the average German changes his shirt every other day, his socks and underwear every three to four days, and his bed linen every four weeks." More than half the population bathe only once a week and brush their teeth only rarely, and approximately 10 per cent bathe once every four weeks. Similarly, it was reported that when the East German army tried to persuade its troops to change underwear more frequently, the men simply sent the fresh underwear to the laundry and continued to wear their old underwear for weeks at a time.[10]

Lest any reader feel smug, it must be noted that the only remarkable thing about this report is simply that the comfortable illusions were shattered by exposure in the press. Physicians in the United States report, for example, that many young people today do not wear underwear at all, and a study in Great Britain a few years back reported that some 9 per cent of the men wore no underwear. The author noted that outward appearances were often deceiving and that "A 'Teddy Boy' is outwardly very smart, his hair well greased, his pointed shoes well polished, and he has a pride in his appearance often contradicted by stripping him. This was true of other grades as well.[11] And in 1971, the British Safety Council felt compelled to distribute some twenty thousand posters to industries urging the workmen to "Wash—Help Stop Skin Disease."

A recent preliminary investigation in Sweden has revealed that in many industrial plants the workers do not use the showering and changing facilities provided but prefer to come and go in their dirty work clothes rather than bathe and change into clean clothing. It is probably a fair supposition that this problem is more widespread than is commonly realized, particularly in Western Europe, where there are great numbers of guest workers, most of whom come from areas where opportunities for personal hygiene were minimal if not virtually nonexistent. This suggests that while the middle class, and its values, may have grown enormously in the past several decades, there is still a large lower class of both native populations and foreigners entering the mainstream of Western middle-class society whose experiences and opportunities in this regard indicate a need for more education.

The matter of the frequency with which underwear is changed is significant here because it is almost axiomatic that one is not going to move back into soiled underwear if one has bathed. The correlation is quite direct—as it is when no underwear is worn and outer garments are not changed and cleaned regularly. Both circumstances also deny the very reasons for the adoption of "linen," that is to say, it is softer to the touch of the skin than most outerwear can be and it is simpler to launder and clean frequently than the more elaborate and costly outer garments. Gandhi, for example, went so far as to urge that everyone wear white clothing because the colored and patterned clothing worn in the West hides dirt too readily.

To a degree, such behavior can be explained away by noting that there is often a fairly high correlation between the frequency of bathing and laundering and the ready availability of bathing facilities, ample hot water, and other requisites. While it is true that even in highly developed countries like Great Britain and Germany, as well as the rest of Europe, only 50 to 80 per cent of households are equipped with private bathing facilities, there is reason to suspect that some of the more extreme patterns—such as deliberately not bathing or changing clothes for a month—are a reflection of other, more subtle psychological factors.

Flugel and others have suggested that among the many functions clothing serves, psychological reassurance and protection can be just as important as physical protection from the environment.[12] In this instance, the psychological reassurance and protection is not that which comes from role or ego identification but the very direct sensory reassurance that comes from physical contact, such as the return to the womb. Just as the newborn infant needs quite literally the physiological and psychological continuation of the sensation of warmth and snugness, so this need persists throughout our lives in varying degrees.[13] Clothing, bed clothes, human contact, and physical affection all fulfill these needs.

It may well be, therefore, that the attraction of month-old underwear and unwashed skin is analogously comforting and emotionally satisfying in certain situations. It certainly possesses the virtue of familiarity in the most direct sensory fashion: the feel of the skin itself, the feel of the garments, as well as the odor of oneself. Lived-in clothing is almost invariably softer, both in surface texture and in general structure, than clean clothing and is "familiar" to us in almost imperceptible ways. The skin, moreover, is, of course, our most basic "clothing," and there is no question that one's skin sensations after bathing are significantly different than before. Although the whole idea will be repugnant to some, there is little doubt that the practice fulfills a significant emotional need. It is basically the same, for example, as the age-old phenomenon of a man's refusing to throw away an old hat. It may be caked with grease, stained through with perspiration, filthy with soot, totally misshapen, but it remains for many a treasured "part of themselves" that is obviously comforting to wear.

Interestingly, much the same sort of pattern can be observed among old people, who commonly begin to resist or abandon bathing and who take to wearing the same clothing day after day. While there are often sound physical reasons for avoiding, or reducing, bathing—such as skin dryness and arthritis—one is led to suspect additional, if unconscious, motivations, particularly in individuals who have previously been scrupulous in their personal hygiene. Similarly, while the restriction of dress is a reflection of a restriction of roles to be played, it also suggests a yearning for a very intimate personal security that is often no longer available from other sources.

We also commonly speak of someone's "getting under our skin," that is, beneath our protective clothing where we are really vulnerable. On occasion we also speak of "getting into someone else's skin," that is to say, knowing another person so intimately that we can almost assume his identity. The concept of identity also figures commonly in the remark that one "feels like a new person" after bathing. Although this often has simply to do with feeling refreshed, there is sometimes an undercurrent of something more profound intended. This is also reflected in the relationship between identity and role and appropriateness. Most of us can tolerate, even with a degree of pleasure, short periods of what we would regard as extreme dirtiness while we are engaged in particular physical activities or dirty jobs. It seems appropriate and sometimes even a welcome change from accustomed routine. In contrast, as the situation and our role expectations change we feel compelled to alter ourselves to suit.

Because this particular aspect of cutaneous sensations and psychological needs is largely unexplored, it may be useful to note briefly that the converse behavior appears to be equally complex. While some enjoy the "pleasures" of the warmth, odor, and moistness of a familiar intimate environment, others will, for example, bathe two and three times a day and insist on fresh bed linens every night, or, in the extreme, change beds several times a night so as to be always in a cool, fresh, crisp bed, as apparently was the custom of Franklin, Disraeli, and Churchill.[14]

In addition to its various ritualistic purposes, body cleansing has, of course, several other fundamental bases. The first is the maintenance of health—in the sense of not harboring vermin, not allowing irritations and rashes to develop into infectious lesions, not allowing the accumulation of waste materials to interfere with the respiratory and secretory functions of the skin, and of not disrupting the delicate bactericidal balance of the skin. The second is the maintenance of a socially acceptable level of aesthetic presence, in both the visual and olfactory senses. The third is the use of water and the washing process as a device for refreshing, reviving, relaxing, cooling, warming, and for simply obtaining sensual pleasure.

By and large, aesthetics and refreshment can be regarded as the primary factors currently governing our attitudes and practices, at least in the developed world. These motivations follow, of course, a normal cultural pattern, for once we have achieved the minimum practical hygiene necessary to avoid vermin and various skin disorders, any further attention to the cleanliness of the body is chiefly a matter of refinement, both intellectual and sensory—or, as some would have it, a matter of effective advertising.

As we have seen, throughout the history of hygiene, aesthetic refinement has followed the development of basic minimal practices. When, however, aesthetic refinement has reached a certain point, a reaction has usually set in, and a period follows wherein overattention to the details of personal hygiene has been considered effete or silly, if not, indeed, actually immoral. At present we appear to have both extremes of viewpoint operating concurrently. On the one hand, much of Western society seems to accept the precepts of basic bodily hygiene and, perhaps, as has been suggested by some, overdoes the superficial emphasis on appearance, particularly in the United States. On the other hand, as we have observed earlier, many of the world's young people in their rebellion have gone so far as to discard not only superficial considerations of appearance but also the fundamentals of bodily hygiene. The unfortunate result of this is that vermin, which had, for all practical purposes, been eradicated from the developed nations of the world, have reappeared in sufficient numbers to constitute a significant medical problem. Scabies *(Sarcoptes scabiei)* has reappeared worldwide in all strata of society and is no longer the sole problem of the poor. Historically scabies has been linked with poverty, overcrowding, and poor hygiene and has not been a problem in the West since World War II. A 1955 survey reported that the disease had almost disappeared, but in 1971 it had broken out worldwide.

Similarly, but far more seriously, we are experiencing a major re-emergence of lice. In the United States alone, public health officials estimate that more than two million persons were infested in 1972 and some have even taken to wearing animal flea collars. They lay the blame to long hair for sheltering head lice *(Pediculus capitis),* the new morality for spreading pubic lice *(Pediculus pubis),* and the disdain for bodily hygiene for spreading body lice *(Pediculus corporis).* We would do well to remember in this respect the connections between hair styles and hygiene. The close-cropped "G. I." haircut was originally neither a fashion nor a perversion but, rather, a means of coping with the problems of hygiene and lice in the difficult circumstances of war. Similarly, the splendid tresses of our ancestors were, more often than not, wigs worn over a head shaved for the same sanitary reasons. In addition to the discomfort caused, the body louse, in particular, poses a major health hazard since it is a carrier of the agents of typhus among other microorganisms and has historically been a primary agent in the epidemics that have ravaged the world.[15] In their enthusiasm for rejection, the young may be said in many instances to "have thrown the baby out with the bathwater."

While it may be true, as many insist, that no one has ever died as a direct result of not washing, millions have died as an indirect result, and millions more have suffered from a variety of illnesses ranging from typhus through polio to hepatitis from being unable, or unwilling, to practice the basics of hygiene. In a recent report on longevity, a study team investigating the inhabitants of a remote Ecuadorian village found that some had not bathed in two years or more (the record being ten). As they noted, cleanliness was obviously not a prerequisite for longevity. On the other hand, it is almost universally related to high rates of infant mortality.[16] The classic anus-to-hand-to-face linkage for disease transmission has not changed, even though many of us have been lulled by the public health successes of the last several decades into a more casual observance of basic safeguards such as washing one's hands after elimination. Even on a more prosaic level, recent research suggests the possibility that the common cold virus is as effectively spread by hand-to-face contact as by airborne or direct oral contamination.[17]

CLEANSING AND AESTHETICS

At the opposite end of the spectrum we find, particularly in the United States, a high degree of advertising-induced concern over cosmetic cleanliness and grooming. Most especially we are concerned that we don't "offend," that is, have any discernible body or mouth odor. Yet we must recognize that while such an objective is relative—like most such matters—it is ultimately futile in a broader context. It has been observed that:

> We imagine that through liberal use of soap and water, decent Caucasian people do not emit any unpleasant odor. But, wash as he may, a meat-eater stinks in the nostrils of a vegetarian, and the odor of a well-soaped Englishman is a stench to a Hottentot who, *per contra,* enjoys the company of his own people who comb their hair with rancid butter.[18]

One might also add that a smoker stinks in the nostrils of a nonsmoker and that a dog will always recognize his master by his smell. Indeed, one suspects that much of the success of the campaign to persuade us to be concerned about offending others is due to the fact that most of the time we are so accustomed to our own odors that we are not aware of them ourselves. We don't know if we might smell to others; therefore, we play it safe and try to make sure we don't.

In 1971 the Federal Trade Commission undertook an advertising substantiation program requiring advertisers to prove their product claims. It appears that the advertisers have responded all too eagerly, swamping the Commission with often conflicting data. Among the research conducted were comparison tests between the various brands of underarm deodorants wherein "trained judges" sniffed armpits to ascertain which product provided better odor control. Since the various tests were ultimately contradictory, the Commission now faces the prospect of organizing its own tests of these (and other?) deodorant products.[19]

This concern is both relatively recent and by no means universal. Europeans, for example, have been highly amused for years by Americans' preoccupation with body odors that they regard as "perfectly natural." Our deodorants, antiperspirants, mouthwashes, chlorophyll tablets, and so on seem to many a somewhat fatuous attempt to achieve a neutral and sterile presence. Ernest Dichter, for example, has noted that, "Some American ad men find it hard to accept, but the fact is that in some countries it is still quite socially acceptable to smell of honest sweat."[20]

And, indeed, a Duke in nineteenth-century England could proclaim that "it is sweat, by God, that keeps a man clean!" Ernie Pyle remarked that if you go long enough without bathing, even the fleas will leave you alone. Perhaps, but certainly mosquitoes, gnats, and black flies will leave you alone, since they appear to be chiefly attracted by the perfume that is an almost inevitable ingredient in soap, after-shave lotion, and hairdressings.

Furthermore, we must also recognize that body odors are not all inevitably unpleasant for everyone, nor even neutral, for that matter. Many people, even in the United States, find a man's, or woman's, perspiration and scent ("B.O.") exciting and sexually stimulating. Marcello Mastroianni has remarked with respect to women that "I like them to smell a little."[21] Victor Emmanuel II complained bitterly on one occasion when a young farm girl he had admired was delivered to him scrubbed and perfumed by overzealous courtiers. The erotic effect of body odors—the odor of the "human flower" as Goethe put it—is not confined only to the body directly but also to the clothing worn by others. Our literature, both erotic books and "respectable classics," is full of references to the stimulus provided by the smell of a garment belonging to one's beloved.

In virtually all of the animal kingdom, various body odors and a highly developed sense of smell play an important role in communication among members of the species—in the detection of fear, death, disease, defeat, and, most important, in mating. In Man, body odors have tended to be regarded as a carry-over from primate Man, unnecessary in the present day, a notion confirmed by the observation that of all the senses Man appears to rely least on his sense of smell. Although the chemistry of our bodies still produces a variety of odors in response to different stimuli, the only ones we regard as functional today are oral odors, which signify that the body is not functioning properly. The odors associated with fear, menstruation, pregnancy, and other states have generally been regarded as redundant and superfluous cues in today's society. Nonetheless, recent research in chemical communication has established that the same fatty acids producing "body odor" in Man also make up the sex pheromone, or chemical message, of the rhesus monkey, raising the possibility that this might also be the case in the higher primates. One scientist has suggested that perhaps our preoccupation with deodorants and the like is in reality an unconscious way of enforcing our Puritan sexual taboos.

Perhaps the most potent sexual stimuli for many people, however, are odors specifically arising from the genital region, from the various vaginal secretions, and from semen. One of the oldest topics in our sexual folklore concerns the attractiveness of vaginal secretions and odors, of female pubic hair—the smell of "pussy" in the common vernacular. In spite of this attractiveness, or perhaps because of it, we have in the last few years attacked it with a questionable variety of perfumed and fruit-scented (and flavored!) vaginal sprays and douches. Interestingly, however, if one reads the various advertisements carefully, one discovers that, while some are promoting the idea of a deodorant pure and simple to protect a woman from "offending" (or attracting?), others are candidly promoting the notion that their product enhances the woman's sexual attractiveness.[22]

This development calls to mind an old, and once seemingly improbable, "dirty(?) joke": A poor pharmacist invents a product to make "pussy" smell like oranges (now true!) but has difficulty finding financial backing (untrue). Years pass and the once poor pharmacist is discovered living in luxury in Paris by an old friend who inquires whether he had made his money on his invention. "No," he replies. "I took the banker's advice that there was no market for that kind of product; so then I figured out how to make oranges smell like 'pussy' and, as you can see, I'm making millions!" (not yet true!). One can only wait in utter fascination for the full sequence of life's imitating art to be completed.

The prospects for such an eventuality's occurring must also be weighed in the light of the following remark made recently by an advertising executive:

> Businessmen ran out of parts of the body. We had headaches for awhile, but we took care of them. The armpit had its moment of glory, and the toes, with their athlete's foot. We went through wrinkles, we went through diets. We conquered hemorrhoids. So the businessman sat back and said, "What's left?" And some smart guy said, "The vagina."[23]

CLEANSING AND REJUVENATION

The third major purpose of body cleansing is to produce the sensations of being refreshed or relaxed and sometimes simply to get warm or to cool off. Simply getting clean, of course, produces a feeling of well-being, but what we are dealing with here we might regard as a "pseudo-bath" in that the primary object is not really to cleanse but rather to use water to produce an easing of muscular and nervous tensions. This practice dates back at least as far as the Roman Empire and unquestionably beyond, since it is essentially the same as "bathing" in the sea, though now we call it swimming.

In some societies this aspect of bathing has been clearly recognized and institutionalized—most notably today among the Japanese, who have very distinct sets of practices and facilities for the cleansing function and for the relaxing function. Most of the rest of us do not make such nice distinctions in purpose, so that if we take a nice long relaxing bath, it is in our dirty bath water. Throughout Europe at least, where every tub is also equipped with a hand shower, it is still possible to rinse oneself clean after soaking. The Japanese soaking bath or "furo" serves another major purpose besides hygiene: water conservation. Because of chronic water shortage on the Japanese islands, the practice, for centuries, has been to treat the soaking bath much as we treat our swimming pools, which is to say that the water remains in the tub for months and is simply reheated by an attached stove or water heater each time it is used. This allows each member of a family to enjoy a hot bath without enormous waste of water, particularly since their tubs, in order to permit full immersion of the body, hold considerably more water than the average American bathtub. In between uses the tub is covered with a tight-fitting lid. Proper body cleansing beforehand is therefore a necessity if this finely balanced system is to work.

Another important, though generally unrecognized purpose of the "pseudo-bath" is to get warm. "It appears to me to be quite evident that it is not the water, but the *warmth,* to which most, if not all, the good effects experienced from warm bathing ought to be ascribed. Among those nations where warm bathing has been most generally practiced, water has seldom been employed, except occasionally, and merely for washing and cleansing the skin."[24] This is especially true in Japan, for example, and in Great Britain, where the bath enjoys particular favor because of a generally damp, raw climate and the lack of central heating. In at least some respects, the popularity of the sauna in Scandinavia is attributable to a similar combination of conditions. At the end of a day when one is always cold and bundled up in heavy clothes, a hot bath is a particular luxury that many of us today can scarcely appreciate. This also accounts in large measure for the general lack of showers throughout most of Europe, for example. To take a shower comfortably one must take it in a heated bathroom. Conversely, the popularity of the shower in the United States is at least partly attributable to central heating and to a milder, if not actually tropical, climate. Indeed, the notorious American penchant for a daily shower or two may well have more to do with revival and refreshment than with cleansing, in view of climatic factors and the stresses of contemporary urban life.

The therapeutic value of water has, of course, long been recognized medically, and water is often used as a treatment for a variety of arthritic and muscular ailments. Although not as much in favor as it once was, mineral water therapy has also been used in the treatment of numerous physical disorders, most particularly in the various spas of Europe, some of which have been in operation since antiquity. Much of the effectiveness of water therapy is due to the remarkable neural and thermal sensitivity of the skin. Water can be soothing enough to lull one to sleep; it can be invigorating and increase blood circulation; or it can be employed as a massage, particularly in the case of some of the recently developed "impulse" shower heads. In addition to producing markedly different physical sensations, each of the two primary bathing methods, the tub bath and the shower, has also had develop around it a set of quite different responses and attitudes.

THE TUB BATH

The tub bath may be said to be generally considered more relaxing, more luxurious, and more feminine in usage than the shower. It is probably true that the tub is the more relaxing since it does, in fact, permit a sitting or semi-recumbent posture, and undoubtedly still or gently moving water can produce a more soothing sensation than a forceful shower spray. This is not to suggest that people do not find a shower relaxing, but there does, however, seem to be a significant difference in how the term "relaxing" is interpreted. The shower is generally described as "refreshing" and "revitalizing" whereas the tub bath calls forth terms such as "soothing" and "calming." The person seeking to calm down or to forget anxieties or tensions is essentially seeking an escape. This is also attested to by the fact that persons who have a choice say that they take a shower bath when they are in a hurry but a tub bath when they have the time and are tense and wish to relax. Some of the popularity of the tub bath is due simply to the fact that it *does* take time—to draw the bath, to soak, to wash, and so forth. For many people, particularly the mothers of young children, the tub bath offers a convenient and socially acceptable way to withdraw into seclusion for a period of time that the shower does not offer. As we have noted elsewhere, a significant function of the bathroom today is its social role in providing more or less guaranteed privacy with no questions asked. Recently, it was discovered that the bathtub has also emerged as a favorite place to study in university dormitories because it was again the only place where some students felt they could escape from their roommates and from the general noise and confusion.

The tub bath also serves, like sleep, as the ultimate escape—the symbolic return to the womb, which in this instance is directly analogous since one's immediate environment is, indeed, warm, wet, and enclosing and presumably offers the user a high degree of psychological security. The relaxing effect is generally pronounced, so much so that a hot bath has long been a recommended procedure for people who have trouble sleeping.

For a variety of cultural and historical reasons, the tub bath also has the connotation of being more luxurious than the shower. Largely this is because of the strong historical association of tub bathing with lavishness and extravagance. We also find ample evidence in the legacy of extravagant and elegant tubs that have survived to the present day. The skill and imagination with which they were fashioned testify to their importance in the lives of their owners. It is probable that this idea of luxury is responsible for the image of tub bathing's being, rightly or wrongly, essentially feminine. Throughout history, and in fiction and the films, desirable women are found languishing in tubs—usually elegant—and often while entertaining intimate friends. The acceptance of this connotation can be explained by the fact that the two concepts, luxury and femininity, go virtually hand in hand in our society. The "desirable" woman has historically been able to command luxury; and luxury, being defined as an "excessive indulgence in creature comforts and sensual pleasures," is regarded in our culture largely as the prerogative and characteristic of women. Some men, to be sure, may equally indulge in luxuries in this sense, but they tend to be somewhat of an exception and are often regarded with some suspicion.

There are, however, persons who take exception to this notion—at least insofar as American bathtubs have been concerned. Professor Parkinson, echoing the sentiments of many, complains that "some Puritanical tradition underlies the American bath in which one can sit but cannot lie. Cleanliness is not to be made the excuse for luxury."[25]

These attitudes are most clearly revealed in advertising, where, for example, men are generally shown in showers—rarely in tubs. Advertising directed at women, on the other hand, tends to divide clearly into two images: the tub image, which suggests luxury and eroticism, and the shower image, which is more neutral—what some commentators on the American scene have described as the new "pal" image of the woman, and what the advertisers themselves term as "the young moderns," "the fun people," "the lively ones," and so on. The models who pose in the shower generally have what is known as the "wholesome American look." The models who pose in the tub are generally of a type that might be called "sultry" and are often depicted only vaguely—in silhouette or through a filmy haze—to create a dream-like quality, a relatively subtle approach to eroticism that is presumably acceptable, since one can scarcely be held accountable for one's dreams.

On the other hand, from a purely practical standpoint, the tub would also seem to offer greater possibilities for both luxury and sensual enjoyment. A tub bath, for example, readily permits the use of a variety of additive substances such as scents, oils, and bubbles, not to mention exotica such as champagne and milk. Or perhaps we should say erotica instead, as exemplified by the following recent advertisements for bath products appearing in national magazines. One advertisement consisted of a virtually blank black page bearing the following message:

> Take a bath in the dark tonight and let the water make love to your skin.*

and at the bottom of the page:

> *Recipe for an intriguing experience: 1. Surround yourself with ———. 2. Turn out the lights. 3. Lean back. Relax. 4. Let the fragrance fire your imagination.

The other asked:

> What's the difference between an American bath and a French bath? What's the difference between an American lover and a French lover? With ———, you get stroked along your arms and legs and under your chin and in the crook of your elbow and kissed on the back of your neck and behind your ear where you love it so, with an expert French softness and sweetness you've never felt in the bath before.

Certainly, little imagination is needed to understand the implications or the appeals in these two very respectable advertisements. This potential for eroticism in the tub is also attested to by the fact, which many psychologists have noted, that a great deal of masturbatory activity is associated with it, particularly among women. When we consider the general atmosphere that can be created, either unconsciously or deliberately, and the natural reasons to explore one's body, this is not too surprising. In some instances, the tub also offers the possibility of shared bathing. Whereas the average American five-foot tub is scarcely more comfortable than a two-seater sports car, many European tubs are large enough to accommodate two in comfort. A number of manufacturers have, however, recently introduced tubs specifically designed to hold two (see Figure 60).

In addition to its erotic possibilities, shared bathing is also very much a family matter in many societies, particularly in Japan and Scandinavia. This concept of a "family" bathroom with a large tub is also finding expression in the recent development of the German *Wohnbäder* or "living bath." Perhaps the most common form of shared bathing the world round, however, is that done by parents and their small children. Many young fathers, in particular, seem to delight in bathing and playing with their infant sons in the tub. Not only is this a practice that finds enthusiastic approval from many psychologists, but also it is a pleasure that is essentially not possible to enjoy in the shower, particularly since many infants are terrified of a shower. The tub, moreover, has traditionally afforded young children the pleasurable opportunity of playing with water toys, an opportunity again absent in the shower.

In conclusion, the tub emerges ultimately as a source of "relaxation" in a variety of ways, some purely physical and direct, some purely psychological. Both conscious "dreaming" or an unconscious state of sensual semi-gratification can be equally diverting and relaxing and may be commonly resorted to not only in this context but in many others.

THE SHOWER BATH

As has been suggested, the shower bath represents a series of attitudes and images that are almost directly opposed to those of the tub. It is "refreshing"; it is fast, efficient, Spartan; it also appears sometimes to be sexless in the sense that it does not seem to be as overtly erotic either in its use or in its image, even though shared showering is fairly common. This neutrality holds, however, only for female use and co-exists with a distinctly masculine image. Its speed and efficiency, its invigorating quality, and its generally businesslike, no-nonsense character are all parts of this image. The shower has also been described as somewhat like getting caught in the rain—casual, uncontrollable, destructive, rough—a circumstance that a man is expected to take in stride.

The popular stereotype of the man singing in the shower may be directly related to this rain–masculine image. In these circumstances, the "singing" is more nearly apt to be akin to a bellowing, in spirit if not in quality, and may be taken to represent a primitive expression of virility rather than an art form. If we consider the circumstances—standing naked under a buffeting stream of water—we can see that at least in a physical sense this represents a free and elemental condition, one that modern urban man does not commonly experience and one that can take on a special significance on occasion.

We can thus see how the shower image can be manipulated in several ways. Primarily, it is masculine; secondarily, it becomes essentially neutral when assumed by a woman, since in using a shower the woman symbolically shares the man's world and behaves like him—in effect, tending to remove sexual differentiation. This general trend toward an assumption by women of what has traditionally, in our culture, been regarded as masculine behavior is a phenomenon that is both widespread and reasonably accepted. The converse situation is also true, though perhaps more limited in its applications. In the last several decades, men have increasingly shared in "woman's work" and relinquished more and more of their former male prerogatives, with a resulting tendency toward a more neutral sex image.[26]

In the past, the shower has also had an association with "public" facilities, an association that has now largely disappeared, showers in the home having become so common. Some elderly persons, however, still maintain that a shower is inappropriate in the house or is impossible to get clean in or is too uncomfortable—presumably because of the standing posture.

The shower also has associated with it certain simple and relatively obvious attitudes. Some women feel, for example, that they "cannot seem to get as clean" in the shower. This may be due to not "soaking" as one commonly does in a tub, though in view of the general frequency of washing, this is more of an imaginary than a real problem, since people, particularly women, are rarely so dirty that this could be a significant factor. The most likely explanation is that this attitude refers, perhaps unconsciously, to genital cleanliness, since it is true that the shower in its present design does make it virtually impossible for a woman to cleanse herself properly there.

The irony in this is, of course, that the shower is, in all other respects, inherently a more hygienic method of body cleansing than the tub bath unless special pains are taken to rinse the body afterwards. In the United States at least, the shower is also becoming the preferred method of hair washing for both men and women for the same reasons of cleanliness. Although the shower has certain limitations, it is probably safe to say that it is the overwhelmingly preferred method of bathing by adults in the United States. In fact, there is good reason to believe that most of the bathtubs in the United States that are also fitted with a shower head are rarely used as a tub but rather as a shower receptor—a circumstance that mitigates to some extent the fact that they are really unsuitable as bathtubs in the first place. Nevertheless, there is little question that tub bathing has devotees equally as dedicated as shower bathers and that both methods will continue to exist for some time to come.

PERINEAL CLEANSING AND THE BIDET

In addition to attitudes and concepts associated with body cleansing in general and with its related equipment, we must also consider the somewhat special circumstances surrounding the cleansing of the perineal region and the use of the bidet. Both the activity and the equipment in this case are, in some instances, highly charged emotionally and offer a striking example of the way in which objects can become invested with powerful associations and psychological sets.

Through misunderstanding and misinformation, not to mention lack of information, the bidet has, in both the United States and Great Britain, become associated in the average person's mind with sex and sex-related usage—if, that is, he or she even had any idea what the fixture was in the first place. Essentially, however, as more and more people today are coming to realize, the bidet is an innocent washing fixture intended for use by both sexes for the general cleansing of the entire perineal or anal-genital region after defecation, urination, or intercourse—or simply for quick partial bathing.

The misconception, unfortunately still widely held, is that the fixture is solely to be used for douching the vagina, contraceptively or otherwise, and for washing the vulvar region after intercourse. The error is sometimes further compounded by the belief that this genital-cleansing fixture is used only by prostitutes or "loose women." From a historical standpoint, it is relatively easy to see how such an association could come about: first, because the veil of secrecy and consequent misinformation about sex has persisted until fairly recently; and, second, because the first large-scale contact Americans and British have had with the fixture was in France during World War I—often presumably under circumstances that could give rise to these impressions, the traditional male double standard also possibly being involved.

The fact that this association has initially and largely been transmitted via men would also account for the fact that American men as well as women tend, by and large, to reject the fixture and its association. Furthermore, the plumbing fixture manufacturers have, in some instances, not helped this situation. One leading United States manufacturer, for example, who is apparently also a victim of this attitude, has seen fit to call its model of bidet the "Carmen"—a name that can scarcely be considered likely to correct the public's image! (It might have better been promoted by borrowing an idea from the marketers of that other unmentionable, the "sanitary napkin," and saying "A bidet because. . . ." On the other hand, one medical wag, with apologies to Rodgers, Hammerstein, and Mary Martin, has suggested the theme song "I'm Gonna Wash That Man Right Out of My Hair.")

It would appear that so long as the bidet is associated in the public mind with the sexual act, whether licit or illicit, there will be some persons who will reject it because of this association. Its acceptance under present circumstances would be, for some, tantamount to according the same unselfconscious status to the role of sex as to the role of elimination physically symbolized by the toilet. The range of responses to the bidet, among persons who knew what it was, extended, for example, from "I don't need it" and "I wouldn't want anyone to know I needed to use it," to "It might be all right if I could have it in a separate compartment where guests couldn't see it" and "What would I tell the children?"! In New York City a few years ago, a number of the people moving into one of the city's most luxurious and expensive new cooperative apartment buildings, fully equipped with bidets by the forward-thinking builder, actually had them torn out at their own expense. This is a particularly interesting situation because one would have expected most of these people to have been abroad and to have developed a certain sophistication. Indeed, for many sophisticates, or would-be sophisticates, a bidet has for years been the ultimate status symbol. At the other end of the spectrum, the "average" American or English tourist, who does in fact exist, asks "What is it?" or "Is that one of those 'European' things?", or uses it for doing hand laundry or for cooling bottled drinks, or, as in one of Henry Miller's novels, assumes that it is simply a different kind of water closet or urinal.

From the standpoint of personal hygiene, however, it is totally immaterial whether there is such a fixture as the bidet or whether this anogenital cleansing is accomplished in some other way. It would not matter seriously if we rejected the bidet on the basis of our prejudices against its supposed sexual connotations if we otherwise observed and practiced proper hygiene with respect to this part of the body.

The blunt fact is that we do not—as every physician and anyone who has ever laundered a pair of drawers can testify, and indeed some have. In the British study cited earlier, not only were approximately 9 per cent of the men found not wearing underpants but also some 44 per cent revealed fecal contamination of their underpants, or trousers in the case of those who wore no underwear, ranging from "wasp-coloured staining" to "frank massive faeces." There was virtually no difference in the percentage so contaminated between "white-collared," "artisan," or "labouring class" workers. Furthermore, the author notes that:

> Under the circumstances in which this survey was conducted, it could be safely presumed that almost all the men concerned would have known that a medical examination was to be expected. From this it may be inferred that a surprise inspection might reveal an even higher proportion of contamination than already shown; for many might take the precaution of presenting themselves in clean linen.

He concludes by observing that many are prepared to complain about a "tomato sauce stain on a restaurant tablecloth, whilst they luxuriate on a plush seat in their faecally-stained pants."[27]

This situation is not, of course, unique to Great Britain nor is it unique to men; it will be found whenever anyone contents himself with simply wiping with dry paper, for the inescapable fact is that, while dry-wiping will remove the bulk of the fecal matter clinging to the anal opening, it will not remove it all. A portion will be absorbed by the underwear and the rest will remain as a dry stain on the skin around the anus and, in some cases, will coat the hair surrounding the anus to form a dense, irritating, and sometimes painful mat. As my friend, a Confucian scholar, notes, undoubtedly apocryphally, "He who goes to bed with unwashed asshole wake up with smelly finger." The only way to get really clean is to wash the anus or, at the very least, to wipe with wet paper, as anyone who has ever suffered from hemorrhoids can testify. Or as Tiny Tim, in a frank interview, put it:

> I take one big shower a day and then a shower, soaping three times, every time nature calls. This is not to offend the public, it avoids stains on the underwear and it gives a feeling of security.[28]

The situation is perhaps best summed up in a perceptive and rare piece of literary candor by Philip Roth's Portnoy, who confesses that:

> [I try] to clear my feet of my undershorts before anybody can peek inside, where, to my chagrin, to my bafflement, to my mortification, I always discover in the bottommost seam a pale and wispy brushstroke of my shit. Oh, Doctor, I wipe and I wipe and I wipe, I spend as much time wiping as I do crapping, maybe even more. I use toilet paper like it grew on trees—so says my envious father—I wipe until that little orifice of mine is red as a raspberry; but still, much as I

would like to please my mother by dropping into her laundry hamper at the end of each day jockey shorts such as might have encased the asshole of an angel, I deliver forth instead (deliberately, Herr Doctor?—or just inevitably?) the fetid little drawers of a boy.[29]

Washing the anus after defecation is not restricted, by any means, to persons using the bidet, nor is the practice as recent as the development of that equipment. It dates back into antiquity and has been an integral part of the religious laws of the Moslems, Hindus, and Jews, each of whom carefully prescribed the proper ritual to be followed. In circumstances when water was not available, then stones, dirt, or sand were to be used for this cleansing—the left hand always being employed, for it is the right hand with which one ate (another nicety we no longer observe). Hindus in the last century refused to believe that Europeans wiped only with paper and thought the story a vicious libel. In a somewhat analogous fashion, many peoples have been disturbed by the Western custom of using a handkerchief. The late Ian Fleming summed it up nicely in one of his novels when a Japanese pointedly observes that it has always seemed so astonishing to see a Westerner take a lovely linen cloth, deposit excrement on it, and then carefully wrap it up like some precious object and store it away in his pocket.[30] In this connection, note that the Japanese originally developed the tampon—a vast hygienic and aesthetic improvement over "the rag" universally used formerly.

Although the story of wiping with paper may not have been a vicious libel, it has, in some instances, seemed to Americans, at least, a vicious practice, most particularly in the case of European papers, which are generally regarded as "unsuitable," being either too coarse, too hard, or too glazed. In terms of cleansing this presents a somewhat curious situation since a classic reply to the American who is used to soft tissue is, "You don't wipe, you blot!" Blotting with a nonabsorbent paper is obviously the least effective cleansing method—and the one most favored in Great Britain.[31] On the continent, blotting is compensated for by the use of the bidet. Americans can be said to strike a middle ground by simply wiping with soft, absorbent tissue. From a historic viewpoint one must suppose that the Anglo-Saxon penchant for mortification of the flesh must have its origins in Puritanism, since before the commercial availability of toilet tissue as such, discarded printed matter was used, often with unhappy results. Not only the texture of the paper (particularly newsprint) but also the chemicals in the paper and ink commonly resulted in skin irritations and inflammations. In those circumstances one would have thought that the idea of simple washing would have occurred to someone. At the other extreme is the recommendation made by Rabelais' character Gargantua that the finest "wipe" in all the world is the neck of a white swan.

While fecal contamination is perhaps the most obvious(?) and widespread problem with our personal hygiene habits, much the same criticism can be leveled against men's urinary hygiene, for the plain fact, again, is that since men, unlike women, don't customarily blot themselves after urinating, their underpants and pants are stained and caked with crystallized urine deposits that no amount of dry cleaning will remove, as every dog unerringly knows.

This situation represents the most curious anomaly in the entire picture of personal hygiene practices and attitudes and is especially striking in view of our preoccupation with cleanliness in most other respects. The most obvious explanation is that our concern is, in many respects, only a cosmetic one—that we are primarily concerned with the appearance of cleanliness, with the appearance of beauty, and with the appearance of youth. What we cannot see or directly experience or what others cannot readily see we ignore.

In the British study cited earlier, the author noted that:

> For the greater part I was amazed that so many of the persons involved considered this state of affairs to be "normal." The question "Does your wife enjoy washing your pants?" usually

brought the reply "No—but she accepts it because she thinks all men are like this."[32]

Aside from some of the medical journals, perineal hygiene is a subject that is virtually ignored except for an occasional article in one of the more sophisticated women's magazines supporting the bidet for feminine hygiene. Obviously, considerably more education is necessary before we will take steps to correct this situation. It is also likely that the only way anal-genital cleansing may ever become a reality in the United States or in Great Britain is by accomplishing it in ways other than using the bidet, which has become so emotionally charged—or possibly by hoping that another "businessman" will discover that here is yet another part of the body that has not been adequately dealt with.

THE ANATOMY AND PHYSIOLOGY OF CLEANSING

3

THE HUMAN SKIN

The human skin is made up of several distinct layers. The outermost layer, the epidermis, is a thin membrane containing pigment and epithelial cells, pierced by sebaceous and sweat glands and hair follicles, and nourished from the layer below, the corium. The corium contains the glands, muscles, blood vessels, nerve endings, and hair follicles. The epidermis has been compared to a perpetual paper pad in the sense that, as each top sheet dies and is discarded or removed, a new sheet grows from the bottom to replace it. In the course of this constant regeneration, the cells that come to the surface die and undergo a chemical transformation into a horn-like material similar to nails. This outermost horny layer is constantly being shed but is held together by the oil from the sebaceous glands and, combined with foreign matter, forms a relatively dense and impervious deposit covering the body. (This deposit is seen most readily in dandruff.) It is this dead layer that protects the skin against damage from most foreign matter, but we must continually remove it if we are to keep the sebaceous and sweat glands clear and the body functioning properly.

Because it is a living organ, the skin can vary considerably in certain aspects, depending upon circumstances, for example, the process of aging. As a person ages, a number of marked changes occur in the skin. These include a decrease of water, a decrease of fat, a decrease in elasticity, and a decrease in the capacity to regenerate.

> The decrease in skin elasticity appears to run parallel with the actual degeneration of the elastic connective tissue fibers. The decrease in the subcutaneous fat may play a minor role. The dryness of the aged skin is probably secondary to decreased secretion of the sebaceous glands. . . .[1]

As a result of these changes the person most commonly suffers from an itching and an irritation, which can largely be overcome by using superfatted soaps and oiling the skin regularly.

In contrast, the so-called "animal" skin, even within the same age group, can vary from an extreme we call "dry" to one we call "oily," though strictly speaking, this refers primarily to the quantity of skin secretions and the appearance of the skin. The skin of infants and young children is obviously a much softer and more delicate covering than the skin of an adult and accordingly needs gentler handling and care. Most particularly, infants appear to secrete very little natural oils, and it is commonly recommended that they occasionally be given an oil bath in place of a regular bath, much the same as in caring for aged skin. In spite of these variations, however, the basic cleansing problems remain essentially the same for all ages.

Functionally, the skin serves a number of distinct, though interrelated, purposes:

Protective The skin protects the body against the elements and the general external environment. When clean and healthy, it acts in a self-disinfecting way to protect against microorganisms, such as streptococci, coliform bacteria, Salmonelleae, and perhaps viruses.[2] An excess of dirt, on the contrary, not only provides additional material for the growth of microorganisms but also inhibits the process of self-disinfection.

Sensory A rich nerve supply gives the skin an important sensory function.

Respiratory As a respiratory organ the skin is capable of eliminating water vapor and carbonic acid gas, though with respect to this function the role of the skin is minor compared with that of the lungs.

Heat Regulating The skin helps to maintain a constant body temperature by regulating the amount of heat lost from the body surface. Surplus heat is thrown off through perspiration. Undue loss of heat from evaporation of the perspiration is prevented by the oily layer of sebum.

Excretory The skin performs an excretory function of eliminating waste materials through both the sweat glands and the sebaceous glands. Sweat is composed principally of water and salt but contains numerous other chemicals that must be excreted as well. Sweat is normally acid and is a factor in protecting the skin from the growth of microorganisms. The sebum prevents the skin and the hair from becoming too dry or from absorbing moisture and holds the horny scales together to form a protective covering. As a result of this glandular activity:

> The skin is practically impermeable to the absorption of water or aqueous solutions of salts, alcohol, or other substances, except at the orifices of the sweat glands and hair follicles.[3]

The various body odors are a natural and inevitable result of the glandular secretions of different substances and of their subsequent chemical alteration as they lie on the skin, are exposed to air, and react with the resident bacteria of the skin. Since special circumstances can give rise to particular and identifiable odors, it is possible that certain kinds of secretions are released only in response to particular stimuli. The hairy parts of the body, the armpits, and the genital area are generally the most troublesome in this respect. First, they are more widely supplied with the apocrine glands, which secrete a relatively highly organic sweat and do so apparently more in response to emotions and exercise than to simple rises in temperature. Second, these regions, because they are confined by the body and by clothing, are ideal sites for bacterial growth.

There are four basic methods of combating body odor. One of the oldest is simply to mask the offending odor with another that is more pleasing, as when perfume or cologne is used with abandon. Some "deodorants" apparently do little more than that. The second, and simplest method, is to bathe and change clothing frequently. Curiously, one often overlooked source of body odor is clothing that has become soaked with perspiration. Thus, a shirt or dress that has not been cleaned may stink, even though the person wearing it may have just stepped from a bath. The third method is to impede the bacterial action by the use of a soap or deodorant containing a bactericide. The fourth is to use an antiperspirant or some combination of antiperspirant and bactericide or other agent. Unfortunately, recent research has considerably complicated the issue by revealing that many of the key ingredients used have produced severely adverse allergic reactions in numbers of users. In fact, many dermatologists are coming to the view that bactericides should not be used generally but should be restricted to special applications. They are not only felt to be generally unnecessary, they also basically attack the normal resident bacteria, which are thought to play an important protective role in combating external disease-producing bacteria. There is considerable concern that, in this instance, as in our enthusiastic overuse of antibiotics, we are seriously weakening our inherent disease resistance.[4] For most people, good hygiene practices and a simple antiperspirant are probably all that is necessary.

The head hair also presents some special cleansing problems. Because of its exposed position and its denseness, the head hair catches and retains more material from the atmosphere than the rest of the body does and also hides and retains the secretions and scales better, especially since it is generally cleansed relatively infrequently. The hair is also generally oilier than other parts of the body—naturally, because the hair is heavily lubricated by the sebaceous glands, and unnaturally, because of the practice of using oily lotions and pomades to enable the hair to be trained to assume desired forms. In some instances, one of which is the so-called "dry-itchy scalp," there is a lack of normal sebaceous secretions, and the dead cells are readily shed as "dandruff." In other cases, there is an overactivity of the sebaceous glands that results in binding the dirt together into a thick paste-like layer if the hair is not washed frequently. In either case, the hair presents an aggravated problem of cleansing.

AGENTS AND TECHNIQUES OF BODY CLEANSING

The essential problem in cleansing the skin is to remove the accumulation of foreign matter, dead cells, horn, and sebum and other secretions. In order to accomplish that most effectively, three things seem to be necessary: (1) a mechanical action that helps to dislodge and break up the horny layer, (2) a chemical agent that breaks down and emulsifies the oils, and (3) a solvent that picks up and carries off the accumulated materials. This is accomplished most commonly by using the hands for a massaging and lathering action, soap for an emulsifier, and warm water as the solvent. The mechanical action may be increased by use of a coarser agent such as a rough cloth or a brush, the temperature of the water may vary considerably, and a variety of soaps and detergents or special solvents may be used, but these are minor variations and the basic steps remain essentially the same.

The mechanical action of soaping, lathering, and scrubbing is also useful in ways other than merely dislodging dirt. It serves purely massage functions as well, increasing the blood circulation, nourishing the skin, and maintaining nerve and muscle tonus. The added abrasion of a brush or washcloth is to be recommended so long as the article is thoroughly cleansed between uses. Dermatologists often, however, advise against the use of a cloth because of the difficulty of keeping it clean and the reluctance to use a fresh one each time. From this standpoint, the hands are obviously best since they can be cleansed more readily than any implement.

Soaps or detergents are necessary in order to emulsify the body oils and render them soluble and hence removable in water. Soaping is particularly important for the hairy parts of the body like the armpits and groin, since they tend to hold secretions more than other parts. Equally important, however, is the thorough removal of all residue of soap because even small traces can continue to react with the body oils and result in irritation and odors. This is especially important with certain kinds of soaps that tend to form a chemical valence bond with the skin and that require extra care in rinsing.[5]

The most common solvent used for rinsing and carrying off all the residues is, of course, water—generally warm water. Although other solvents might be used, water is an almost universal solvent, is cheaper and more readily available than any other suitable substance, and is likely to continue to be the normal agent for cleansing in spite of possible localized water shortages.

Research has shown, however, that not all water is equally effective as a cleansing agent. "Hard" water, for example, which has a high mineral content, particularly of calcium and magnesium, reacts chemically with soaps, not only resulting in the need for more soap to get a decent lather but also making it more difficult to rinse the soap from the body. Incomplete rinsing with extremely hard water can leave a residue of precipitated soap curds on the skin that can hold bacteria and leave one with a sticky feeling. This is particularly true in the case of hair washing and was the basis for the time-hallowed practice of collecting rain water for washing purposes. "Soft" water, in contrast, takes less soap and permits greater cleanliness in that it is a more efficient solvent for carrying off waste matter, including the soap residue.

The temperature of the water is also a factor in cleansing. Aside from the fact that "warm" water (approximately 32°C to 38°C [90°F to 100°F]) is more comfortable than either hot or cold, it is also functional in two respects. First, the higher temperature helps break down the oils and makes it easier to carry them off; second, it dilates the blood vessels and the pores and permits more of the secretions to be removed. Cold water is less efficient from this functional standpoint. Warm water also tends to have a marked sedative effect and, as we know, is used as much for this reason as for its cleansing properties.

Hot water (temperatures over 38°C [100°F]) tends to be stimulating in its effect—as does cold water (approximately 18°C [65°F]); in fact, cold water is particularly useful for its tonic effects after warm water, since it acts to contract the blood vessels and pores and stimulates the muscles and nerves in an opposed way. Because of their effects on the vascular system, cold baths are often used purely as a therapeutic device. This tonic effect is the basic premise underlying the Scandinavian practice of going directly from the heat of the sauna into a cold lake or frolicking in the snow. Because the skin temperature is so high, one does not initially feel the cold, and as long as one times the cold exposure properly one feels only exhilarated. This phenomenon has also been exploited in a sophisticated transistorized impulse "Futurum" shower developed in Sweden in which programmed hot and cold water alternate in a multidirectional spray.

The method by which we supply and use the water, that is, the passive pool or tub and the active stream or shower, also has an effect on the cleansing possibilities. While the tub possesses certain real and psychological advantages over the shower, there is no question that it is the least effective cleansing method as it is commonly used. There is no escaping the fact that in the tub the water becomes increasingly dirty and inevitably leaves a film of dissolved and suspended dirt and soap on the body. Depending upon a variety of circumstances, including the kind of water, soap, or other substance used, it is possible to see a more or less thick scum on the surface of the water, a scum that clings as tenaciously to the body as to the sides of the container. This is true irrespective of how "clean" or "dirty" one was upon entering the bath, because a certain flaking of dead skin cells will inevitably take place, and so long as any soap or other additive is used, they will remain in suspension in the bath water. This problem can, of course, be dealt with relatively simply by showering or rinsing with a hand shower after emerging through the scum. Other, more sophisticated systems have also been proposed, such as providing continuous cycling as in a swimming pool where the scum can be drawn off at the top and fresh water constantly added. Although technically possible they are not particularly feasible economically.

In this regard tub bathing has, for many years, been forbidden to pregnant women, because of the fear of contaminated bath water entering the patient's vagina. While recent research tends to disprove this possibility, many physicians remain apprehensive because of the basic unhygienic conditions.[6]

Perhaps a more compelling argument against a

tub bath during pregnancy is the very real safety hazard posed by the average tub installation in which no grab bars are available. Getting from a standing to a supine position in a hard slippery tub is not easy for any of us but is particularly treacherous and difficult for a woman in the late stages of pregnancy.

Curiously enough, this problem—and its solution—is almost universally recognized with respect to face and hand washing and hair washing where virtually everyone today uses running water for face and hand washing instead of stoppering the basin as formerly and uses a shower whenever possible for hair washing instead of attempting to do it in the tub as formerly. Although some find the idea offensive, one measure of this recognition is that in many households where there is no shower, hair washing is performed in the kitchen sink where there is usually either a hand spray or the possibility of rinsing the hair under the tap. In both activities, however, there is a universal and clear recognition of the problem—a recognition that thus far has not extended to body cleansing. This may be, again, another instance of ignoring something we don't readily see or feel. But like all arguments, the one against the sanitariness of the tub is relative, particularly when viewed in the broad framework of human hygiene. Yet, since our goal is the clarification and establishment of objective standards, the present American usage of the tub must be condemned.

There are several other unique methods of water delivery and body cleansing that might also be mentioned. One is the "fog gun" developed by Buckminster Fuller during the 1930s. Extrapolating from his earlier Navy experiences, Fuller found that a combination of wind and heavy fog was extremely effective as a cleansing technique and developed a system employing the kinetic force of compressed air and atomized water together with liquid soap to cleanse and accelerate the surface oxidation of the skin. The system would presumably save enormous quantities of water since a one-hour "bath" apparently used only one pint of water. Such a system would obviously also drastically change the requirements for a bathroom. While such a system might perform satisfactorily as far as cleansing is concerned, it leaves a great deal to be desired as far as the many other reasons for bathing are concerned. Pure functional efficiency is not something most people seek, or even accept, much of the time.

There are always exceptions to every generalization, of course, such as the person who complained in a letter to *The New York Times* some years ago: "In these days of complicated machines for cleaning floors, dishes, clothes, etc., how come nobody has invented a gadget to help poor old homo sapiens 'come clean' in less than the fifteen minutes or so which the average shower takes? After all, even a car gets cleaned in one-third of this time in a five minute car wash!"

Another highly specialized system, designed for space use by the Fairchild-Hiller Corporation, is the "Astrovac," which superficially resembles a hand shower. It contains a sponge fed with water and a cleansing agent and cleaned of excess water and dirt by a vacuum line. Somewhat like the system just mentioned, this permits body cleansing with a minimum of water and eliminates the need for a container. Interestingly enough, in the Skylab missions, where space and weight are not nearly as critical as they were on the earlier Apollo flights, a version of a regular shower has been provided for the crews so that they could enjoy the pleasures of "real" bathing. Unfortunately, as in many space-performed activities, the "shower" takes up to an hour and a half to prepare and use, with the result that on the 59-day Skylab II mission apparently one crew member showered twice, one once, and one not at all. As Johnny Carson later quipped, "The three astronauts are fine. The guy who opened the hatch is on the critical list."

Perhaps the ultimate in bathing systems is the ultrasonic bathing machine shown at Expo 70 by the Sanyo Electric Company of Japan. The bather enters a capsule with his head outside, selects the desired water temperature and kind of soap, and pushes a button, and the machine does the rest. It soaks, washes with suds produced by ultrasonic waves, rinses, massages the body with rubber balls, and finally dries the body with heat lamps.

Although not strictly a bathing technique in our normal sense, mention should also be made of the various versions of the "steam bath," which might be considered to be deep-cleansing adjuncts to regular bathing, since normal soaping, scrubbing, and rinsing invariably precede and follow it. Although the distinctions are not commonly recognized, there are two distinct, though related, techniques involved: one using steam and one using dry heat. Both, however, rely on the application of intense heat to stimulate a profuse sweating and secretion of body wastes and an increase in vasomotor activity.

The Turkish bath, as well as the Russian and most contemporary steam baths, rely on steam and an air temperature ranging from 43° C to 54° C (110° F to 130° F). Although such a temperature is easier to achieve, it does not produce as profuse a sweating as the higher dry heat. More often than not, what one assumes to be perspiration is simply condensate.

The Finnish sauna, like the ancient Roman "sudatorium," relies on dry heat in the temperature range of 71° C (160° F) up to 104° C (220° F) and has a very low relative humidity, generally under 50 per cent. Under these conditions, perspiration begins quickly and is more profuse.[7]

Although not medically advisable for everyone, this "sweat bath," which is perhaps a more appropriate description, has enjoyed a wide and dedicated following for centuries. It appears to have been one of the earliest cleansing techniques and was common not only throughout northern Europe but also in Asia Minor, Japan, and among the North American Indians.

As we move further and further away from simple body cleansing, we find a wide variety of "baths" being used for therapeutic and pleasurable purposes such as whirlpool baths, mud baths, hot sawdust baths, and so on. The basic premise underlying all of them, however, is the application of heat in one form or another to induce perspiration and to stimulate blood circulation and rests on the ancient Hippocratic concept that states: "Give me the power to create a fever and I shall cure every illness."

4

DESIGN CRITERIA FOR CLEANSING HANDS, FACE, AND HAIR

The term *body cleansing* as used thus far has embraced not only total body cleansing, or what we normally refer to as bathing or showering, but also the separate cleansing of the hands alone, or the hands and face, or the hair, or the perineal region. Since there is no reason to suppose that there will be, or need be, any drastic change in this almost universal habit of sometimes cleansing only selected portions of the body at a time, each of these activities will be treated separately in the following discussion.

When we examine the totality of body cleansing as a physical activity in terms of what a person actually needs to do and the postures one needs to assume, we find that it is almost always active, often strenuous, and sometimes even potentially hazardous, compared with one's other habitual activities. One must be able to reach all parts of the body, climb in and out of containers, stand on slippery surfaces, and work with one's eyes shut—tasks that most of us perform unhesitatingly in this context but would balk at in another. It is a tribute to human adaptability. If, however, we accept the premise that the equipment should be designed to fit the task rather than the other way around, then we must first examine each of these activities in the light of the convenience, comfort, and safety of the user.

CLEANSING THE HANDS

Although we have studied hand washing as a separate activity and report on it separately here, the practice is inherently a part of face washing, which is more demanding as an activity. Consequently, the discussion here will be brief and merely point up some of the problems, since the obvious necessity of evolving one fixture to accommodate both activities means that the design criteria will largely be determined by the more demanding requirements of face washing,

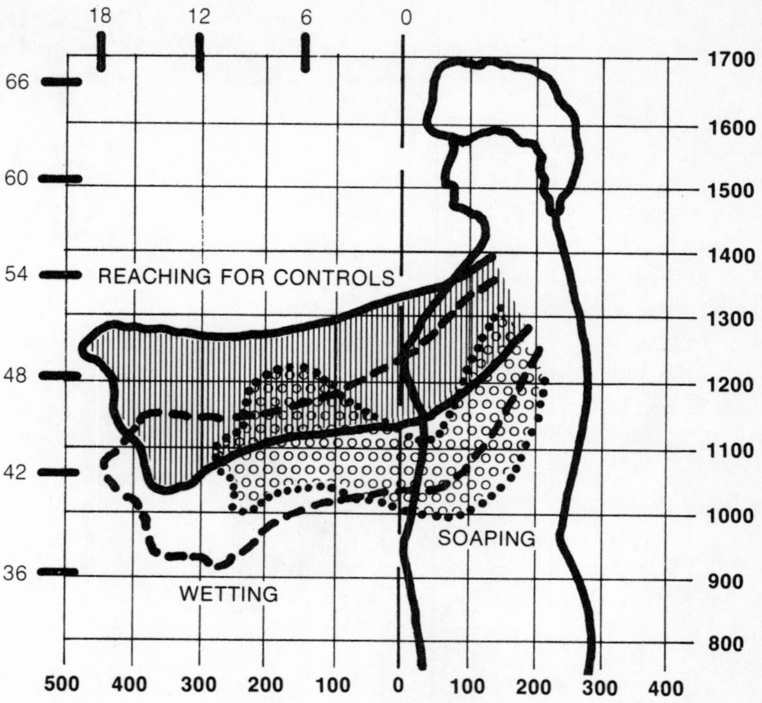

1 / RANGES OF BODY
AND ARM MOVEMENTS
WHILE ONE IS WASHING HANDS
WITHOUT REFERENCE TO EQUIPMENT

or in some cases, the still more demanding requirements of hair washing. Obviously the lavatory is used for a number of other hygiene and non-hygiene activities as well, but none are as critical in determining the basic design criteria as these fundamental washing activities.

DESCRIPTION OF ACTIVITY

Hand washing is probably the simplest and most frequently performed cleansing activity, largely because, in addition to being performed as an independent activity, it is performed in connection with many other personal hygiene functions—after grooming, oral hygiene, urination, and defecation and in conjunction with other washing activities.

Viewed as a separate activity, hand washing is performed relatively quickly, most often while fully dressed, and most conveniently while standing erect. The process itself is simple and similar to other washing activities; the parts must be wetted, soaped, massaged and/or scrubbed, and rinsed with clean water. Except when the hands are exceptionally dirty and need prolonged scrubbing or repeated washing, the process is accomplished in a single cycle usually lasting less than a minute.

Proper rinsing (and cleansing) can, however, be achieved only by using clean running water rather than a pool of water unless, of course, it is changed several times during the process. Since, in fact, the overwhelming majority of people today (94 per cent) regularly wash their hands under a stream, this is not as much of an issue as it was in the past when the habits established during the era of the hand-filled wash basin still prevailed.[1] In this respect, most conventional lavatories are totally unfunctional since they are still nothing more than the old-fashioned wash basin fitted up with a water supply and a drain and take no cognizance of the fact that when running water was supplied it changed our habits totally. Almost without exception, the water source is obviously intended solely for filling the basin and is located so that the spout is at, or even below, the rim of the basin and only 25 mm (1 inch) or so from the back wall of the basin. The results are that it is virtually impossible to get one's hands under the stream and that one is forced to assume a very tiring and uncomfortable posture because of the low heights at which lavatories have traditionally been mounted.

In terms of ideal posture, the body should be in a relaxed vertical position and the hands should be manipulated just in front of the body, with the upper arm vertical and the forearm extended horizontally. During the wetting and rinsing part of the process the hands are generally held slightly lower to prevent water from running down the arm and slightly further forward to prevent any water from splashing on clothing. Present lavatory installation practices and recommended standards, however, preclude such a posture. As will be demonstrated, the heights used at present are so low as to be ideal only for small children.

DESIGN CONSIDERATIONS

Our study involved observations of volunteer subjects under controlled conditions. In beginning our study of the activity itself, divorced from all considerations of equipment, the subjects were asked to pretend to wash their hands purely in the abstract. Then they were given a basin height but no water source and finally a water source but no basin. From these initial investigations several key points emerged. First, with no equipment to refer to, the subjects invariably proceeded to "wash" their hands while maintaining a relaxed but erect posture (see Figure 1). Second, with equipment introduced, the subjects oriented themselves to the water source while wetting and rinsing but maintained an erect posture while soaping. Only when the overall height of both basin and water source was as radically different from the freely assumed postures as that posed by conventional installations did subjects perform the whole operation while doubled over (see Figure 2).

Studies in other areas indicate that the optimum "work height" of the hands is 25 to 75 mm (1 to 3 inches) below the level of the elbow, a relaxed standing posture being assumed.[2] All the experiments substantiated this posture. There was, in addition, a rather constant relationship of approximately 100 mm (4 inches) below the water source at which the subjects tended to hold their hands—regardless of how the water source was positioned.

If we begin with the premise of accommodating the average of the total population, the comfortable working height of the hands can be set at roughly 965 mm (38 inches), with the water source at approximately 1,065 mm (42 inches) and the height of the basin rim at approximately 915 to 965 mm (36 to 38 inches). Present standards, by comparison, set the basin rim at approximately 760 mm (30 inches) with a water source height of approximately 735 mm (29 inches), forcing a working height for the hands of approximately 660 mm (26 inches). This is roughly 305 mm (12 inches)

2 / POSTURE ASSUMED
WHILE ONE IS WASHING HANDS AND FACE
USING CONVENTIONAL EQUIPMENT
AT CONVENTIONAL HEIGHT

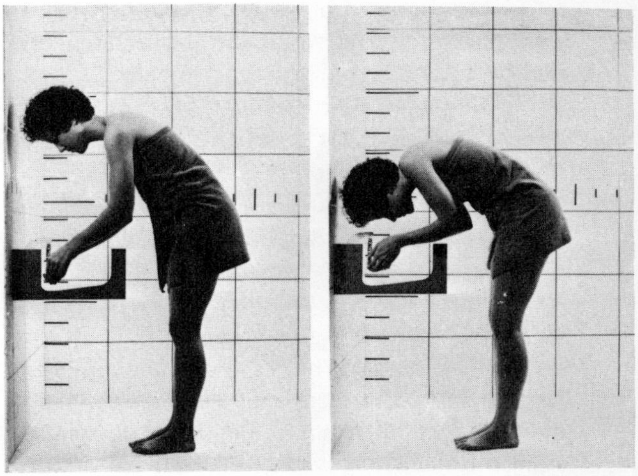

lower than the heights desirable for the use of the adult population (see Table 1). The existing situation is, however, worse than is indicated in Table 1 since the water source that was used was considerably higher, rather than lower, than the basin rim (see Figure 2). It does, nevertheless, show quite dramatically the extent of the problem.

TABLE 1 / COMPARISON BETWEEN HEIGHT AND OPTIMUM DIMENSIONS OF LAVATORY HEIGHT

Subject Height	Basin Height	Water-Source Height
1,238 mm (4′0¾″)	686 mm (27″)	838 mm (33″)
1,372 mm (4′6″)	787 mm (31″)	991 mm (39″)
1,626 mm (5′4″)	940 mm (37″)	1,143 mm (45″)
1,880 mm (6′2″)	1,092 mm (43″)	1,270 mm (50″)

In the horizontal plane, the position of the hands averaged 180 mm (7 inches) from the front of the body while soaping and massaging, or 150 mm (6 inches) from the front of the basin since, in almost all instances, the subject stood almost touching the front of the basin. The comfortable distance to the water source averaged approximately 280 mm (11 inches) from the body. A minimum of 100 to 125 mm (4 to 5 inches) is necessary from the water source to any back obstruction so as to allow room for the hands while rinsing. In contrast, most present lavatories offer only 25 to 50 mm (1 to 2 inches) of clearance from the water source to the back wall of the basin. Thus, the minimum dimension of the basin from front to back, for hand washing only, would be approximately 380 to 430 mm (15 to 17 inches).

The side-to-side dimension of the container is also a function of the position of the hands and their movements, in terms of catching water and of comfortable clearances. Since the hands are generally held close together during the entire washing process, a side-to-side distance of approximately 305 to 380 mm (12 to 15 inches) would be adequate in this case.

In terms of washing hands, the only requirement for the depth and cross-sectional configurations of the basin is the minimization of splash from the stream striking the surface of the basin. In this respect the use of aerators or other means of reducing impact and consequent splash is desirable. For this activity, however, the depth can be set at approximately 150 mm (6 inches), a water source 100 to 150 mm (4 to 6 inches) higher being assumed, since the depth depends largely on the position of the water source and the space necessary for the hands.

CLEANSING THE FACE

For purposes of this discussion, face washing is considered to include the face, neck, ears, and all parts of the head except the hair, which will be discussed separately since this is probably the activity least often performed in the lavatory.

The face is one of the most sensitive areas of the body in terms of hygiene and is easily subject to skin problems of various sorts. It is also highly sensitive to differences in soaps, and consequently there are great variations in the manner in which cleansing of the face is accomplished, particularly among women, for many of whom face cleansing becomes more a part of a grooming than a purely hygiene function. Most people use water, but some use only creams (approximately 1 per cent of the survey sample). Some use soap, others never do. Some commonly use a washcloth, others do not. For our purposes the activity is defined as washing with soap and a running stream of water. In this instance, 70 per cent of the survey respondents reported washing their faces by using a running stream of water rather than a pool.[3] Because of the variations in basic practice, however, this 70 per cent figure is in a sense quite comparable to the 94 per cent who used this method for hand washing.

DESCRIPTION OF ACTIVITY

Although far less frequent an activity than simple hand washing, face washing is also performed relatively quickly, most often while fully or partially dressed, and from a standing position. The pro-

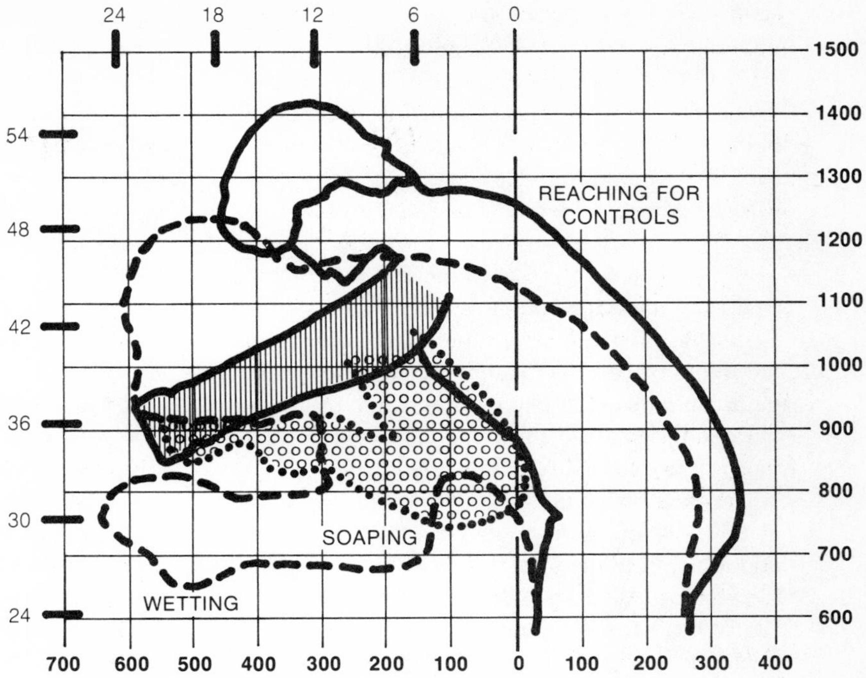

3 / RANGES OF BODY AND ARM MOVEMENTS WHILE ONE IS WASHING FACE WITHOUT REFERENCE TO EQUIPMENT

cess is again one of wetting, soaping and/or massaging, and rinsing with clean running water.

In terms of posture, face washing is more complex than hand washing in that more body movement is involved, but it is still essentially performed in a standing position. The normal sequence of steps is to: stand more or less erect and wet the hands, bend over and bring water to the face with cupped hands, stand erect and soap the hands, bend over and soap and massage the face, remain bent over while rinsing the face with water repeatedly brought to the face with cupped hands. The degree of bend assumed—and the height of the basin—are determined, respectively, by the maximum amount one can physically and comfortably bend and by how little one can bend and still keep from dribbling water down the arms and body while bringing water up to the face. Because of their low heights, present installations force one to assume virtually the maximum comfortable bend (see Figure 3).

DESIGN CONSIDERATIONS

The height of the source of water is dependent upon two aspects: the minimum degree of trunk flexion which is physically comfortable and at which the clothes remain dry and the desired distance (and direction) that water is brought from the stream to the face. Other considerations are that the container be high enough in relation to the water source to minimize splash and that the height not be such that it interferes with the movements of the elbows.

As with hand washing, tests were conducted both in the abstract, without equipment, and with equipment arranged in a variety of ways. From these studies it was found that the optimum basin height for face washing falls in the area of 865 to 915 mm (34 to 36 inches), while the optimum water source height is approximately 1,015 to 1,065 mm (40 to 42 inches). The posture assumed under these conditions is illustrated in Figure 4.

Note that these heights are slightly lower than the optimum heights for hand washing alone, but they are still significantly higher than present practice.

The horizontal distance from the front of the body to the water source, when the subject bent over in the comfortable range during wetting and rinsing, tended to average between 430 and 485 mm (17 and 19 inches). This was true irrespective of the actual distance between the front of the basin and the water source, as might be expected, since the orientation is to the water source, and the angle of bend was fairly constant. The minimum space needed beyond the water source for the hands remained the same as for hand washing: 100 to 150 mm (4 to 6 inches).

The side-to-side dimension is, again, a function of the positioning and movements of the hands and arms, in terms of catching water and providing comfortable clearances. In this case, the arms form a basic triangular pattern in this position that must be recognized. A circle of 305 mm (12 inches) in diameter centered on the water source would provide sufficient space at the back of the container. Since the span of the elbows ranges from 455 to 610 mm (18 to 24 inches), a shape that measured approximately 560 mm (22 inches) across the front and that tapered back and was tangent to the circle would provide ample space and result in a shape that was adequate and natural to the activity. Additional space across the back would only be unused, and any narrowing at the front would only result in cramping the arms and in dripping water.

The requirements for depth and configuration are essentially the same as for hand washing. The greatest depth is required at the back of the basin to provide sufficient room for the hands: approximately 150 to 205 mm (6 to 8 inches). Similarly, the front portion can be shallow since it serves essentially only to catch the drip from the arms.

One highly significant difference between the requirements for hand washing and for face washing (which will be even more critical in the case of hair washing) is in the potential methods of water delivery. Whereas the point of contact between the water stream and the hands remains approximately the same for both activities, in the case of hand washing a conventional faucet with a long reach, as is common on kitchen sinks, would be one way of solving the problem. Such a solution is, however, unsuitable for face or hair washing because of the hazard and obstruction such a faucet would present when bending over. For universal use, which a residential lavatory must accommodate in view of the range of uses to which it is put, a different approach is needed—one that delivers the water to the appropriate spot without presenting an obstacle. It may also be noted that the front-to-back dimension of the basin is a significant variable in this respect. With a longer than necessary dimension, for example, where one had to reach forward for the water and had to carry it back as well as up, the faucet itself assumes less importance in that it could be out of range of the head. The more compact the basin, the more critical the various relationships and the specific design resolutions become.

CLEANSING THE HAIR

Although not nearly as frequently performed at the lavatory as hand or face washing, hair washing is, nevertheless, still significant both in terms of frequency and the additional demands it makes of the fixture. The preferred method of hair washing from all viewpoints—comfort, convenience, and cleanliness—is in the shower. Failing that, the choice of equipment and/or locations is dependent upon available space and facilities for adequate rinsing. Combining hair washing with tub bathing, for example, would largely be a measure of desperation unless a hand spray were available; otherwise one is faced with the problem of how to obtain clean water for rinsing—interestingly, a point people seem to be more conscious of in this respect than with regard to bathing the body generally. In any event, one is forced in this situation into assuming awkward and uncomfortable postures at best. Although some people find the idea repugnant, one of the favored places to wash hair

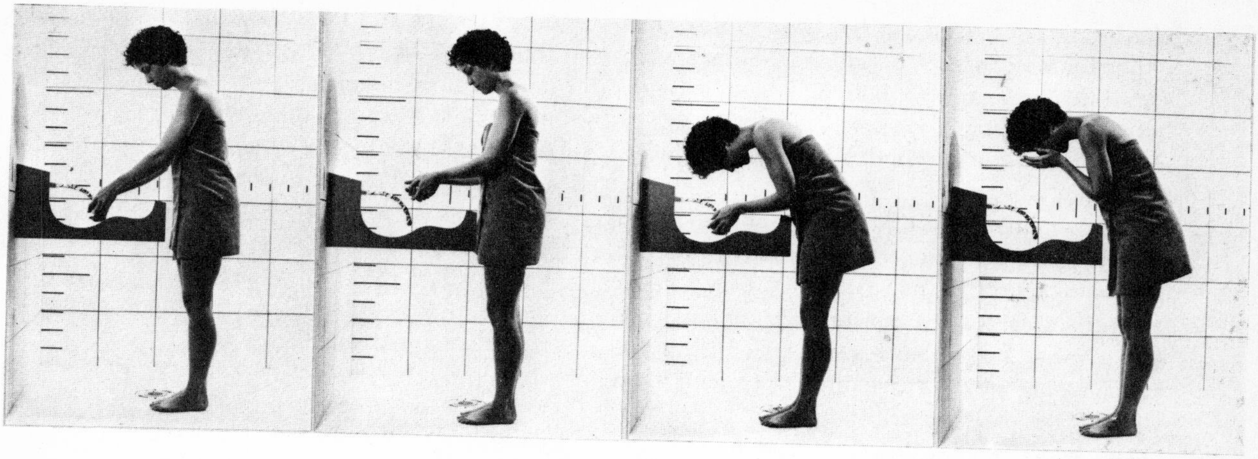

4 / POSTURE ASSUMED WHILE ONE IS WASHING HANDS AND FACE USING PROPOSED EQUIPMENT AT OPTIMAL HEIGHT

is at the kitchen sink.[4] This should not be surprising since there are many advantages to this location relative to the average conventional bathroom lavatory. The height is more comfortable—915 mm (36 inches) as opposed to 760 mm (30 inches); the sink is generally substantially larger; there is either a hand spray or a long swinging faucet to use for rinsing; and there is generally adequate counter space for shampoo, dryers, curlers, and other needed articles.

DESCRIPTION OF ACTIVITY

In terms of the actual steps involved, hair washing is basically similar to the other washing activities. The basic sequence is still wetting, soaping, massaging, and rinsing, and the basic posture must be a standing one in order to keep the body dry. One important difference is, however, that hair washing is to some extent a "blind" operation in that the eyes are kept closed for a major part of the sequence. Relative to hand or face washing, moreover, hair washing takes a much longer time and tends to be extremely sloppy, particularly for persons with long hair. Comfort and water containment are major problems and are largely responsible for the high percentage of persons who use the kitchen sink for this purpose in preference to the lavatory.

Another significant problem, and one also related to the use of the kitchen sink, is that of adequate rinsing. The hair tends to be the dirtiest part of the body as well as one of the most difficult to clean properly. On the assumption that all the accumulated materials have been dislodged, dissolved, and picked up in suspension, the key problem is carrying this material off. This can be accomplished only by thorough rinsing with clean water supplied in a stream or spray. Because of the relative difficulty of accomplishing this, many persons tend to wash, and especially to rinse, their hair more than once during each cleansing operation. Another important difference between this activity and face washing is that, for effective rinsing, the head must be directly rinsed by a stream or spray, rather than indirectly by water brought to the head with the hands.

DESIGN CONSIDERATIONS

The height of the water source is determined by the maximum degree of head and trunk flexion which is physiologically comfortable and at which the clothes remain dry and the desired and/or safe clearance from the top of the head in this position to the water source, a stationary water source rather than a hand-held mobile source being assumed. (This latter is generally impractical for self-operation unless random splashing and wetting is not a factor.)

The container in turn must be high enough in relation to the water source to minimize splashing and low enough for the individual to bend over comfortably and have full freedom for the arms and elbows. In this last respect, hair washing is considerably more active and strenuous than either of the previous activities.

The tests were again conducted both in the abstract and with a variety of equipment arrangements. The results are summarized below.

Persons tend to straighten up and stand almost erect, though with the head bent over the container, when soaping and massaging so that the position of the water source depends primarily on their allowing for a comfortable posture while wetting and rinsing. In this respect, the activity pattern is similar to that for face washing, in which the same tendency toward maintaining full flexion only while absolutely necessary was exhibited.

The preferred water source height was 1,040 mm (41 inches), though this was partially dependent upon the particular basin height. Generally, the most consistently acceptable water source heights were 205 to 255 mm (8 to 10 inches) above the rim of the basin; these allowed a clearance of 25 to 50 mm (1 to 2 inches) between the water source and the top of the head. (The front-to-back dimension of the head varies between 150 to 205 mm [6 and 8 inches] approximately.) In order to accommodate the total adult population, however, the desirable heights would range from 1,120 to 1,220 mm (44 to 48 inches) for the water source and from 865 to 965 mm (34 to 38 inches) for the basin, 1,170 mm (46 inches) and 915 mm (36 inches) being optimum (an overhead water source being assumed) (see Figure 5).

The use of a stream of water for wetting and rinsing results in a basic orientation to the water source rather than to the basin itself. The horizontal distance from the front of the body to the water source, when the subject was bent over in the comfortable range during wetting and rinsing, tended to average between 430 and 485 mm (17 and 19 inches), the same as for face washing.

Because of the relatively extreme bend, however, and the fact that much of the activity is performed with the eyes shut, there is also a tendency to shy away from obstructions such as the back of the basin. It is desirable, therefore, to maintain a minimum sensory clearance of at least 50 mm (2 inches) from the head to any obstruction. In this case, the distance from the water source to the back of the basin should be a minimum of 150 mm (6 inches).

In order to accommodate the shortest segment of the population, the distance from the front of

5 / POSTURE ASSUMED
WHILE ONE IS WASHING HAIR
USING PROPOSED EQUIPMENT
AT OPTIMAL HEIGHT

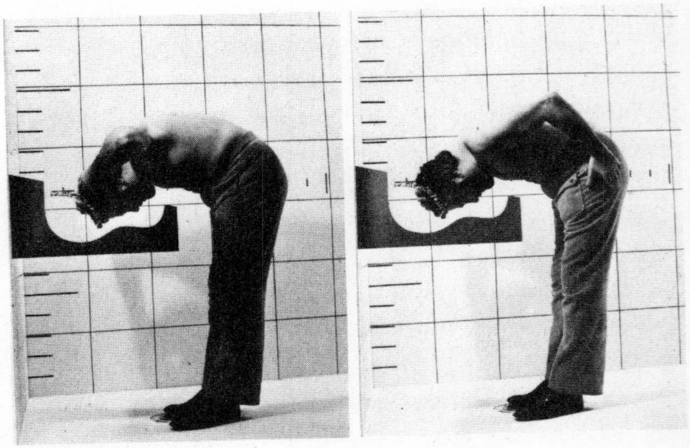

the basin to the water source should be no more than 380 mm (15 inches) (a 915-mm [36-inch] basin height being assumed), nor less than 305 mm (12 inches). This gives an overall front-to-back dimension of from 455 to 535 mm (18 to 21 inches), larger than that necessitated by hand or face washing.

The basic pattern of the arms is similar to that for face washing but larger in its dimensions because the hands are now used to massage the top and sides of the head rather than cupped under the head. The most extreme condition is produced during the rinsing phase when the head is moved from side to side under the stream and the hands are used to fluff the hair. Thus the head moves in an arc extending approximately 150 mm (6 inches) to either side of the water source and the elbows extend an average of 305 mm (12 inches) to either side. This suggests a minimum side-to-side dimension at the back of approximately 355 mm (14 inches) and a minimum dimension at the front of approximately 635 mm (25 inches).

Since the principal differences between this activity and hand and face washing are in the horizontal dimensions necessary, the vertical configuration and dimensions can remain essentially the same as proposed earlier. The one essential difference lies, however, in the water source. In both hand and face washing the point of water delivery is below the head. In head washing it must be above the head. In any case, however, the method of water delivery must be substantially different than has been customary.

Summary — Design Possibilities Although the lavatory must, from a practical viewpoint, accommodate a wide range of personal hygiene (and non-hygiene) activities from hand and face washing to hair washing, grooming, and oral hygiene, it is essentially face washing that poses the most severe demands in normal usage and hence can be regarded as the basic determinant of the design criteria.

The necessary dimensions, relationships, and general configurations are summarized in Figure 6. The dimensions in the low end of the range are

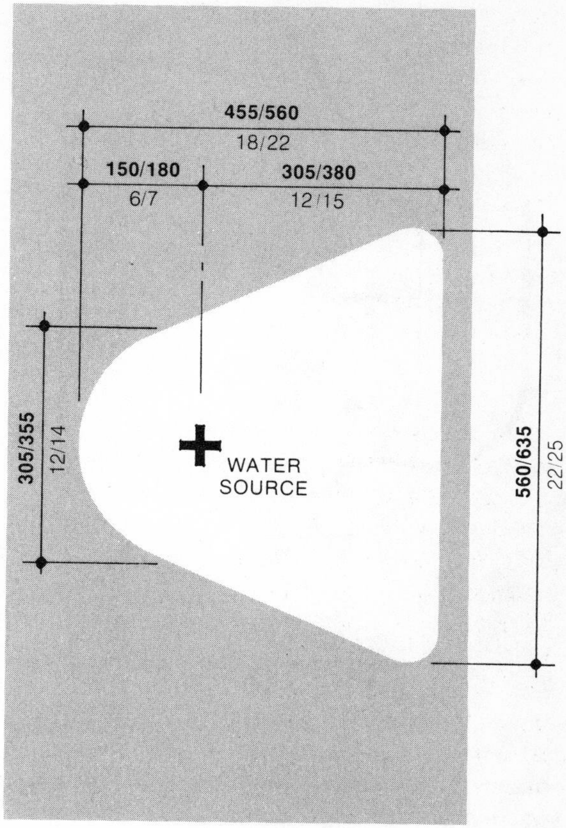

6 / DIMENSIONS AND CONFIGURATIONS NECESSARY FOR EQUIPMENT FOR WASHING HANDS AND FACE

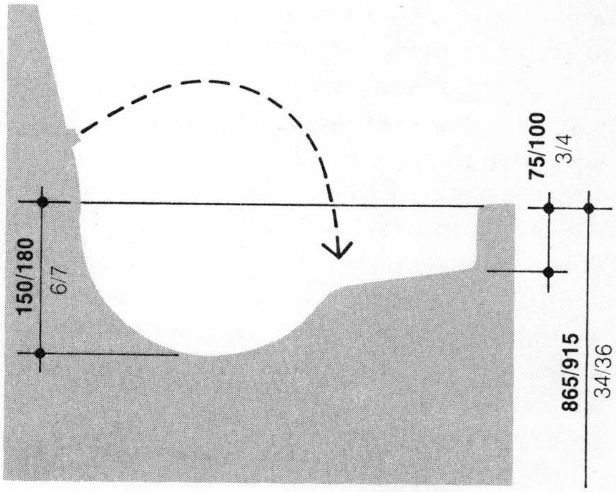

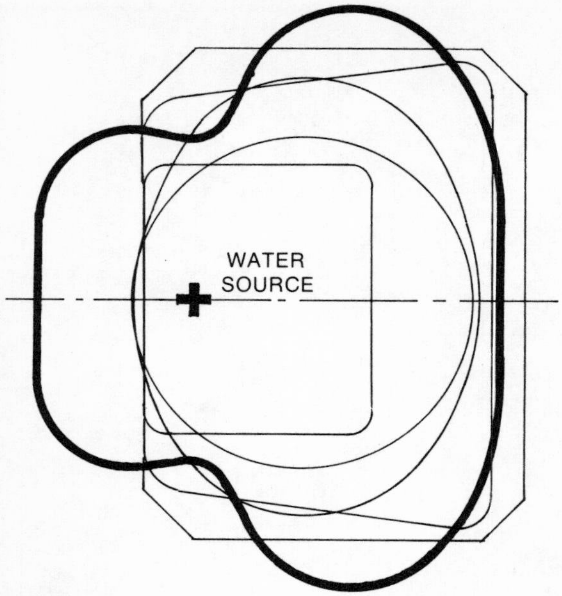

7 / COMPARISON BETWEEN COMMON LAVATORY SIZES AND NEEDED DIMENSIONS

based on the requirements for hand and face washing and the larger dimensions on the accommodation of hair washing.

Figure 7 compares these optimum dimensions and configurations with the immense variety of shapes and sizes generally available. The matter of available lavatory sizes offers as good a commentary on the attitudes of builders and architects with respect to the bathroom as anything else. An examination of virtually any manufacturer's catalog reveals a preponderance of undersized basins and invariably a few special models intended and advertised as "space savers" for those cramped spaces—some of which measure no more than 205 mm (8 inches) from front to back! Whereas this is perfectly understandable from a historical point of view since, fifty years ago, bathrooms were still being fitted into existing houses wherever possible, it does seem a bit odd that we are deliberately designing and building bathrooms today that necessitate the use of such inadequate fixtures.

Water Supply The method of water delivery and the positioning of the source are critical factors in the design of the basin. In addition, the water delivery should be from a single source capable of supplying mixed water. An aerated stream would minimize splashing, and consideration should be given to the use of a spray rather than a solid stream, because a spray would minimize both splashing and water consumption.[5] In general, using a running stream of water for normal hand and face washing requires less water than filling the basin. Probably the biggest single waste of water is in bringing hot water up to desired temperature from the supply main temperature. In this respect, use of a unit heater on each fixture, as is common in many parts of Europe, can effect significant reductions in water consumption, most particularly on the upper floors.

Controls The basic criteria for water supply controls are that they be readily and comfortably accessible, that they be direct and simple to understand and operate, and that they permit varying both the water temperature and pressure.

Experiments with various types of controls suggest that those operated by hand, rather than foot, knee, or elbow, are most convenient and comfortable for general use, particularly if two controls are necessary for regulating water temperature. Using foot controls tends to throw one off balance, is tiring, and is uncomfortable with bare feet.

Controls should also observe the "expected relationship" between the movement of the control device and the direction of what is being controlled. Faucets of the handle or lever type that turn in opposition to one another permit movement in the opposite direction by each hand. The relationship is direct and obvious and recognizes the basic opposition of hot and cold (or right- and left-hand actions). "Modern" or "decorator" faucets are commonly of the wheel type and some-

8 / POSSIBLE APPROACH TO A LAVATORY

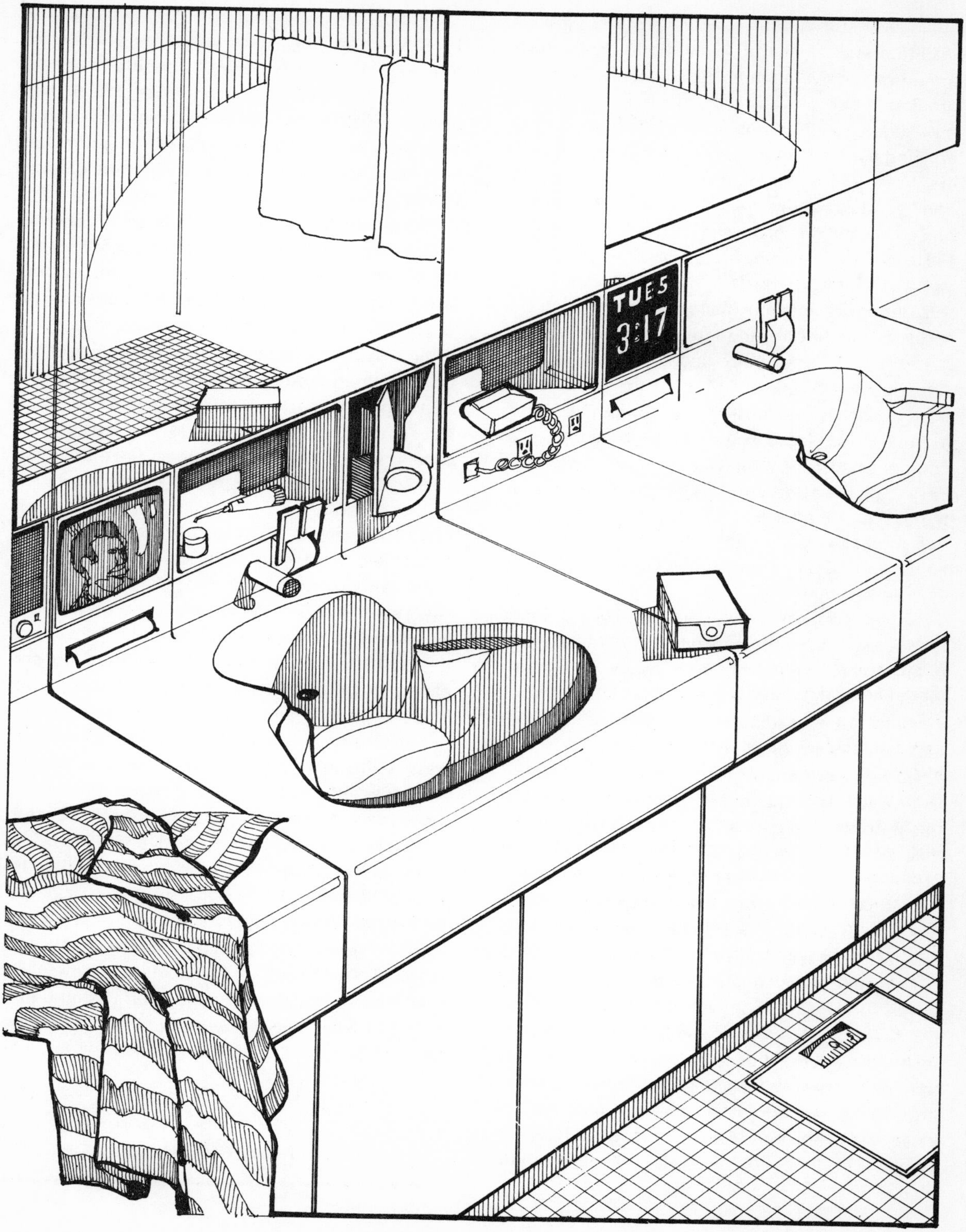
TUES
3:17

times even turn in the same direction, with a resultant lack of clarity, frustration arising from unnatural movements. When there are a great number of valves or faucets to be controlled, such a uniformity of operation is obvious and logical. In this case, however, the designers have lost sight of the essential "pairing" and "opposition" involved in bringing together hot and cold water and of the simultaneousness of use. Furthermore, lever controls are easier to grasp with wet and soapy hands.

In terms of location, paired controls such as these are commonly and logically mounted symmetrically on the back ledge of the basin. Although the proposed width of the basin from front to back is greater than that commonly found at present, the increased reach to the controls is compensated for by the additional height of the basin. Because the controls intersect the arc of the arm at a higher and farther point, it was also found that the operation of the controls is more comfortable if they are mounted more or less vertically rather than horizontally. With the arm outstretched at approximately counter height (915 mm [36 inches]), the arm, as well as the consequent natural rotational movement of the wrist, is at an approximate 60-degree angle. Operating a horizontally mounted rotating control forces the wrist into an awkward position.

Storage For hand or face washing, no particular storage demands are associated with the use of the basin other than for soap. Related activities, however, such as hair washing, shaving, grooming, and medicating pose considerable demands, primarily for a flat surface to put things down on temporarily where they will not be in the way of the arms. As we shall examine in more detail later, inadequate counter and storage space in the bathroom has long been a major shortcoming. An absolute minimum of 305 mm^2 (one square foot) is necessary for temporary storage at the lavatory for one person. In this respect countertop-mounted lavatories are vastly superior to even the grandest old-fashioned pedestal lavatory in terms of safe and usable storage space.

Cleaning A design consideration that is frequently overlooked is the ease with which a fixture can be kept clean. Fittings should be simple in design and shape and arranged so that all their parts are easily accessible, with no hidden surfaces. One approach, illustrated in Figure 9, is simply to incorporate the fittings into the body of the fixture itself.

Pop-up drains tend to be a special problem in this regard. It may be questioned whether they are really necessary at all in view of the fact that the lavatory is so rarely stoppered. Quite possibly an easily removable screen or strainer, such as those commonly used in kitchen sinks, would be preferable. Such an arrangement would not only make cleaning vastly easier, particularly with respect to hair removal, but would also provide a safeguard against accidentally losing things down the drain and would still allow the basin to be stoppered when necessary.

With respect to the fixture itself, it would be desirable if it could be designed to be essentially self-cleaning. Although a lavatory does not generally have a "ring" of scum around it after use, it is subject to considerable soiling from the various related hygiene activities such as grooming and particularly oral hygiene. Probably because there tends to be little actual physical contact with the fixture and because the lavatory is almost always used with running water, there also tends to be relatively little regular cleansing of the fixture. Although self-cleaning might be accomplished in a variety of ways, even a device as simple as locating the drain other than directly under the stream of water can be effective because of the swirling action set up.

Other criteria for ease of cleaning are that all parts of the fixture—particularly soap receptacles—be self-draining, that the fixture be mounted in such a way that any joints with adjoining surfaces can be easily cleaned (see Figure 48), and

9 / CURRENT APPROACHES TO LAVATORIES AND FITTINGS

"ARMADA" BASIN: VILLEROY & BOCH, METTLACH, WEST GERMANY, WITH "TASTAMAT" PUSH-BUTTON FITTING: HANSA, STUTTGART, WEST GERMANY

"ROHAGLAS" BASIN WITH INTEGRAL FITTINGS: RÖHM, DARMSTADT, WEST GERMANY

"CORALUX" BASIN: BUDERUS, WETZLAR, WEST GERMANY

"TASTAMAT" PUSH-BUTTON FITTING: HANSA, STUTTGART, WEST GERMANY

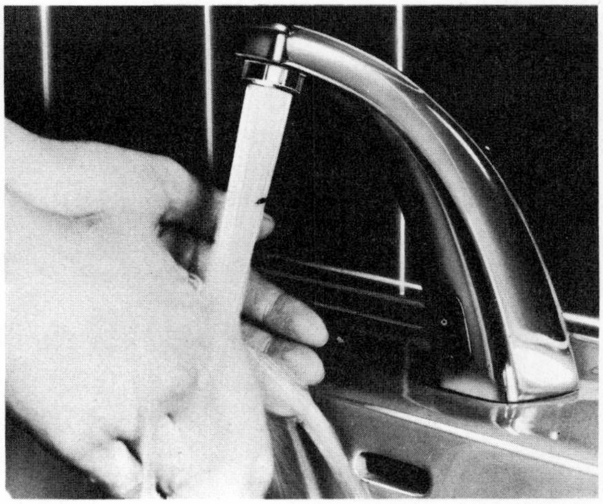

"AQUAMAT 2000" ELECTRONIC FITTING: BUTZKE-WERKE, BERLIN, WEST GERMANY

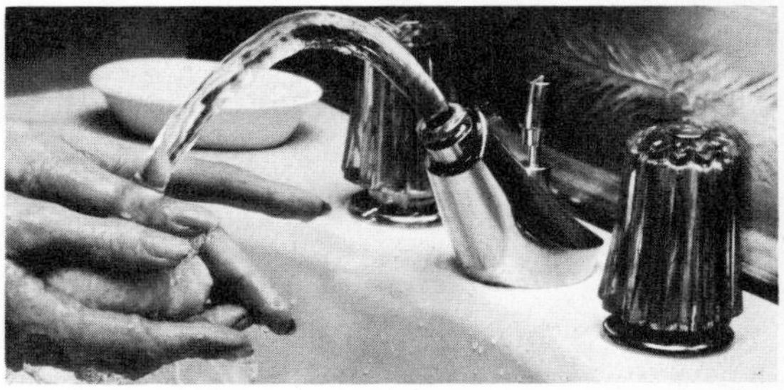

"ULTRAFONT" FOUNTAIN-TYPE FITTING: AMERICAN STANDARD, NEW BRUNSWICK, NEW JERSEY, U.S.A.

that no part of the fixture surface be inaccessible because of insufficient clearance between it and an adjacent surface.

One possible approach to such a facility is illustrated in Figure 8. The form of the container follows very closely the activity pattern described earlier (see Figure 6). As indicated, the forms are completely rounded sections, more or less spherical, and deeper at the back than at the front. The center portion, where the two concavities intersect—and where the stream normally hits—is convex. This configuration allows for ease in cleaning, but more significantly, it sets up a full swirling action so that the runoff effectively rinses most of the basin. The rim around the basin is slightly pitched around the front, not only for drainage but also for maximum freedom of arm movement.

A fountain type of water source is used in order to resolve the problem of interference with a spout. On the obvious assumption that a pressure-regulating device is employed to keep the stream always within the container, this arrangement also offers the considerable advantage of providing a water source at variable distances or locations. Thus, persons of different size can bring the stream to them and modify it at will rather than have to adapt to a fixed position. For hand washing, for example, the stream can be brought quite close; for face washing it can be "pushed back" out of the way. Interference from the spout is eliminated and cleaning also becomes simpler, in terms both of the basin and the fitting itself. An incidental advantage is its natural usefulness as a drinking fountain.

The controls illustrated are of the "throttle" type. Pulling either the hot or cold lever forward (or both simultaneously) turns the water on—or brings it forward. Pushing the levers back pushes the water back—or turns it off. The action of such a control is obvious and direct and is particularly well suited to the type of water source used. In fact, it would be difficult to imagine another type of control operation that would be as well fitted. Several recent innovative approaches to these problems are illustrated in Figure 9.

DESIGN CRITERIA FOR CLEANSING THE BODY—BATH

5

Although the two common methods of body cleansing (the tub and the shower) have significant differences psychologically and operationally, they also share certain common functional characteristics. Whereas standing or sitting under a stream, for example, is radically different from lying back comfortably in a pool, there is a significant convergence in the activity of washing itself. Of necessity, the postures and difficulties are essentially the same, even though, in some instances, the postures may be rotated 90 degrees, as illustrated in Figure 10.

There is also a convergence in terms of the need for a seat, multiple or flexible water sources for rinsing all parts of the body, auxiliary support devices, storage shelves, control locations, and even overall size. While, on the one hand, this suggests a design that could serve both approaches equally well, the differences between standing and reclining postures are substantial enough not to preclude designs focusing specifically on the unique characteristics of each approach taken separately. Any bathtub, however, that has a shower head installed in conjunction with it will have to serve as a shower receptor as well, and this must be clearly recognized in the design. In fact, it is likely that, in the United States particularly, most bathtubs see service primarily as shower receptors.

For example, in 19 per cent of the households that had only a tub-shower combination, no member of the household ever used the fixture for taking a tub bath. Considering only adults, the figure rises to 40 per cent, and in households composed solely of adults, 43 per cent never used the fixture for taking a tub bath. Given the increasing trend toward the use of showers among the young, it is likely that the figure is considerably higher today, a decade later.[1]

In view of these considerations, the two methods of body cleansing have been analyzed in terms of both their unique and their common

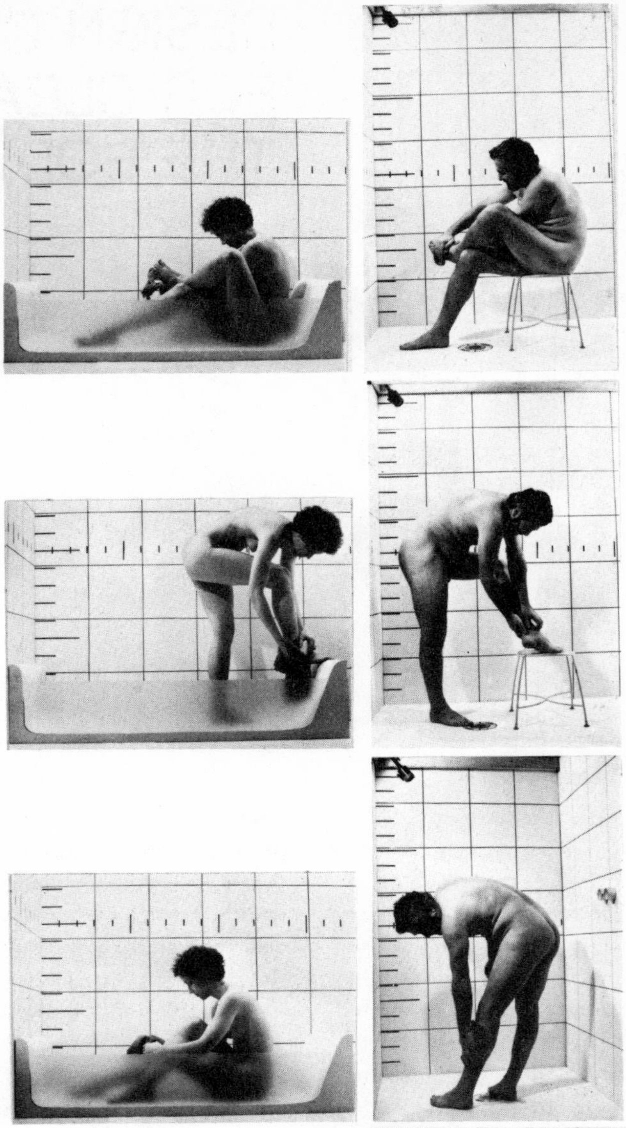

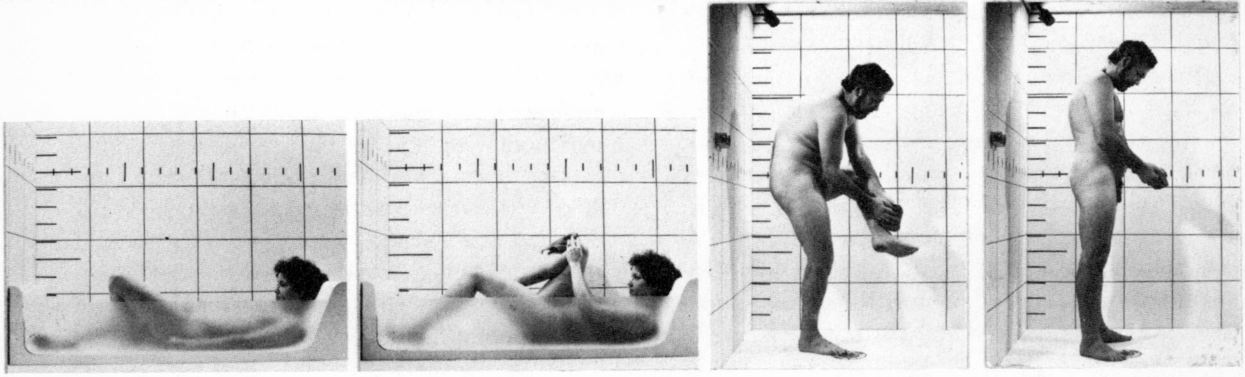

10 / SIMILARITY OF BASIC POSTURES ASSUMED FOR WASHING PARTS OF THE BODY IN TUB AND SHOWER METHODS OF BODY CLEANSING

characteristics, though for the sake of clarity they are presented separately.

DESCRIPTION OF ACTIVITY

Relative to other personal hygiene activities, body cleansing is a complex, strenuous, time-consuming, and sometimes potentially hazardous undertaking. In 1972, the U.S. Department of Housing and Urban Development estimated that 275,000 persons are injured annually in the United States using bathtubs and showers, a number ranking these fixtures second as a source of injuries involving home equipment.

Studies by the Bureau of Product Safety of the U.S. Department of Health, Education, and Welfare indicated that among such injuries lacerations accounted for almost half (49.1 per cent); contusions/abrasions (22.7 per cent) and fractures (10.6 per cent) were next most frequent. A more intensive follow-up study revealed that falls and slips accounted for almost half the accidents.[2]

Several recent experimental approaches have tried to solve these problems by the creation of "soft" bathrooms in which virtually all the fixtures, fittings, and room surfaces were covered with varying densities of plastic foams of one sort or another so as to create a completely energy-absorbing environment. While it is not possible at this time to assess fully the potential problems of such a solution with respect to longevity, cleanability, repairability, and fire hazards, it does represent the ultimate "idiot-proof" approach. On the other hand, it is possible, even with conventional materials and finishes, to achieve significant gains in user comfort and safety simply by paying attention to certain basic design criteria that are commonly ignored.[3]

When we examine body cleansing from an overall point of view, we find that it is composed of several major components, of which the actual washing process is only one. These include getting in and out of the fixture; relaxing, which in this case must be viewed as a distinct and major subactivity; and cleansing, which consists of wetting, soaping, massaging, and rinsing.

Getting In and Out of the Tub Because a bathtub, by definition, must be a vessel capable of containing the body and a quantity of water sufficient to cover most of the body, its dimensions become such that even getting in and out of the tub needs to be regarded as a major component of the overall activity. It is a maneuver that is difficult for infirm persons and potentially hazardous for all persons.

In general, there are three basic methods of getting into (and out of) a tub: 1 / stepping over the rim with the body held erect; 2 / bending forward and supporting the body by holding on to the rim and swinging the legs over in back; 3 / sitting on the rim and lifting the legs over in front. (There is also the somewhat special fourth category that involves a sunken tub and poses unique and extreme problems of safety.)

There are also some basic differences between getting in and getting out. Getting in involves lowering the body from a standing (or sitting) to a squat position, by using mainly the body's own restraint mechanisms, and then shifting each (weight-bearing) leg into an outstretched position and lowering that side of the buttocks onto the tub bottom while simultaneously shifting much of the body weight to it.

Getting out involves shifting the weight of the body from the buttocks onto the feet, which must become positioned underneath the major weight of the body, and then pulling or pushing the body into an upright position.

Relaxing Relaxing in the tub is largely a matter of assuming a passive and static position in which the body is relieved of all muscular tension and strain. This results when individual stable positions are assumed by achieving the lowest center of gravity and providing support for every body segment, including the head.

It is probably fair to say that the only substantive reason for taking a tub bath (other than pure personal idiosyncrasy) is to "relax," and yet it is precisely this that the vast majority of tubs have not permitted the user to do, particularly in the United States. This unquestionably has to do with the fact that most American tubs are used as shower receptors. Conversely, in Europe where tub bathing still appears to be by far preferred, the tubs are generally much more satisfactory—but are frequently unsuitable as shower receptors. This analysis consequently must concern itself equally with the possibilities and problems of relaxing as well as with those of cleansing the body in a pool of water.

Washing Although the basic cleansing process remains more or less constant, namely wetting, soaping, massaging, and rinsing, it is essential that it be possible to reach all parts of the body easily and comfortably, both in and out of the water. Wetting is customarily accomplished by immersing the body as nearly completely as possible, though in many instances this presents a gymnastic challenge because of the size and configuration of the tub (see Figure 11). Soaping and massaging, on the contrary, must, in order to be effective, be done while the body part is out of the water, and this requirement often necessitates numerous changes in position, as indicated in Figure 10. From a safety viewpoint, however, it would be desirable to minimize the amount of movement that must take place and to be sure that all the postures assumed are stable. The rinsing operation is, of course, effectively accomplished only by means of clear running water, though it is most commonly managed after a fashion by immersing the body again in the by now dirty bath water.

DESIGN CONSIDERATIONS

If we accept the fact that tub bathing, by definition, involves the assumption of a fully reclining posture with only the head kept above the water, whether for relaxing or merely for wetting the body, we might well begin with the requirements posed by this aspect since it is what most clearly distinguishes this fixture from one designed for showering.

The first and most obvious (and also the most ignored) criterion is that the user be able to lie back and stretch out comfortably. This suggests an elongated, directional shape of sufficient size, contoured so as to provide an integral back- and headrest, together with some provisions for aiding the assumption or termination of this posture. Most modern bathtubs are totally inadequate in these respects, as indicated by the postures illustrated in Figure 11.

Angle and Configuration of the Back For maximum comfort while fully reclining, complete support must be provided for all parts of the body, particularly the back and the head. The provision of full support requires, however, careful analysis and design because it must bear a major part of the body's weight and do so on a hard, unyielding surface uncushioned by any layers of clothing.

A related and critical factor is the basic angle at which the backrest is set. This not only affects the user's comfort but is also a major determinant of the basic size of the fixture. The more nearly vertical the backrest, for example, the higher the sides will have to be to allow the body to be fully under water, and the shorter the overall length can be. Conversely, a nearly horizontal backrest permits lower sides but also necessitates a considerably longer fixture. Other considerations are the relative ease with which a person can lower and raise himself from the reclining position and the maximum angle at which the head can be comfortably kept out of the water while the shoulders are covered.

Tests of the angle of the back were made at 5-degree intervals from 90 degrees (vertical) to 0 degrees (horizontal). At each angle tested, comfort was measured in terms of the position of the ischial tuberosities and of the coccyx (whether or not they were "digging into" the bottom of the tub), the existence of support at the small of the back, and the subjects' opinions of their relative comfort.

The various angles were tested both when the subjects sat with their buttocks to the back of the tub and when they slumped (let the buttocks slide forward—away from the back of the tub). The angle found to be most comfortable was in the range from 25 to 40 degrees. At any angle less than 25 degrees, a water level sufficient to cover

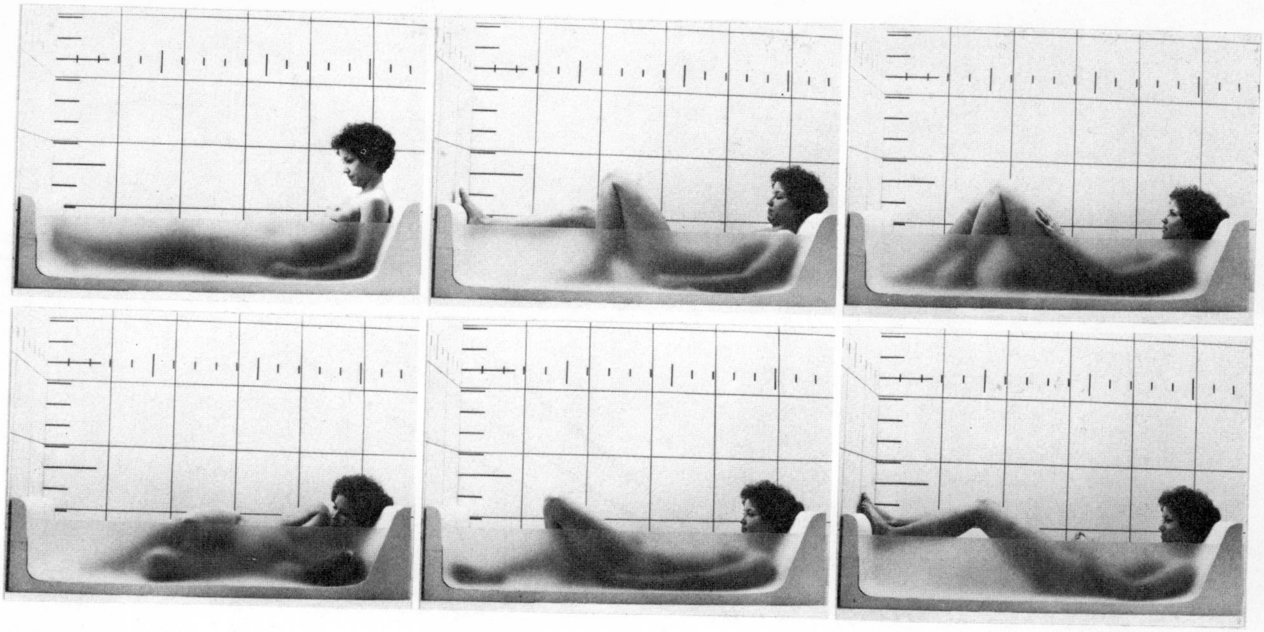

11 / POSTURES ASSUMED FOR RELAXING IN A CONVENTIONAL TUB

the shoulders of an average adult would also uncomfortably reach part of the back of the head and neck and cause the hair to get wet. At angles greater than 40 degrees so much of the body weight was transferred to the buttocks as to be uncomfortable. This is in part due to the fact that a flat bottom was used that caused pressure on the ischial tuberosities at an unaccustomed angle and that also resulted in a tendency to slide downward. This can be overcome by providing a contoured sitting area as well, but this would magnify the problems of getting up from a reclining position and would also violate one of the basic safety criteria, namely that the bottom of the tub be essentially planar and flat for possible standing. There is, however, a tendency to float away from the backrest at any angle if the body is not braced by the feet. This can, however, be overcome by reversing the longitudinal slope of the bottom of the tub so that the bottom slopes toward the back rather than away from it. This also involves, of course, reversing the customary location of the drain outlet, but as will be demonstrated later this, too, offers several functional advantages, one of which is that the user's comfort is increased.

An investigation of the rather extensive literature on seating indicates a general consensus on several points that are applicable to the determination of the back contour.[4] These are that the backrest be vertically contoured to approximate the natural curvature of the spine so that support can be given to the lumbosacral (lower) area of the back and to the shoulder, and that the back support begin a minimum of 100 mm (4 inches) above the level of the seat and thus allow for the greatest variations in posture. The specific criteria evolved from these principles and illustrated in Figure 12 follow.

In order for support to be given to the user's lower back, the back of the tub should begin to curve at least 100 mm (4 inches) above the bottom of the tub. This will allow the initial point of con-

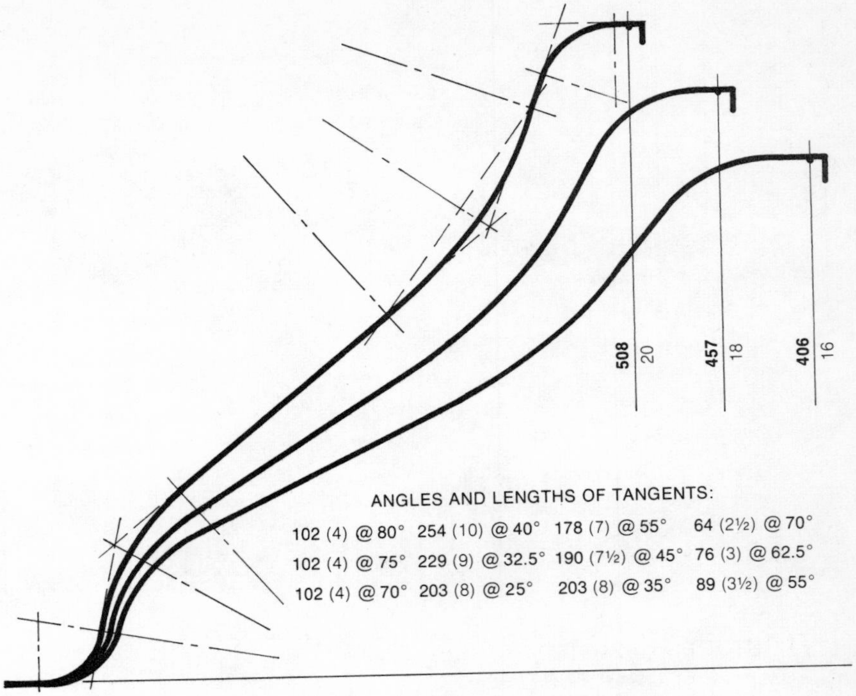

102 (4) @ 80°	254 (10) @ 40°	178 (7) @ 55°	64 (2½) @ 70°
102 (4) @ 75°	229 (9) @ 32.5°	190 (7½) @ 45°	76 (3) @ 62.5°
102 (4) @ 70°	203 (8) @ 25°	203 (8) @ 35°	89 (3½) @ 55°

12 / PROPOSED CONTOURS AND ANGLES OF TUB BACKREST

tact with the back of the tub to be at approximately waist level and will allow space for the buttocks and the coccyx.

The subjects studied in the laboratory chose an angle for the back of the tub, below shoulder level, of at least 40 degrees but wanted their heads raised somewhat. This coincides basically with the findings regarding seating in general. The back of the tub, then, should become gradually steeper toward shoulder level, which would be 330 to 405 mm (13 to 16 inches) from the point at which the back of the tub begins to angle back.

The tub should be contoured even more steeply under the neck and head, at an angle of approximately 55 degrees. This should begin at 405 mm (16 inches) from the point at which the back of the tub begins its 25- to 40-degree angle and continue to 510 mm (20 inches), where it should round off to form the rim of the tub. Shorter persons would receive support from the nape of the neck to the prominent part of the occipital bone where the back of the tub steepens, while taller persons would be supported at the nape of the neck where the back of the tub levels off to form the rim. Differences in the sizes of people occur primarily in the lower part of the body; the range in total sitting height for 90 per cent of the adult population is less than 100 mm (4 inches), so that it is not unreasonable to assume that a single fixed contour can comfortably accommodate most of the adult population. Figure 13 illustrates various relaxing postures possible for persons of varying body dimensions with a median basic back angle of 32.5 degrees.

For maximum comfort it is also necessary that the back of the tub be similarly contoured in the transverse direction as well. A full semicircular horizontal contour, as is commonly found, is too pronounced and tends to cramp the shoulders. A perfectly flat section, in contrast, generally results in discomfort both at the lower back and at the neck where the spinal column tends to be exposed. The most likely solution would appear to be a gentle compound curve.

In this case, adequate space must be allowed for the largest persons to lean back comfortably. The greatest sitting breadth to be accommodated is 411 mm (16.2 inches) and the greatest shoulder breadth 460 mm (18.1 inches). Room for clearance being added, the width of the tub at shoulder level, 330 to 405 mm (13 to 16 inches) from the beginning of the angle of the tub back, should be a minimum of 560 mm (22 inches).

Length of Tub The overall length of the tub is a function of the angle of the back of the tub, on the assumption that a fully reclining posture must be accommodated. In determining a suitable length we must consider, besides purely anthropometric dimensions, the fact that there is a tendency for the body to float away from the backrest and slide down until the feet find support. Therefore, an overall tub length that is not *too long* for the shorter segment of the population is equally as important as one that is long enough for taller people, especially in view of the fact that taller people can always bend their legs somewhat if necessary. This does suggest, however, that some arrangement that allowed for several lengths might prove desirable (see Figure 14).

If we begin with the shortest segment of the adult population, whose length from the back of the buttocks to the feet in a sitting position is approximately 940 mm (37 inches), we can establish the minimum length of the bottom at approximately 1,065 mm (42 inches), defining "bottom" as the portion of the bottom that is flat enough to stand on, measured from the front wall to the point where the slope of the backrest begins. This allows for the distance from the buttocks to the actual start of the back contour (see Figure 12). For the largest segment of the population, the comparable length is approximately 1,090 mm (43 inches), yielding a maximum bottom length of

13 / POSTURES ASSUMED FOR RELAXING IN PROPOSED TUB

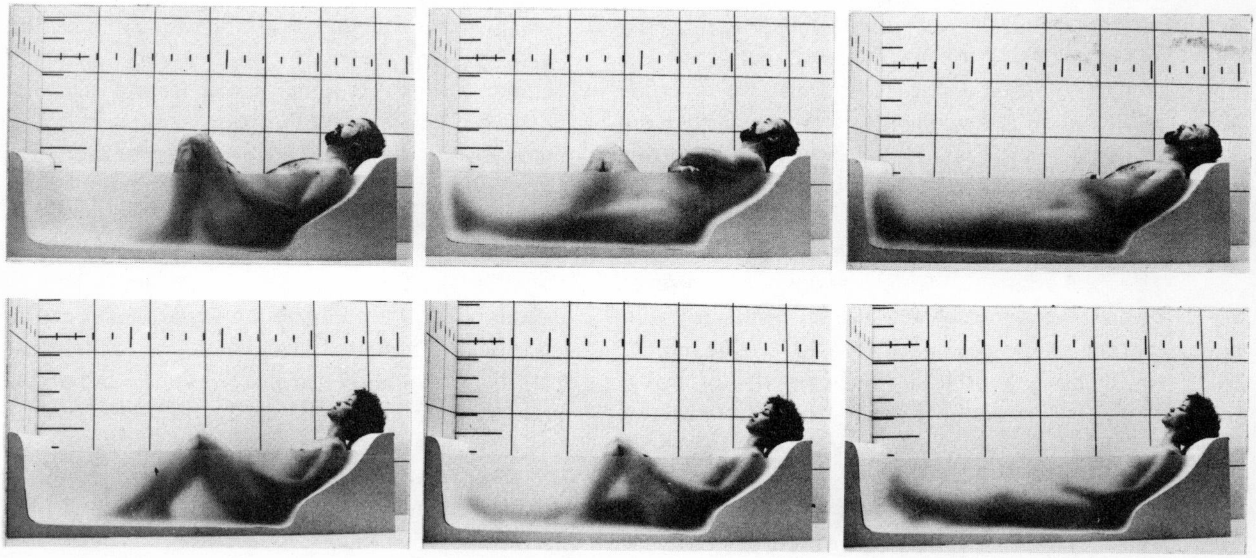

approximately 1,220 mm (48 inches). In this instance, the compromise length of 1,145 mm (45 inches) would still be acceptable and would yield comfortable, relaxed postures to both groups if each made slight adjustments. In terms of actual washing operations these dimensions are more than adequate since the basic posture that must be assumed in order to reach all parts of the body is a doubled-over sitting one, as illustrated in Figure 10.

When these length figures are combined with the desirable configuration for the back, the *overall* maximum length of the tub becomes more nearly 1,830 mm (6 feet) than the 1,525 mm (5 feet) customarily found. If, for economic reasons, one wished to keep the overall length to 1,525 mm (5 feet), it would be necessary to resort to the proportions commonly found in the early free-standing tubs, in which the more steeply sloped back (a 40-degree back angle, which gave a shorter length) was compensated for by a considerably greater depth so that the user could remain comfortably submerged.

Depth of Tub (Inside) As stated above, the inside depth of the tub is determined largely by its relationship to the angle and contour of the back and to the length. If the general slope of the back is set within the comfortable 25- to 40-degree range, the depth of water needed to cover the shoulders of large adults while fully reclining would be 305 to 405 mm (12 to 16 inches respectively). The total inside depth must, however, be sufficient to prevent water from splashing out while the person is washing or otherwise moving about. For this, another 100 mm (4 inches) is necessary as a minimum, yielding a total inside depth of from 405 to 510 mm (16 to 20 inches). The total volume of water used would, however, be approximately the same as is now used in tubs that have total depths of from 305 to 405 mm (12 to 16 inches), primarily because the proposed configuration with the backrest would result in a smaller volume than present configurations require.

In making a final determination of the depth, consideration must also be given to the height of the side in relation to the ease of using it as a support and in relation to the width of the tub. The higher the sides, the wider the tub must be in order to have sufficient clearance for washing movements while the person is seated in the tub.

Width of Tub The inside tub width at a minimum would have to accommodate the seat breadth of the largest members of the population with at least 50 mm (2 inches) of clearance on each side. This would mean a width of approximately 535 mm (21 inches). This would not, however, allow sufficient room for any of the body movements commonly involved in bathing, on the assumption that the person is seated in the bottom of the tub while engaging in the washing operations. On the other hand, it may be seriously questioned whether the entire washing operation ought to have to take place from such a posture. As suggested in Figure 10, a person has a limited number of ways in which he can reach all the parts of the body, regardless of whether his essential posture is reclining, sitting, or standing. Significantly, however, some of these positions are far easier and more comfortable to assume and maintain from one posture than from another. Washing the arms and upper torso can be accomplished while one is sitting flat, sitting upright, or standing. It is easiest, however, from a standing position in that the entire trunk of the body is freer to rotate. Washing of the midsection can be managed while one is sitting upright or standing, but it is again easier from a standing position. The most difficult task is the washing of the feet and legs, which, while it can be managed from all three basic positions, is simplest from an upright sitting position, as suggested by Figure 10. Attempting this operation from a flat sitting position is extremely strenuous, while from a standing position it is both awkward and hazardous because of the unstable position of the body, even if the foot being washed is supported on the rim. In short, sitting flat on the bottom of the tub is the most difficult posture from which to attempt to wash oneself. In actual practice it is likely, however, that most persons use a combination of postures.

Returning to the question of optimum width, if we assume that the washing will be performed while sitting flat, then a width of from 610 to 685 mm (24 to 27 inches) is needed at the midpoint to accommodate the legs and the movements of the elbows. On the contrary, if we assume that a seat is provided for the washing operations, then a width of 560 mm (22 inches) is adequate for all but the largest segment of the population.

From the standpoint of getting in and out of the tub, however, the width should not exceed 915 mm (36 inches). When the side rims (or grab bars parallel to rims) are used for support and for aid in raising or lowering the body, the width of the tub should not be more than would allow small persons to keep their forearm flexed at 90 degrees or less when the upper arm is abducted to the maximum.

Seat If an integral seat is to be provided for foot washing or other operations, this may or may not influence the overall dimensions of the tub, depending on how such a seat is incorporated into the design, as Figure 14 suggests. If the seat is simply added to the length of the tub as, for example, in Figure 14-A, either as part of the tub or as part of the tub surround, then another 305 mm (12 inches) is needed. The seat might, however, be included within the basic volume of the tub, as suggested in Figure 14-B and 14-C, and also serve as a prop for short persons to brace themselves against in the relaxing position. In particular, the proposal illustrated in Figure 14-C could accommodate three different sizes of persons if they assumed slightly rotated positions.

The "Lotus" tub by Adamsez (England), shown in Figure 14-D, illustrates an ingenious approach in that the seat extends as a shelf over the recessed foot end of the tub. This allows for a seat within the normal length of the tub and also for two different sizes of persons to be accommodated. A different but equally interesting approach is

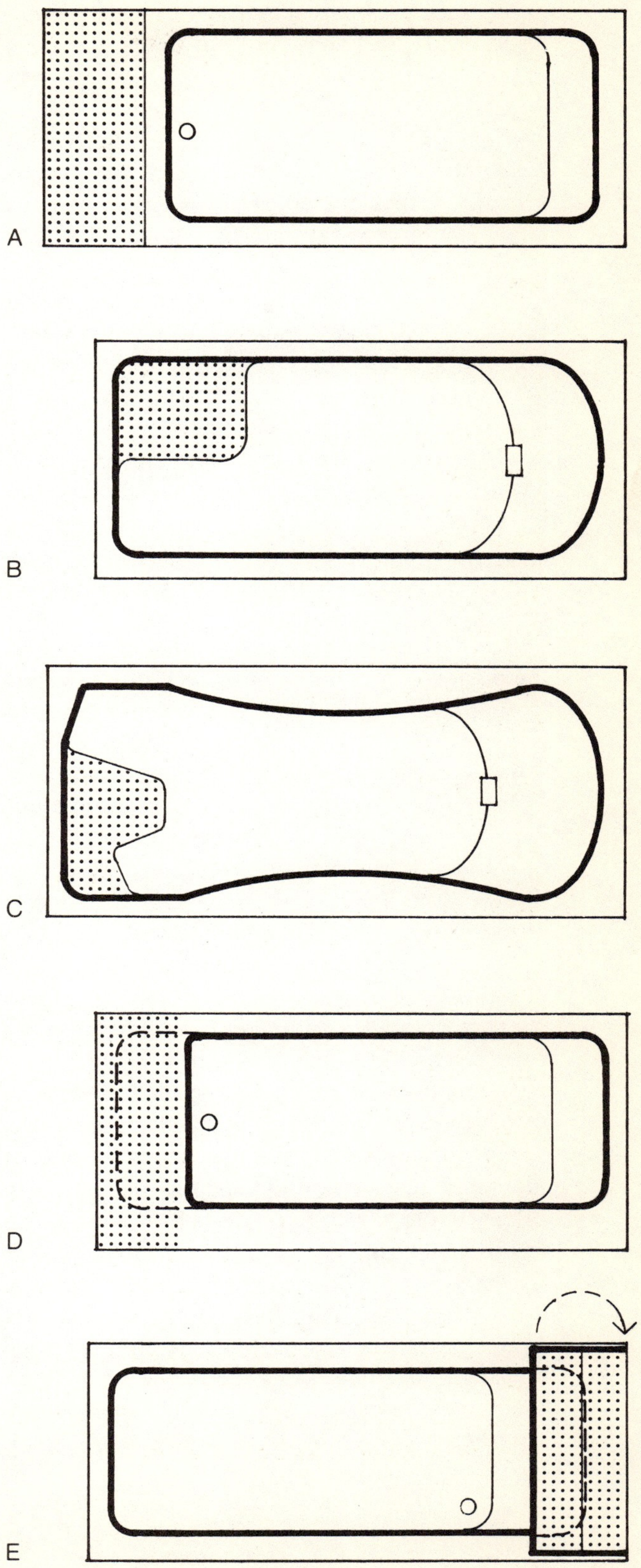

14 / APPROACHES TO PROVIDING A SEAT AS AN INTEGRAL PART OF AN IMPROVED TUB

the "Vogue" tub by Allied Iron Founders (England), shown in Figure 14-E, in which a foamed plastic headrest unfolds to form a seat over the backrest end of the tub.

In existing installations, a separate bath stool would be a perfectly good substitute, particularly for aged, overweight, pregnant, and other persons for whom the normal gymnastics are unsuitable or unfeasible.

In any event, such a seat should be a minimum of 305 mm (12 inches) square and should be self-draining. In this respect, seats that are part of the tub surround are not as satisfactory as those incorporated into the basic design of the fixture itself. A height in the normal tub depth range of 305 to 405 mm (12 to 16 inches) is satisfactory. The relationship of the seat to the controls and hand spray must be determined on the basis of the particular configurations involved. We are dealing here, of course, with fixtures intended for single-person occupancy, but there is virtually no limit to the degree of lavishness possible if one assumes fixtures intended for two or more bathers (see Figure 59).

Requirements for Access The matter of getting in and out of the tub presents major design problems, primarily from the viewpoint of safety. The operation is inherently hazardous, and the design of the fixture should be such as to minimize this hazard as much as possible.

The basic process of entering the tub is one of stepping or climbing over a barrier into a hard and slippery container and then lowering the body from a standing to a reclining position, and then reversing the process for leaving the tub. At each step, the body is momentarily off balance and is in danger of slipping and falling because the normal functional resistances that keep us balanced are greatly reduced with a wet glass-like surface. The key to minimizing these hazards is to provide for auxiliary support devices on which the body can be braced. The "old-fashioned" high-sided tub, which has been criticized as being unsafe, is actually safer from the standpoint of access than the modern low-sided tub, *if* no convenient support is provided—and almost universally it is not. The higher the side, the easier it is merely to reach out and steady oneself on the rim of the tub. A tub in the normal range of 305 to 405 mm (12 to 16 inches) is so low that it is almost impossible to steady oneself on the rim, and one is forced to find some other source of support.

Height of Tub Rim from Floor (Outside) When no grab bar or other convenient support is provided, there is a tendency to try to maintain an erect body position upon getting into a tub up to 405 mm (16 inches) in height and to bend forward and grasp the rim on getting into a tub of 430 mm (17 inches) or more. Generally, all the heights from 255 to 405 mm (10 to 16 inches) were acceptable to the subjects when using the erect approach, while a range from 430 to 610 mm (17 to 24 inches) was most acceptable to them when using the bending approach (see Figures 15 and 19).

When grab bars are provided, the subjects always use the bars and retain an erect position. The most acceptable rim heights ranged from 355 to 455 mm (14 to 18 inches).

Any rim height that was less than the inside depth of the tub, 355 mm (14 inches) in this case, was unacceptable. The subjects seemed to feel insecure and confused about the relative difference in depth, inside and out. In the case of fully sunken tubs this perceptual ambiguity is lessened somewhat insofar as one is clearly aware that one is stepping down, but water obscures one's ability to make a precise judgment of depth. The more serious problem, illustrated in Figure 16, is simply the awkwardness of taking such a big step onto an unsure footing.

If we accept the premise that the optimum height of the tub rim for an erect approach would be what could be stepped over easily (with auxiliary support), all but the smallest persons in the total population could easily step over a rim height of 380 mm (15 inches) and 50 per cent of the population could step over a height of 455 mm (18 inches).

Taken by themselves, however, these figures are misleading. As Figures 15 and 16 show, there is a tendency to step in sideways rather than straight on. Largely this is necessitated and determined by the width of the rim, the degree of curvature of the tub bottom, and the relationship of both with the rim height. The figures just given presume, therefore, a barrier of zero thickness. If the rim width is in the range of 150 to 205 mm (6 to 8 inches), as it often is, the problem then becomes one of not only stepping over but also of stepping out, as illustrated in Figure 16. Obviously, the greater the rim width the lower the height must be. (Note that the rim width of the tubs used in the experiments described earlier was 65 mm [2½ inches].) As Figure 16 also demonstrates, the greater the horizontal barrier the greater the danger of slipping and the greater the need for hand support, since the horizontal force component varies directly with the distance. The basic movement is much like walking except for the timing involved.

> In the human gait the equilibrium is lost and regained with every step; lost with the take off of the propelling foot when the body's center of gravity momentarily lies beyond the anterior border of the supporting surface. It is regained as soon as the swinging leg is extended forward and its heel touches the ground. The horizontal component of the force applied by the foot when it touches the floor acts forward and is counteracted in ordinary walking by a friction force which is just as large but acts in the opposite direction. It is this play of forces which reestablishes the momentarily lost balance at each step. But if the friction force is less than the horizontal force applied by the feet, the foot skids along the floor and we slip.[5]

Stepping in and out is a much slower and more deliberate movement than walking, with a consequent loss of momentum and of coordinated reflex action. Moreover, the greater the rim width the greater the tendency to step into the tub sideways. This tendency is always, of course, present to some extent because of the ultimate necessity of turning in the direction of the long axis of the tub in order to sit down. In summary, therefore, on the basis of a careful study of the relationship between the height and the width of the rim, the actual desirable height will be several inches less than those listed.

One other critical factor with respect to the safety of stepping in and out is the degree of curvature of the bottom of the tub and the radius of curvature between the horizontal and vertical surfaces. In tubs that are also, or primarily, used as shower receptors this matter becomes critical because of the basic standing posture used. The radius of the fillet is particularly of concern in stepping in and out because it effectively increases the distance to be stepped over, before a secure footing can be found. The greater the radius of curvature, the greater the distance to be stepped over. A fully curved bottom, most commonly found in Europe, presents the further hazard that the foot has no secure or stable position available to it at all when one is standing (see Figure 17 and p. 62).

If, however, we presume a tub with relatively high sides, 510 mm (20 inches) or more, as in the old-fashioned tub on legs, this relationship between height and rim width is not critical, because a person naturally climbs over sideways, as illustrated in Figure 19. The constant bent-over posture assumed in that approach is inherently safer than the erect approach, primarily because a person is always braced and supported and because the person never stands upright. Consequently, the shift in posture is from a bent-over one to a sitting, and then a reclining, one. There is far less movement and a surer footing because the body does not have to rotate, and the distance down is much less.

The criticism of the high tub has largely centered around difficulties encountered by special groups: for example, very young children, for whom getting in and out is difficult and potentially dangerous, and aged and infirm persons, who find it difficult to pull themselves up out of a high tub. (The specialized problems of these groups will be discussed in more detail in a later chapter.)

Another approach, novel in the United States but common in many parts of Europe, is to raise the tub by some 280 mm (11 inches) or more. In their case this is generally done to keep the drains and piping above the floor; it has, however, some

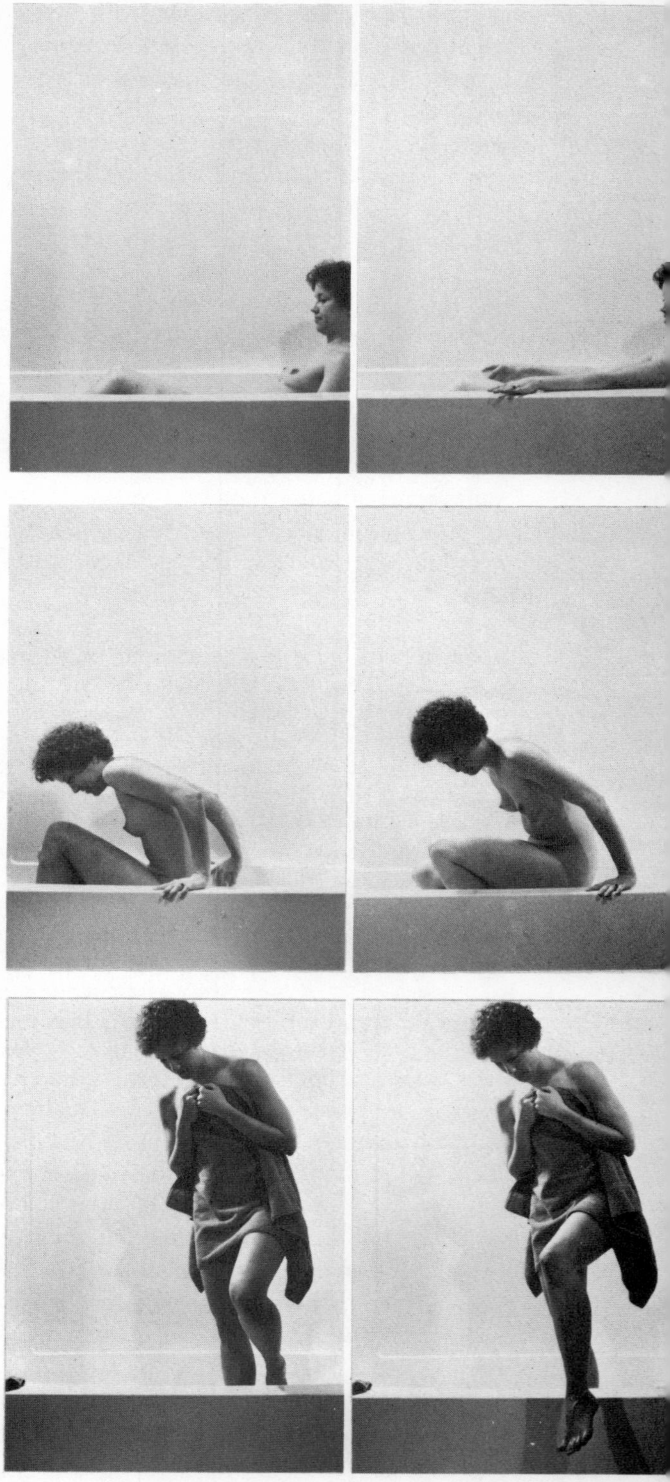

15 / TYPICAL MOVEMENTS INVOLVED IN ENTERING AND LEAVING A CONVENTIONAL TUB AND IN SHIFTING FROM A RECLINING TO A STANDING POSTURE

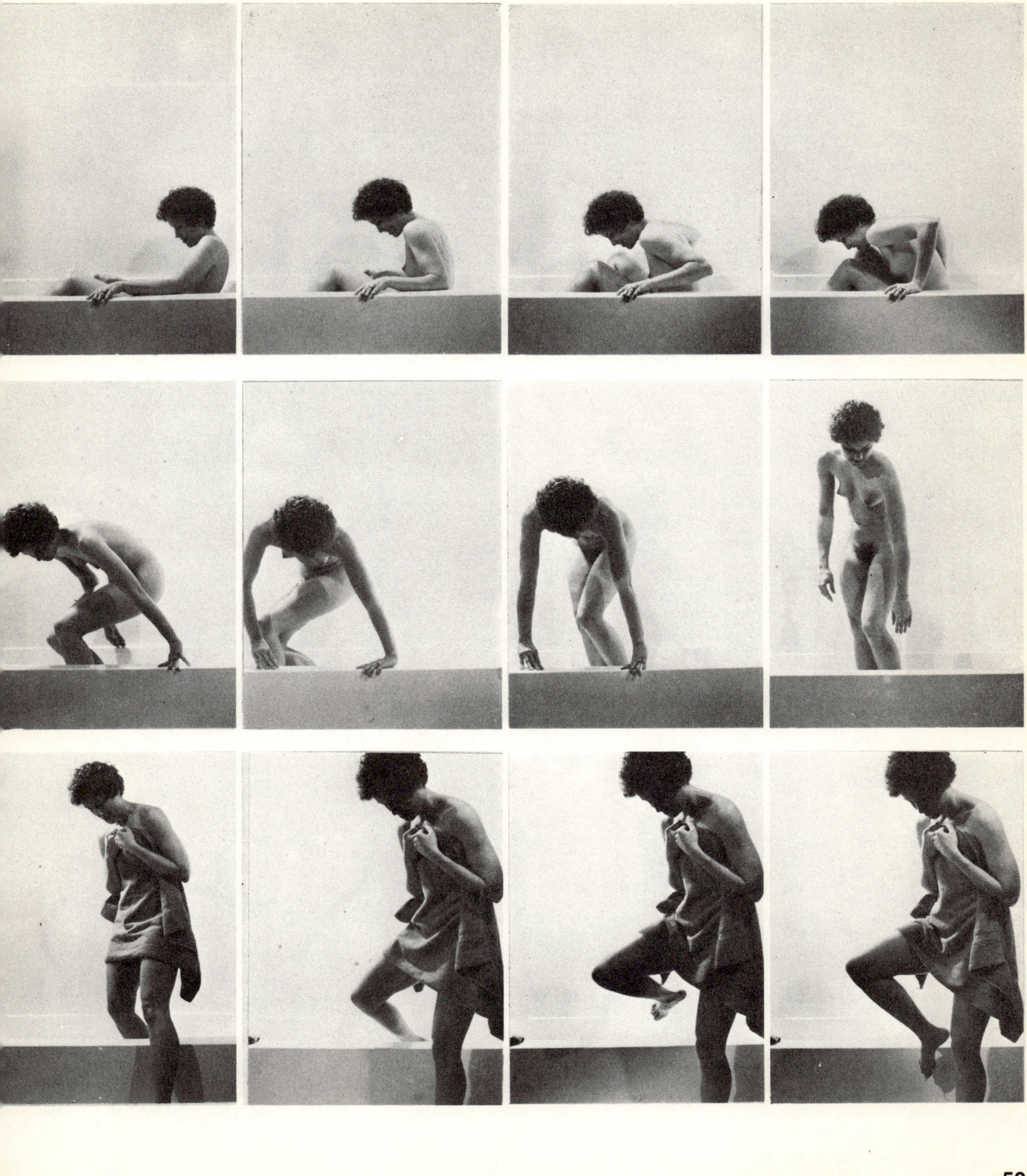

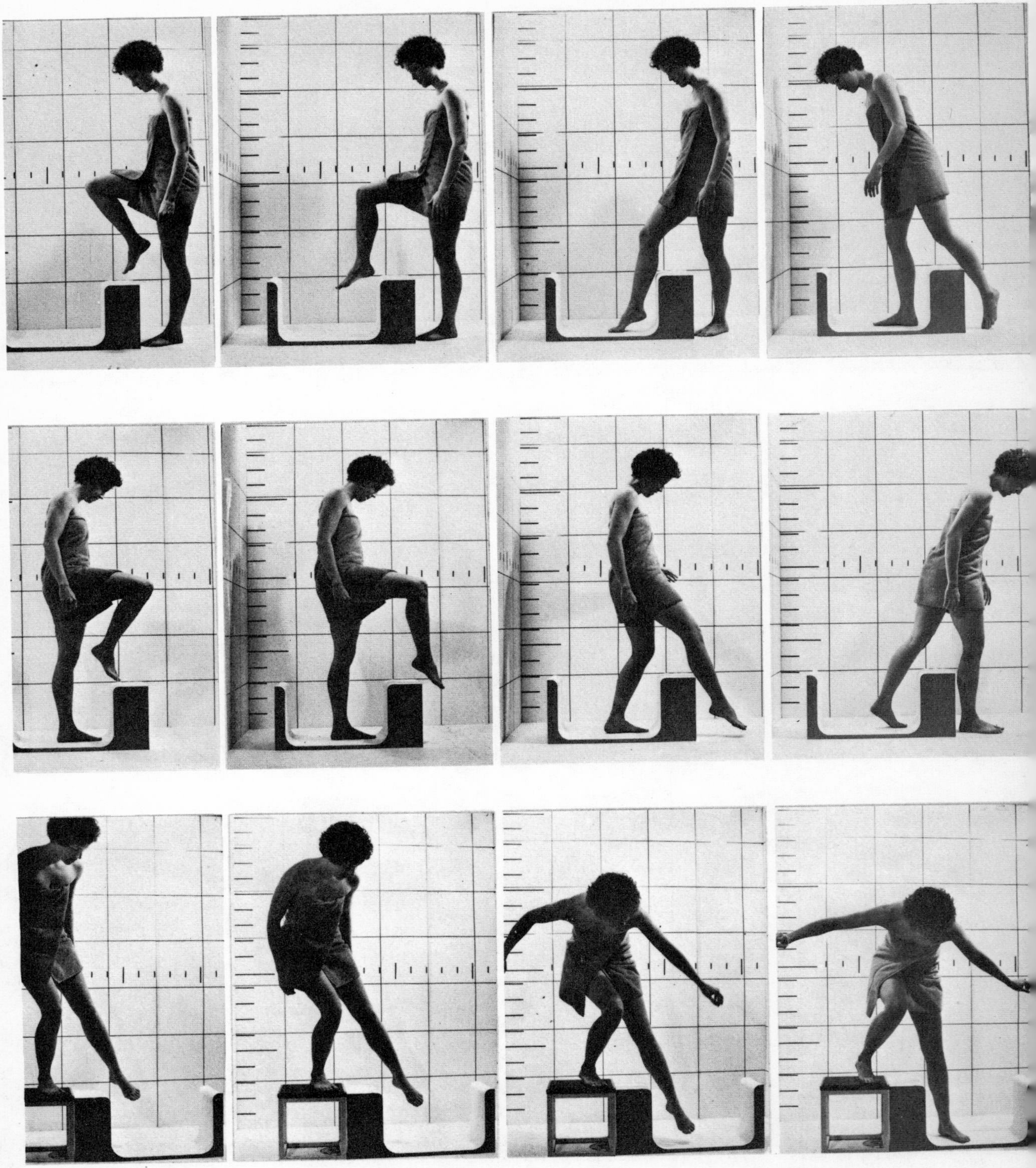

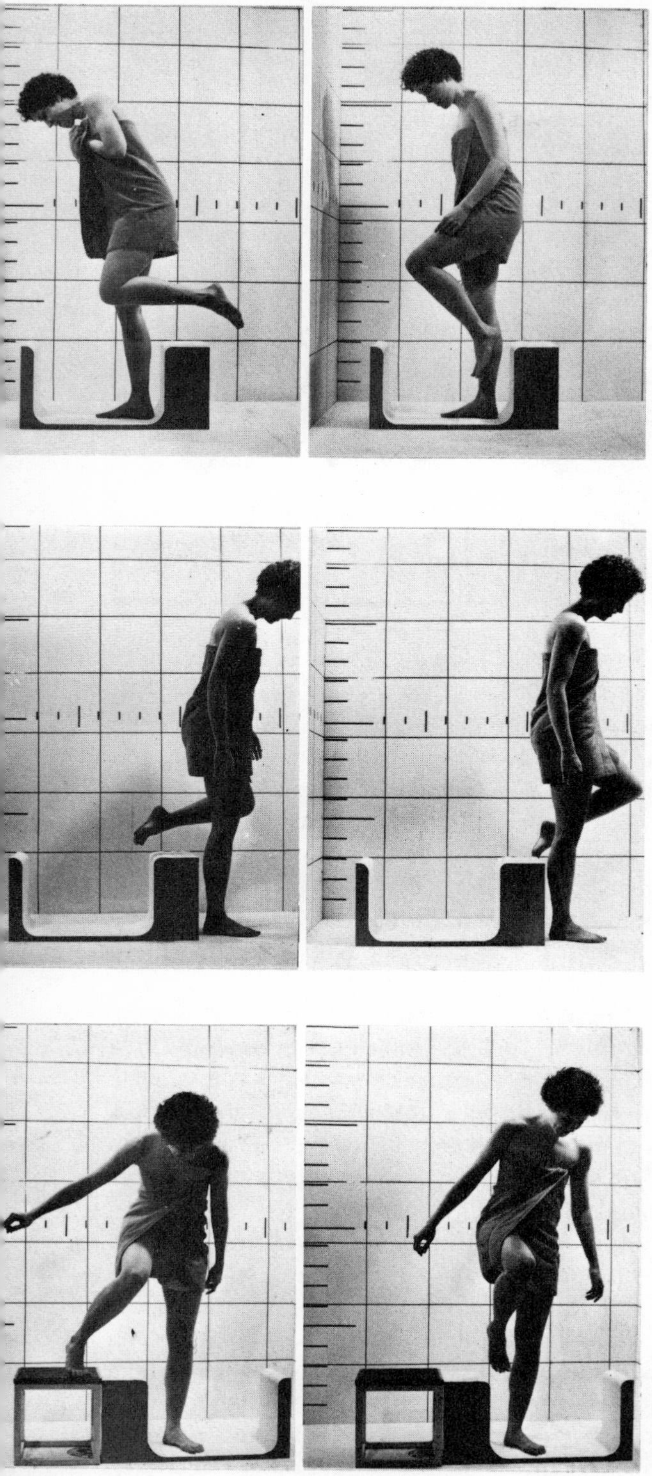

16 / MECHANICS INVOLVED IN
STEPPING OVER AND IN STEPPING DOWN
WHEN ENTERING AND LEAVING A TUB

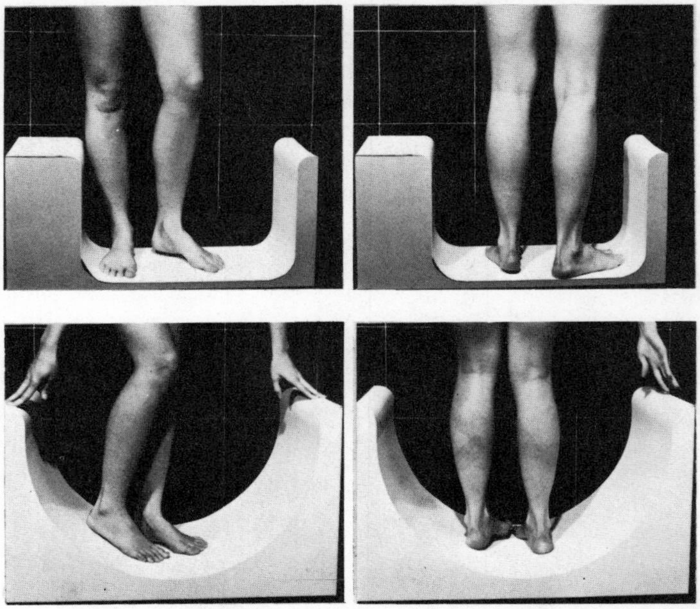

17 / CONFIGURATION OF TUB CROSS-SECTION IN RELATION TO A STANDING POSTURE

significant advantages as far as ease and safety of entry and exit are concerned. This approach, illustrated in Figure 19, is based on minimizing the amount of movement required and also the distance that one could potentially fall since it assumes that one need never stand. It assumes that a conventional-depth tub of 405 mm (16 inches) is raised so that the rim height is approximately 660 to 760 mm (26 to 30 inches) from the floor. As shown in Figure 19, this allows a person to lean against the rim and gradually shift to a sitting position on the rim and thence to a sitting position in the bottom of the tub. If proper support is provided, this approach is in many ways the safest of the lot since the person need never shift from what is basically a sitting position. Because of the posture assumed in this method of entry, however, the front edge of the tub must be free of obstructions such as bars, controls, and so on, which need to be either recessed or relocated.

Width of Tub Rim The width of the rim is related to the height of the rim in the case of a step-over approach. In general, it may be safe to say that for the sake of ease and safety of access the rim width should be as small as possible, as should be the degree of curvature of the tub bottom and the fillet between the side and the bottom.

The width of the rim must also, however, be considered from the viewpoint of its use as an aid in offering support and in raising and lowering the body once in the tub. If the rim is to be grasped by the hand, the optimum width appears to be about 65 mm (2½ inches).[6]

These recommendations conflict, of course, with current practice, which has generally been to make the rim as wide as possible so as to provide a seat—primarily, presumably, for mothers bathing small children. If, however, we assume the high sitting method of entry, then a partial wider rim is necessary for seating comfort.

Auxiliary Support Devices In terms of safety while one is getting in and out and operating within a tub, two major types of support appear necessary: for use in an erect position while one is getting in and out and for use in raising and lowering the body to and from a sitting/reclining position. The first source of support must, accordingly, be located at the outer rim and be easily accessible from both within and without. Experiments suggest that a vertical bar located above the rim is perhaps the most useful since it is used also as a pivot point, as illustrated in Figure 18, the body making a 90-degree turn in entering and leaving. It further seems desirable that such a bar always be located at the foot end of the tub—both to ensure facing in the proper direction and to avoid entering onto the sloping surface of the backrest. This location would also be useful when one is leaning over the tub to operate the water controls, which generally are, and should continue to be, at the foot of the tub. The most convenient height centers around 1,000 mm (40 inches) from the floor, the height of the forearm with the hand outstretched. The useful length of such a bar is limited to a foot in either direction from this point. To be most useful, the bar should be so positioned that it can also be reached from a sitting position.

A second area of support must be provided to assist the process of raising and lowering the body from a standing to a sitting or reclining position. As illustrated in Figures 15 and 19, this process inevitably involves the use of both hands for support. The first critical point in lowering the body comes when a full squat has been achieved and the body is still balanced and when the weight must be transferred to a sitting position. During that transition, balance is completely lost unless the arms are used to provide a temporary second support. Most commonly this is accomplished by placing the hands on the floor and then gently sliding out the feet until all the weight has been transferred to the buttocks and the hands. The second critical point comes in the shifting of the

18 / CHANGES IN DIRECTION INVOLVED IN ENTERING AND LEAVING A TUB

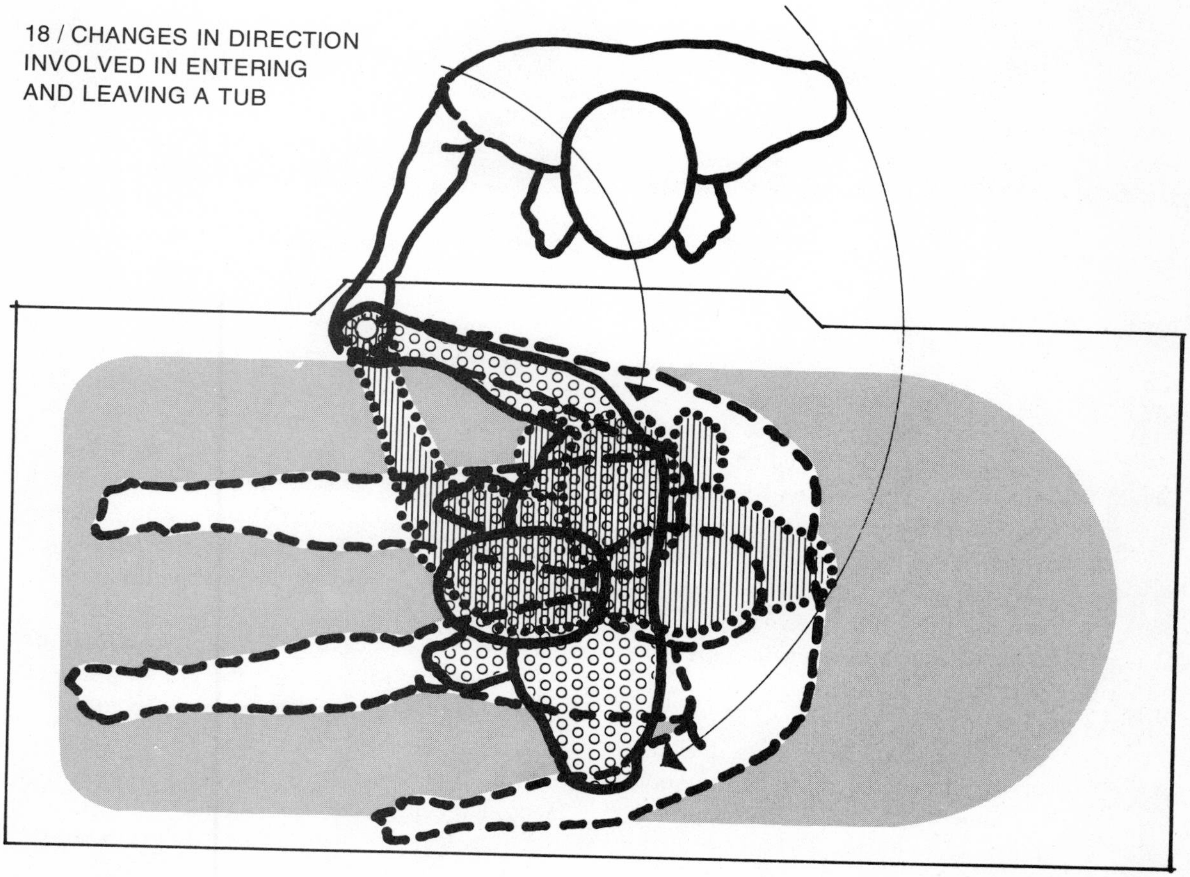

19 / ALTERNATIVE METHODS OF GETT

body weight from a balanced vertical sitting position to a reclining one. Whereas this maneuver can be accomplished by using the legs as a counterbalance, similar to a "sit-up," this is not an easy task for most people. Again, most commonly, the weight is transferred to first one elbow and then both until finally the weight is borne by the back and the buttocks in a semi-reclining position. Reversing this process and getting up again is generally more difficult (as suggested in Figures 15 and 19), largely because the muscles must now do all the work rather than merely cushion the effect of gravity.

During the lowering phase, it would be desirable to provide support that would be used throughout the process, in other words, horizontal support on two sides that could be grasped almost at the outset when one is still standing and until one is sitting. This support can be furnished by the outer rim provided it is narrow enough to be easily grasped and by either a special rim configuration on the wall side or by a horizontal bar. With such support, it is possible to loosen one's grip sufficiently to allow the hands to slide along the support and thus ease the body down gradually and securely from a squatting to a sitting and then a reclining position.

During the raising phase, the process is essentially reversed. After pulling the body up to a sitting position, one can push the body up sufficiently to allow the legs to take over.

In both of these cases the effectiveness of the approach is obviously dependent upon the inside depth of the container. If the depth is about 305

AND OUT OF A HIGH-SIDED TUB

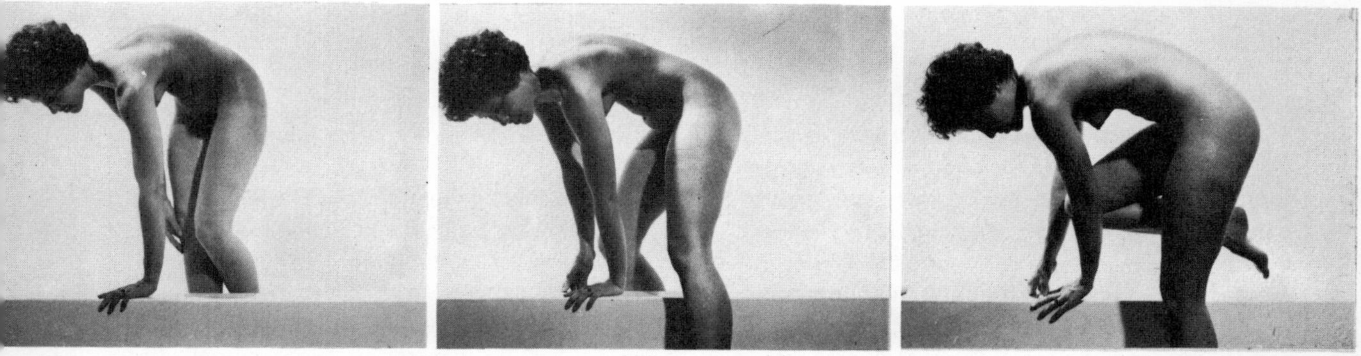

mm (12 inches), it is not possible to get sufficient leverage. Conversely, if the depth is 510 mm (20 inches) or more, it is impossible to do more than exert a pulling force.

Another approach sometimes suggested is a pulling approach using a sloping bar on the side wall. The premise seems to be that one can pull oneself up hand over hand to a standing position and vice versa. Such a technique is, however, totally dependent upon a secure footing since the feet act as a pivot point about which the body is caused to rotate. Bathtubs, by and large, cannot be counted on necessarily to provide such secure footing.

Needless to say, support devices are only as effective as the solidity of their construction and security of mounting. In this respect, the matter of integrated and comprehensive design becomes important once again for, in attempting to install such devices after the fact, one often finds it impossible to locate a suitable anchorage where necessary. Similarly, inadequate support devices can break a fall, but they also can give one a dangerously false sense of security; unfortunately there are inexpensive devices on the market that are adequate for holding on to but not if one is in the process of falling and bringing one's entire body weight to bear under conditions of dynamic loading.

Water Supply The first, most obvious, and traditional source of water is that necessary for filling the tub. In addition, however, a second source is needed for properly rinsing the body with clean running water at the conclusion of the

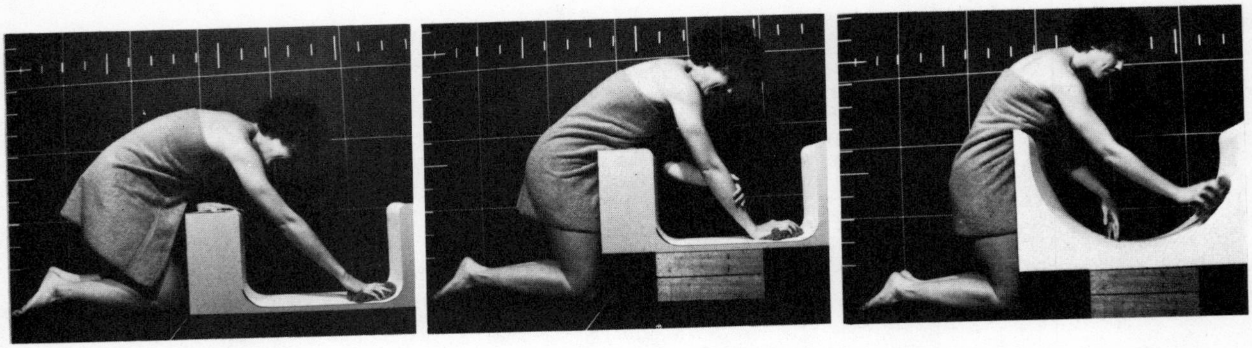

20 / POSTURES ASSUMED FOR CLEANING AND FOR BATHING CHILDREN NECESSITATED BY DIFFERENT HEIGHTS OF TUB RIM

bathing process. The argument for a rinsing device is based on the fact that one cannot get thoroughly clean by rinsing oneself with the dirty bath water. The problem can actually be resolved in two ways: by the provision of either a supplementary rinsing device or a recirculating system in the container similar in effect to that used in swimming pools. This latter approach also offers the not inconsiderable advantages of keeping the water temperature constant and also providing the therapeutic benefits of a circulating system. Conversely, such a system would not only increase water and energy consumption but would also, for most purposes, be prohibitively expensive.

The water source fitting (and the controls) should be located where it can be easily reached for testing the temperature of the water both from within and without the tub, rather than centered, arbitrarily and awkwardly, over the foot of the tub as is present practice. The location should also be such that it does not present a hazard or become an obstruction to the user. The most logical placement lies in the area of the foot end of the outer rim together with the controls. The specific location must obviously be determined on the basis of the particular overall situation since this is only one of many interacting variables and will change as the basic dimensions and configurations of the tub change.

A single mixing faucet is desirable from the standpoint of convenience in testing temperature. In the interest of the time required to fill a tub, it may also be convenient to have a larger supply line than is commonly provided. Presumably the grossly oversized chromed housing generally furnished to cover the normal supply line is meant to give one this illusion.

A rinsing supply may be built in, in the form of a shower head (as is now commonly available and largely unused) or, preferably, in the form of a permanent hand spray with a flexible hose, which would seem to be psychologically more appropriate to a supplementary rinsing function than using the regular shower. The hand spray is more flexible than the single semifixed shower head and would allow for proper rinsing of all parts of the body including genitourinary and anal areas. One would also be likely to use less water than with a regular shower. In addition, if we presume that a seat is provided in the tub for ease in the actual cleansing operation, a hand spray would be far more convenient and would permit rinsing in the same sitting position. The ideal placement of a hand spray is in the same area as the other fittings and the controls so that it is easily accessible from within and without the tub and from the seat. A further advantage offered by the hand spray is its usefulness in cleansing the tub. In terms of operation, it would be desirable to have the spray function through a diverter mechanism controlled from the handset itself. This would both conserve water and ensure a certain measure of protection against misdirecting the stream.

Controls As suggested, the first criterion for the controls is that they be located in such a way as to be easily accessible from within and without the fixture, that is, along the outer rim at the foot end of the tub. For convenience, the controls should also be located higher than has been common practice. A height of from 760 to 865 mm (30 to 34 inches) places them advantageously for a person standing outside or sitting on a seat and still allows them to be reached from a sitting position in the bottom of the tub if necessary.

The particular controls used, and their mechanics of operation, should, in addition to being simple and direct, reflect the postures from which they will be used—inside or outside the tub, sitting, and standing. Experiments with various control types suggest that some form of lever or throttle control is easier to use from a variety of positions than the common wheel type.

Drain The location of the drain fittings also needs particular attention and re-evaluation. If the bottom of the tub has a reverse slope, that is, if it slopes down from the foot to the back, in order to counteract the tendency of the body to slide or float away from the backrest, the drain must obviously be located at the back. This reversed location would also aid in washing out the tub during the cleaning process, since the drain would now be located at the opposite end of the tub from the supply fitting.

Storage Space or facilities must also be provided for the wide variety of articles commonly used in conjunction with relaxing and washing. These may range from the very obvious soap, sponge, brush or washcloth, and safety razors, manicure implements, and shampoo to ash trays, reading matter, and drinks. In this respect, present-day tubs with their wide rims do offer the possibility of shelf space, though their use is not to be recommended because of the danger of knocking things off. Ideally a shelf or tray should be provided, sufficiently out of the way so as not to be an obstruction or hazard and readily accessible whether the bather is reclining or sitting up and washing. This shelf should have a minimum usable depth of 100 mm (4 inches), a clear height of approximately 305 mm (12 inches), and a minimum length of approximately 405 mm (16 inches). The surface must be easily cleanable, nonbreakable, self-draining, and reasonably nonskid. The location for this temporary storage or active-use shelf seems most reasonable on the inside wall above the tub where it can be easily reached. For both comfort and safety this shelf should not be more than 455 mm (18 inches) from the bottom of the tub—at the shoulder height of the shorter segment of the population.

Cleaning Problems A subsidiary but still important activity to be considered is that of cleaning the fixture, from the standpoint of both the cleanability and the ease with which a person can accomplish this. In the case of the bathtub this is a major problem compared with other fixtures principally because of the deposit of scum that forms the proverbial ring and because of the size of the fixture. This ring is inevitable and is as much a function of soap and bath oils as it is of dirt. The more things added to the bath water, with the exception of certain bath salts which are water softeners, the more there is to deposit on the fixture.

The activity may be described as that of scrubbing all parts of the fixture (with or without a cleansing agent), generally with a sponge, brush, or cloth, while one remains outside the fixture, and then rinsing it clean. The posture assumed may range from kneeling on the floor and leaning over the fixture to standing and leaning over it.

If we examine the posture assumed in terms of either convenience or comfort, we find that it is a function of the size and configuration of the container. For the general range of tub sizes and shapes, the two key variables are the overall width and the height of the side rim. The higher the rim and/or the greater the depth, the more likely a standing–leaning posture. The lower the rim the more feasible the kneeling–leaning posture.

On the assumption that the maximum tub width is less than 760 mm (30 inches), the principal variable is the height of the rim. Tests, with heights ranging from 305 to 735 mm (12 to 29 inches), indicate that a standing–leaning position is most satisfactory at heights of 610 mm (24 inches) or more, where one hand can provide convenient support and where the body can be braced by the lower thigh; a kneeling–leaning position is satisfactory at heights of 430 to 610 mm (17 to 24 inches), where the body can brace and support itself on the rim and in some instances allow the use of both hands; a kneeling–leaning position can be managed at lower heights, down to 305 mm (12 inches), but it necessitates bending one arm under the body on top of the rim, in effect raising the height so as to keep from toppling in (see Figure 20). Aside from the obvious problem of effective armreach, the critical issue appears to be one of arranging adequate support and balance for the body. From this standpoint a height of 405 to 455 mm (16 to 18 inches) appears to be the most satisfactory.

In terms of cleanability the principal issue is one of washing out or rinsing the fixture at the conclusion of cleaning. In this regard, two of the features mentioned earlier would be useful. The first is the provision of a hand spray and the second the location of the drain at the opposite end from the water source.

The problem of cleanability can, of course, be further complicated by unusual dimensions and configurations. A sunken tub or an oversize tub for two virtually necessitates cleaning the tub from the inside. In such situations, a hand spray is essential for rinsing out the tub after cleaning.

Small Children In general, children do not achieve independence in bathing until about the age of six or seven, at which age they are also generally capable of coping safely with getting in and out of a tub with heights of 455 mm (18 inches) or less. In other words, the age at which independence in performance is developed coincides with the age at which a fixture, as designed for a "normal" population, should be able to be used without assistance. It can be reasonably assumed then that special problems will arise principally with bathing children between the ages of one year and six or seven years, since children under one are almost universally bathed in a special container, such as a bathinette.

The essential problems arise, however, not with respect to the child's use of the tub but rather with respect to the posture of the person outside the fixture who is helping or actually washing the child. The problem in this instance is very similar to that involved in cleaning and revolves around the height of the rim of the tub. Tests conducted of this activity indicate that, because of the greater time involved and the generally more passive activity, comfort and a stable, balanced posture are ultimately critical, particularly because the person must have both hands free to wash and hold the child. Even after a child develops to the point where he no longer needs to be held while being bathed, the person bathing a small child must still, however, use both hands, one hand counteracting the pressure of the scrubbing hand.

Sitting on the rim of the tub, even the lowest and widest, was totally unsatisfactory except for passive observation of the child. A person in such a position was incapable of accomplishing anything without radically shifting positions. In the first position, kneeling back, the most comfortable height for the rim proved to be 405 to 455 mm (16 to 18 inches); in the kneeling–upright position, the comfortable heights ranged from 455 to 710 mm (18 to 28 inches); and in the standing position, over 710 mm (28 inches). As with cleaning, it appears that the most satisfactory position involves support from the rim, generally somewhere in the region from the waist to the third rib. This accounts also for the spread of acceptable

21 / POSSIBLE APPROACH
TO A WASHING/RELAXING TUB

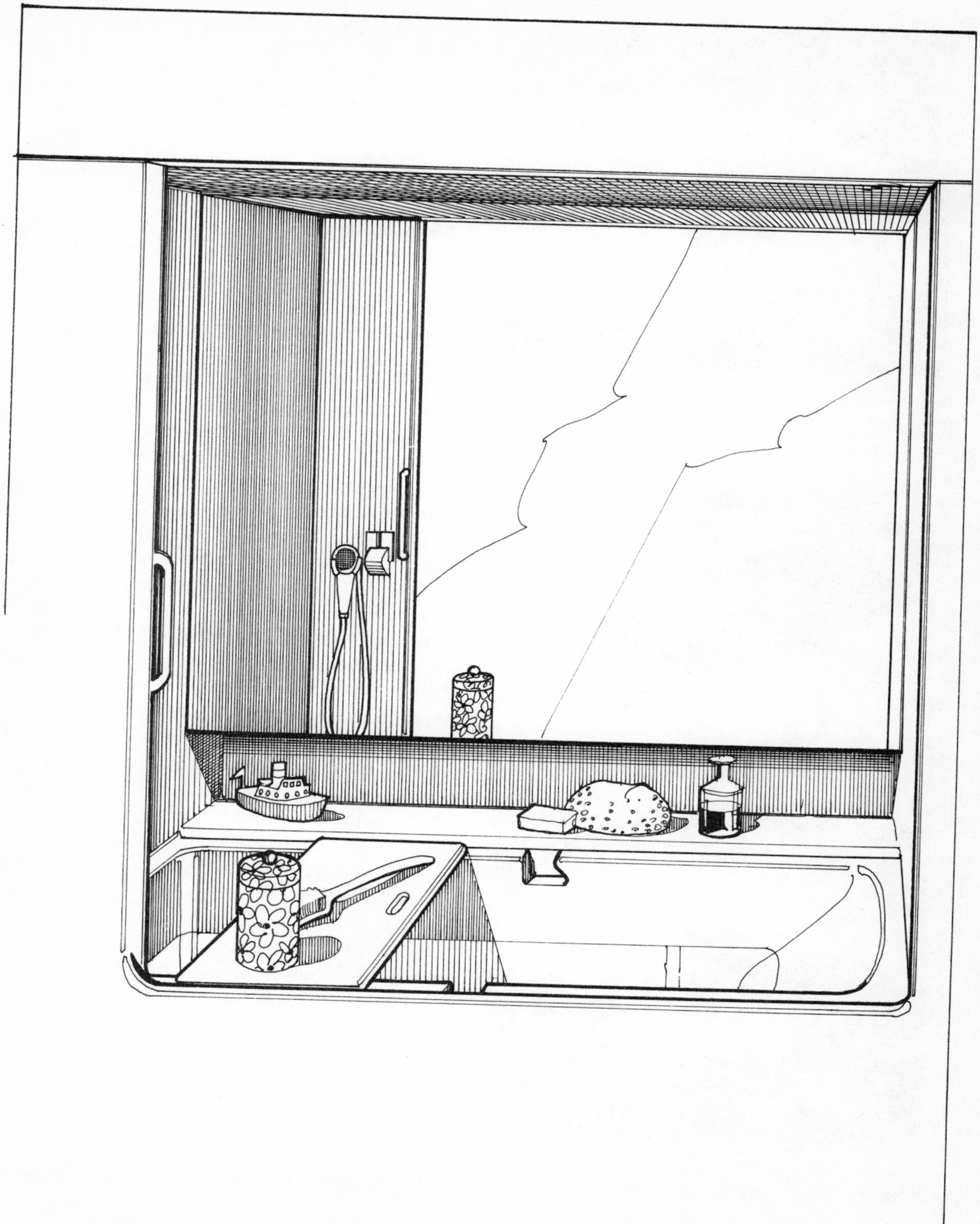

"REPOS" BATHTUB:
JACOB DELAFON, PARIS, FRANCE

"CORALUX" BATHTUB:
BUDERUS, WETZLAR, WEST GERMANY

"STEEPING" BATHTUB:
KOHLER, KOHLER, WISCONSIN, U.S.A

heights since the applicable dimensions of the adult female population are:

	Hip Height	*Top of Diaphragm*
Small:	541 mm (21.3″)	655 mm (25.8″)
Large:	617 mm (24.3″)	770 mm (30.3″)

These figures indicate that a tub rim height of 610 to 635 mm (24 to 25 inches) would be suitable for the greatest number of adult females for this particular purpose. Note that women have asked for years for tubs with higher sides, or raised tubs, for ease in bathing children.[7] Note also that these dimensions are higher than those cited for cleaning, because in this instance the body must receive all its support from the front wall of the tub whereas in cleaning, one arm was generally used to support or brace the body.

Summary — Design Possibilities When we examine the process of body cleansing and its various component parts, it is obvious that our customary provision of a simple container for water is grossly inadequate. From the standpoints of function, comfort, and safety, many things are necessary, and they are necessary in the proper relationship to one another. A complete bathing facility involves not only a properly sized and shaped container but also storage, seating, support devices, controls, and rinsing devices, which must be provided as part of a comprehensive fixture package. There is ample evidence that, if this is not done, the completion of the bathing facility is simply left to the ultimate user to solve in whatever haphazard fashion he can. An integrated facility can ensure not only the inclusion of the essential items but also their proper location and design. While such an integrated bathing facility will cost more *initially* than a simple conventional tub, the final costs of the latter, when the user is through adding all the necessary components, will not be very different.

The range of possible approaches to this inte-

22 / CURRENT APPROACHES
TO WASHING/RELAXING TUBS

grated bathing facility is broad—all the way from an oversize tub for two to a minimum fixture without a complete surround, to one that includes a surround and a ceiling, to one that serves as a combination tub/shower. In addition, there are possible variations based on the height of tub rim and the method of entry. In each situation it must, however, be remembered that, while the basic criteria remain constant, certain conditions change each time and necessitate making adjustments in dimensions, configurations, and relative locations. This is not to suggest that highly specialized facilities are necessarily desirable but rather that facilities should be designed for specific purposes. The attempt to provide a universal facility that attempts to accommodate all possible functions almost invariably fails to fulfill any function adequately.

One possible approach to an integrated facility is illustrated in Figure 21. Other, currently available approaches are illustrated in Figures 14, 22, and 59.

DESIGN CRITERIA FOR CLEANSING THE BODY—SHOWER

6

As Ogden Nash points out in a witty and perceptive analysis of the difference between a tub bath and a shower, in a poem entitled "Splash," there are three things that simply cannot be done in a shower:

> . . . one is read, and the other is smoke, and the other is get wet all over.[1]

The shower is, from both a psychological and an operational viewpoint, a relatively fast and efficient method of body cleansing. This is not to suggest that people do not relax in a shower, but when they do, the relaxing generally consists simply of standing still and letting the water beat down on them, a circumstance that makes little demand on the design of the fixture as compared with the bathtub. By attaching a reservoir to the shower arm, it is even possible to take a "bubble-shower." The principal criterion, nevertheless, for a showering facility is that of accommodating the washing function.

DESCRIPTION OF ACTIVITY

In relation to tub bathing, showering may be regarded as a simpler, faster, and safer activity. As we saw in Figure 10, it involves, basically, the washing function, which is most comfortably and conveniently performed while one is standing or sitting upright—both inherently simple and stable postures. In contrast to using the tub, the process of getting in and out of the fixture presents little difficulty or hazard since it involves only walking into an enclosure rather than climbing into a pool of water and then turning and assuming a reclining position. In addition, one does not have to wait for the tub to fill nor expend as much time or effort afterwards in cleaning the fixture.

Since the shower by its very nature is based on a running stream of water that is continually drained away, the essential job of the fixture is to furnish sufficient enclosure to contain the stream, any splash, and any accumulated water. Accordingly, the enclosure can be one that a person can simply walk into. A low barrier of 75 to 100 mm (3 to 4 inches) is necessary at the entrance to contain the water on the floor—and as a precaution in the event of a partially stopped drain. It is preferable to step over a barrier rather than down or up the same distance. It is easier to judge accurately the heights involved, and the body is in a more stable position when both feet are on the same level. The only significant considerations in this regard are that one will be on a wet, soapy floor, so that provisions will need to be made for nonskid floor surfaces and for auxiliary support devices.

Whereas the showering process is inherently safer than the tub method of bathing, this potential must be exploited in the design of a particular installation if it is also to be safer in practice. In a great many instances this, unfortunately, is not the case, most especially when we use the tub as a shower receptor. This problem becomes acute in the case of certain European installations where tubs with fully rounded bottoms—designed for sitting and relaxing comfort and raised above the floor for a seated entry—are also equipped to function as showers. In such cases, not only is a standing entry and exit awkward and dangerous but it also proves virtually impossible to stand in such a tub because of the curved cross-section. Turning, as one must do during a shower, is completely out of the question without holding on to the sides of the tub and readjusting the position of one's feet, one foot at a time (see Figure 17).

The essential cleansing procedures—wetting, soaping, massaging, and rinsing—and the basic postures involved remain much the same as described earlier for the tub method (see Figures 10 and 23). The various body parts can best be reached from either a standing or an upright sitting position, which in this instance is the natural thing to do. The chief difficulty arises again with respect to the legs and feet, which are reached most comfortably from a seated position (see Figure 23). This is particularly important for related activities such as shaving legs, which for many women is almost an integral part of the washing function.

Soaping and massaging are done most effectively while the body is wet but out of the water. This might be accomplished in either of two ways—by providing a large enough enclosure so that there is room to move out from under the stream or by arranging to shut off the water temporarily. This latter possibility, however, not only poses formidable technical problems of ensuring foolproof water regulation but also becomes somewhat absurd since one does not soap and scrub one's entire body at one time and then rinse off, but rather, one soaps and rinses one body part at a time, and the time interval between each operation is measured in seconds. Moving in and out of the stream is far simpler and more natural than endless turning on and off of the water and also helps maintain a reasonable uniformity of skin temperature, which is more comfortable.

Rinsing is, of course, ideally accomplished in a shower and poses little problem except, as noted by Mr. Nash, that of getting wet all over at one time. This observation presumes, of course, a single conventional source of water, but there is little reason why multiple sources cannot be used or a source that provides a larger volume of coverage than the cone of the conventional shower head. A vigorous shower is regarded by many people as a relaxing or invigorating form of hydrotherapy and, indeed, several shower heads have been especially designed with this aspect in mind. This is an aspect, however, that appears to have eluded much of Europe, where showers commonly consist of the hand shower simply hung on a wall bracket. While perfectly adequate for washing and rinsing, the restricted volume of coverage and low water pressure leave much to be desired from a purely sensual viewpoint. In any event it is important to bear in mind the various prejudices of people with respect to water temperature, pressure, coarseness of spray, and location of stream and to provide fittings that permit individual adjustment.

DESIGN CONSIDERATIONS

To a large extent, the configuration of the basic container or enclosure and its dimensions are

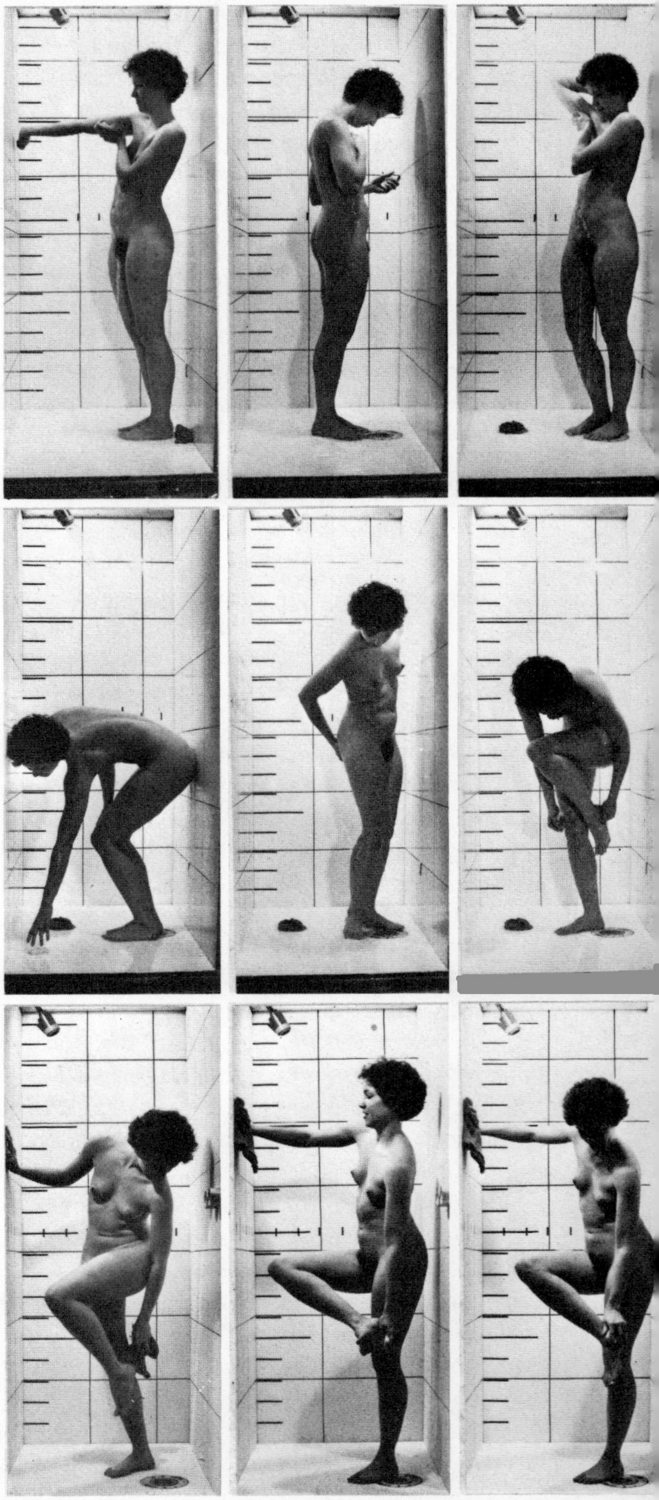

23 / COMPARISON OF TYPICAL
SHOWERING POSTURES IN
760-MM (30-INCH) AND
1220-MM (48-INCH) SHOWER ENCLOSURES

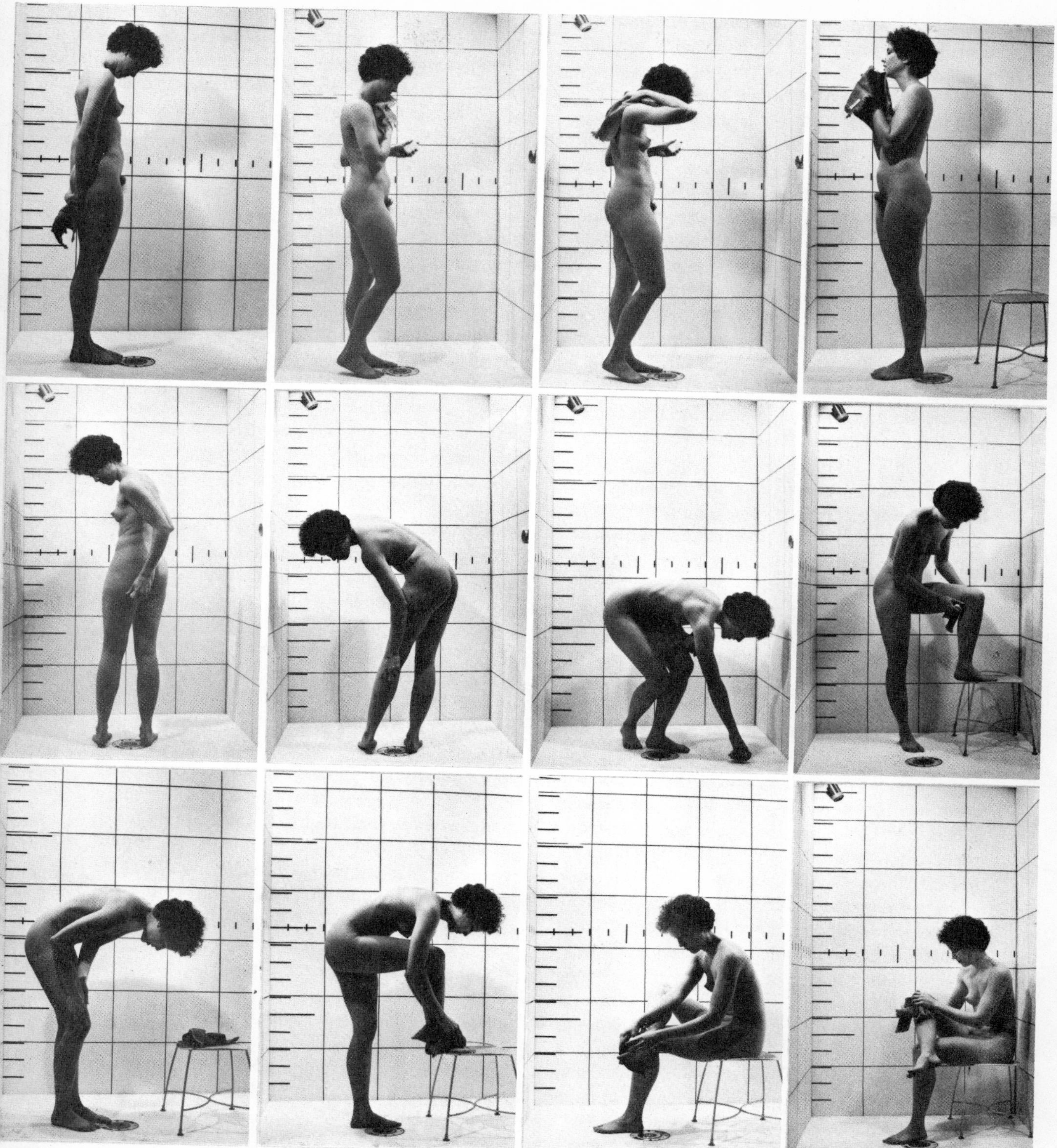

dependent upon the number, nature, and location of the water sources, since a person's primary orientation is to the water source and one will adjust one's range of movements accordingly.

Size of Enclosure If we accept the premise of a constantly running stream rather than one that is alternately on and off, a premise both more common and demanding, then the minimum size of the enclosure is the space necessary to accommodate in comfort the normal range of bodily movements while one is washing in a fixed position, in addition to the space necessary to allow for moving in and out from under the stream for soaping and the space for a seat and/or footrest.

Experiments with varying sizes and arrangements of enclosure indicate that the total space actually used in a standing position ranges from 915 to 965 mm (36 to 38 inches) along the axis of the stream and from 840 to 865 mm (33 to 34 inches) in the transverse direction. These figures are, however, based on washing in a virtually unlimited enclosure that presents no restrictions to the person's movements. They represent, therefore, the space used, not the space needed. The actual enclosure would need to allow an additional 100 to 150 mm (4 to 6 inches) in both directions for sensory clearance, giving a minimum comfortable enclosure size for washing of 1,065 by 915 mm (42 by 36 inches). When an enclosure is provided that is precisely the same dimensions as the actual area used, people begin to restrict their range of movements to accommodate the body in a more or less constant relationship to the space actually available. Thus, we can, after a fashion, manage to wash in a standard 760-mm (30-inch)-square shower enclosure, but we constrict our movements and move more slowly and deliberately to keep from hitting the sides. The only exception to this sensory avoidance behavior is that in such an undersized container there is a tendency to use the sides for support. Figure 23 illustrates typical postures in both a 760-mm (30-inch) and 1,220-mm (48-inch) enclosure and shows that it is virtually impossible to bend over in the 760-mm (30-inch) enclosure, either to wash the feet or to pick up something that may have been dropped. This can, of course, be demonstrated simply on the basis of bodily dimensions, since the distance from the buttocks to the top of the head in a bent-over position ranges from 840 to 940 mm (33 to 37 inches) for the adult population. Furthermore, and most important, in such a substandard enclosure it is impossible to move out from under the stream.

The directional quality of the space needed is related to the directional and angular quality of the stream and to its conical shape. In virtually every instance, there is a tendency to move out from under the stream in the direction of the stream rather than sideways, a maneuver that seems to be related to maintaining a specific relationship with the stream. In moving in the direction of the stream one is certain of where the water will hit, but in moving in and out sideways one could get completely doused, depending on how one turned back into the stream. With multiple streams this pattern still holds so long as there is a free area to which one can move. In this case, the pattern of movement and orientation is still axial or linear but with respect to water/no water rather than to the axis of a single stream.

Positioning of Water Source The dimensions of the enclosure (and one's freedom of movement) are also dependent on the positioning of the shower head and the angle of the stream. If the angle of the stream is too flat, for example, then it becomes impossible to move out of the range of the stream unless the enclosure is excessively large, and it is also impossible to wet the entire body. A nearly vertical stream, on the other hand, makes it difficult to keep one's hair dry, if desired, and also severely restricts one's possible range of movements while under the stream. The essential relationship is between the stream and the area actually available for use by the bather rather than that between the stream and the wall, as is often carelessly assumed. In all too many instances, particularly where a tub used as a shower receptor has been built into a recess, the tub has not been set tight to the wet wall but has been set back by a ledge. In such a situation, the use of a standard shower arm fitting will only cause the stream to fall in an area where the bather cannot possibly be.

In general, the optimal arrangement is to have the stream cover slightly less than half the diagonal volume of the enclosure, as illustrated in Figure 24. The water source, which should be adjustable both to angle and coarseness of spray, should be set so that at a height of 1,525 to 1,675 mm (5 to 5½ feet) the center of the stream would be 305 to 380 mm (12 to 15 inches) from the wall. The bottom of the shower head itself should be no less than 1,980 mm (6½ feet) from the floor.

Seat and/or Footrest The basic dimensions just given for the size of the enclosure are based on performing the entire washing operation from a standing position. Ideally, however, a seat should be provided, or at the very least, a footrest. The most critical problem comes with washing the feet, a task that may be accomplished from several postures, as illustrated in Figures 10 and 23. The two most comfortable—and safest—postures are sitting upright on a seat and standing on one foot with the other foot propped up on a support. In either case, the proper location for such support is at the dry end of the enclosure so that the soaping process can take place out of the water. If only a footrest is provided, it can be incorporated within the same area. Provision of a seat, contrariwise, necessitates increasing the size of the enclosure proportionately. A footrest need be, for example, no larger than approximately 150 by 150 mm (6 by 6 inches) and could be absorbed diagonally across one corner. A seat should have a minimum width of 405 mm (16 inches) and a minimum depth of 255 mm (10 inches) and should be so arranged as to allow for adequate elbow room. If the seat were set diagonally into a corner, the overall length should be increased from 1,065 to 1,220 mm (42 to 48 inches). If a full bench were located across the dry end of the enclosure, it would be necessary to add another 305 mm (12 inches), making the total length 1,370 to 1,525 mm (54 to 60 inches). The most comfortable height, for both the seat and the footrest, is approximately 380 mm (15 inches). (These dimensions approximate very closely the dimensions of a bathtub, which may explain at least partially why tubs frequently appear to have been chosen for use as shower receptors in preference to commonly available shower stalls.)

Shape of Enclosure So long as certain essential relationships are maintained, the precise configuration of the shower enclosure can vary over a considerable range. In its most basic form, the enclosure is simply a room-height rectangular volume with both wet and dry areas, as indicated in Figure 24. Because the basic posture assumed is a standing one, the floor of the enclosure should be essentially flat with just enough slope to provide effective drainage. A positive nonslip surface should be provided—a feature that is somewhat simpler to provide here than in the tub bottom, where one must also be concerned with the tactile properties of the surface relative to sensitive parts of the body.

The entrance to the enclosure should be located in one of the long walls at the dry end and have a minimum opening of 610 mm (24 inches) and a sill height of not more than 100 mm (4 inches). A support device should be located at the entrance for use in stepping in and out and while one is adjusting and testing the water.

Unless the enclosure is particularly large, some form of closure is generally necessary at the opening to keep the spray and splash contained. Although the traditional shower curtain is both inexpensive and sometimes highly decorative, it is often less than satisfactory in use. A shower stream tends to set up a negative air pressure that causes the curtain to billow inwards and envelop the bather, unless it is restrained. If doors are provided, it is important (and in some instances mandatory) that they be made of safety glass or plastic and be so arranged in their operation that they do not interfere with easy access from the dry to the wet area nor with access to the controls.

Storage Another important, and generally overlooked, aspect of a shower is the provision for temporary storage or shelf space. Although, in general, people take fewer things into the shower than they do into the bathtub, there is still

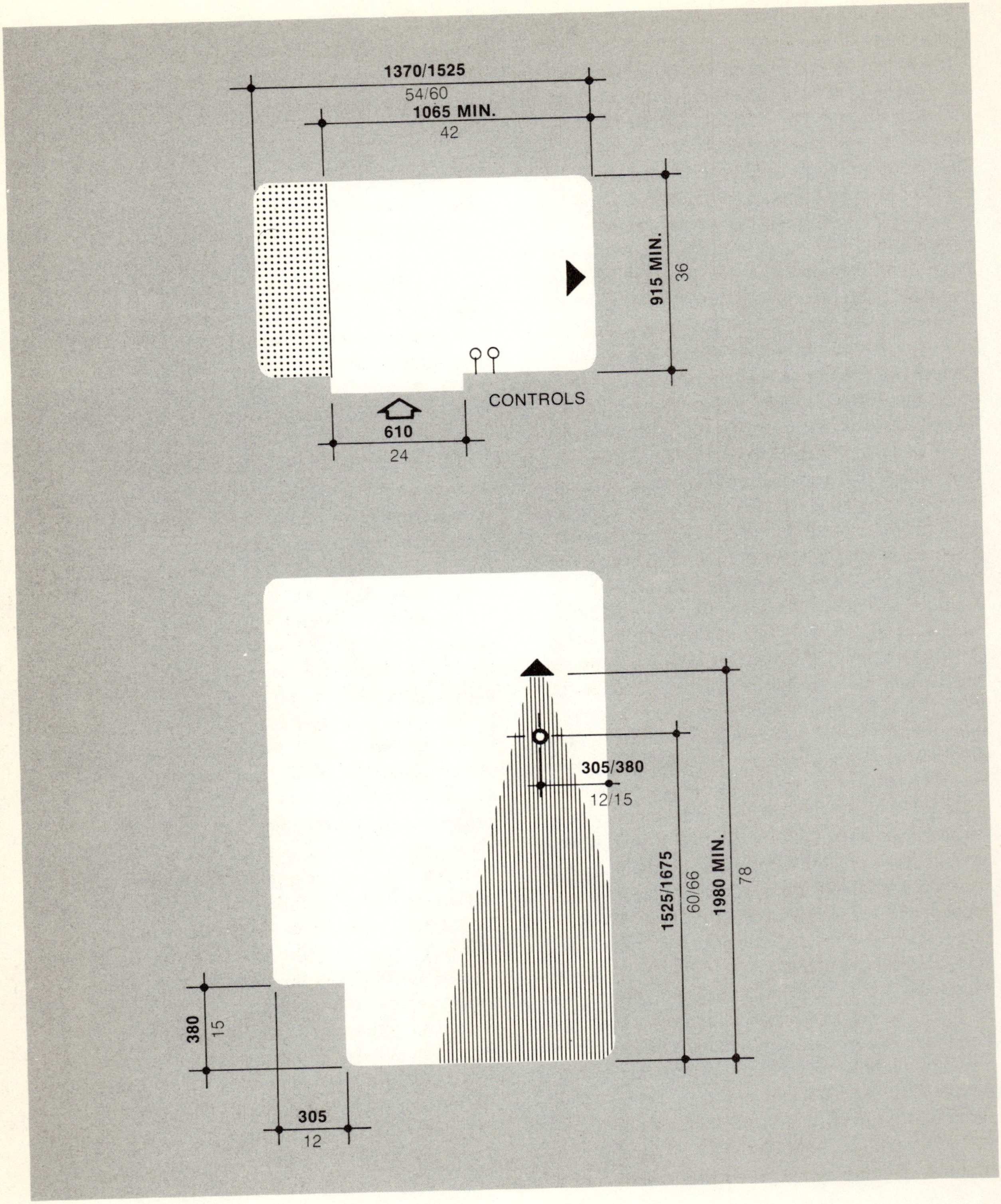
1370/1525
54/60
1065 MIN.
42
915 MIN.
36
CONTROLS
610
24
305/380
12/15
1525/1675
60/66
1980 MIN.
78
380
15
305
12

a need to provide shelf space—at a standing height—for items such as soap, sponges, brushes, shampoo and various other hair preparations, safety razors and pumice stones.

These unmet needs are attested to by all the best-selling gadgets and accessory items that attempt in patchwork fashion to solve some of these problems, such as various wire contraptions that one can hang on the shower head arm or stick onto the wall with suction cups, and shower curtains with pockets.

The criteria for such temporary storage are essentially the same as for the tub: it must be readily accessible but not present a hazard to the user by bumping or knocking things over; it must be dry and easily cleanable; it must be of adequate size, approximately 100 by 405 mm (4 by 16 inches) by 305 mm (12 inches) high, set at a height of 1,000 mm (40 inches).

Support Support devices must also be provided in conjunction with entering and leaving the enclosure, using the seat or footrest, and standing under the stream. Depending upon the particular design, it may be possible to have one continuous bar serve all these functions, or several may be necessary. For entering and leaving and for operating the controls a vertical bar at the entrance would be most desirable. In addition, a vertical or sloping bar should be provided at the seat, as well as a bar that can be easily reached in the wet area. For most effective reaches, bars should not be lower than 865 mm (34 inches) or higher than 1,270 mm (50 inches). The most comfortable height is generally 1,000 mm (40 inches).

Controls Perhaps the single most important consideration in the design of a comfortable and safe shower unit—and the one almost universally ignored—is the proper placement of the controls in relation to the water source and the entrance. Almost without exception, the controls are located directly under the water source and, in the case of most installations where a tub is used as the shower receptor, at a height so low as to be usable only from a sitting and not from a standing position. As a consequence, the matter of making adjustments in the water temperature, which virtually everyone does for one reason or

24 / NECESSARY DIMENSIONS
AND CONFIGURATIONS
FOR A SHOWER ENCLOSURE

25 / COMPARATIVE POSTURES ASSUMED
IN REACHING FOR CONTROLS
WHEN THEY ARE LOCATED AT ENTRY
AND UNDER STREAM

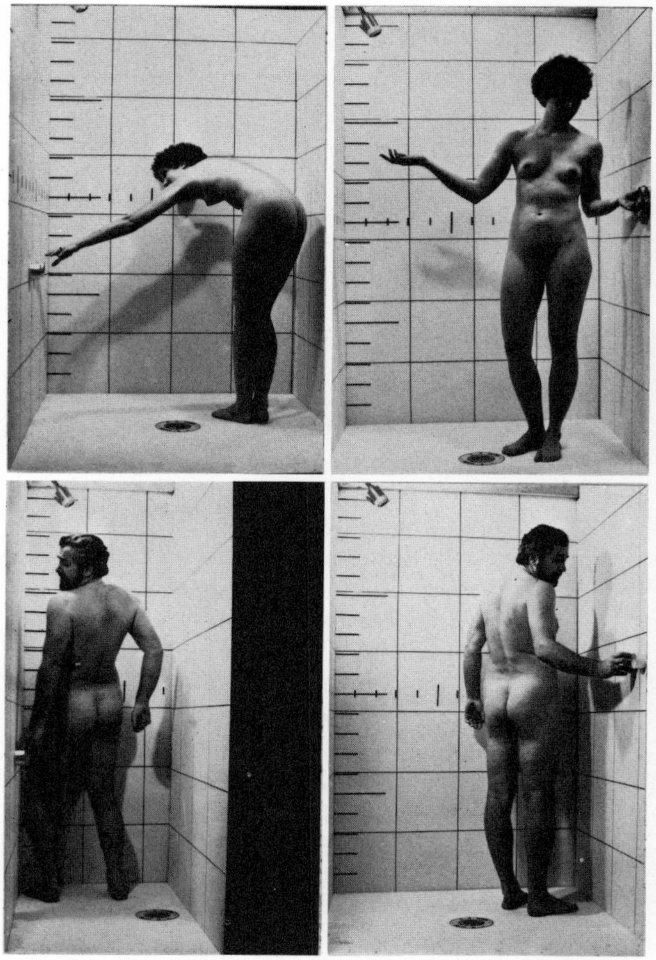

another, becomes an extremely hazardous undertaking (see Figure 25). Any number of serious accidents have occurred either through scalding or through the violent evasive movements made by the bather's trying to reach and adjust the controls while avoiding the stream. This is a problem both so serious and so widespread that its importance cannot be overemphasized. It reinforces the need both for support devices and for ample room to move out of the path of the stream if need be. In particular, it points up the importance of location.

One of the most common shortcomings of water delivery systems worldwide is their relative unreliability with respect to the pressure and, most especially, to the temperature of the water delivered to a given source at a given moment in time. Depending upon the circumstances, the water either tends to get hotter as one gets down to the supply in the heater or it gets hotter or colder if other users suddenly drain off or release quantities of hot water. In any such circumstance, because the bather is directly subject to immediate water delivery as it comes from the mains, the bather must be able to regulate and readjust the water from a point outside the stream. While good-quality thermostatic controls can alleviate this problem to a very large extent, these are still not in widespread use. Even with thermostatic controls there is no reason to locate them directly under the streams.

Aside from variations inherent in the water system itself, many people like, for example, to increase the temperature of the water as time goes along; others like to finish off a shower with cold water. Whatever the practice, it gives rise to seemingly endless adjusting of the controls. Because the body is alternately exposed to both the water and the air, which are at different temperatures, it is particularly sensitive and responsive to even minute variations in water temperature. It is important that the controls be simple and direct in their operation and that there be an obvious and predictable cause-and-effect relationship between the operation of the controls and the resulting water temperature. A throttle or lever type of control of the kind described earlier would be ideal in this situation.

Ideally, it should be possible to control the water supply from both inside and outside the fixture, and from both in and out of the water. The optimal location in the basic enclosure described earlier is, as suggested in Figure 24, at the side of the entrance closest to the stream. This location, which is similar to the preferred location for the tub, is central to all parts of the enclosure and allows for comfortable adjusting and testing of the water from outside the enclosure. An alternate location, necessary, for example, when a tub is used as a shower receptor, is on the end wall opposite the shower head and as close to the front face of the container as possible, rather than in the center of the fixture as has traditionally been the case. In either situation, the controls should be set at a height of from 1,000 to 1,300 mm (approximately 40 to 50 inches) so as to be comfortably and safely operated from the basic standing position (see Figure 25).

The shower head itself should be adjustable both to angle or height and to coarseness and intensity of spray. Many of the better-quality contemporary adjustable shower heads employ various plastic parts for the internal working mechanisms, which have the important property of being essentially self-cleaning as far as hard water deposits are concerned. Ordinary adjustable shower heads, by contrast, employ machined metal parts that soon become totally inoperable as far as adjustability is concerned and so clogged that only the familiar faint and erratic drizzle is obtained.

For those desiring them, a variety of specialized features can also be incorporated, such as multiple needle sprays, pulsating "massage" shower

26 / POSSIBLE APPROACH TO A SHOWER

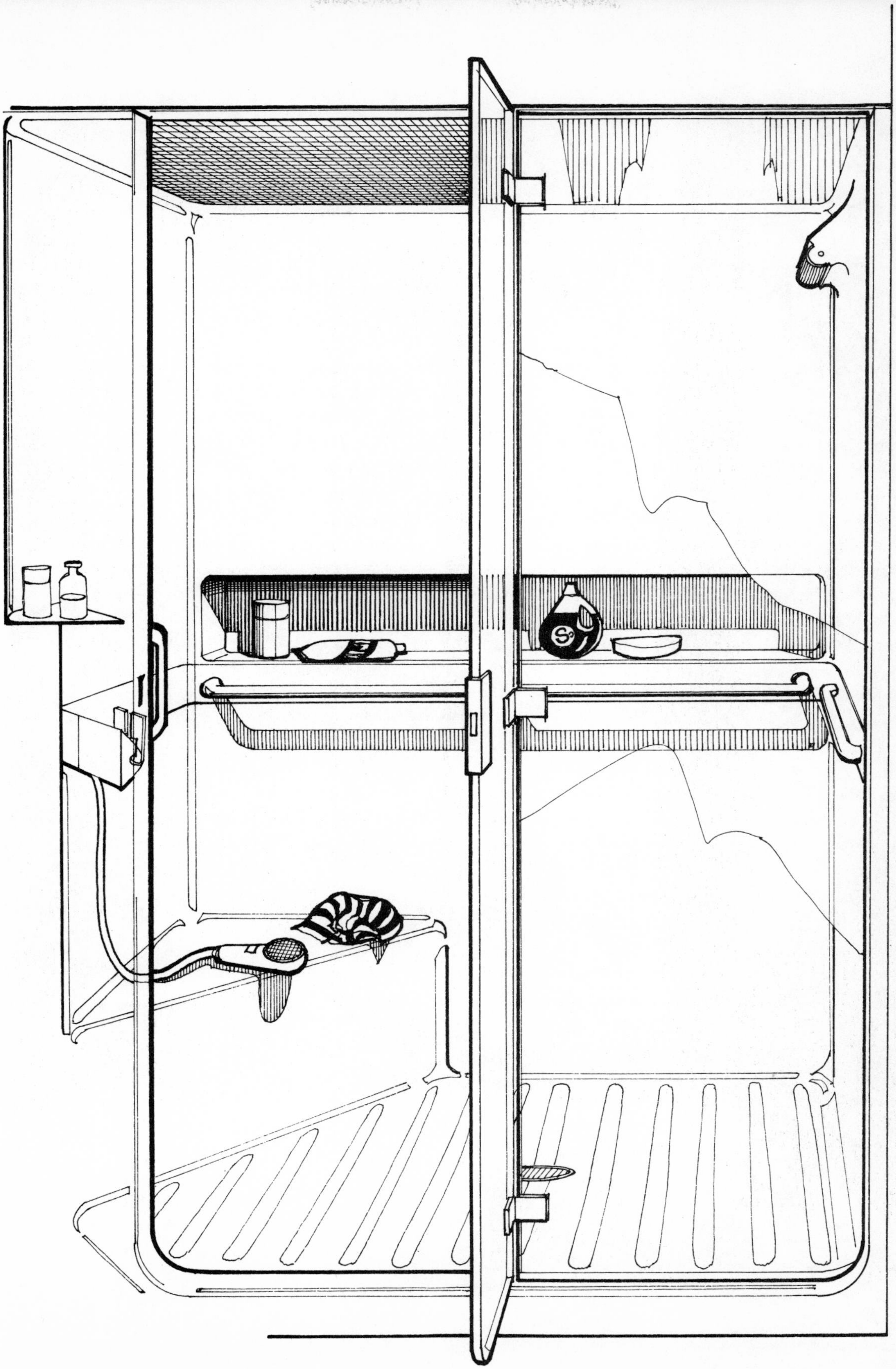

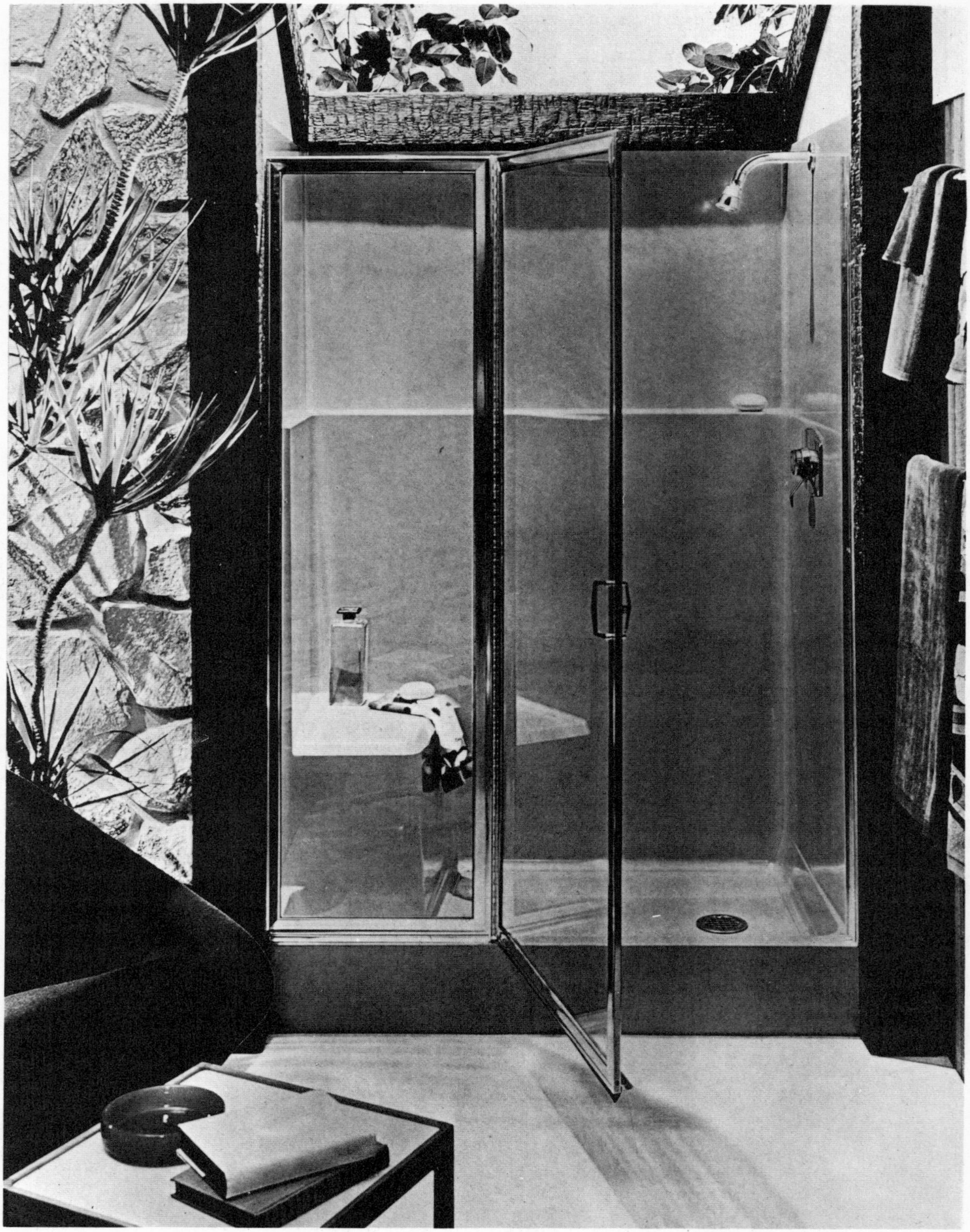

ABOVE: "CONCEPT III" TUB-SHOWER COMBINATION: ELJER, PITTSBURGH, PENNSYLVANIA, U.S.A.

LEFT: "DESIGNER LINE" ONE-PIECE SHOWER: AMERICAN STANDARD, NEW BRUNSWICK, NEW JERSEY, U.S.A.

27 / CURRENT APPROACHES TO SHOWERS AND TUB-SHOWER COMBINATIONS

heads, and preprogrammed alternating hot and cold water. It would also be possible to equip shower heads to dispense automatically bath salts or soap, or both, if one wished.

Lighting and Ventilation The shower, by its very nature and by virtue of the necessity for a nearly complete enclosure, poses two problems that are often the cause of complaints—poor lighting and poor ventilation.[2] Both of these problems are easily enough resolved by incorporating a separate mechanical exhaust system and separate lighting within the shower enclosure. As in so many other instances, this simply points up once again the necessity for conceiving of hygiene facilities as a functional entity rather than as a collection of pieces, the assembly of which is left to the whim of a first-cost-conscious builder.

Whenever a shower is provided, a mechanical exhaust is desirable, if not one directly incorporated within the shower itself, then one that serves the entire bathroom. A shower inherently and inevitably releases far more moisture into the air than a bathtub, and this substantially raises the relative humidity. Adequate insulation of the bathroom and adequate heat will also substantially cut down on the problems of condensation on windows and mirrors. A fully enclosed shower enclosure from which the moisture cannot escape can also reduce the problem. In such a situation, briefly turning on cold water will cause the moisture to condense inside the shower enclosure before it has a chance to escape into the room. In a minimal bathroom where a shower is equipped only with a curtain, a mechanical exhaust is a necessity if one is to avoid serious moisture problems.

Cleaning Problems In some respects, cleaning a shower enclosure presents fewer difficulties than cleaning a tub, even though it is as large, if not larger. Physically, the shower enclosure does not get as dirty, because there is no appreciable retention of water and no scum or ring to be scrubbed away. It also does not appear to get very dirty simply from a visual standpoint, because of the colors and materials commonly used. From a psychological standpoint we do not seem to mind whatever dirt there may be as much as in a tub because we have so little actual physical contact with the fixture. In addition, we seem to accept the fact that for a thorough cleaning there is little alternative except to get into the enclosure and clean. Once one is in, however, the openness and size of the enclosure are such that cleaning is relatively simple in terms of accessibility and posture, and much of it can actually be done while one is standing.

There are several obvious features that would make the shower both more self-cleaning and more easily cleanable: there should be a minimum number of surfaces; all surfaces must be self-draining, including the seat or shelf; there should be a minimum of joints and seams; the junction of different surfaces should be seamless; the provision of a supplementary flexible spray hose would allow the entire enclosure to be rinsed with running water; the drain should not clog easily and it should have a strainer that can be removed for cleaning.

Summary — Design Possibilities Figure 26 illustrates one of the possible approaches that might be taken to a total facility for showering based on this analysis. As shown, the enclosure is treated as a single unit and incorporates a built-in seat and a recessed shelf with a light. The plan configuration and the overall dimensions are basically the same as those developed in the analysis. Grab bars are located at the entry and horizontally along the far side where they would always be accessible from within the shower. The controls are located at the entry in such a way that they can be easily reached from outside the enclosure while one is making the initial water adjustments and from any point within the enclosure. The controls themselves are based on the direct and obvious action of a throttle—pulling either the hot or cold lever down (or both simultaneously) to turn the water on, both volume and temperature being directly related to the position of the lever, and pulling the lever up to shut off the water. A single adjustable shower head is used, supplemented by a hand spray. The ceiling incorporates a built-in ventilating and lighting system.

Obviously, numerous other approaches may be taken, both generalized and specialized. As with the other fixtures, however, it is imperative that the entire facility be conceived and executed as a single entity if the essential relationships and component parts are not to be lost. (Several recent approaches to a comprehensive shower module are illustrated in Figure 27.)

PERINEAL CLEANSING

7

DESCRIPTION OF ACTIVITY

Perineal hygiene is the general term used to describe the cleansing of the genital, urinary, and anal regions of the body, both male and female. Of all the normal body cleansing activities these are undoubtedly the least understood, the least discussed, and the least performed.

Although it is convenient for purposes of discussion to group these areas together, each must be examined separately in terms of its own unique problems and requirements.

Genitourinary The principal concern here from the viewpoints of hygiene, health, and aesthetics is the external cleansing of the vulvar region of the female. This comprises the area surrounding the urethral and vaginal openings, the mucous membrane of the labial folds, and the pubic hair.

Unlike other areas of the body, the vulvar region poses particular hygiene problems, chiefly because the labial folds and hair that protect the body openings also retain urine and other body secretions from urination, menstruation, and coitus. This makes effective cleansing difficult and often results in odors, irritations, and discomfort. In addition, the hairy parts of the body are inherently difficult to clean.

In terms of cleansing, vulvar hygiene may be divided into two separate components: after urination and during and after menstruation, pregnancy, and coitus. The first stage is fairly simple and rarely presents any particular problem since women tend, by and large, to keep themselves reasonably clean by blotting with tissue—a practice men would do well to copy—or by using the bidet to wash the vulvar region. In addition, regular washing of the region as a part of the normal bathing routine is generally sufficient in most cases. Topical cleansing following coitus or pregnancy or during menstruation poses a greater problem in that positive washing is generally indicated. This again is commonly taken care of by use of the bidet, by partial or complete bathing in the tub or shower, or by vaginal irrigation.

Medical opinion is divided on the advisability or harmfulness of using the various recent "feminine hygiene" deodorants. The argument against them rests on the point made earlier—that a normal healthy vagina needs nothing more than normal care with soap and water and that such deodorant sprays can mask a more serious sign of possible infection and generally lower the body's inherent resistance to infection by destroying the normal resident bacteria. As with many of the bactericidal soaps and underarm deodorants, there are numerous people who have developed severe allergic reactions. Somewhat ironically, women are also cautioned not to use these sprays immediately before coitus in an effort to be more alluring, because this use has resulted in a number of instances of genital irritation in both partners.

For the male, little is ever said about genitourinary hygiene and, consequently, little is ever done. Several matters, however, deserve attention. One is the blotting of the penis after urination—and after "jiggling"—to remove those last drops of urine that otherwise are absorbed by the clothing. Contrary to the age-old and universal jingle: "No matter how much you jiggle and squeeze, those last few drops always go down your knees!", more times than not those last few drops are simply absorbed by the underwear and soak through to the trousers, particularly if they are tight-fitting. ("Speaking of the Mahometans," Tournefort says, "when they make water, they squat down like women, for fear some drops of urine should fall into their breeches. To prevent this evil, they squeeze the part very carefully, and rub the head of it against a wall; and one may see the stones worn in several places by this custom.")[1] In this respect, tight-fitting underwear, jock straps, "jockey"-style shorts, and the like pose a special problem since confinement of the genitals tends to result in more perspiration and to hinder evaporation of both urine and perspiration so that "jock itch" and chafing are common if cleansing is not frequent and thorough. In this respect loose-fitting underwear is preferable, if unfashionable at the moment.

Thorough washing of the genitals is also particularly important in uncircumcised males. Although circumcision is still widely practiced today as a hygienic measure, it is by no means universal, and careful washing under the foreskin is essential. Indeed, some physicians observe that if one can be taught to brush one's teeth, one can be taught to wash one's penis and that circumcision is a wholly unnecessary bit of ritualistic mutilation in the guise of hygiene.

Vaginal Irrigation Internal cleansing, or vaginal douching, has long been a part of "feminine hygiene" though it is not nearly as widespread today as in the past. This internal irrigation is sometimes accomplished by using the spray (douche) feature of the bidet but more commonly is accomplished by means of a syringe inserted into the vagina. (The word *douche,* which is not quite polite these days, is simply the French word for shower and refers not only to the spray in the bidet but also to any shower; this term was, in fact, in common usage in this context in the last century, even in the English-speaking world.) Although plain water is most commonly used, various other solutions, medicated or not, are also used for special purposes. Until fairly recently it was popularly believed that douching immediately after coitus with a mildly acid solution was also an effective means of contraception. Modern medical opinion holds this to be totally erroneous, and, in fact, appears to be divided on its desirability or necessity under any circumstances. In general, its use today seems to be recommended largely for therapeutic reasons in the treatment of vaginal infections, which are quite common, and occasionally for just plain cleansing after coitus or menstruation. The arguments against regular douching rest on the fact that the body normally produces certain acid substances that have a bactericidal action and that would be washed away and thereby lower resistance to infection. Even its therapeutic use is opposed by some physicians on the grounds that douching merely removes the evidence of infection and relieves the symptoms so that patients are tempted to discontinue treatment.

Anal Hygiene The anus and the area immedi-

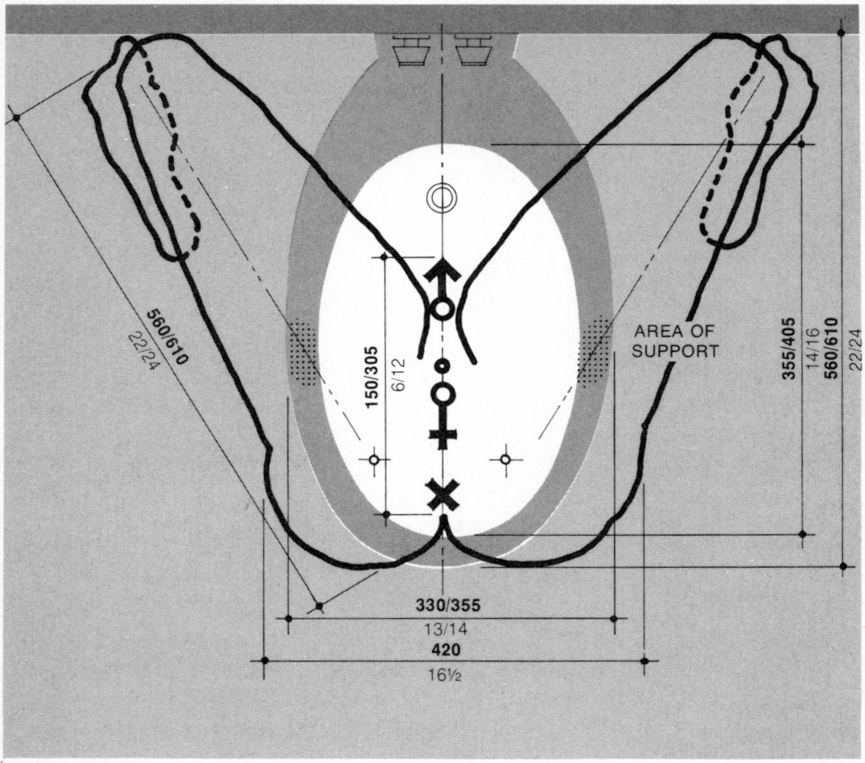

28 / PLAN VIEW OF SITTING POSITION ON A CONVENTIONAL BIDET

ately surrounding it are unquestionably the most soiled parts of the body because of the fecal smear that is left following defecation. Dry wiping with paper, as commonly practiced, removes some of this fecal matter but obviously not all. This is particularly true of persons with an abundance of hair surrounding the anus. In addition to soiling undergarments, this partial cleansing also results in odors, chafing, and, in persons with hemorrhoids, the possibility of contamination and infection.

Thorough cleansing can be achieved only by washing the anus after each defecation or by wet-wiping—using either wetted paper or one of the proprietary cleansing foams currently marketed as medical preparations for hemorrhoid patients. Actual washing, as done today, is generally through the use of the bidet or one of the special water closets or water closet seats that incorporate a washing device. Normal body cleansing, whether performed daily or not, is generally inadequate unless special attention is paid to this area, particularly since this region is rarely washed any more than the vulvar region is. To some extent this is inevitable since both of these areas are relatively sensitive and likely to be irritated by soaps and by scrubbing. This can be compensated for by regular washing with water or by wet-wiping. This cleansing is an essential procedure in the case of persons with hemorrhoids.

DESIGN CONSIDERATIONS

General cleansing of the vulvar and anal regions can be accomplished during regular body cleansing by using either the tub or the shower method. The only particular requirement is for adequate rinsing, especially of the vulvar area. This can be provided for most readily by the inclusion of a hand spray or other flexible and mobile water source as a part of the washing facility.

29 / PLAN VIEW OF NECESSARY DIMENSIONS AND CLEARANCES FOR A BIDET

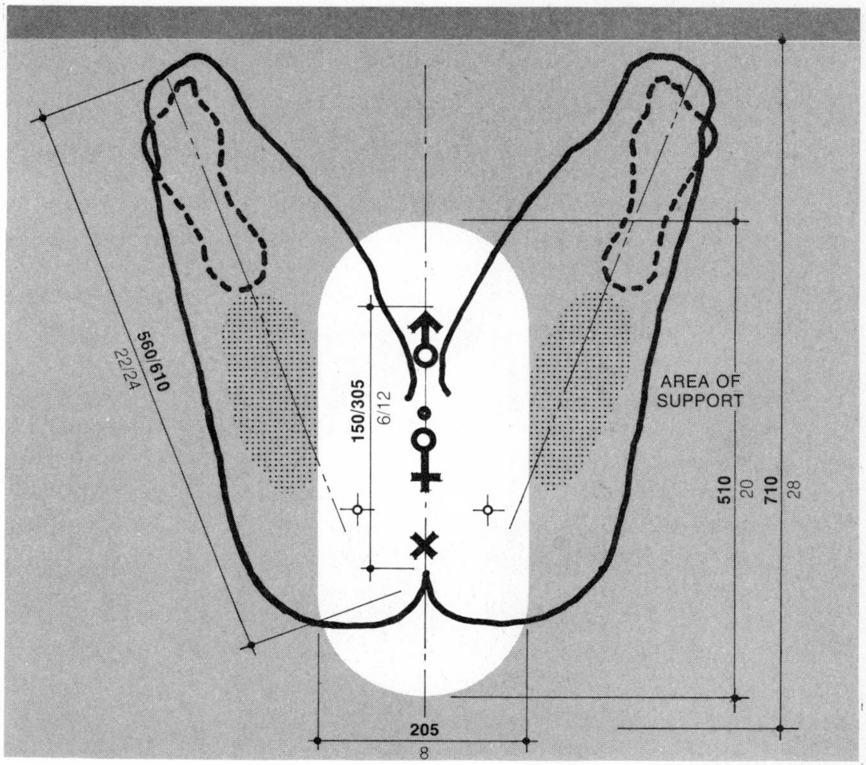

In terms of accommodating specific topical vulvar and anal cleansing, let us consider two basic approaches. The first is the provision of a special washing facility, in effect, a bidet or some variation thereof. The second is the elaboration of the water closet to accommodate the washing function as well as the elimination function.

The bidet offers the advantages of additional uses such as for sitz baths and foot baths, and it can also serve as a facility for generalized cleansing of the anal–genital area under circumstances where bathing facilities are generally lacking or in warm climates where especially frequent and thorough cleansing is desirable. Conversely, the bidet has a number of disadvantages: additional space requirements, extra cost, and, perhaps most significant, the inconvenience of having to move from one fixture to another following elimination. And for some people, of course, the psychological barriers to its use are formidable.

The second approach, the incorporation of provisions for washing within the basic elimination facility, offers the fundamental advantage of naturally allowing the related elimination and cleansing processes to be accomplished at one sitting, as it were—a circumstance that would greatly encourage proper cleansing. The disadvantages of this approach are the greater mechanical sophistication required of the water closet and the specific limited usefulness of the washing capability compared with the versatility of the bidet. Because, however, this approach is such an integral part of our examination of the water closet, further discussion of it will be found in chapter 10.

Although the bidet is used for a wide range of washing and soaking purposes, it is generally treated as an adjunct to the water closet, primarily for the sake of convenience for anal cleaning. Unfortunately it has also come to be designed as a companion piece to the water closet—so much so that in many instances its functional utility has

30 / CURRENT APPROACH TO A BIDET

"ARMADA" BIDET: VILLEROY-BOCH, METTLACH, WEST GERMANY, WITH "TASTAMAT" SPRAY FITTING: HANSA, STUTTGART, WEST GERMANY

been sacrificed for the sake of a matching appearance. Although the basic size and shape are roughly similar, the sitting posture on the bidet is quite different in that the bidet must be fully straddled and have ample room front and back for the hand to reach comfortably the anogenital parts of the body. In this respect, the original bidet shape, which approximated a figure eight, was more suitable than the oval shape commonly found today in terms of permitting a more comfortable posture and providing better support.

At a conventional height of 405 mm (16 inches), which matches the water closet generally, one sits in a normal upright posture with the legs spread, straddling the fixture. In this position one's weight must be supported along the backs of the thighs and for maximum comfort should receive as much support as possible. As indicated in Figure 28, support under the buttocks is not possible without encroaching on the free area needed for anal washing. In this respect many contemporary bidets are inadequate in that the front-to-back dimension is so short as to force one to sit back on the rim for vulvar cleansing and then shift into an awkward forward crouch for anal cleansing unless one attempts to do so from the front, which is also awkward and, in females, inadvisable because of the risks of cross-contamination of the genitourinary region. The seated, buttocks-to-knees dimension ranges from 560 to 610 mm (22 to 24 inches) in the adult population. Spreading the legs decreases this dimension slightly, by 25 to 50 mm (1 to 2 inches). Most contemporary fixtures, however, have only an overall length of 560 to 610 mm (22 to 24 inches) and a clear opening size of 355 to 405 mm (14 to 16 inches) where a minimum of 510 mm (20 inches) is desirable (see Figure 29). In part, this becomes awkward because most fix-

31 / POSSIBLE APPROACH TO A BIDET

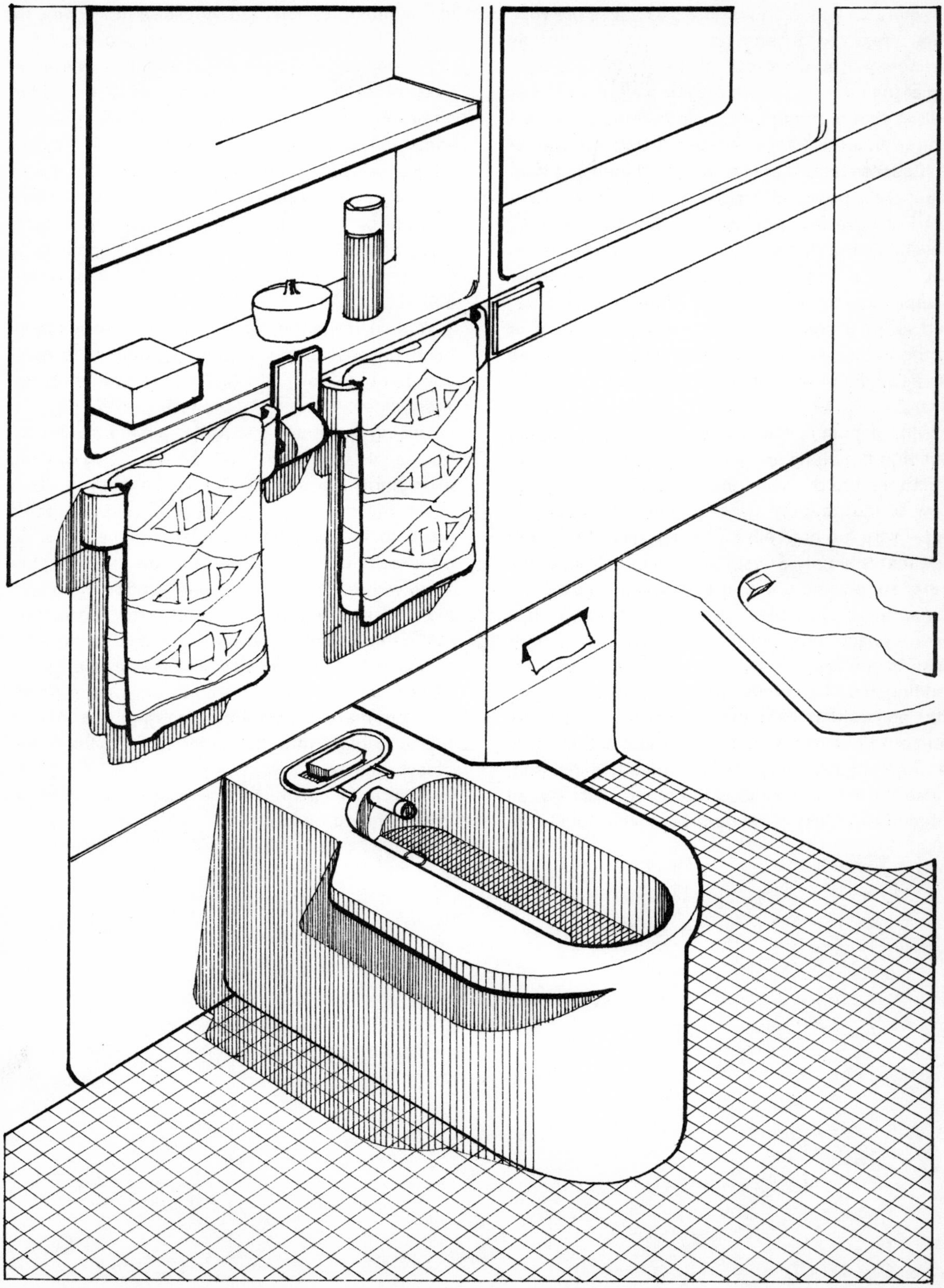

tures are designed so that the user faces the wall. This offers the advantages of a simpler fittings arrangement and more flexibility in the positioning of the controls, which may be wall-mounted as well as fixture-mounted. It also permits a convenient arrangement for soap and towels. Conversely, it necessitates a greater overall dimension than is generally provided if one is to sit at the midpoint of the fixture and not have to change positions. Reversing the direction of use so that one faces out into the room, as has sometimes been done, complicates the arrangement of fittings, controls, and so on, which must now be located at the front of the fixture, but it does offer more flexibility as far as accommodating persons of varying body size.

With respect to the manner in which the actual washing functions are accomplished a number of variations are possible and generally desirable in view of the range of uses to which the fixture is put. There are basically two versions of the bidet: one that is simply a basin fitted with a drain and a water supply and one that additionally has a vertical spray or "douche." Over the years there has been considerable controversy over the sanitariness of the built-in spray, some authorities contending that infectious material can drain back into, and contaminate, the water supply. The spray version, while common in many parts of the world, is generally prohibited in the United States and, indeed, in some localities the bidet is prohibited altogether unless a vacuum breaker is built into the plumbing system. The question has obviously been of particular concern with respect to maternity wards and other public installations where the risks of cross-infection are higher than in the home. Although a pool of water is desirable for some activities, it is not the ideal cleansing method. For vulvar and anal washing, a stream of running water is preferable. This may be accomplished by providing an adjustable horizontal spray nozzle or a separate small hand spray, as is sometimes done with maternity bidets (see Figure 30).

Vaginal irrigation, or douching, has generally been unsatisfactorily accommodated. It is most commonly performed while one is seated on the water closet, though the preferred method from a cleansing viewpoint is to perform it in a horizontal position. In the home, this is possible only by lying in an empty tub, and it is awkward at best. In either case, one common problem is to find a suitable place to hang the bag containing the water or other solution. (The same difficulties are encountered with respect to the administration of an enema.) There are, however, devices on the market that can be built in and provide a mixing valve for tempered water, a retractable hose, and a variety of nozzles suitable for vaginal or colonic irrigation. Another possible approach might be to build this capability into the bidet or into the water closet module.

(Figure 31 illustrates one way in which these criteria might be met.)

SOCIAL AND PSYCHOLOGICAL ASPECTS OF ELIMINATION

8

ATTITUDES TO ELIMINATION PROCESSES AND PRODUCTS

Whereas our attitudes surrounding the cleansing processes tend to be essentially positive in outlook and focus on concepts of hygiene and symbolic cleanliness, our attitudes surrounding the elimination processes—urination, defecation, flatulence, spitting, and so on—tend by and large to be negative in outlook and focus on dirt and filth and a variety of notions about real and symbolic defilement. Urine and feces, in particular, are generally regarded by contemporary Western societies as filth of the worst sort, so much so that the individual not only wants to dispose of them as thoroughly and quickly as possible but also wishes in many instances to be completely disassociated from the act of producing them. In fact, it is probably fair to say that for many people urine and feces are the most repulsive and worthless substances imaginable. Indeed, the degree of feeling sometimes encountered has its roots in something more than aesthetic or hygienic rejection.[1]

Although "dirt" can be almost any unwelcome foreign or displaced substance or thing, we reserve our worst proscription for body wastes: fingernail parings, hair, spittle, sweat, semen, menstrual discharge, mucus, gas, urine, feces, and so on. Interestingly, most of these body wastes are viewed either neutrally or positively until the moment they are cast off, when they undergo a drastic role transformation. Feces, on the other hand, has often been regarded as intrinsically undesirable, even while being formed in the body. Until quite recently, in fact, it was commonly believed, even by the medical profession, that constipation and prolonged retention of feces within the body would result in autointoxication and contribute to a wide variety of ailments.[2] On the other hand, at least a few scientists have recently begun to speculate that there may be a link between colon–rectal cancer and the rate of digestion, Western peoples generally having a markedly higher incidence of colon–rectal cancer than peoples who live on a high-bulk, low-fat, vegetarian diet and who pass food more rapidly. It must be noted, however, that there is a considerable difference between such natural regularity and self-induced regularity which can produce problems of its own, as we shall examine later. It is highly doubtful, however, that there is any basis for this in normal healthy individuals, though regrettably these attitudes and their associated purges continue to persist. Indeed, the condemnatory expression "He's full of shit," amply demonstrates the persistence of these attitudes.

This negativism is, however, a learned response rather than rooted in our instincts. Very young children, for example, feel no particular revulsion or disgust for feces or urine or for the elimination processes. Over a period of time, children learn that excrement is not really all that pleasant to be in contact with but:

> It is seldom . . . that the child is left alone to acquire an aversion to his waste products or an attitude of secrecy and shame with respect to the processes of elimination.[3]

On the contrary, children often find feces and urine pleasurable, or at least neutral, and "things" that can be manipulated in relationships with parents. Franz Alexander points out, for example, that:

> The child's earliest attitude toward his excreta is a coprophilic one. The excrement is a valuable possession, a source of pleasure and something which can be exchanged for other goods.[4]

What is of more immediate concern is that the attitudes replacing this early outlook may be more permanent, as Alexander goes on to describe:

> This coprophilic attitude, however, is inhibited by educational procedures and changed into its opposite, disgust and depreciation, which becomes the basis of the sadistic aggressive-and-soiling connotation of the excremental act. . . . In later life all these emotional connections, to a greater or lesser degree, disappear from the conscious personality but remain deeply rooted in the emotional life.[4]

Elimination is often also used in a punitive way. A classic situation, standard in psychological literature, is the one wherein the child either withholds its feces or, more commonly, soils the fixture or the surroundings as an obvious and early learned means of punishing the parent. This is a relatively subtle way of causing annoyance and displeasure because it cannot be established clearly that the action was intentional rather than accidental.

> There was chamber pot etiquette in the nursery. Number One was applauded, but Number Two was a severe breach. I imagine Rose, our nursery-maid who waited on Nanny and brought up the meals, was not too keen on emptying pots: piss plus turd produced revolutionary rumbling and upset nursery hierarchy. It was an accident with agreeably sinful overtones.[5]

This infantile pattern may carry over into adulthood, and a grown man, frustrated in his attempts to cope with a situation, may release his aggressions (or indirectly express his dissatisfaction with himself) by such deliberate soiling. In more extreme instances, as we shall examine in more detail later, deliberate defecation is employed as a gesture of contempt for authority figures. A certain amount of soiling, as will be demonstrated later, is inevitable and unavoidable when men use the water closet for urination. There is, however, a fairly wide area of discretion within which the man can elect to be cautious or careless.

The behavior of children also provides insight into another aspect of our attitude toward elimination, namely, that the products are part of ourselves. Fliess, for example, states that, to small children

> . . . feces are both an object and a part of the individual, who is prone to identify with them. . . . It is thus that young children exhibit a fear of defecating because the act is equivalent to the relinquishment of a part of themselves. . . .
>
> In adults one observes not infrequently that this fear has persisted and merely led to a modification of the procedure, attenuating the loss through delay: they inspect excrement before flushing it down.[6]

Interestingly, this pattern appears to be quite widespread in parts of Europe, particularly Germany, where the old-fashioned "wash-down" closet with its inevitable scrub brush is still the norm. My medical friends there assure me that the daily examination of one's feces is still considered a sound and common health practice, as it was in Pliny's time. At the opposite extreme, we find persons who are so anxious to dispose of the offending matter that they flush away each fecal bolus as it is deposited, while seated. Still others flush only once after defecation is complete but while still seated and then carefully close the lid and never look back.

One also finds that among adolescents, for example, the self-discovery and awareness of one's body and its functionings that are common at this stage extend to elimination functions and to rivalries over the largest bowel movement or the longest trajectory while urinating. Contrary to common supposition, the practice is not confined to adolescent boys: "On Saturday afternoons the girls (in an English girls boarding school) would buy chocolates, pool them, and engage in a trial of skill which consisted in attempting to perform the feat of urinating in the erect position into a bottle placed on the floor. The victor was entitled to carry off the chocolates."[7]

Even adults sometimes exhibit a rather more casual than common attitude toward elimination when preoccupied with other matters. James I of England is said to have regularly and splendidly beshat himself while in the saddle since he refused to pause in the hunt for any reason. More recently it was reported that in Las Vegas, women slot-machine players had occasionally to be ". . . forcibly dragged from their stations by security guards when they refused to quit long enough to attend to basic biological needs."[8]

Not only are our negative attitudes toward body wastes learned rather than "natural" or instinctive, they are also of relatively recent origin. Most commonly, the originator of these attitudes is thought to be Luther, who was vexed by the Devil while closeted. In other times, both urine and feces have been regarded as useful and valuable commodities not only in primitive cultures but also in our own. Body wastes were, for our ancestors, a dependable, readily available raw material that possessed valuable properties and could be used in a wide variety of ways.[9]

Urine, for example, has been one of mankind's oldest known forms of "soap," since oxidized urine produces ammonia compounds that are a standard agent for dissolving fats. The Eskimos carefully stored urine for use in washing their cooking utensils and employed a bundle of grass wetted with urine to wipe their mouths after eating. Various North American Indian tribes urinated on one another before scrubbing and going into the steam bath. As late as the turn of the century, ladies would urinate on their hands with the idea of cleaning and softening them. Even today, persons such as fishermen and loggers who work outdoors in all kinds of weather urinate on their hands simply to warm them. Urine has also had a number of medicinal uses, both external and internal: because of its urea content, urine has been used effectively as an antiseptic agent to promote healing of cuts and wounds, and urea compounds are still used for these purposes today. Urine has also been used, at least from the time of the Roman Empire, for fixing dyes in cloth. One of the oldest (and in a way most contemporary) uses of urine has been as an intoxicant and hallucinogenic vehicle. Many peoples, for example, have concocted preparations using urine that were then drunk for a "high." In some instances, the urine of the drinker was then passed along to another who got his high secondhand and only slightly diluted. In many tropical regions, urine is drunk as a quick tonic or pick-me-up, again quite logically, for the salts and trace minerals might otherwise be seriously depleted in hot climates through perspiration and urination. On the other hand, in Siberia human urine is given to the reindeer to drink in lieu of otherwise unobtainable salt. Diderot's *Encyclopédie* lists dozens of other practical uses ranging from the manufacture of saltpeter to phosphorus, which should not be surprising if we can regard urine neutrally as simply a chemical compound and a potential raw material.

Not surprisingly, urine has also played an important role in many religious rituals and is generally thought to be the origin of holy water as it is used today. It has been used in the marriage and fertility rituals of many peoples and also been regarded as an aphrodisiac.

In similar fashion, feces has had a long and varied history of symbolic and practical uses. Among the Tibetans and Mongols, for example, the feces of the Dalai Lama was venerated and worn as an amulet in a little pouch—much as we would treasure a lock of hair or the finger joint of a saint. Among certain Hindu sects the feces of the sacred cow was eaten as a magic potion to guarantee purity. Feces, like urine, has also been ingested medicinally in our own culture until relatively recently, though usually as only one ingredient in a preparation. And, indeed, human excrement has even slyly found its way into the preparation of foodstuffs such as bread and cheese, where it was sometimes used to help fermentation and to impart "a special piquancy to the flavor." Feces has also been burned as fuel and used to cure tobacco.

The most common and universal use for fecal matter has, however, been as fertilizer, or "night soil" as it was once quaintly put. In many parts of the world human excrement is used along with animal excrement, even today. According to one, possibly apocryphal, account a fertilizer salesman sent to the Orient before the war cabled back in despair after several months that he was getting nowhere with 500 million competitors!

In recent years, however, considerable attention has once again been given to the recycling of sewage sludge for use in commercial farming operations and land reclamation projects. Although the value of sewage has been amply demonstrated, along with its innocuousness, communities are reluctant to accept it because of its despised origins. On the contrary, Australia has used sewage to irrigate farm lands for decades, and in many parts of Europe "sludge farms" have existed for years for growing various specialty crops. Increased research is also under way to explore the large-scale feasibility of collecting and burning the methane gas generated in raw sewage. An old youthful prank is to light a match while someone is farting profusely and see who can produce the longest blue jet flame. Similarly, an old deodorizing remedy calls for lighting a match and waving it about to burn off the offending odor.

In the early days of the U.S. space program the authorities decided that it would be acceptable to jettison various waste materials from the capsules but *not* solid body wastes, even though these would also completely vaporize and disappear in space. The idea was diplomatically unacceptable. Parenthetically, it may be noted that urine was often vented out and was suspected of being responsible for the crystalline build-up that fogged the capsule windows.

As our ecological awareness grows, perhaps we can in time again overcome our squeamishness in these respects and begin to do a more intelligent and productive job of recycling our own wastes. Flushing the toilet, after all, only removes the offending matter from our immediate presence; it does not *really* disappear; it merely pollutes some other place—unless we deal with it in a positive and deliberate way. Interestingly, in some quarters there is a movement afoot (so to speak) to reinstate the outdoor "privy" as an ecologically sound practice. In a 1972 broadcast Arthur Godfrey advocated a return to the "two-holer" as a way of combatting water pollution, and in 1973 the New Hampshire State Legislature passed a bill to legalize and regulate outhouses again.[10]

ATTITUDES, LANGUAGE, AND BEHAVIOR

The clearest and commonest evidence of our negative attitudes toward elimination processes and products is to be found in our language usages, both verbal and symbolic, for it is here that our notions about worthlessness and defilement find rich and varied expression vis-a-vis contempt and hostility.

Only one positive usage comes to mind though it is somewhat indirect: "She's built like a brick shit-house." This curious approbation also suggests not only the positive pleasures of a commodious accommodation but also the positive pleasures of a satisfying defecation.

One other possibly positive example is to be found in the expression "He thinks he's hot stuff," sometimes rendered as "He thinks he's hot shit."

On the other hand, feces also appear positively, though unconsciously, with respect to the feces/money/time equation suggested by many psychologists: "to be filthy rich, to be rolling in it, to have money up the ass, to make one's pile . . . to piddle the time away . . . to make it big, or make a splash, he has to produce, to put out. He can't *sit tight*; he can't sit on his material."[11]

Since feces is the most worthless and despised thing we know, it becomes a convenient and universal analogue for all our imputations about others' ideas and motives. The expression "He's full of shit" (or in its more acceptable form, "He's full of it.") unmistakably conveys the speaker's estimation of his subject's good sense or honesty. A similar usage is to be found in the expressions "He's an asshole," the more recent "Don't shit me," or in the simple expletives "Crap!" "Horse shit!" or "Bull shit!" delivered in response to a statement that one disbelieves or disagrees with. Curiously, only "Bull!" can stand alone in this respect or "That's a crock" (of shit), apparently derived from the chamber pot.

One of the more interesting recent expressions favored by teenagers and college students is "dump on"—most commonly used in reference to an action taken against the speaker, as in "He dumped on my report." Here we find a subtle shift, for shit is now not only worthless but is also defiling and used by the recipient of the action.

As single expletives these same excretory terms have also entered our vocabulary as almost universal expressions of anger and frustration and follow a common pattern of invoking the unmentionable in times of stress. Depending on the individual and the circumstances, we find the term in a variety of guises from "shit!" to "sheet," "shoot," "shucks," and "sugar."

Our society's attitude toward the body and elimination is also expressed by its violent responses to the calculated use of language such as "shit," "piss," and "fuck." The degree of "uptightness" of society in this respect has not escaped the notice of the alienated and the radical, who have, ever since the "Free Speech Movement" in Berkeley in the sixties, brought some segments of society to the verge of hysteria and apoplexy with such usage and with their general tactics. Their tactics for expressing contempt center almost exclusively around the body/sex/elimination amalgam and encompass dress, appearance, hygiene habits, nudity, sexuality, and their respective terminologies. It has been endlessly argued, with respect to both the tactics and behavior of the alienated and the definitions of pornography and obscenity, whether the human body and its biological functions are as "obscene" as some of the deliberate activities of people. Obviously for many people it still is, and, as has been noted by many observers, it is not only the language of elimination that is the source of our worst condemnatory expressions but also the language of sex. It is claimed by some students of language that English is the only language in which virtually the entire vocabulary of sexual activity is essentially hostile in tone and the source of most of our swearing vocabulary. Be that as it may, there is no question that the issue is a central one in our current social confrontations. The attitudes are perhaps best summed up in the somewhat cryptic expression "Fuck that shit!" Here shit has now come to signify everything that the enemy, that is, established society, says or does and society's usage of fuck has been ironically borrowed as a hostile rather than a loving term.[12]

With respect to symbolic communication, perhaps the most dramatic gesture of contempt is actual defecation. At one time, for example, many English households favored a chamberpot with a portrait of Napoleon in the bottom. More recently, Rudi the Red stunned a German court by lowering his trousers and defecating on the judge's table! In another recent instance, a book critical of television programming in the United States featured a cover photo of the author sitting, with his trousers lowered, on top of a television set. The symbolism in this instance is particularly rich, for not only is the author "dumping on" television but he is also commenting on the programming that is passing through the "receiver."

Although such overt actions are relatively rare, at least insofar as society in general is concerned, it is a common tactic in some quarters. The so-called "Phantom Shitter"—another version of "Kilroy"—has been a traditional phenomenon in the Navy for years—a folk hero to the ordinary seaman and a considerable irritant to the officers against whom his activities are directed, since his "messages" almost invariably appear in the most sacrosanct and embarrassing places such as the Captain's bridge and the officers' mess.

Apparently this method of venting one's hostility is also common in the construction industry, where workmen will often single out finished work or tools or supplies on which to defecate. The circumstances here are somewhat mitigated by the fact that on large construction jobs toilets are generally few and far between, so that the workman often has little choice but to defecate wherever he happens to be. But even in such circumstances he obviously has a choice between committing a minor nuisance or deliberately giving maximum offense.

While it can be argued that such tactics are nothing more than a regression to infantile behavior patterns, it is also true that our response, as the victim, is generally not that of a tolerant parent. Quite the contrary; it is undoubtedly the ultimate gesture of contempt when deliberately performed, even though there is generally a symbolic parent–child relationship involved.

Much the same is true of deliberate farting, which has long been regarded as a major insult, particularly when timed to serve as a response to someone's remarks. This is most commonly engaged in as a kind of good-natured banter among friends; the insult is too grave to be risked except when one is prepared to face the consequences, since, in contrast to shitting, farting must be done to one's face. Generally we resort to the more familiar simulated oral version that we term "the raspberry" or "the Bronx cheer."

In fact, "that lowest of all human expressions," as farting has been called, is also employed in somewhat milder fashion—for example, to deflate pomposity and formality. The means of expression in such instances may equally well be auditory or olfactory, since curiously enough the production of maximum noise and maximum odor are generally mutually exclusive. Farting is also commonly employed by persons in authority to demonstrate to underlings that they are one of the "boys" too, and one bit of folk wisdom holds that "the honeymoon is over when the husband farts in front of his wife."[13]

These same general attitudes also extend to the whole anal region. If we return to the Devil for a moment, we find numerous associations with the rectum as well as feces. Witches supposedly kissed his rear and "those especially damned were obliged to live beneath his tail." In this regard, deliberate exposure of the buttocks, as practiced by Luther, was an early form of exorcising the evil influence. Although the spiritual significance of this act has faded away, the act survives among many Western peoples as a major gesture of contempt—even when performed as a pantomime without baring the buttocks. The invitation to "Kiss my ass!" also still survives as demeaning and contemptuous. (President L. B. Johnson: "I don't want loyalty. I want *Loyalty.* I want him to kiss my ass in Macy's window at high noon and tell me it smells like roses.")[14]

The other major form of insult surviving from Roman times in both spoken and gesture form is the extended middle finger—the *digitus impudicus* or "shameless finger" and the invitation: "Shove it!" (up your ass) or, "Up yours, Mac!" In the still favored Italian version, the entire right forearm is used. As with most such gestures, considerable variation appears in their usage and meaning. "The finger," for example, is currently employed rather extensively as a silent and surreptitious gesture, often among associates and signifying anything from "Fuck him" to "Fuck you." Obviously, the degree of insult can vary enormously, depending on identity of the respective participants and the boldness with which the gestures are performed. In an interesting variation, there is the story of the defeated Indian chief who "gives the finger" to the victorious cavalry major every time he rides by camp. He first gives him the standard gesture with the finger upright and then extends it horizontally. After several such episodes, the major, somewhat perplexed, stops one day as he is riding by and asks the chief what he means by the horizontal gesture. The chief replies, "I feel the same way about your horse!"

One consequence of these attitudes toward the elimination processes and products is that, having invested them with strong negative meanings and having borrowed the vocabulary for swearing purposes, we regard such topics as "unspeakable" in polite society and resort to the development of a totally new vocabulary that is socially acceptable. This recourse to euphemisms, which Havelock Ellis aptly calls "the clothing of language," applies not only to the processes and products but also to the equipment used and the room where it is located. Further, as the meaning of a euphemism becomes too obvious, we replace it by some other term so that we may continue to conceal at least our specific need, if not our general purpose.

Thus, shit, piss, and fart, which were standard Anglo-Saxon words until the eighteenth century both in speech and literature, have become feces, urine, and flatulence respectively, or "number two," "number one," and "passing wind." Similarly, we "defecate" or "pass a stool" or we micturate or "go wee wee." Or, more generally, we "powder our noses," "wash our hands," "do our business," "use the facilities," "see a man about a dog," or possibly "heed nature's call" or "take a leak." If we should do any of these things in public, we "commit a nuisance." In an (apocryphal?) anecdote regarding President Truman, the President is delivering a speech to a farm group and makes repeated reference to the importance of manure. Mrs. Truman and a lady friend are in the audience. Afterward, the friend turns to Mrs. Truman and asks if she couldn't persuade the President to use some "more suitable" term. Mrs. Truman supposedly replied, "Helen, it took me thirty years to get him to say manure."

Having been "shown the geography of the house," we do these things in the "powder room," "little girl's room," "ladies' (men's) room," "restroom," "washroom," "lounge," "can," "john," "head," or possibly in the "lavatory" and, sometimes, even in the "bathroom." In a New York City park we do them in the "comfort station." When we reach the sanctuary of these places we use the "john," "can," "pot," "throne," "commode," "crapper," and so on. Unfortunately, perhaps the most logical term, "arsenal," which complements urinal rather neatly, has thus far found little favor.

The term *crapper* has an interesting and inverted history since, contrary to common supposition, it is, or rather was, a perfectly "proper" trade name like "Fridgidaire" for refrigerator. Thomas Crapper was an early developer of water closets and a major English manufacturer who put his name on his fixtures as does every manufacturer. American troops in World War I apparently picked it up and began to use it as a generic name for all water closets and in time derived "crap" from it. By inversion and association, the terms have by now been transformed into improper slang terms.[15]

If we are bold, we use "toilet" or "water closet." Such boldness, however, rarely extends to public mention. A public health campaign in Britain some years ago was stymied because the newspapers refused to print key words such as "water closet" and "bowel movement." One could get as far as "Wash your hands after. . . ." but could never say after what. Stranger still, when the first edition of this book appeared in 1966, dozens of newspapers across the country made cryptic reference to "the watchamacallit" in their stories. And indeed, the television broadcaster's code in the United States, despite all the other obscenities it permits to be shown, will not allow even advertising of plumbing fixtures on national television programs.

In our penchant for euphemisms we advertise "facial quality tissue" that is not intended for facial use. We do not have pimples, merely facial blemishes. In the past, only horses sweated; men perspired, and ladies glowed. Now we simply offend. In this endless game there are some dangers, however, particularly when we borrow from foreign sources or forget the origins. Thus our adoption of toilet for water closet was at one time perfectly acceptable since we took it from the French *toilette* meaning dressing, derived from the word *toile,* or linen cloth. In Canadian usage, a napkin refers to the unmentionable "sanitary" variety; table linen there is referred to as a *serviette.* In the United States we use lavatory for wash basin, which is perfectly proper since it means washing place and derives from the French *laver*—to wash. In Britain, however, lavatory is somewhat taboo and plainly means bathroom, and, as we all know, bathroom is too plain for polite usage.

Not only do we resort to euphemisms to modify our speech with respect to elimination, we do so only when absolutely necessary, for in general we don't speak of the subject at all. It is simply something one doesn't talk about. For example, during the heyday of the space program, all the missions were given elaborate and detailed news coverage about all facets of the operation, but the one that was never mentioned, except indirectly, was elimination. There were a few cryptic references to problems with odors and the fact that several members of the crew opted to wear their oxygen masks. It wasn't until almost a decade later during the Skylab missions that the news media reported in detail on the hygiene arrangements. There is, however, a particular irony in this situation, because such delicacy extended not only to the news media but actually to the persons in the space program itself who were charged with the development of the operational systems. It wasn't until 1968, after bitter crew complaints about the management of elimination functions, that a major conference involving NASA and contractor personnel was held on the subject. The proceedings began with an impassioned address by Dr. C. A. Berry, the NASA Director of Life Sciences, who stressed the importance of the subject and pleaded with the participants to please get over snickering and giggling and take seriously what had become a significant problem. Toward the conclusion of the conference one engineer looked around and confided that probably more man-hours had been devoted to this problem in those two days than had been spent since the inception of the program!

Unfortunately, this is not an isolated example, though it is perhaps somewhat more extreme than most. Our reluctance to discuss such matters shows up in all of our lives with respect to our own bathroom facilities and their adequacy or inadequacy. It is the rare woman, for instance, who is going to tell a builder or plumber that she wants a urinal in the downstairs bath because she is tired of mopping up pee. The same situation also occurs in the architectural profession, which is one reason we have endless repetition of the same dismal, minimal bathrooms. In the first place, architectural students are rarely interested in, or taught about, such mundane things; and in the second, bathrooms are traditionally one of the first assignments entrusted to the fresh graduate in his first job. Obviously, the boss doesn't feel it is very important or he wouldn't have entrusted it to a beginning employee and, equally obviously, the new employee knows it, too. As in the military, beginning at the bottom means you have to put in your time at "latrine duty," which this assignment symbolically is.

On the other hand, one of the more interesting things about this subject, like most forbidden ones, is the ambivalence that crops up in terms of the absolute fascination and curiosity people have about the subject in spite of their horror of it. For example, a further irony with regard to the space program is that the greatest curiosity shown all around the world concerned the very provisions for elimination that were carefully never discussed. Indeed, Dr. Berry has observed that, no matter where in the world he happened to be, or whom he happened to be visiting with, from taxi drivers to heads of state, sooner or later, he would be asked in an aside "How do they do. . .you know, *it*?" The answer, for the curious, is generally "Not very well." Beginning with what were, in effect, diapers, the techniques progressed to plastic bags taped to the buttocks and finally to a specialized water closet on the Skylab missions. Urination was accommodated by condom catheters and similar devices familiar to military pilots. In all instances, however, the major difficulty, aside from restrictions on weight, size, and energy consumption, has been the lack of gravity, which has necessitated extraordinary measures to ensure positive entrapment of the body wastes. Neither feces nor urine (nor anything else) drops; it floats and must be captured; thus the elimination processes are at best time consuming and at worst distasteful in the extreme. The same sort of curiosity has also been remarked on with respect to the seemingly endless coronation ceremonies of Queen Elizabeth II.[16]

ATTITUDES AND HUMOR

Still another common subterfuge we employ to make acceptable our meanings is humor. As the man says: "Smile when you say that, pardner!" The most outrageous, hostile, and suggestive things can be spoken of, either generally or directed at a given individual, so long as one smiles, or makes the remark in the context of a "joke," or, when challenged, says, "I was only kidding." Like euphemisms, humor is the universally accepted disguise for the naked statement.

Thus, what we commonly understand as "bathroom humor," or scatology, is almost exclusively concerned with elimination functions. (The exceptions tend to center on one of the few other hygiene or bathroom unmentionables that is not directly sexual, the dirty bathtub ring: "Liz Taylor's tub has a 14-karat gold ring," "Why did the Polish couple want to get married in the bathtub? So they could have a double-ring ceremony!" and so on.) These are the essentially forbidden topics and more logically "humorous" than, say, brushing teeth. In this regard, bathroom humor serves two different but related purposes, or perhaps we should say clientele. First, it serves as a sexual surrogate and, second, as an acceptable way to deal with elimination anxieties.[17] As we shall examine in more detail in a later section, there is, for many people, a degree of ambiguity or correspondence between elimination organs and activities and sexual ones. Thus, all the "laff-riot party gags" that feature one of the endless variations of the drink dispenser employing a boy peeing the liquor are simply one way of bringing the penis to the attention of the group. Others escalate the subterfuge and bring sex into play immediately by telling sexual jokes directly. In part, this accounts for the relatively strong class distinctions that are often made between sexual humor, which is generally considered relatively chic, and bathroom humor, which is considered coarse and lower class. Persons who feel relatively more comfortable with sex tend to proceed directly to the more immediately personal, verbal form of humor. This is borne out by psychologists who have noted that, in general, higher socioeconomic and educational levels correspond fairly directly with levels of sexual comfort, freedom, and experimentation. The imputation has been that earthy, coarse types may have quantity but certainly not quality, if one defines quality as subtlety and variety.

The sex-surrogate role of elimination humor has also been remarked on by a number of commentators who observe that many of the great historical scatologists have been clergymen, who presumably could not deal with sexual themes directly, for example, Rabelais. One also finds evidence of this among many older persons who, when they venture into a forbidden area, will do so only in terms of rather infantile elimination jokes.

Although the sex-surrogate humor centers mainly on urination, particularly male urination (with the recent exception of a spate of humor directed at women's liberation), the predominant subject of bathroom humor is defecatory and centers on the toilet, the outhouse, toilet paper, feces, farting, the anus, and so on. The themes are generally elementary and depend primarily on the simple statement or exposure of the forbidden, or on being "caught short." Thus we find an abundance of postcards, calendars, and so-called novelty items such as imitation turds, pillows that make a farting sound when sat on, "horse's ash" trays, toilet ashtrays, miniature outhouses that serve as ashtrays with a sign on the door that says "Rest your butt here," and the old favorite, the picture of a man sitting on a water closet with the inscription "The only guy in the place who knows what he's doing." In a great many instances the "joke" depends almost exclusively on the double entendre, for example: "Innuendo—is that the Italian name for Preparation H?"

The other favorite theme appears to be toilet paper, which is printed with a variety of things from Christmas greetings to cartoons and double entendres such as "If at first you don't succeed, try, try again." Perhaps the most revealing is the toilet paper printed as hundred-dollar bills. (Freud's gold?) And for the ubiquitous "man who has everything," there is even an "electric corncob."

Another aspect, particularly beloved by early Hollywood, is the practical joke. In one instance, a figure of a male, nude except for an obviously applied fig leaf, is placed in the ladies' powder room. As the story goes, nine out of ten visitors could not resist lifting the fig leaf, which was rigged up to a siren—much to the chagrin of the visitor and the mirth of the host and other guests. Another fellow

> designed an outdoor house to which he likes his guests to retire. As soon as the guest flushes the toilet, an elaborate mechanical device is set in operation, causing the walls of the house to open and fall to the ground, much like the opening of the petals of a beautiful flower, leaving the victim of the jest exposed to the howls of the host and the other guests.[18]

The history of such foolishness is quite old, for apparently the early Jews would sometimes manage to pepper the stones in Jerusalem where the Mohammedans would dry their penises after urination.

ELIMINATION AND ART

Interestingly, although personal hygiene activities are certainly one of the universals of human experience, they rarely figure as a theme in art, especially as far as elimination functions are concerned.

With the exception of the questions, or suggestions, sometimes raised about Rodin's *The Thinker,* defecation is an almost nonexistent theme except in satire. Urination, though equally rare in most respects, has at least been a theme for sculptural fountains for centuries, the most famous probably being the *Manneken-Pis,* the statue of a small boy urinating, in Brussels.

On the other hand, water closets and urinals have figured in the modern art movements, presumably as much for their shock value as their aesthetic merit, as, for example, Marcel Duchamp's urinal proffered to (and refused by) the New York Independents' Show in 1917. (This theme of an out-of-context urinal has surfaced again in recent years among the "joke" items as a plastic urinal complete with simulated flush valve and an adhesive backing so that it can be mounted anywhere—on your golf bag, and so on. "This gag bowls them over.") A water closet has figured several times among the sculptures of Claes Oldenburg, as a "soft toilet," "ghost toilet," and so forth. A water closet was also the basis for a somewhat whimsical sculpture by François-Xavier and Claude Lalannes: *Le Moucheron Éblouissante et Utile,* a huge and elegantly wrought house fly that unfolds to reveal a water closet. With respect to whimsy, perhaps the ultimate in this respect is the *Metatunic Dryer* created by Canadian Marc Lepage. This is a "spectator sculpture": by standing on a central platform one activates two fans that blow warm air through two large opposed half-spheres of terrycloth that "gradually become breast-like and caress the moisture away." On the other hand, one can still buy a bath mat made of molded rubber that simulates rows of upturned breasts, indulging the fantasy of "walking barefoot over acres of tits."

Bathing has, however, been the one favored and universal theme that occurs in all periods of history, in all societies, and in all media, from Japanese *ukiyo-e* prints to heroic classical paintings. Indeed, the circumstance of the bath has, in many instances, provided, one suspects, the excuse or rationale for the study of the nude figure.

EQUIPMENT AND FACILITIES

By extension, our attitudes toward elimination processes and products are also reflected in our direct responses to the equipment itself and to the spaces housing it. This is apparent not only in our language usage but also in the marvelous powers we ascribe to that nasty, but marvelous, monster that swallows everything without so much as a trace. Obviously, since feces is about the nastiest substance known and the water closet can cope satisfactorily with "that," it can cope with anything. It is our universal dispose-all. We use it, sometimes quite indiscriminately, to dispose of anything that is in the least unpleasant, that we don't wish to handle unnecessarily, and that we wish to be rid of without a trace. Thus it is particularly used to dispose of body-sex-related items such as condoms and sanitary supplies. In more extreme instances, it is used to dispose of fetuses and dead or unwanted pets such as the baby alligators that, according to legend, turned up in great numbers some years ago in the New York sewer system. It is also today the standard method of disposing of drugs ("shit") that might otherwise prove incriminating.[19]

Obviously not everyone shares these feelings, and in fairness it must be noted that the water closet has also enjoyed some positive, though incidental, uses like cooling beer or wine bottles or for temporarily storing cut flowers. One lady reports that "When you're really down, take one shoe and sock off, put your foot in the toilet and flush it. The feeling is fabulous—it's cool and it tickles, relieving tension."

Just as the water closet is an anathema as far as public mention and viewing are concerned, similarly we often find that in the home an attempt is made to "pretty up" that "ugly" thing. Of course, in the past, one could buy extremely elaborately decorated fixtures that were made by some of the most famous names in European ceramics like Royal Doulton. Even today, famous firms like Arabia, Richard Ginori, Sphinx, and Villeroy-Boch make both elegant table china and sanitaryware. If one is relatively well-to-do and has a sophisticated decorator, one simply hides "it" in a lovely wickerwork *chaise percée* or a marble shroud. Failing that, we more commonly use a "decorator" seat embellished with posies or a gilded eagle if our taste runs to Early Americana, or we fit a plush fabric cover to match the bath mat. One U.S. manufacturer recently introduced a splendid innovation: a tank (cistern) lid that incorporates a planter and space for half a dozen books. And if one is a dedicated dyed-in-the-wool alumnus, one can have a special seat emblazoned with the school seal and, for a few dollars more, the deluxe model, which features a music box that plays the school song when the lid is raised. A curious tribute, all things considered.[20]

A particularly forceful attitude of rejection was evidenced some years ago in Brazil, where the longshoremen struck for 20 per cent "shame pay" for handling cargo such as water closets and sanitary supplies![21] A few years ago a great controversy raged in a St. Louis suburb over the appropriate degree of restoration and preservation of a Civil War plantation home; that is, whether or not the outdoor privy should be maintained. The preservation committee felt yes, but some of the neighbors felt it "frightful," "inappropriate," "a laughing stock," and "in poor taste." As one newspaper editorialized, "Since when did history become a matter of good taste? Should our children be led to assume that we brought plumbing with us out of the Garden of Eden?" Happily for good sense, the committee's view prevailed.

ATTITUDES AND PERFORMANCE

As we might expect, even the manner in which we perform elimination activities and the postures we assume are subject to censure or approval, depending on our respective points of view. In particular, this is true of urination, since today almost all Western peoples have adopted the standard high water closet for defecation.

Havelock Ellis notes that, in respect to urination:

> It would be a mistake to suppose that that attitude (squatting) has been everywhere and always customary with women, just as it would be a mistake to conclude from prevalent European custom that the erect attitude has been everywhere and always prevalent among men. As a matter of fact, there are widespread variations, though it is comparatively rare for both men and women to adopt the same attitude, and with the usual sexual contrariness, where the women adopt one attitude the men tend to adopt another, or vice versa.[22]

In general, however, postures have been the reverse of our current ones among almost all peoples. In Egypt, Herodotus states that "women stand erect to make water, the men stoop." Among the Irish, where women similarly enjoyed a relatively high social status, it is reported that "the men discharge their urine sitting; the women standing." Notions about the Amazon come into play here, and, of course, sexism is at least in part responsible for the almost constant differences in the behavior of the sexes. Our current attitudes tend to be quite clear in this respect, for example: "Hearing that one member of his administration was becoming a dove on Vietnam, (President) Johnson said, 'Hell, he has to squat to piss!'"[23]

The subject also appears to have caught the male fancy in its obvious "improbability" vis-a-vis women's liberation and resulted in a number of posters, cartoons, and jokes depicting a female using, or attempting to use, a male urinal.

Among the Moslem peoples, who are exceptional as far as this form of sexual differentiation is concerned, tradition dictates that each sex squat to defecate and urinate. It is considered shameful to be seen otherwise and remarked that "such a one pisses like a dog, standing." And indeed, some young children today do piss like dogs, on trees, having learned their "toilet training" from observation rather than from their "modern" parents. Contrariwise, some men do sit to urinate, especially when they are guests in someone's home, essentially to obviate the noise and spare themselves and their hosts any possible embarrassment—essentially President Johnson's point though interpreted differently by each.

Aside from our respective attitudes toward sex-role differentiation, the principal factors in determining our postures are the equipment, or lack of it, that may be available and, especially, the restrictions posed by the clothing a given people wear—an aspect we shall examine in more detail later on. In Japan, for example, women traditionally urinated in a standing position because their tight, narrow costumes would not permit easy raising of their skirts. In ancient China, noblemen generally used "polished canes, a cubit long and open at both ends, sufficiently large to introduce the penis. When one wants to make water, therefore, one stands and turning the tube away from oneself, one discharges the urine." An examination of the elaborate court costumes would suggest that this was an eminently sensible technique. Among the Maori, the woman stands because it is possible for her to avoid wetting her clothes or exposing herself; the man, on the other hand, squats so as not to expose himself or wet his skirt. Exposure of the genitals in many cultures was undesirable, not so much from any notions about modesty, but in order to protect their reproductive powers from evil influences.

In point of fact, European women sometimes urinated in a standing position, even into this century, when out and away from facilities. We must remember, in this connection, that drawers, or "bloomers," for women did not come into general use until quite late in the last century. (Trousers for women originated with the harem costume of the Middle East, were then adopted by Venetian courtesans, and were thus, obviously, totally unsuitable garments for "ladies.") It was possible, therefore, for a lady, wearing the voluminous floor-length dress of the period but not wearing drawers, simply to stand innocently on a path, or in a crowd, and discharge her duty as necessary without much fear of exposure. And, of course, we must not overlook the fact that virtually all women today urinate in a standing, or at least hovering, posture when using a public toilet, as we shall examine in more detail later. The impetus here, as all ladies know, is not perversity but simply avoidance of a wet, soiled seat.

CORRESPONDENCE AND CONFUSION BETWEEN ELIMINATION AND SEX ORGANS AND FUNCTIONS

If our attitudes toward the elimination process were based only on our training to keep away from contact with obnoxious substances that can soil or cause us harm, it is likely that, once that particular difficulty were resolved, we could accept the demands of this physiological need with the same grace, humor, and possibly enjoyment that we accept our other physiological needs. Many people are able to do this. In fact, most normal people are inclined to worry more—and with reason—over nonfunctioning than over the embarrassment attending the performance of acts of elimination. There is, however, another factor that enters into our attitudes, one held by many authorities to be the prime reason for our embarrassment and the basis for our attempts to conceal our purpose when we withdraw from a social setting to seek out the place of many names.

Because of a fairly direct anatomical and neuromuscular correspondence between the body parts used for elimination and those used for sex, our attitudes toward sex are also linked to our attitudes toward elimination. This is, of course, most obvious in the case of the penis, where the same organ serves both functions, but it is also present in the case of the vagina, because of its proximity to the urethra within the labial folds. As a consequence, urination tends for many people to be irrevocably associated with attitudes toward sexual matters. Fliess, for example, commenting particularly on neurotic personalities, speaks of the "fantasy" of confusing sexual and urethral organs and functions, and of the apparent frequency with which it is retained into adolescence and even adulthood by both males and females.

> A surprising characteristic of the fantasy is its long persistence. Adolescent girls, or girls of college age or above, will eventually inspect themselves while urinating in order "to find out where the urine really comes from". . . .[24]

Albert Ellis notes, for example, that a linkage between elimination and sex is implied in:

> . . . virtually every twentieth-century statement about and attitude toward scatological things: since the main reason why such things *are* considered to be intrinsically wicked, laugh-provoking, and exciting is patently their underlying sexual content. True, urinary and fecal matters are to some extent aesthetically and odoriferously obnoxious in themselves; but little of the highly emotionalized disgust which modern Americans feel about toilet matters seems to be specifically traceable to this type of obnoxiousness alone, and much more of it seems to be related to their sexual connotations.[25]

Conversely, it has been argued that the problem is "rather the disastrous discovery by the young that the organs of sex are the very same despised organs of elimination." Another commentator notes that: "If the vulva and the vagina were situated between a woman's shoulder blades, and a man had a separate instrument for coitus, not used for any excretory purpose, I do not think women would feel about intercourse as they sometimes do."[26]

For all practical purposes we do not have to resolve this matter of original sin, since the end result is that both elimination and sex are still linked and still taboo. Because of this, it is not difficult to understand how the act of elimination may easily, if unconsciously, be associated with the violation of some of the moral taboos that are deeply rooted in our culture, as, for example, not handling the genitals in public and keeping this area of the body concealed from view. There appears to be, for example, considerable fear of urinating noisily, among men as well as women, at least when others are within hearing range, presumably because of the sexual connotation of the act. A male noisily urinating might be said to be handling his sex and proclaiming to all within earshot that he has a penis. A consequence, significant for design, is that men usually go to considerable lengths to avoid being heard. A woman, with less choice in positioning her body to avoid making noise, commonly resorts to masking the sound by turning on a faucet and running water. Similar tactics of masking the sounds of defecation are also resorted to by both sexes, though the association with "obnoxiousness" probably supplies part of the motivation for this.

Such devices add chiefly, of course, to the mental comfort of the individual performing the act and do not deceive any other persons nearby, though they may appreciate not having their auditory privacy intruded upon. Masking sounds in private households where a number of persons may use the same bathroom serves the additional purpose of indicating that the room is in use and that the user wants privacy.

It is also likely that the association of the elimination functions with sexual functions is responsible, in part at least, for the tendency on the part of many women to disapprove strongly of having a urinal in the home. Such a fixture is, in a sense, all too obviously a one-sex, one-organ, one-function fixture and serves as a constant reminder of the sexual differentiation, and possibly of the male's tendency to a certain indifference when urinating. Pursuing this further, the possession of a urinal could also be regarded as unnecessary pampering of the genitals, a notion that would be alien and embarrassing to most of us if taken this way. In terms of Freudian symbolism, it may be postulated that the urinal could also be taken as a representation of the vagina, both in terms of the shape of the fixture and the nature of the act of urination, which, incidentally, also ultimately provides "relief." "The pause that *really* refreshes!" as some wags put it. In contrast, nearly a quarter of the survey respondents were willing to have a urinal and a full third expressed a willingness to have one when there were male children in the household.[27] The most significant point perhaps, with respect to this discussion, is that the reactions to having a urinal were rather sharply differentiated and the group responding negatively left little doubt about their sentiments. While the reasons for a particular response were not probed, it seems reasonable to assume that something more basic than extra cost or extra space was involved in the reaction. Interestingly, the same very sharp differentiation in attitude toward a home urinal has also since surfaced among men, many of whom insist with great indignation, even in the face of clear evidence to the contrary, that "they don't need one." While the overt response is one of being insulted by the suggestion of carelessness, we may also speculate that the covert response is, rather, one of indignation at having been found out, particularly if the soiling were deliberate.

While the elimination–sex link is perhaps most obvious with respect to urination it is also true of defecation. Not only is the act of defecation pleasurable; for many it is also sensual.

> Defecation was not considered an unclean thing, as evidenced by the openness with which it was performed; it was a natural function, comparable to a sexual orgasm. . . . To defecate and to copulate were similarly compared in what to me was a much more distressing manner . . . for when I said that copulation, as opposed to masturbation, gave pleasure to two whereas defecation gave pleasure, if at all, to only one, I got the bland reply: "Who knows what the other is feeling? In each you only know your own feeling."[28]

On the one hand, defecation is postponed until the last possible moment so as to extract the greatest "relief" from the act and, on the other, laxatives and enemas are used, often unconsciously, so as to heighten the sensations by persons who would be highly embarrassed if they understood their actions.

In point of fact, the anus directly serves both defecatory and sexual purposes so that the ambiguity of attitude and response is, in some instances, even more extreme. It is not only the primary organ of defecation but it also serves directly as a sexual orifice in both heterosexual and homosexual relationships for oral, digital, and penile stimulation and entry. Lest the reader dismiss this as a rare aberration, consider the long history and commonness of "goosing." Indeed, the catalog of sex-related practices to which the anus has been put, from narcotic suppositories to alcoholic enemas, is limited only by the imagination of man.[29]

For some, even the act of defecation is apparently a source of stimulation:

> In Parisian brothels provision is made for those who are sexually excited by the spectacle of the act of defecation by means of a "tabouret de verre," from under the glass floor of which the spectacle of the defecating woman may be closely observed. It may be added that the erotic nature of such a spectacle is referred to in the Marquis de Sade's novels.[30]

Apparently such a spectacle was also featured in an Off-Broadway show several years ago.

This is not to suggest that a sense of physical well-being or gratification resulting from elimination is to be taken as a sign of a perverted sense of sexuality, but it does suggest how closely linked the two areas are in fact and how easily given individuals could fuse them. As Havelock Ellis notes, however, "There is, indeed, no excretion or product of the body which has not been a source of ecstasy" for some. Similarly, there is no body part that has not been regarded as a source of sexual gratification for some and, of course, conversely, no body part or bodily activity that someone has not found offensive at some time or other.

MODESTY AND INDIVIDUAL PRIVACY

Since the entire sex–elimination amalgam is something we tend to think of as "dirty" and something to be somewhat ashamed of, we also tend to want to hide and disguise our involvement with it; in other words, we seek privacy for it. We seek this privacy beginning with our language usage; we cannot even state directly what our needs are or where we wish to go, and once there we resort to all sorts of stratagems to avoid anyone's knowing where we are or what we are about. Even nudists, who otherwise are relatively relaxed with respect to the body, apparently still insist on privacy for elimination as well as sexual activities.

Probably the most common, obvious, and clear-cut example of the sex–elimination linkage is to be found in the Anglo-Saxon insistence on privacy on a sexual basis: the existence of men's and women's rooms, which guarantee complete privacy from the opposite sex but only limited privacy from members of the same sex. It is also likely that it is because of this sex linkage that our society virtually guarantees a person privacy for elimination, though we must remember that we are unique in this respect, both historically and relative to other nations and cultures. Significantly, the only substantial exceptions to this unspoken guarantee are in the case of married persons, where the sexual-privacy aspect is not always observed, and in the case of very young children who have not yet learned the rules.[31] Otherwise, if the bathroom is shared by members of the family, the tendency is to respect both the sexual segregation and privacy for elimination functions.

The consequences of such a guaranteed-privacy situation are not, however, always favorable. Some persons, for example, come to rely on it so heavily that it becomes an effective triggering mechanism for elimination functions and is essential for normal responses. Although the following observation was made some years ago, it is, for many people, as applicable today as it was then:

> It is unfortunate that false modesty also places a heavy burden upon our intestinal functions. From early childhood we are taught to see in excretory functions of the body something debasing and evil. Instead of considering them in the same natural way that we think of eating, drinking, and sleeping, we come to regard them with a sense of shame or guilt. Many people with rectal trouble or constipation defer consultation with a physician because the disorders pertain to the "unmentionables."[32]

Similarly, as almost anyone who has ever had to provide a urine specimen can testify, modesty and privacy play a big role in our ability to perform.

SOCIAL PRIVACY

In contrast, the guarantee of privacy has also led to situations wherein the privacy has been exploited for a variety of non-hygiene purposes—most generally, simply for its own sake. This category might be termed "socially useful" and be defined as that circumstance in which the person's activity (i.e., elimination) is common knowledge and in which, therefore, his right to pursue it in peace is inviolable and, most significantly, free from any questioning or social censure. This usage represents a species of "having your cake and eating it too," for it is necessary to establish or reveal one's destination (thereby giving up privacy) in order to be assured of privacy! This device is commonly used at work, where generally any interruption is a welcome one, and where a mild prolongation is the rule—especially if one has not finished reading the morning paper. Or it may be used as a delaying tactic at school when a pupil may ask to be excused if the questioning gets to be dangerously close. It also serves as a popular means of escape from family noise, quarrels, pressures, or sometimes simply from a person's own activities, without arousing any feelings of guilt.

There are, of course, exceptions—persons who accord only partial respect to these conventions, most generally, those who are compulsive about their work and who cannot bear to let any time go to waste, those who maintain telephones in their bathrooms, or those who insist on carrying on business conversations with associates they happen to encounter.

This guarantee of privacy for elimination functions has also been exploited historically for a variety of forbidden activities ranging from masturbation, to smoking, to sneaking a drink.[33] One fascinating testimonial to this is that old outhouse sites have proved to be a rich mine for old bottle fanciers. As one collector explains it:

> When Dad didn't want Mom to know what he was doing, he would go out to the privy and have a nip of whiskey. Then he'd throw the bottle down the privy to get rid of the evidence.[34]

ATTITUDE FORMATION AND TRAINING

As Freud and any number of investigators since have pointed out, "toilet training" represents one of the more crucial periods in our psychological development. On the one hand, it produces the first major conflict between the child and the parent and represents the child's first encounter with self-discipline and external discipline; on the other hand, it underlies the formation of our attitudes toward the body, elimination, sex, and the self. Stern training in this area often produces stern self-discipline and guilt and repression in other areas.

The first problem is to teach the child to develop voluntary controls over elimination in place of normal involuntary reflexes, and further, to exercise these controls in response to proper stimuli, such as being in the proper place and removing clothing.

It is now generally conceded that such training cannot properly or successfully begin before the child is at least eight months to a year old when its neuromuscular system has become sufficiently developed and coordinated and when it is able to comprehend what is expected of it, as well as to understand that it is indeed able to control these actions. Any toilet training before this time is largely a matter of catching the stool in time, though some degree of voluntary reflex action can apparently be built up by rote. An insistence on what might be termed "premature" training can, however, be considered to be actually punitive since it places demands upon the child for which it is not developmentally prepared. This circumstance has, however, not always been recognized, with results that have proved most unfortunate in later life.

The coercive training program of years past was based on the assumptions that the child, regardless of how young it might be, was capable of being trained to exercise voluntary bowel control and that the parents were responsible for seeing to it that this skill was developed as soon as possible. Some of the recommended methods of the day would likely curl the hair of contemporary child psychologists: shaming the child for lapses, keeping the child on the toilet until defecation has occurred, using suppositories as a training aid, and exerting psychological pressure, such as making the child feel that parental affection or approval depended upon meeting the demands being imposed upon him. This type of training, which probably was as difficult for parents as for the child, was once widely recommended by physicians and other advisers, and instructions for carrying out the program were quite specific, as may be seen from the following excerpt from a government bulletin on child care:

> Training of the bowels may be begun as early as the end of the first month. It should always be begun by the third month and may be completed during the eighth month.

The writer goes on to urge "absolute regularity" and drives home the importance of this by a picture of a mother and a baby with a clock nearby and advises "not varying the time by five minutes." Then follow detailed instructions for using the soap stick as an aid in conditioning the rectum.[35]

One observer, writing of upper-class British life in Victorian and Edwardian times, notes that "the best potty is a full potty" and that:

> The quicker a baby could be pot trained the less work for Nurse and nursery-maid. A clean child is one who pleases Nurse, and a child who pleases Nurse is good. So arrived the equation of cleanliness and goodness which was later raised by those who had suffered the regime into something almost mystic—Cleanliness is next to Godliness.[36]

IMPLICATIONS OF TOILET TRAINING ON PERSONALITY STRUCTURE

One of the more controversial and yet seemingly more obvious facets of toilet training is the extent to which it actually conditions and influences our personality structure and our adult attitudes and habits. Over the years, and among various schools of psychology, the significance of these basic Freudian concepts has varied enormously, at times being very fashionable, at times not. Several fundamental facts stand out, however, in spite of fashion or school and in spite of various inconclusive attempts over the years to verify experimentally some of the more far-reaching concepts.[37]

First, the attitude that the parent (most commonly the mother) displays with respect to toilet training is indicative of the parent's attitude toward the child in general and of her own personality in particular. From this standpoint, toilet training can be legitimately regarded as one of the highly significant indicators of the child's developmental experiences. Jersild points out that:

> If a parent is strongly competitive in his approach to child rearing it is likely that he will wish the child to hurry to get the dry habit and prove himself in this humble enterprise, as in other activities, to be better than the next fellow. If he is a self-accepting kind of person, able to abide the demands of his own nature, without ascribing filthy and self-demeaning implications to the fact that his bladder gets full and that his bowels need to be emptied and without deploring the "lower" part of his nature (and thereby repudiating himself) the likelihood is that he will view the operations of his child's bladder and bowels in the same light.[38]

These parental attitudes are part of the interpersonal communication between parent and child and may exercise considerable influence on the attitudes and images the child acquires concerning himself. In view of the fact that such attitudes often are expressed with great vehemence by the parent, it is not surprising that many psychologists can hypothesize far-reachingly about the causal relationships involved.

The second critical aspect of toilet training, and the one most significant for this discussion, is the fact that it is during this period that the basic attitudes toward elimination functions and organs are developed.

> At this age, the child may not differentiate clearly between the process, organs, and products of elimination. Fears and anxieties which arise in connection with elimination may generalize to

> the organs of elimination. The physical proximity of genitals, urethra, and anus makes it easy for these reactions to generalize further to the sex organs and sexual activities. . . . If anxieties connected with sexuality persist, the individual may find it extremely difficult to make mature sexual adjustments later on.[39]

In some instances this correspondence or confusion is encouraged by the parent; in others, it is allowed to develop through indifference or embarrassment. In either case, however, the result is ultimately unhappy. Although this "anal period" of the child's development is to be regarded as only one of the significant formative episodes, it is the period during which his basic and, most significantly, unconscious, bodily attitudes are formed:

> Weaning accomplished, libidinal drives center on functions of elimination. If during these two periods the child has found pleasure in his sensuality and yet learned to integrate and control it, he is well on the road to incorporating into his adult personality his sexual impulses, which appear in a more conventional form during his fourth year of life.[40]

STIMULI AND INHIBITIONS

Another highly important aspect of the elimination processes, and one that often grows out of proportion, is the whole matter of stimuli and the conditions that encourage or inhibit elimination. This is an essential part of the toilet training process and certainly necessary in a highly "civilized" society. Depending, however, on the conditions of this training and various individual circumstances, it is possible for the defecation reflex, for example, to become overdeveloped in the sense that it becomes almost entirely dependent upon external stimuli. As T. P. Almy points out, this can lead to difficulties since, no matter how well ordered one's life, there are still innumerable disruptions:

> In the highly civilized adult having a well-ordered existence, the "negative" signals have accordingly multiplied and the "positive" signals are few: the bowel movement can be had only in the same bathroom after the same breakfast while checking on the same watch to make sure that there is time to make the 8:08 train.[41]

In addition to allowing ourselves to become too dependent upon a few positive signals, there is also the problem of the various actively negative signals to which we respond. These might be unsanitary facilities or simply pressures of time and traffic in a crowded household. Foremost among these negative signals, however, is lack of privacy. This may range from having another person in the same room in a public toilet to having a child or one's spouse wander into the bathroom. Among the survey respondents, for example, 60 per cent "interrupted or postponed" this activity if they did not have sufficient privacy.[42]

READING

People who experience shame or guilt in connection with elimination, particularly defecation, very often must take their minds off the act in order to defecate at all. Otherwise, tensions produced by guilt or ugliness associated with the act will prevent completion. One of the most common methods of accomplishing this is reading:

> Many people cannot properly perform the act of defecation without reading a newspaper or book. Reading gives the initial feeling of relaxation so useful for proper performance. As one patient said to his doctor, "When I try too hard I do not succeed; but when I put on my glasses and read a newspaper it comes of itself."[43]

There is little doubt that the widespread practice of reading on the water closet came into being either because of the waiting for a bowel movement or because of the need to distract the mind from the activity. While this stratagem, often advised by physicians, may be effective in lessening or removing psychological blocks to normal functioning, the fact also remains that "physical relaxation" as a neuromuscular state is not conducive to efficient defecation. As is so often the case, this may well represent another instance of a vicious cycle. It may be hypothesized that a comfortable and properly designed water closet, while it may not remove basic psychological difficulties, may materially help those persons whose psychological difficulties have arisen because of functional problems.

Contrariwise, reading for many persons may well also be an independent activity, in which case there would be posed the problem of reconciling the criterion for reading comfort with the criterion for the proper posture for defecation. Most likely, reading on the toilet represents merely another dimension of the escape/privacy/leisure continuum with respect to the bathroom—as exemplified by the comment, "It's the only chance I get to catch up on my reading without interruption by the children."

In most instances, it is probable that reading on the toilet assumes both roles—particularly for tense, compulsive persons. Tension and the compulsion to be busy constantly are common traits of the anal character and are frequently contributing causes to the constipation from which they invariably suffer, constipation that seems to have its origins in psychological problems. It has been suggested by some psychologists that reading also serves as a symbolic way of replacing the material lost through defecation and helps to prolong the act of defecation and the consequent loss. In this sense, constipation is, on the one hand, psychologically desirable and, on the other, psychologically devastating if one cannot (or will not) "produce" as expected.[44]

A common prescription or treatment for this type of simple nonpathological constipation is to read or find some other diversion that will relieve the direct anxieties—either before or during defecation. Persons so treated usually take to the treatment with alacrity and generally find it moderately successful, but it often leads them then to a compulsive desire to engage in this diversion, particularly if it is a more or less productive activity. (One survey respondent wanted a mirror at the water closet so she could set her hair and put on her makeup while otherwise engaged.) In some instances, this may well be self-defeating since the joy in doing two things at once often leads to greater and greater concentration on the diverting activity—which, if it is reading, is often reading that is anxiety-producing, such as business correspondence or stock market quotations. If such a person should be deprived of this diversion for any reason, the consequences may well be painful—literally and figuratively.

The denial aspect is also quite old, for we find examples of the same moralistic attitudes in the sixteenth and seventeenth centuries expressed generally in more eloquent phrases to the effect that man is the noblest of creatures and that in order to counteract the vile and base obeisances to Nature he must pay, he should occupy himself the while with the great works of philosophy. In the mid-eighteenth century, Lord Chesterfield in his famous *Letters to His Son* advised that he "knew a gentleman who was so good a manager of his time that he would not even lose that small portion of it which the call of nature obliged him to pass in the necessary-house; but gradually went through all the Latin poets, in those moments."

There are also many "readers" who argue that they pursue this activity totally independently of defecation—those who read before, during, and after. While reading in this instance may appear to be an independent activity totally unrelated to the defecation process, it may also be argued that, in many such circumstances, defecation has been so sublimated that, aside from a barely conscious tripping of the flushing lever, they are not even aware that defecation has taken place. It would seem a reasonable hypothesis that such cases represent a total denial of, and unwillingness to accept, the defecation process. In cases, such as the one cited earlier, where reading is pursued as a concomitant activity because there is no other opportunity or place, one can only conclude that this represents a sad commentary on the organization of family life.

On the other hand, we should not forget the innocent and fortuitous circumstances that have historically led to this practice of reading on the toilet, for it is an old one. The simple fact is that for centuries man has had a variety of reading materials available to him in the toilet—basically for wiping purposes, though it is easy to see how readily it would have been used for diversion if circumstances demanded. During the Reformation in England, for example, quantities of monastic manuscripts found their way into the great houses, not for their content or their beauty but for their value as "tissue." In recent American history, outdated mail order catalogs and newspapers have served the same functions. Today, reading matter is not simply at hand, so to speak; it is institutionalized in the form either of a library to furnish diversion or distraction, or of business reading in order to accomplish more. In at least one instance, this proclivity has also been exploited with a fair degree of commercial success. The Starlite Tissue Company in West Germany is producing toilet paper with English language lessons printed on it for "those Germans who have always said they wanted to learn English but never had the time." In a somewhat analogous fashion, Dylan Thomas once suggested that novels might well be serialized on rolls of toilet paper.

Actually, this idea has been exploited in a number of other ways; for example: the "joke" tissue with sayings like "All's well that ends well" is presumably intended to divert in every sense. One of the boldest schemes has been to use the inside of public toilet stall doors for advertising messages, which is, in some ways, only an institutionalizing of graffiti. Although graffiti is a complex phenomenon (which will be explored in more detail in the section on public facilities), certainly one link, seldom noted, is with the psychologically diverting tactics associated with defecation.

In conclusion, it is obvious that elimination is even more burdened with a variety of attitudes that must be accounted for in the design of equipment and facilities than body cleansing is. In particular, the topic is considered at least in poor taste by many and obscene by others, and whatever attitudes one holds are apt to be pursued with vehemence, if not vengeance. As proctologists and some microbacteriologists are fond of pointing out, however, "It may be shit to you, but it's my 'bread and butter.'"

ANATOMY AND PHYSIOLOGY OF DEFECATION

9

THE PROCESS OF DEFECATION

Defecation is the process of emptying the bowels of feces—waste materials left from the digestive and other body processes. Literally translated from the Latin *defaecare,* it means "to cleanse from the dregs."

The feces of an average healthy adult varies in size from 100 to 205 mm (4 to 8 inches) long by 15 to 40 mm (½ to 1½ inches) and in weight from 100 to 200 grams. Both the consistency and odor as well as the size and weight may vary considerably, depending upon a person's diet, general state of health, and the particular state of the gastrointestinal system. The stool resulting from a basically vegetarian diet, for example, is generally larger, softer, and less odoriferous than the stool resulting from a high-protein diet. Food residues account, however, for only a part of the total bulk of the feces. The remainder is made up of bacteria, dead cells, and a variety of other internal body secretions and fluids. In terms of chemical composition, feces generally consists of approximately 65 per cent water, 10 to 20 per cent ash, 10 to 20 per cent soluble substances, and 5 to 10 per cent nitrogen.[1]

The process of defecation may be said to begin when the basic digestive processes have been completed and the residue of the food leaves the stomach and passes through the small intestine into the cecum, or pouch, at the beginning of the colon. Here the fecal mass progresses more slowly, taking about twelve hours to pass through the colon. Normally the fecal mass does not pass into the rectum until the act of defecation is about to occur. The sigmoid, or the end of the colon, is where the fecal matter is stored, and the rectum is merely a passageway and "notification chamber." The entrance of the fecal mass into the rectum is brought about by a massive peristaltic movement, a propelling motion set up by the muscles. The desire to defecate is initiated by a distention of the rectum caused by this peristaltic movement. If defecation does not follow the original notification, the rectum again relaxes and the desire to defecate does not return until a further increment of fecal matter enters the rectum and distends it further, or unless the action is consciously initiated.

Although this phase of the defecation process is largely involuntary, the final act of expulsion itself can be controlled and regulated through a conscious use of the related musculature. It is this control, which we refer to as "toilet training," that every child is required to learn. In its simplest terms, this voluntary or controlled phase consists of: 1 / contracting the diaphragm and the muscles of the abdominal wall, which we commonly know as "straining"; 2 / assuming a doubled-over or squatting posture so that the thighs provide support, or resistance, to the abdominal wall, and thus permit a greater intra-abdominal pressure; and 3 / relaxing the external sphincter muscle that controls the opening of the anal canal. Normally, the anal canal is totally collapsed by the contracted sphincter, and the anus is a mere slit. Control of this sphincter muscle is particularly vital, as everyone who has ever had to postpone defecation is aware.

Of all the various sets of neuromuscular actions over which man must develop control, defecation is probably one of the most difficult and complex, largely because of the potent psychological factors involved in its development. In spite of the degree of conscious control we may achieve over this process, there still remains a substantial area that may be considered to be controlled purely by reflex action. For example, a person with highly regular habits accompanied by a set of ritual procedures may experience all sorts of difficulties if this routine is disturbed, even though that person may be quite adult and otherwise capable of controlling his actions. Most abnormal defecation—constipation and diarrhea—results directly or indirectly from an interruption of the reflex pattern or disturbance of the normal mental set, such as extreme fright or anxiety. In still other instances, disturbances of the central nervous system or of cerebral functioning can lead to abnormalities of defecation.

DIARRHEA

Diarrhea is the passing of feces in a liquid or semi-liquid state, often with great expulsive force. Usually it is brief in its duration and ascribable to a toxic, infectious, or dietary origin, and occasionally to nervous disorders. The most common form is often described as "emotional diarrhea" and may in some instances persist together with other functional anomalies for some time. For the purposes of this discussion, it is a condition that can be neither assisted nor aggravated by the physical accommodation provided for defecation, but it is a condition that occurs universally and frequently enough to be considered in the ultimate design of any fixture.

CONSTIPATION

"Constipation may be defined as an abnormal retention of fecal matter in the intestinal canal or an undue delay in the discharge of excreta from the rectum."[2] The most significant point with respect to constipation is that it means simply an unusually long interval between bowel movements, whether caused by a retention of feces or by a *lack* of feces. This last point is largely unknown as far as the public is concerned, with unfortunate results. It is still a popular belief that at least one bowel movement daily is essential to proper health and that a person must purge himself of the toxins and poisons that build up in his system. One recent survey in the United States indicates that "two-thirds of the American population have the belief that a bowel movement every day is necessary for health, and nearly a third believe it is appropriate to do something regularly to help with bowel movements." Of the latter group, 76 per cent use laxatives, 22 per cent eat special foods, 5 per cent use an enema, 4 per cent a suppository and 3 per cent some other aid. The total is more than 100 per cent because some persons use more than one method. Approximately 2 per cent of the total population, some two and one-half million persons, use some aid every day.[3]

While this practice may have a general usefulness, it cannot be regarded as an absolute rule to be applied to all circumstances, as any number of normal everyday changes in routine or diet may cause a temporary change in a person's accustomed pace. Many people become disturbed, however, at any such change and resort to laxatives or purges that clean out the colon so thoroughly that several days are necessary before a sufficient bulk is built up again for normal functioning. It is not realized that the feces is less than half food residue. The remainder is made up of dead cells and other residues of the body's constant regenerative activity. During this "normal" and necessary period of inactivity, there is little or no desire to defecate or even the possibility of doing so, but the person often becomes increasingly anxious and starts off a vicious circle of events by again purging himself.[4] These persons will often develop gastrointestinal disorders because of the strain such practices put on the system.

The other, and probably more common, form of constipation, and the one most directly related to fixture design, is the undue retention of feces. This may be brought about by a variety of factors: 1 / an insufficient reflex activity of the intestines; 2 / a lack of normal stimulus; 3 / a resistance to movement of the feces by an internal obstruction, a disorder of the anal sphincter, or a pressure on the bowel such as from pregnancy; or 4 / what might be termed "the effects of civilization," that is, unbalanced diet, laxative abuses, improper posture, and weaknesses of the diaphragm, abdominal wall, and intestinal musculature. In many such instances the fecal mass has become so large and so hard that it must be broken up manually before it can be finally ejected. So long as feces remains in the gastrointestinal tract the body continues to draw off water, with the result that the longer the feces remains in the body the drier and firmer it becomes. This condition is further aggravated by the average American and western European diet, with its high protein content.

The significance of this form of constipation, which has often been referred to as "the Great American Disease," is not to be taken lightly. Many physicians regard habitual constipation as one of their commonest and most difficult problems.

> This condition is reflected in the statistics of illness in industrial populations where the functional gastrointestinal disorders rank second only to the common cold as a cause of absence from work due to illness. Patients affected by functional colonic disorders seldom are very sick but, in the aggregate, they constitute a large medical and socio-economic problem.[5]

Chronic constipation, whether organic or self-induced, is also often a major cause of hemorrhoids, or piles, which essentially is a dilating or rupturing of the blood vessels of the rectum and anus brought about by habitual hard straining while one is attempting to defecate or by the use of strong laxatives. The ultimate irony is that persons who develop hemorrhoids as a result of their imaginary constipation often then hold back defecation because of the pain of defecation and develop organic constipation. Estimates of the incidence of hemorrhoid sufferers run as high as one-third of the population.[6] In addition, habitual hard straining also stresses the heart through the Valsalva maneuver and can result in serious complications for persons with heart conditions.[7]

POSTURAL CONSIDERATIONS

Virtually every physician and physiologist who has ever troubled to write on the subject agrees that there is a natural and physiologically sound posture that encourages the defecation process. As the following sampling from the literature illustrates, there has also been substantial agreement over the years that contemporary water closets do not permit this posture.

> The ideal posture for defecation is the squatting position, with the thighs flexed upon the abdomen. In this way the capacity of the abdominal cavity is greatly diminished and intra-abdominal pressure increased, thus encouraging the expulsion of the fecal mass. The modern toilet

seat in many instances is too high even for some adults. The practice of having young children use adult toilet seats is to be deplored. It is often necessary for them to sit with their feet dangling. Unless the toilet seat is low enough that the feet may rest firmly on the floor and some flexion of the thighs is possible, the accessory muscles which aid in defecation normally have little opportunity to fulfill their function.[8]

Man's natural attitude during defaecation is a squatting one, such as may be observed amongst field workers or natives. Fashion, in the guise of the ordinary water closet, forbids the emptying of the lower bowel in the way Nature intended. Now in this act of defaecation great strains are imposed on all the internal organs. . . . It is no overstatement to say that the adoption of the squatting attitude would in itself help in no small measure to remedy the greatest physical vice of the white race, the constipation that has become a contentment.[9]

It should be mentioned in this connection that a very common cause for unsatisfactory results . . . is improper height of the toilet seat. It is usually too high. An ideal seat would place the body in the position naturally assumed by man in primitive conditions. The seat should be low enough to bring the knees above the seat level.[10]

. . . the high toilet seat may prevent complete evacuation. The natural position for defecation, assumed by primitive races, is the squatting position. Dr. Hurst points out that in Japan there are no seats in the toilets. The pan is sunk in the floor, and in some places a shoe is fixed to the ground on each side of it so that a firmer foothold may be obtained when the individual squats. When the thighs are pressed against the abdominal muscles in this position, the pressure within the abdomen is greatly increased, so that the rectum is more completely emptied.

Our toilets are not constructed according to physiological requirements. Toilet designers can do a good deal for people if they will study a little physiology and construct seats intended for proper defecation.[11]

In view of the fact that proper posture can contribute substantially to ease of defecation, it becomes obvious that if we are going to continue to accept the notion of a water closet as we have known it, we must begin to pay attention to the basic functional problems associated with its use. While on the one hand, there is little doubt about the fact that a full squat posture would be difficult and uncomfortable for most of us to assume and maintain for any length of time—primarily because of a lack of exercise, we must also bear in mind that while we regard the use of the water closet as natural, we represent only a relatively small percentage of the world's population, and a percentage that may be said, in an absolute sense, to be wrong, insofar as we have allowed civilization to interfere with our biological functioning.[12] The irony is that virtually all of the "squat plates" used elsewhere in the world are manufactured in the "civilized" Western countries. In a World Health Organization report dealing with hygiene facilities for developing nations, no mention is made of water closets, but elaborate instructions are provided for the construction of squat plates.[13]

The problem we are ultimately faced with is that the body must have a certain amount of exercise in order to keep functioning optimally; the musculature that needs to be brought into play during the defecation process is also the musculature we need to use in assuming or rising from a squatting position. The unfortunate consequences of this circular dilemma is perhaps best illustrated with reference to the aged, many of whom suffer from functional constipation caused in large measure by a natural decline in muscle tone. H. L. Bockus observes that:

A marked atrophy of the oblique muscles of the lower abdominal wall and diastasis recti are quite common in elderly constipated patients. . . .In patients with an atony of the abdominal musculature, certain procedures may be recommended which may increase the efficiency of the voluntary aids to defecation. Among the more important is the advice to assume the normal posture for moving the bowels. In some instances constipation may be corrected by the simple expedient of having the patient squat over a bed chamber rather than use an ordinary toilet seat. Another alternative is the use of a block of wood or stool on the floor

> in front of the toilet fixture so that adequate support may be available for the feet while permitting the thighs to be flexed upon the abdomen.[14]

Our actual practice is, however, generally to the contrary. This weakness of the abdominal and upper leg muscles also tends to make it difficult for such persons to accommodate themselves to a normal sitting height, let alone to a squat position. The "solution" has been to provide "seat extenders" of various sorts to raise the height, or to provide higher water closets. This has obviously helped the problem of raising and lowering the body, but it has just as obviously aggravated the functional and physiological problems of defecation. Admittedly the problems of the aged will not be resolved by expecting them to use a squat plate, but it is not unreasonable to suppose that the use of a substantially lower water closet over the years will provide us with some of the exercise we need and keep the problems from assuming such major proportions in our later years. In short, the more apathetic we are about making the necessary effort the more difficult it will become.

DESIGN CRITERIA FOR DEFECATION

10

DESCRIPTION OF ACTIVITY

For the purposes of analysis we can divide the activity of defecation into several distinct phases: adjustment or removal of clothing; assumption of a squatting or sitting position; initiation of defecation by straining and relaxing the anal sphincter; defecating, urinating, and farting; wiping, cleansing, flushing; and readjusting one's clothing. While this sequence may be more or less complicated by incidental activities such as reading or by personal idiosyncrasies such as repeated flushing or examination of one's feces, these do not essentially alter the basic pattern. From a design standpoint, the major variable in this activity is the particular posture assumed for which the fixture will have to be designed. The management of clothing, wiping and flushing procedures, and so on are secondary, and the treatment of specific applications will vary, depending upon the precise posture and fixture involved.

The ideal posture for defecation is the full squat, which provides the stomach muscles with the proper support during the straining/expulsion process, as contrasted with the familiar casual "sitting-on-a-chair" posture so often assumed on a standard water closet, particularly by those who read there. In this posture the individual is essentially passive and unable to do much to aid the body's natural mechanisms. Conversely, it is possible, by doubling over, folding the arms across the stomach, and drawing the feet back, to assume a fair approximation of the desirable squat posture even on a standard closet. As Figure 32 illustrates, the squat posture can thus be assumed in a variety of attitudes, particularly since the most important relationship is that between the trunk and the upper leg. Stressing the legs is also helpful and can be achieved by drawing the legs back, which automatically transfers some of the body's weight from the buttocks to the legs. In this respect the concept of a water closet as a "throne" is particularly invidious in terms of its suggestion about sitting posture, particularly when the water closet has been encased in a *chaise percée*, a decorative marble shroud, or some other bit of disguising cabinetwork, since in all such instances one is prevented from drawing one's feet back.

Although we can postulate that the free full-squatting posture for defecation practiced by most of the world's population is ideal from the viewpoint of physiological functioning, this posture is an unaccustomed and difficult one for most Western people to assume, let alone maintain, for any length of time, particularly if unaided. While this difficulty can easily be overcome with sufficient practice and exercise, a more serious impediment to its adoption is the problem posed by contemporary Western clothing. In large measure the problem of clothing is responsible for the gradual shift in Japan from their traditional squat closets to Western-style water closets. Having largely adopted Western dress, they also have to adopt the Western closet. In societies where some version of a loose gown is the traditional costume for both men and women, this can easily be gathered up around one's waist, out of the way, leaving the legs free. Western clothing, in contrast, almost invariably involves some form of under or outer garment—trousers, shorts, girdles, panty hose, and so on—that must be lowered around one's legs or else removed entirely. If simply lowered, as is now customary, these garments would interfere with the assumption of a properly balanced stance, which involves spreading the feet. Furthermore, they would be in danger of being soiled in the fixture or by one's own actions. Urination, for example, would be impossible in this situation. In addition, one is liable to lose the contents of one's pockets, as many unfortunate souls can wryly testify. In short, the only satisfactory way to use the traditonal form of hole-in-the-floor squat closet is to disrobe completely from the waist down. Given our accustomed habits and in light of the practical, not to mention the psychological, difficulties,

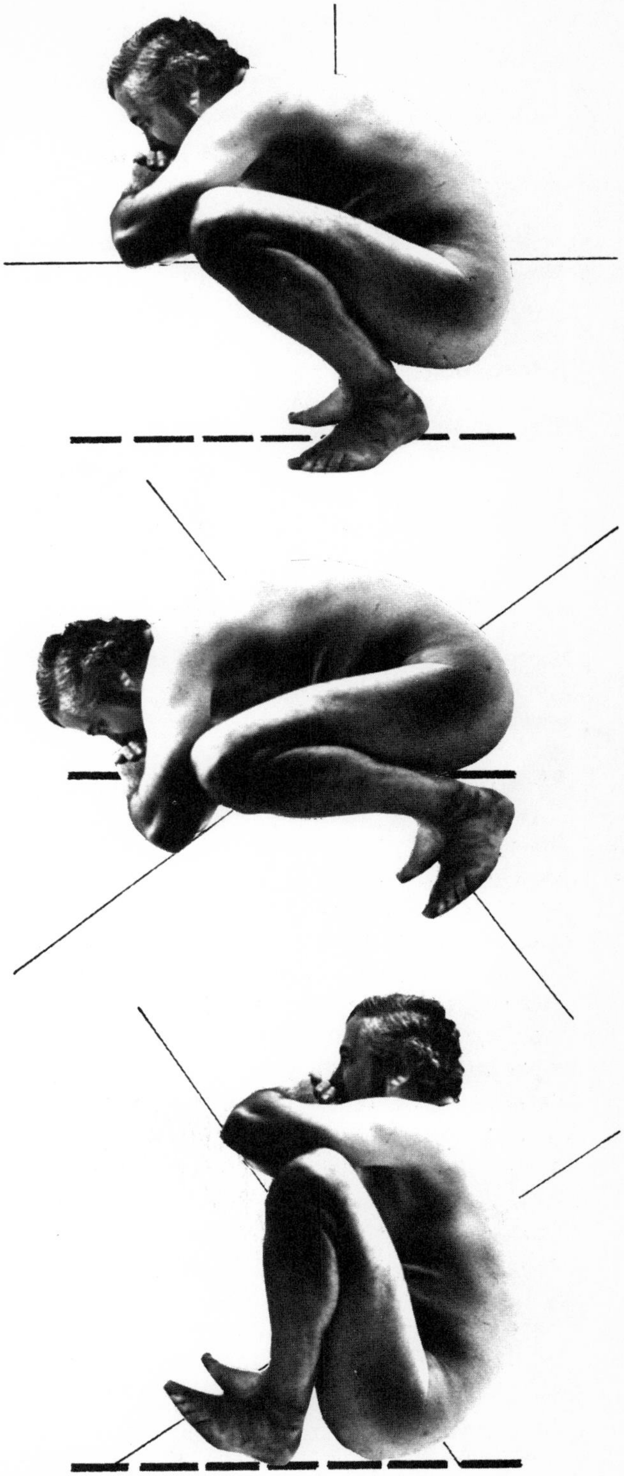

32 / POSSIBLE ROTATIONS OF SQUAT POSTURE

it is probably reasonable to conclude that the adoption of the squat closet is not a proposition that can be seriously entertained in the present context. From a design viewpoint, however, it possesses the one great virtue of being foolproof: it simply leaves the user no choice except to assume the proper posture.

If we leave aside a full squat posture and the fixtures based on it, there are still, however, a number of other modified approaches to the problem to be considered, as shown in Figure 33. These range all the way from a modified squat closet to a modified seat for use on existing water closets. In each instance the premise is that a reasonable approximation of the desirable posture can be achieved. The problem is to make appropriate modifications that will actively encourage the assumption of such a posture with reasonable ease and comfort. While we recognize that none of these modified approaches are foolproof, in the sense that an uninformed or determined user could still ignore the proper posture, they do promise to find wider acceptance and to be of benefit to a larger population.

Modified Squat Closet When we assume a full free-squat posture, the degree of that squat is very much a matter of body size, agility, joint flexibility, and so on. Most Western people unaccustomed to the posture cannot begin to achieve the position commonly achieved by most primitive peoples or by people who are accustomed to the posture. In this connection, age appears to have very little, if any, relationship to one's ability to assume the posture, as the experience of primitive peoples testify, though in the Western world one of the commonest problems of elderly people is their inability to cope with low seating.

In the assumption of a full squat, the height of the buttocks from the floor varies from 150 to 205 mm (6 to 8 inches), and though these heights can be reached with reasonable comfort, they place a considerable strain on the calf muscles and are difficult to rise from, particularly because of the problems of balance. This is true even when support is available at those heights. In part this is because the legs need to be spread far apart in a flat-footed stance so that the trunk can lean far enough forward to maintain balance. Rising from such a position is complicated because the entire body must be brought into play in order to maintain equilibrium. Put another way, there is a considerable horizontal force component to be overcome.

A somewhat modified squat, which we are more accustomed to assume, ranges in height from 230 to 280 mm (9 to 11 inches) and involves balancing on the balls of one's feet. In this position, lowering and raising the body is considerably easier, as is the problem of maintaining balance, since the force exerted by the legs is essentially vertical and the distance to be traveled is less. In the assumption of either posture, however, that posture must be assumed initially by straddling the fixture or support and then lowering and raising the body from that position. It is exceedingly difficult first to sit, as we do normally, and then pull one's legs back or, conversely, to undo the posture once one has assumed it. For all practical purposes a height of approximately 255 mm (10 inches) would represent a workable figure for this approach.

One of the most important design consequences of assuming any such squat or semi-squat posture is that the conditions of support are drastically different from a normal sitting posture, requiring a radically different seat or supporting structure. The essential difference, illustrated in Figure 34, is that in a squat posture only "point" support is possible and this support is at the ischial tuberosities, the bottom-most protuberances of the pelvic structure. If one sits normally on a standard seat, the bulk of the body weight is placed on the thighs. Sitting on a standard seat in a squat position is acutely uncomfortable and causes one to fall partway through the seat opening, since the sole support for the body is at the sides of the buttocks and on unaccustomed points of the pelvic structure. For proper and comfortable seating,

33 / POSSIBLE APPROACHES TO A MODIFIED SQUAT POSTURE

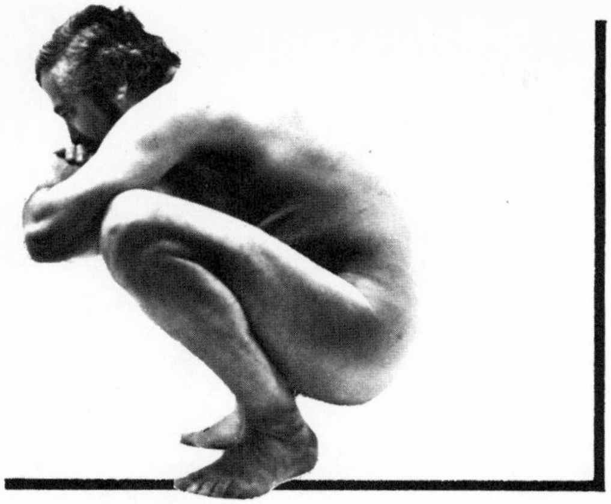

FULL FREE SQUAT

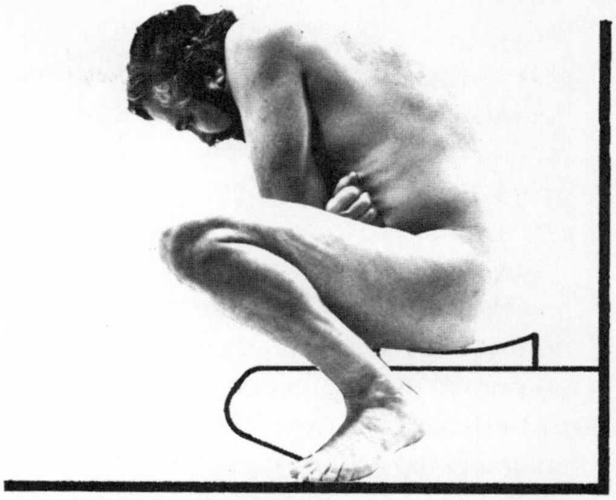

SUPPORTED SEMI-SQUAT

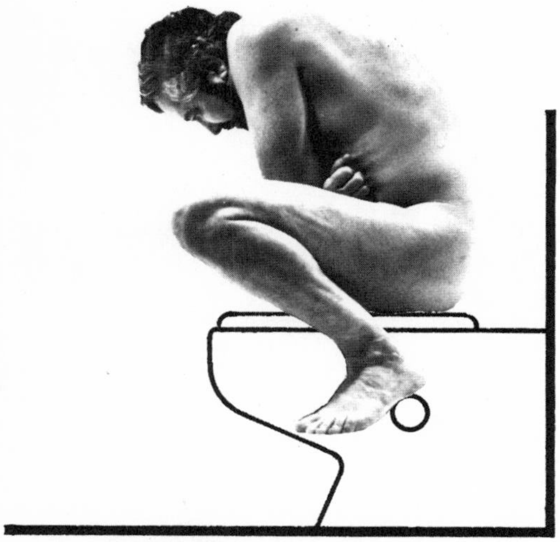

MODIFIED CONVENTIONAL WATER CLOSET
WITH FOOT REST

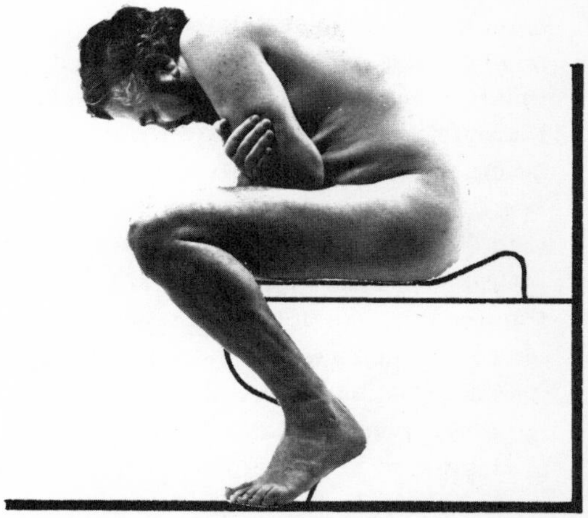

MODIFIED CONVENTIONAL SEAT

LEAN-ON WATER CLOSET

MODIFIED CONVENTIONAL WATER CLOSET

therefore, the seat must be designed to offer support directly to the tuberosities. Since the ischial tuberosities are quite close together, this design requires a narrowing at the midpoint of the seat opening, a radical change from the shape of the present seat.

Point support of this sort necessarily involves, however, a greater concentration of force than is normally the case. Some preliminary experiments on normal seating and buttock loads conducted by Hertzberg at the Wright Air Development Center indicated "that loads under the tuberosities can run in certain body types to as high as 4,218 g/cm^2 (60 pounds per square inch), and perhaps higher. . . ."[1] Figure 35 illustrates the approximate pressure pattern that develops. With respect to the modified squat closet the loading is, however, nowhere near as great, primarily because of the different distribution of weight that results from the squat posture. As we saw in Figure 34, a semi-sitting squat results in less than half the total body weight's being supported by the seat, compared with 70 per cent or more when one is sitting normally. Nevertheless, it is apparent that to provide the greatest comfort, the seat should still be shaped in such a way as to distribute the total load over a somewhat greater area than would be possible by a perfectly flat seat.

This support of the tuberosities is in many ways preferable to the kind of support provided by conventional seats. With a conventional seat the body weight is largely borne by the thighs, often in an unsatisfactory manner, as we shall learn in more detail later. In this position, tissues are compressed, and, in addition to some potentially injurious effects to muscles and nerves, considerable discomfort results. A very common complaint, particularly among the elderly and those with constipation problems, is that their legs go numb from having the circulation cut off. Consequently, people are inclined to sit far forward in their seats in

POINT SUPPORT: 40–50%

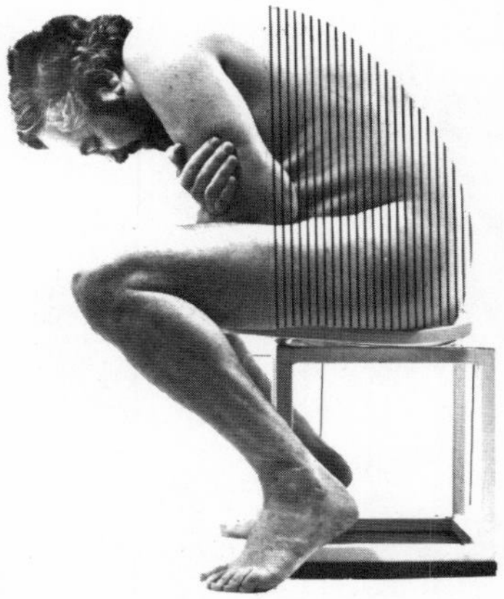

BUTTOCK SUPPORT: 60–70%

BUTTOCK AND THIGH SUPPORT: 70–75%

34 / VARIATIONS IN SUPPORT AND WEIGHT DISTRIBUTION BY POSTURE ASSUMED

order that the ischial tuberosities and not the thighs may support their weight. A better solution is to modify the design of seating:

> To avoid undue pressure on the sensitive soft parts of the thigh, the chair must be so constructed that the weight of the body is borne on the ischial tuberosities. The thigh should be able to hang freely or only rest gently on the seat. The height of the seat should therefore be less than the length of the lower leg. If the chair is low enough to suit those with short legs, these conditions will also be fulfilled for those with longer legs.[2]

In considering the actual dimensions for such a support and its related opening, we must turn to the anthropometric measurements illustrated in Figure 36, which show that the ischial tuberosities are approximately 25 mm (1 inch) in width and 40 to 50 mm (1½ to 2 inches) in length and vary in span from 120 to 160 mm (4¾ to 6¼ inches), females tending to have a larger bi-ischiatic diameter than males, generally by about 20 mm (¾ inch). This suggests that the maximum opening on the transverse axis of the tuberosities can be no greater than 75 to 90 mm (3 to 3½ inches) since, for comfort, the tuberosities must be fully supported. Partial support, so that the pelvic structure is supported at the sides, is acutely uncomfortable.

It will be noted from Figure 36 that both the anus and urethra lie within what must necessarily be the narrowest point in the seat opening if the tuberosities are to be supported. Although extremely narrow, compared with the average 205-mm (8-inch) width of opening in present seats, this opening width of 75 to 90 mm (3 to 3½ inches) is sufficient to prevent soiling the seat, particularly since this proposed type of seat has the effect of "locking" one into position. While minor movement is possible, radical changes of position from the one intended are not really possible without considerable discomfort.

Other considerations necessitate, however, enlarging the opening both in front and back of the point of actual support. One is for purely psychological purposes—to remove the fear of soiling the fixture. When the openings in front and back appear more or less normal in size, the user is likely to feel more secure in this respect. One doesn't realize that the anus is actually located at the narrowest point. The practical, and more important, reason for enlarging the opening is to provide room so that the hand can reach in to wipe both the anus and urethra, since wiping the anus must be done from the back instead of the side as is common on conventional water closets. In a squat or semi-squat posture it proves exceedingly difficult to perform this operation from the side because one cannot shift one's weight so as to reach under from the side. For this, clear openings of approximately 150 to 205 mm (6 to 8 inches) in diameter are necessary both front and back. Another reason is to keep the penis from touching the fixture. In this respect, most conventional water closets are woefully inadequate. This is particularly true of the standard round or egg-shaped bowls in which the front-to-back dimension is usually so small as to necessitate a delicate balance in finding the proper location on the seat—to avoid soiling the back of the seat and to

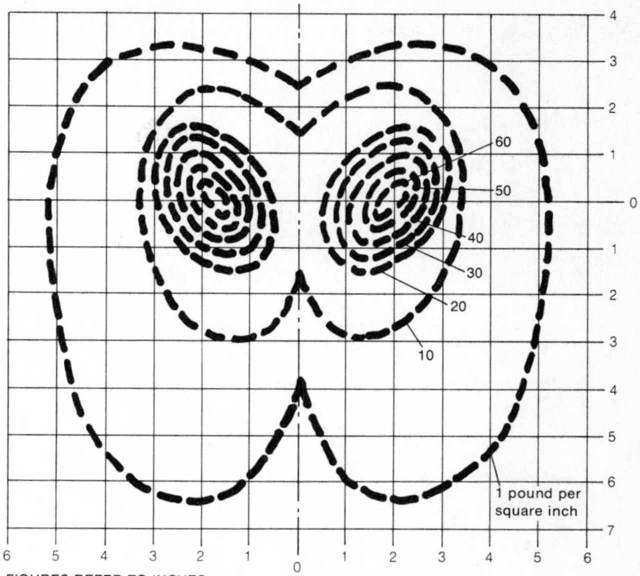

35 / PRESSURES DEVELOPED IN SITTING

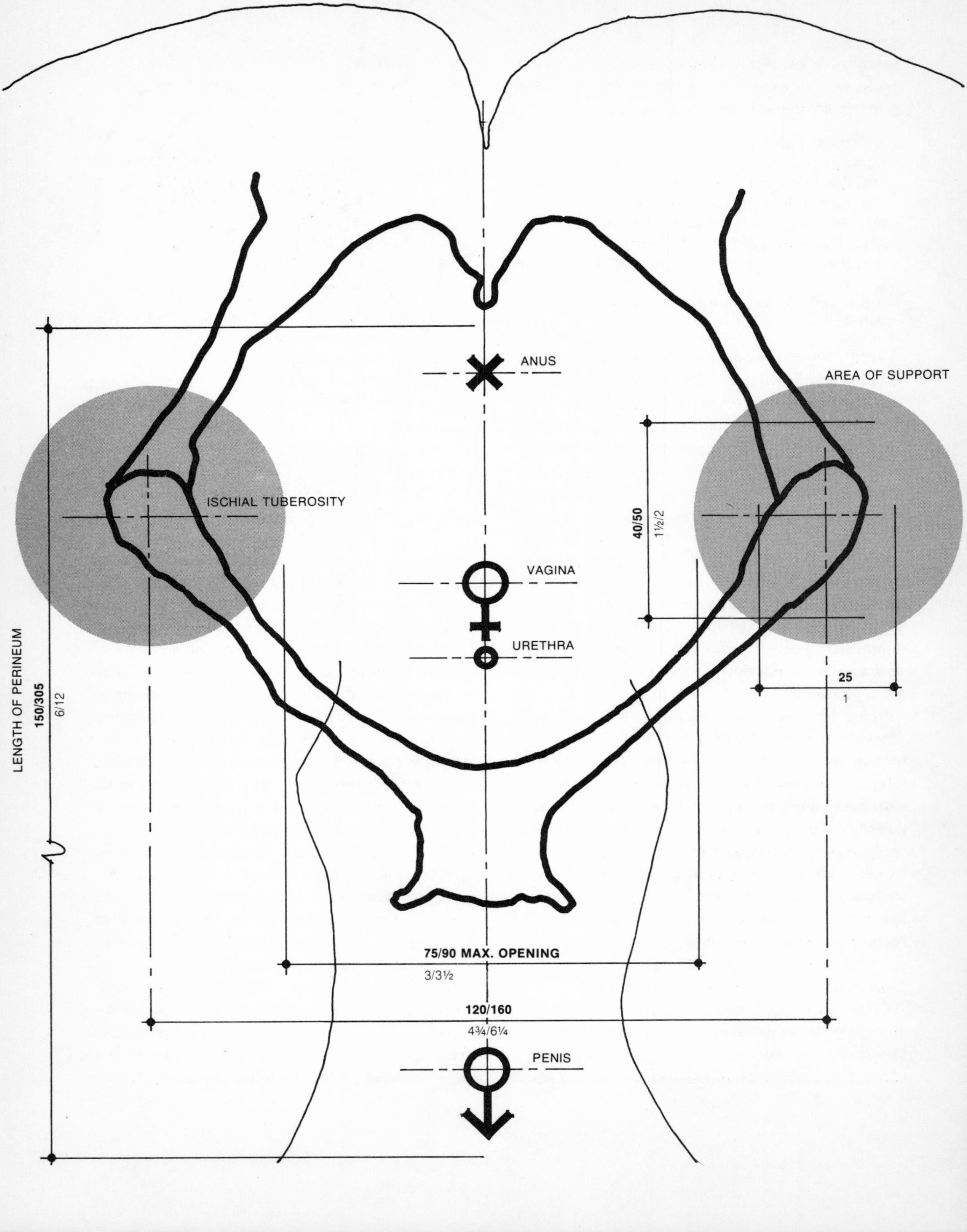

ANUS
AREA OF SUPPORT
ISCHIAL TUBEROSITY
40/50
1½/2
VAGINA
URETHRA
LENGTH OF PERINEUM
150/305
6/12
25
1
75/90 MAX. OPENING
3/3½
120/160
4¾/6¼
PENIS

avoid touching the front lip of the bowl with the penis. As indicated in Figure 36, the length of the perineum from the cleavage of the buttocks to the front of the genitals ranges from a minimum of approximately 150 mm (6 inches) to 305 mm (12 inches).[3] Conventional water closets, as indicated in Figure 37, often meet these dimensions exactly, with no room for error, wiping, or a slightly erect penis.

As suggested in Figure 38, the minimum overall inside front-to-back dimension should be approximately 455 mm (18 inches) and the overall minimum width approximately 205 mm (8 inches). The height from the floor to the low point of the seat can be established at approximately 255 mm (10 inches). In order, however, to contain seated male urination properly, the front lip of the container should be raised higher than the level of the seat. A sitting height of 255 mm (10 inches) being assumed, the front lip could be raised 50 or 65 mm (2 or 2½ inches). At the same time, however, that the front lip is raised, it must also be lengthened in order that the thighs be kept free of contact with the fixture. The vertical profile of the container is directly related to the posture assumed and to the height of the seat—largely because of the problem of clothing. In this regard, the distance from the center of support to the front of the container should not exceed 305 mm (12 inches) in order that clothing gathered around the knees be kept clear of the container. At this 305-mm (12-inch) distance the front lip should not be more than 150 mm (6 inches) wide in order that the fixture may be comfortably straddled. The front of the fixture must also taper back both vertically and horizontally in order to accommodate the desirable posture. In addition (on the assumption that such a fixture would be floor-mounted), the support for the fixture must be cut back a minimum of 150 mm (6 inches) to accommodate the feet—both while one is mounting the fixture and while one is seated.

36 / ANATOMICAL PLAN VIEW
OF PERINEAL REGION

In this instance, particularly, the shape of the fixture is very largely determined by the posture of the user, which, of necessity, is relatively inflexible, and by the basic dimensions established by this posture. Although these recommendations should not be regarded as absolute, they do represent an approximation of the size and shape criteria to be met. Obviously, a number of minor variations are possible, but it should also be obvious that, because of the high degree of interrelatedness between the various components, the design must be considered in its entirety.

One of the possibilities to be considered in the design of such a fixture is the elimination of a separate seat. In this regard, the primary purpose of the separate seat was to provide a warm seating surface in what were once upon a time largely unheated bathrooms. Indeed, some hardy individuals like Churchill are reported to have had the seats removed from their water closets, a taste acquired during their public school days when the closets had no seats. Be that as it may, the separate two-piece seat and lid represent a major cleaning problem and could be considered superfluous in these days of heated bathrooms. (In Japan, where central heating, or heating at all, is still rather rare, one of the most popular luxuries is an electrically heated toilet seat.) An additional justification for eliminating the separate seat is that the actual contact area is so small. If, however, a seat were felt to be necessary from the viewpoint of user comfort, it might well be no more than two permanently affixed pads of a material warmer to the touch than china. Two contemporary fixtures designed to be used without a seat are shown in Figure 39.

Modified Conventional Closet Referring back to Figure 33, we can examine several other possibilities with reference to modification of a conventional water closet. Essentially, these approaches are based upon the premise that, while a squat or semi-squat posture is desirable, it poses major difficulties in getting up and down relative to a low seat height. It would appear obvious,

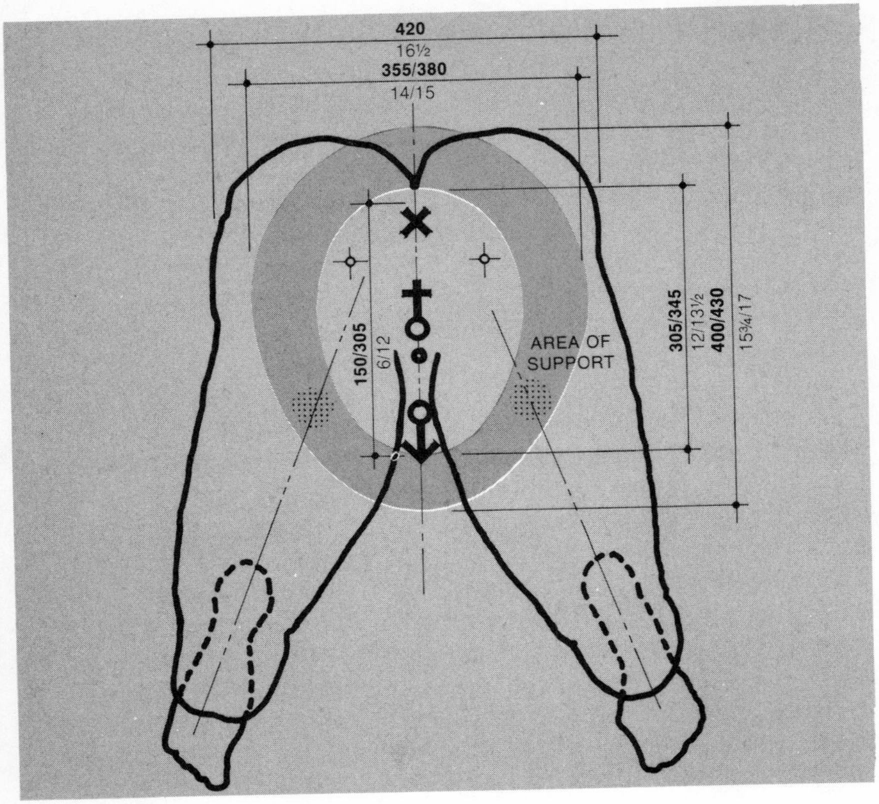

37 / PLAN VIEW OF SITTING POSITION ON A CONVENTIONAL WATER CLOSET AT A CONVENTIONAL 380/400-MM (15/16-INCH) HEIGHT

therefore, that, by beginning with a conventional-height water closet and equipping it with some form of footrest so that one could assume a squat posture after being seated, one could resolve both problems. Indeed, several such fixtures have been tried over the years, as illustrated in Figure 40. Unfortunately, however, the matter is not so simple, as we shall see in a moment.

If we assume a conventional fixture approximately 405 mm (16 inches) high equipped with integral footrests at a height of 205 mm (8 inches), similar to the illustration in Figure 40, we have theoretically established the proper relationship for a full squat as described earlier. It proves to be virtually impossible, however, to assume such a squat posture after one is once seated—except perhaps for a trained gymnast. In order to assume the posture and lift one's feet up into position, it is necessary first to lean back, bring up the feet, position them properly on the footrests, and then try to rise from a leaning-backwards position forward to a balanced squatting posture, without tumbling over forward in the process. Even when possible to execute, this maneuver is more awkward and strenuous than getting up and down from a simple squat posture, particularly in terms of balance.

Clothing again provides a further complication. With one's feet effectively bound by lowered clothing one must either try to lift both legs simultaneously or else disrobe in order to lift one leg at a time. Shoes aggravate matters even more since the feet must be lifted higher in order to hook the heels behind the footrests.

Another approach in this situation is not to assume a horizontal squat position but to remain

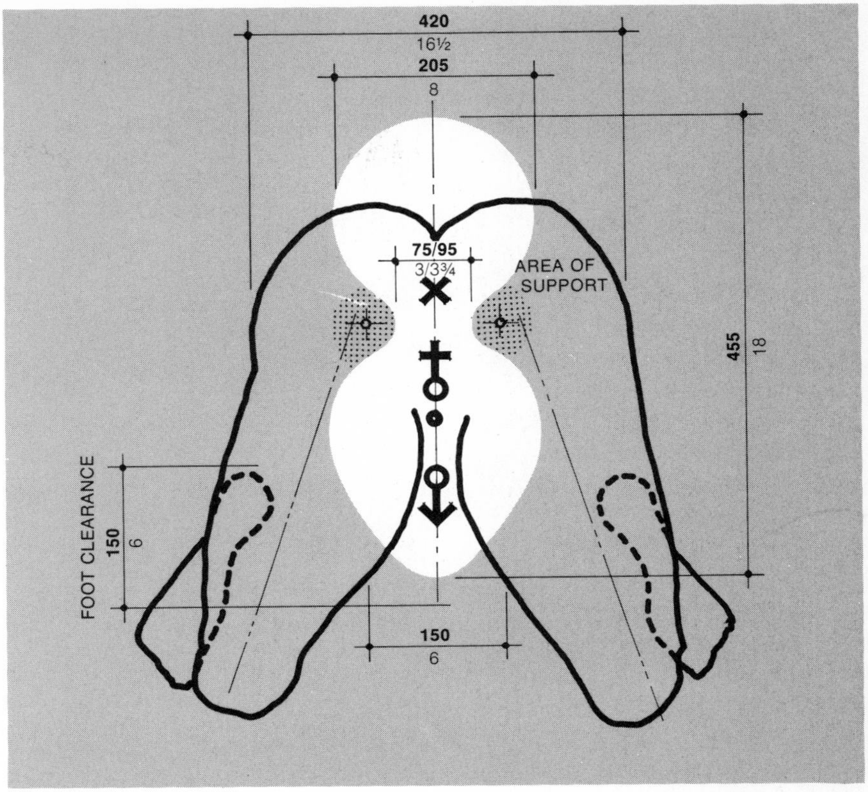

38 / PLAN VIEW OF NECESSARY DIMENSIONS AND CLEARANCES FOR A SEMI-SQUAT WATER CLOSET AT 255-MM (10-INCH) HEIGHT

in a rotated 45 degree squat position. This, in some ways, is similar to the position assumed, for example, when one is using some temporary form of footrest in conjunction with a conventional closet, as has sometimes been recommended, or when one is using some of the "health closets," which are based on the idea of simply having the knees higher than the pelvis. Theoretically these are all based on the assumption, as illustrated in Figure 32, that once a tight squat posture is assumed it can be rotated. This is true but only within limits. The difficulty with many of these rotated positions is that they are rendered ineffective as a defecation posture because one's energy and musculature are working to maintain one's balance and cannot at the same time be employed for expulsion, nor can one relax the anal sphincter while in a strained posture. In order for the posture to be effective one must first be relaxed, comfortable, and properly balanced; only then can one fully bring into play the musculature for defecation. The most important relationship is between the trunk and the thighs; the positioning of the legs is of secondary benefit.

One rather extreme way in which such a rotated posture might be made to work is to provide a full backrest that would effectively lock one into position so that maintaining one's balance and posture is no longer a problem (see Figures 41 and 32). In such a case, one would not only be locked into the proper posture but would also be free to devote one's efforts to the task at hand. For greatest ease of assuming such a posture, the backrest could be made adjustable so that one would sit, lean back, place one's feet on the footrests, and then raise the back, bringing one into proper posi-

"ROHAGLAS" WATER CLOSET:
RÖHM, DARMSTADT, WEST GERMANY

"ARMADA" WALL-HUNG WATER CLOSET:
VILLEROY-BOCH, METTLACH, WEST GERMANY

tion. Conversely, the backrest could be fixed and the footrests made adjustable.

In the assumption of any such drastically rotated position, the conditions of support change once again—this time to the coccyx, or to the ischial tuberosities, depending on the degree of rotation. While this can be resolved in the case of any new fixture based on the possible approach just outlined, it is one more problem with respect to any attempt to assume such postures on a conventional closet equipped with a conventional seat designed for a flat horizontal sitting posture. Rotation of the body also means that the body orifices are rotated relative to the horizontal plane so that the front of the bowl would have to be raised and shaped to contain the expelled body wastes properly. In this respect, there is obviously a limit beyond which such rotation ceases to serve any purpose and becomes a hindrance. Wiping can, moreover, become difficult if one cannot shift one's body weight to one side or if the opening is not sufficient for free hand access.

Another variation, shown in Figure 40, uses footrests that are sloped back and up from the floor, allowing one to work one's feet into the proper position without the strain and difficulty encountered previously. If, however, the footrests are too far forward, one is faced with much the same problems as before—either of adjusting one's posture once seated or of remaining in a rotated and strained position. Conversely, if the footrests are sufficiently far back so as not to involve a postural change once seated, they do offer some support or resistance to the feet, but once one has pulled one's feet that far back under the body the footrests are largely superfluous. In either case, they interfere with the placement of the feet if we assume that the water closet will continue to be used for standing male urination. In addition, the determination of a suitable angle is complicated, if not rendered insoluble, by the dif-

39 / CURRENT APPROACHES
TO WATER CLOSETS

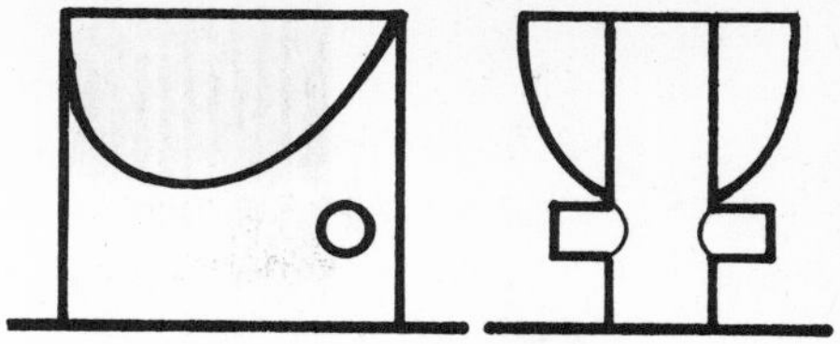

POSTURE CLOSET BY LE CORBUSIER
FOR POZZI, MILAN, ITALY

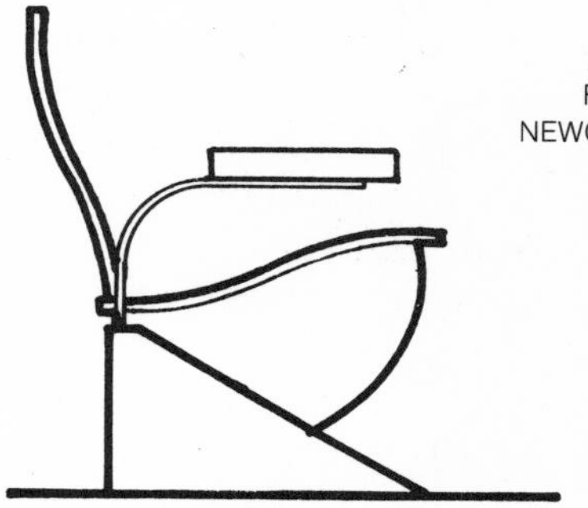

POSTURE CLOSET
BY J. GARDNER
FOR ADAMSEZ, LTD.,
NEWCASTLE-UPON-TYNE,
ENGLAND

40 / APPROACHES TO SEMI-SQUAT WATER CLOSETS

ferences between what would be optimal for a bare foot and what would be suitable for a woman wearing high-heeled shoes.

In virtually every instance, the adaptations examined are sufficiently drastic in terms of altering all the normal relationships between the body and the fixture that they cannot be seriously considered as workable approaches. The complexity of these relationships is such that it is necessary to begin from the beginning.

The last and least drastic, not to mention least foolproof, approach, suggested in Figure 42, is to provide an improved seat for use on existing conventional closets. The premises underlying this approach are that a reasonable approximation of a semi-squat posture can be assumed even on a 405-mm (16-inch)-high conventional closet and that a properly designed seat can assist in the comfortable assumption and maintenance of that posture. While this is obviously a compromise, it does have the merit of permitting existing installations to be more effective and comfortable. Most conventional seats (and closets) have two major shortcomings: a front-to-back opening dimension that is too small for hygienic use and a configuration based more on appearance than seating comfort. Although one obviously cannot stretch existing fixtures, it is possible to lengthen substantially the actual effective opening, which is determined by the seat rather than the bowl. In the common range of residential water closets, particularly European ones, the front-to-back dimension of the bowl opening varies from 305 to 345 mm (12 to 13½ inches). Almost all seats have, however, a considerably wider rim than the rim of the bowl and overhang the inside of the bowl by 20 to 40 mm (¾ to 1½ inches), thus further reducing the effective opening to as little as 255 mm (10 inches) in extreme cases. By cutting the rim away and eliminating these overhangs at the front and back, we can at least have the maximum opening possible on any given closet, even though it still falls short of the 370 to 400 mm (14½ to 15¾ inches) desirable.

With respect to configuration, most often one finds seats that have a doughnut-like constant convex cross-section or, worse yet, a sharply tapered constant cross-section (see Figure 42). Such configurations obviously have little to do with seating. They are essentially decorative, and, as we are seeing increasingly, such seats have become a major fashion item for the bathroom. Because of one's seated posture, however, as shown in Figure 34, such configurations provide only point support for the thighs, where some 70 per cent of one's body weight is concentrated. In the bolt-upright posture this is not so serious since the buttocks receive support as well, but the more one leans forward and pulls one's feet back to assume a semi-squat posture, the more one concentrates one's weight on the thighs. In fact, the moment one leans forward at all—enough, for example, to part the buttocks as one must—one has shifted the weight to the thighs. When that happens, the weight is essentially concentrated on two pivot points approximately midway along the femur with the familiar result that one then complains about one's legs' "falling asleep" from having the blood circulation cut off. The possible pressures at those two pivot points can exceed those encountered under the ischial tuberosities.

In order to accommodate such a seated posture properly so that the weight is borne by the thighs, it is necessary to maximize the area of support. This can be accomplished by providing a constant and slightly concave cross-section all along the axis of the thighs, as shown in Figure 42. In some respects, the overall configuration would be much like a cut-away tractor seat with a complex continuously variable cross-section based on the sitting posture rather than the symmetry of the bowl.

In order to encourage further the assumption of a doubled-over semi-squat, the back of the seat might be raised slightly (rather than lowered). With a high back and a slight forward tilt the seat is somewhat awkward and uncomfortable to use if one attempts to sit on it in a bolt-upright position but is very natural in the proper position. Such a high-back seat could also incorporate the mechanism necessary for a washing/drying function within the back seat cavity.

One new seat based on these principles, designed in this case for use on existing elongated closets, is shown in Figure 43. Obviously, similar seats can be designed to accommodate other sizes and configurations of conventional closets. Seats can also be designed to accommodate other approaches such as the proposal for the ultimate reading seat shown in Figure 44.

High-Rise Closet The approach just described could also be applied to the design of an entirely new fixture as well, as suggested in Figure 33. In this case, the features could be incorporated in optimal form into the fixture itself and, as suggested earlier, the seat itself might be eliminated altogether (see Figure 45).

Another variant on this approach would be to raise the point of contact sufficiently so as to require a lean-on posture, to approximately 610 mm (24 inches), as suggested in Figure 33. In this case the only way the fixture could be used would be in the doubled-over position, which is necessary in order to remain in place. Such an extreme approach poses problems, however, with the management of clothing, which must be dropped to the floor, proves tiring after a short while, and thereby violates the principle of a relaxed posture. In addition, it is unsatisfactory for urination from a seated position unless there were a pronounced projecting front lip similar to some of the early female urinals, which, in fact, such a fixture would closely resemble, though it would serve admirably for standing male urination. On balance, however, this approach does not appear as promising as others reviewed.

41 / POSSIBLE APPROACH
TO A FORCED-SQUAT POSTURE

Anal and Urethral Hygiene The techniques for anal wiping will vary according to the posture assumed on a given fixture—from either the side or the back. Urethral blotting is simply done from the front regardless of posture. In either case, however, the ideal location for the toilet tissue is in front of the seated user where it can easily be reached and folded. A side-wall location is acceptable if the dispenser is located just even with the front of the fixture. Unfortunately, all too

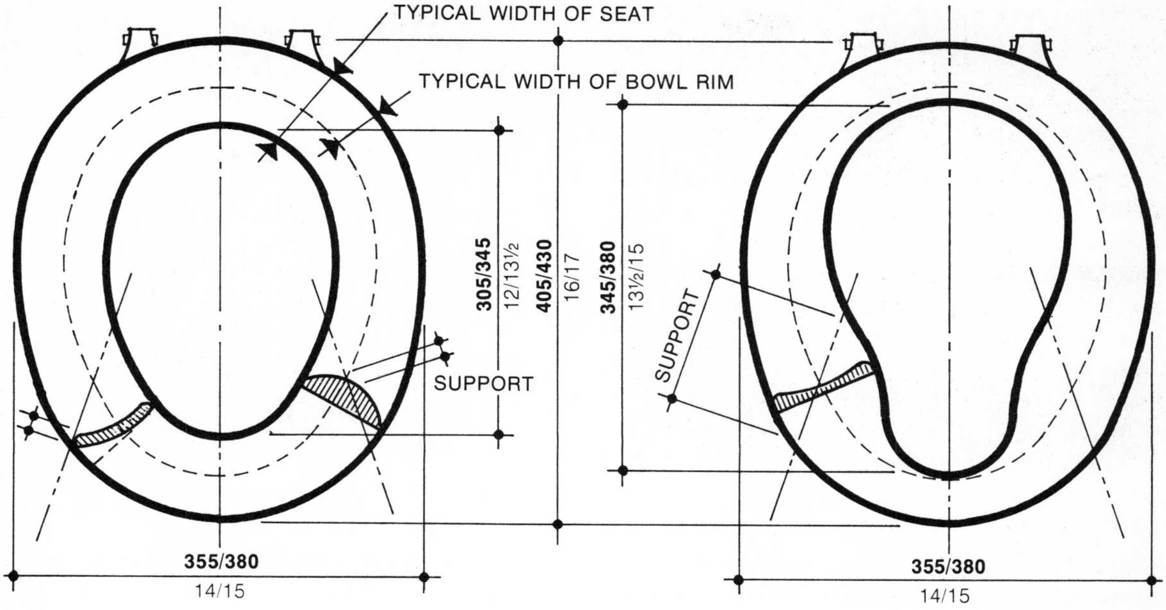

42 / POSSIBLE MODIFICATIONS OF EXISTING WATER CLOSET SEATS

often it is located behind the user, necessitating considerable contortions to reach it. Indeed, it is curious that we persist in regarding paper-holders as "accessories," an attitude that implies they are optional rather than essential.

For proper cleansing the anus should, at the very least, be wet-wiped if not actually washed. Most commonly, such washing is done at the bidet. For maximum convenience, however, such cleansing would logically take place as a natural part of the wiping process while one is still seated on the water closet. The most direct approach to this is to build a washing and drying function into the water closet itself, as is illustrated in Figure 46. This requires a fairly sophisticated design: separate controls, tempered water, an aerated stream, a precise and dependable stream trajectory, a warm-air drying jet, and other features. The precise dimensions and mechanics involved are obviously determined by the posture assumed and the precise configuration of the fixture in question, and they cannot be detailed further here. Another variant on this approach is to build such functions into the toilet seat, which offers the advantage of use on existing water closets. Several such seats are on the market in the United States and in Europe.

Several early models of water closet used a washing jet relying only on water from the tank. If the closet had not been used for some time and the water was at room temperature the result was reasonably satisfactory, but when fresh cold water from the mains happened to be used, the result was a very pronounced shock to the system. No such fixtures are on the market any longer.

In some circumstances it is possible, of course, to wet the tissue by using another nearby water source such as a lavatory or a bathtub, which is the stratagem used by most hemorrhoid patients. It would be far preferable, however, to make this operation an integral part of the elimination and hygiene processes by making it as convenient and natural as possible.

For the benefit of the sceptics or the guilt-ridden, note that the sensation resulting from our common habit of dry-wiping—once one has become ac-

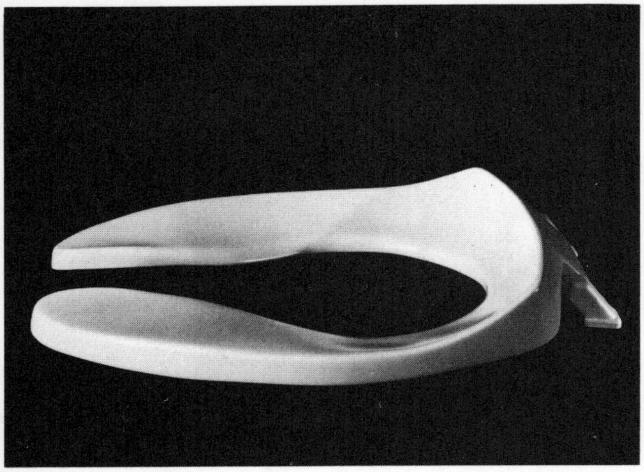

"POSTURE MOLD" SEAT: AMERICAN STANDARD, NEW BRUNSWICK, NEW JERSEY, U.S.A. (COLLECTION THE MUSEUM OF MODERN ART, NEW YORK)

43 / CURRENT APPROACH TO A POSTURE WATER CLOSET SEAT

customed to washing—has been compared by some to the sensation resulting from not brushing one's teeth from one week to the next.

One other relatively simple and adaptable approach is to use one of the proprietary cleansing foams (commonly marketed as hemorrhoidal preparations) with regular tissue, a usage that would require only a new combination holder for the foam and the paper. Most such preparations have the additional advantage of containing some lanolin-like substance and consequently are extremely soothing, almost voluptuously so. Still another variant is the use of packaged prewetted papers, again commonly marketed for hemorrhoidal use.

Odor and Noise Privacy in the bathroom, particularly for elimination functions, is a major concern for some people. All manner of verbal and social conventions are resorted to in an attempt to disguise or mitigate our activities, such as running water to mask the sound of other running water. While such stratagems are more or less successful, they all ultimately fail with respect to telltale odors—a source of considerable concern and embarrassment for many. Probably the oldest, and still the commonest, approach to this problem is to use some other, presumably more pleasant odor to mask the offending odor. As a solution this is rarely satisfactory: either the chemistry of the combination is unfortunate, or the masking odor is so strong as to be repellent in its own right, or the masking odor becomes so familiar, as in public urinals, as to be equally as offensive as the original.

A more recent though actually quite old, and certainly more satisfactory, approach is to use some form of positive chemical or hydromechanical exhaust system. There are a number of commercially available systems today that perform satisfactorily. Some are built into the water closet and use a syphonic action to induce venting of the bowl itself. Others rely on a mechanical exhaust to the outside and still others use a chemical, generally charcoal, filtration system.

One of the more promising recent approaches employs a chemical attack on the problems not only of odor but also of noise. It is based on the deployment of a complex chemical foam blanket on the pan water, which reduces the noise and splash back of urination and of defecation and is a deodorant, a germicide, and a cleansing agent.[4]

Controls If we examine the matter of controls from the viewpoint of user comfort and convenience rather than of mere mechanical convenience, it becomes readily apparent that most flushing mechanisms are poorly located. The most common arrangement in the United States, for example, is a lever handle mounted on the top lefthand face of the tank. This is convenient only if the user flushes the closet after rising and turning around. A sizeable number of persons prefer, however, for one reason or another (odor, peace of mind, and so on), to flush the closet while seated and after each bowel movement and must engage in some contortions to do so.[5] Since the water closet is presently also used for standing male urination, this might be regarded as a justification for its location. Conversely, many of the modern low one-piece water closets have a flushing mechanism that can be readily reached from the seated position but that is awkward to reach from a standing position.

Throughout much of Europe the most common arrangement is a pull-up knob located on the top of the tank. While this has the virtue of mechanical simplicity, it effectively precludes use from any but a standing position. It also has the not inconsiderable drawback of negating the use of the space over the tank for much needed storage or for a counter.

Although most commonly found in public installations, possibly the worst arrangement from a functional viewpoint is the ambiguous positioning generally used for flushometer installations where the flushing lever is approximately 455 mm (18 inches) off the floor and where it is not clear whether the device should be operated by hand or by foot and where either method is ultimately awkward and unsanitary.

More suitable arrangements are, of course, possible and have, in fact, been available for many years. In 1891, Thomas Crapper patented a "Seat Action Automatic Flush," for example. Another venerable solution with much to recommend it is the use of a spring-loaded flushing button set into the floor just in front of the fixture, an arrangement that permits use from either a standing or sitting position, before, during, or after elimination. Contemporary versions of this floor-mounted button now operate electronically rather than

44 / APPROACH TO A
WATER CLOSET READING SEAT

"AD 2000 COMFORT CONTROL CENTER":
OLSONITE, DETROIT, MICHIGAN, U.S.A.
(FEATURES INCLUDE READING LIGHT,
ASHTRAY, RADIO, T.V., TIMER,
TILTING MASSAGE BACK, BIDET)

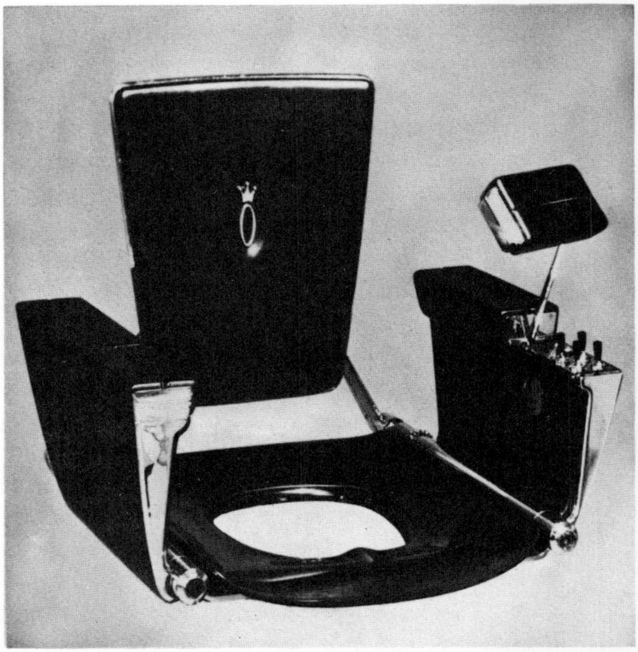

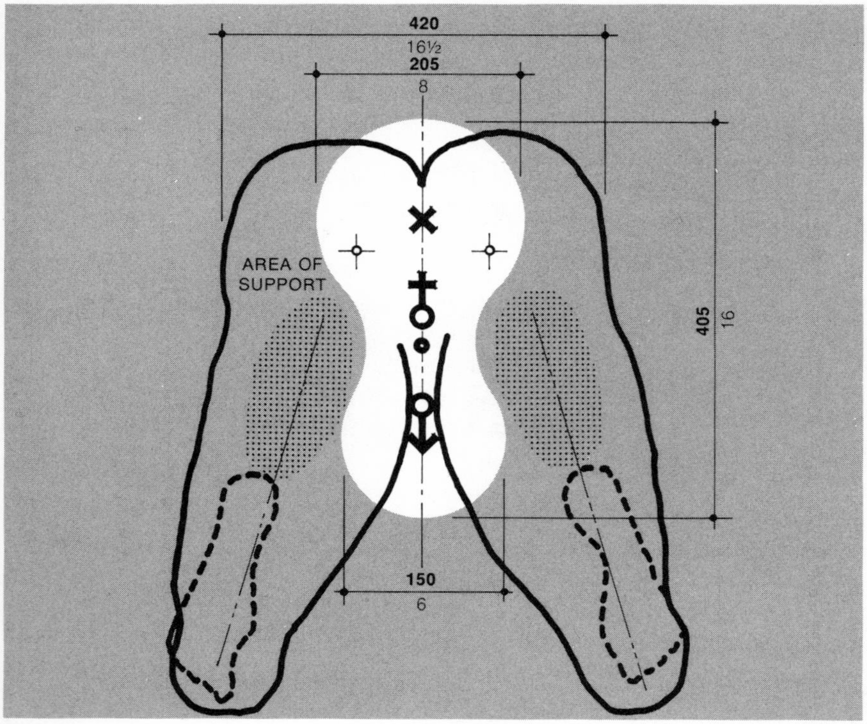

45 / PLAN VIEW OF NECESSARY DIMENSIONS AND CLEARANCES FOR A HIGH-RISE WATER CLOSET

through a complex mechanical linkage. The increasing use of electronic control devices, especially in Europe, is extremely promising in that it permits the triggering switch to be located virtually anywhere that is appropriate without regard to where the actual flushing mechanism itself may be located. These new devices are also a much cleaner and simpler solution than the "electric-eye," which has been in use in public facilities for many years. Another effective approach to this problem is illustrated in Figure 46. In this instance the flushing mechanism is activated by the pressure bar extending horizontally across the face of the tank, an arrangement that permits operation by leaning back or hitting the bar with an elbow from a seated position or with a hand from a standing position if desired. This approach is particularly well suited for use by the elderly and by the disabled.

When the fixture is also equipped with built-in washing and drying functions, odor control devices, etc., the same criteria should apply: that the controls be easily accessible from the posture of primary use, that they be easy to identify and distinguish one from another, and that their operation be apparent.

Soilability and Cleanability Although cleaning is not strictly speaking a personal hygiene activity, it is, nevertheless, an aspect that must be taken into account in the design of any fixture. This is particularly true of the water closet since it and its immediate surroundings have long presented an aggravated and especially disagreeable cleaning problem, both in and out of the home.[6] Not only is the water closet more readily

46 / CURRENT APPROACH TO A BIDET/WATER CLOSET

"ATLANTIC"BIDET/WATER CLOSET:
CLOSOMAT, ZURICH, SWITZERLAND

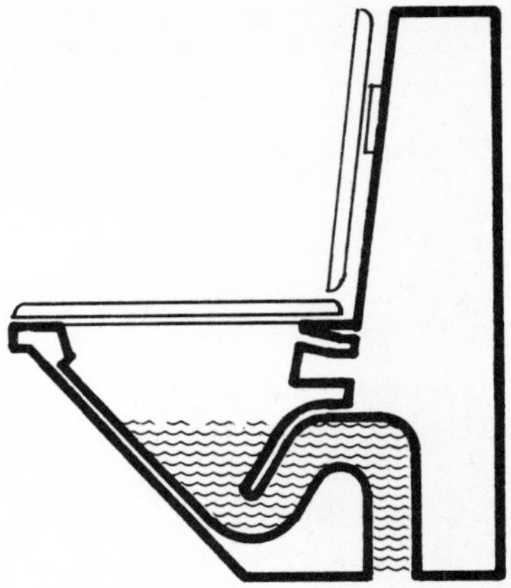

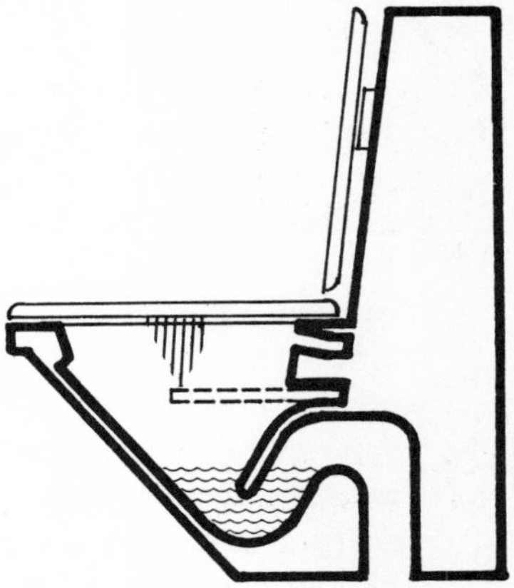

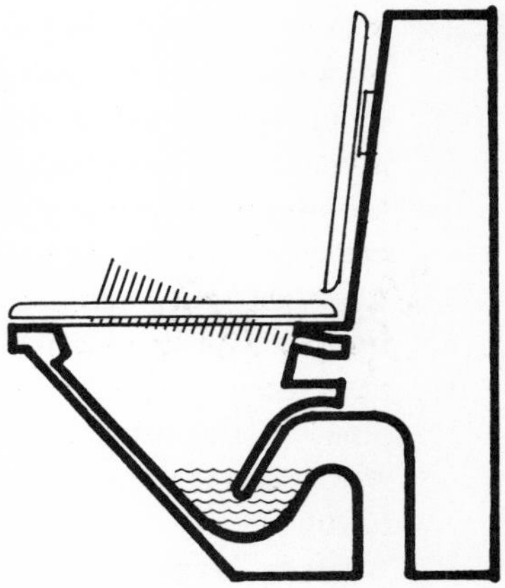

soiled than most other fixtures, but its overall design and configuration also commonly make cleaning needlessly difficult. In addition, the particular nature of that soiling is such as to provoke in many people a strong psychological revulsion.

While there are a number of common soiling agents—urine, feces, vomit, spittle, blood, etc., as well as water deposits and precipitates—the single biggest problem is probably that of standing male urination. As we shall examine in more detail in the next section, such urination inevitably results in urine's being deposited on the rim of the closet, the seat, floor, and walls. If not cleaned frequently, such deposits produce an odor, attract dust, and can ultimately cause rotting or blistering of seats and adjacent nonceramic surfaces (see Figure 65). Insofar as this problem can be alleviated by the provision of a separate stand-up urinal or by specifically adapting the suggested high-rise water closet to accommodate such urination, an enormous improvement will have been made. The semi-squat closet suggested earlier is not intended to be employed in this fashion, for it would only aggravate the problems further. A separate urinal would be a necessity. As long as existing water closets are employed for urination, there is, unfortunately, little or nothing that can be done to improve the situation.

The soiling problem due to the adhesion of fecal matter or menstrual blood is, in most instances, a question of the design of the particular type of water closet. In most contemporary top-of-the-line syphonic-action water closets the standing pan water surface is sufficiently large to eliminate the problems of adhesion to a dry surface. With many older types of water closet, however, such fecal adhesion is a common problem. This is most pronounced in the case of the flat-pan wash-out closets still favored in many parts of Europe, where the fecal matter is deposited onto a barely wet shallow ledge, ostensibly so that the feces may be examined before flushing (see Figure 47). With such closets, fecal adhesion is virtually guaranteed, a fact that is recognized in that every such closet is inevitably accompanied by a scrub brush or "Johnny Mop." Even the fixture manufacturers

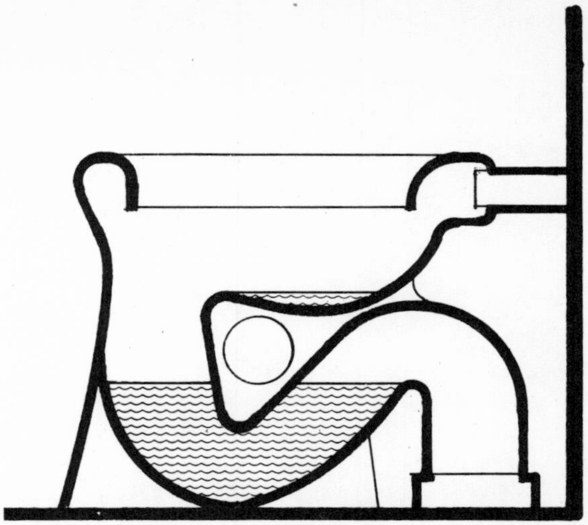

47 / CROSS-SECTION THROUGH TYPICAL EUROPEAN FLAT-PAN WASHOUT WATER CLOSET

recognize this, since many of them manufacture matching ceramic brush holders! Even if one accepts the desirability of such examination, the examination is essentially visual and can just as well be accomplished with a syphonic closet without the eternal necessity to scrub the fixture after every use. The flat-pan type of closet was originally designed for hospital use, for the collection of uncontaminated fecal samples—a use to which it is still put in many hospitals around the world. As a home fixture, however, it remains an unsightly, if not unsanitary, anachronism. Perhaps the strangest view of functional design is to be found in parts of Latin America and Spain where an unfortunate combination of coarse, heavy toilet paper and water closets with traps too small to pass the paper has resulted in the rather unpleasant institution of the waste basket next to the water closet into which the used paper is put. This is not simply a rural phenomenon but is also common in the cities and can be found in hotels and public toilets.

The most common, and inescapable, soiling arises from the water's leaving behind various

48 / CURRENT APPROACH TO MODULAR FIXTURE DESIGN

"MERIDIAN ONE" FIXTURES:
ADAMSEZ, LTD., NEWCASTLE-UPON-TYNE, ENGLAND

organic and inorganic deposits and precipitates. Depending upon the relative hardness of the water and whether or not it has been treated in a municipal treatment plant, the precise composition of these deposits will vary rather substantially, hard water resulting in the greatest proportion of inorganic scale build-up. In addition, many of the compounds in the water react chemically with the urea in the urine and produce ideal conditions for bacterial growth. This is particularly true in areas such as the underside of the rim, which retains splashed urine, is alternately wet and dry, and is rarely cleaned. Allowing urine to stand in the bowl in order to conserve water, as is sometimes done, accelerates bacterial growth, which in turn provides more base for the adhesion of inorganic solids. There appears to be little that can be done in these respects except to clean the fixture regularly, preferably with a cleaning product formulated for the purpose.

From a design standpoint, however, there is a good deal that can be done to improve the cleanability of fixtures as far as configuration and accessibility are concerned. Placement of the fixture can also be important since often a fixture that appeared easily cleanable in isolation proves virtually impossible to clean after installation because of inaccessible spaces in and around the fixture.

Perhaps the most important criteria are the simplicity of the shape and the simplicity of the joints the fixture makes with the wall and the floor. In this respect, the wall-hung fixture possesses the one considerable advantage of eliminating the most bothersome juncture. Its use is, however, limited by the additional costs involved in providing the special mounting arrangements necessary. One of the simplest, most direct, and effective approaches to this problem is illustrated in Figure 48, where the base and back of every fixture is straight-sided and modular with respect to common tile dimensions; this permits the fixtures to become integral with the wall and floor surfaces instead of being applied to the surface as is commonly done. A further refinement of this approach would be to provide a cove at these junctures so that the finished joint is rounded and the surfaces flow smoothly together.

49 / TYPICAL DIFFICULT-TO-CLEAN EUROPEAN MODEL OF WATER CLOSET

Probably the worst configurations as far as cleaning is concerned are those found in the inexpensive European water closets that resemble Rube Goldberg contraptions where every turn of the trap is left exposed (see Figure 49). The complexity of these shapes renders them virtually impossible to clean properly. Such fixtures are actually no more complex than others; the problem is that the enclosing shroud normally used has been omitted, presumably for cost reasons, leaving the functioning parts exposed. While this may raise, in the minds of some, the aesthetic arguments about form following function, it can

50 / POSSIBLE APPROACH TO A SEMI-SQUAT WATER CLOSET

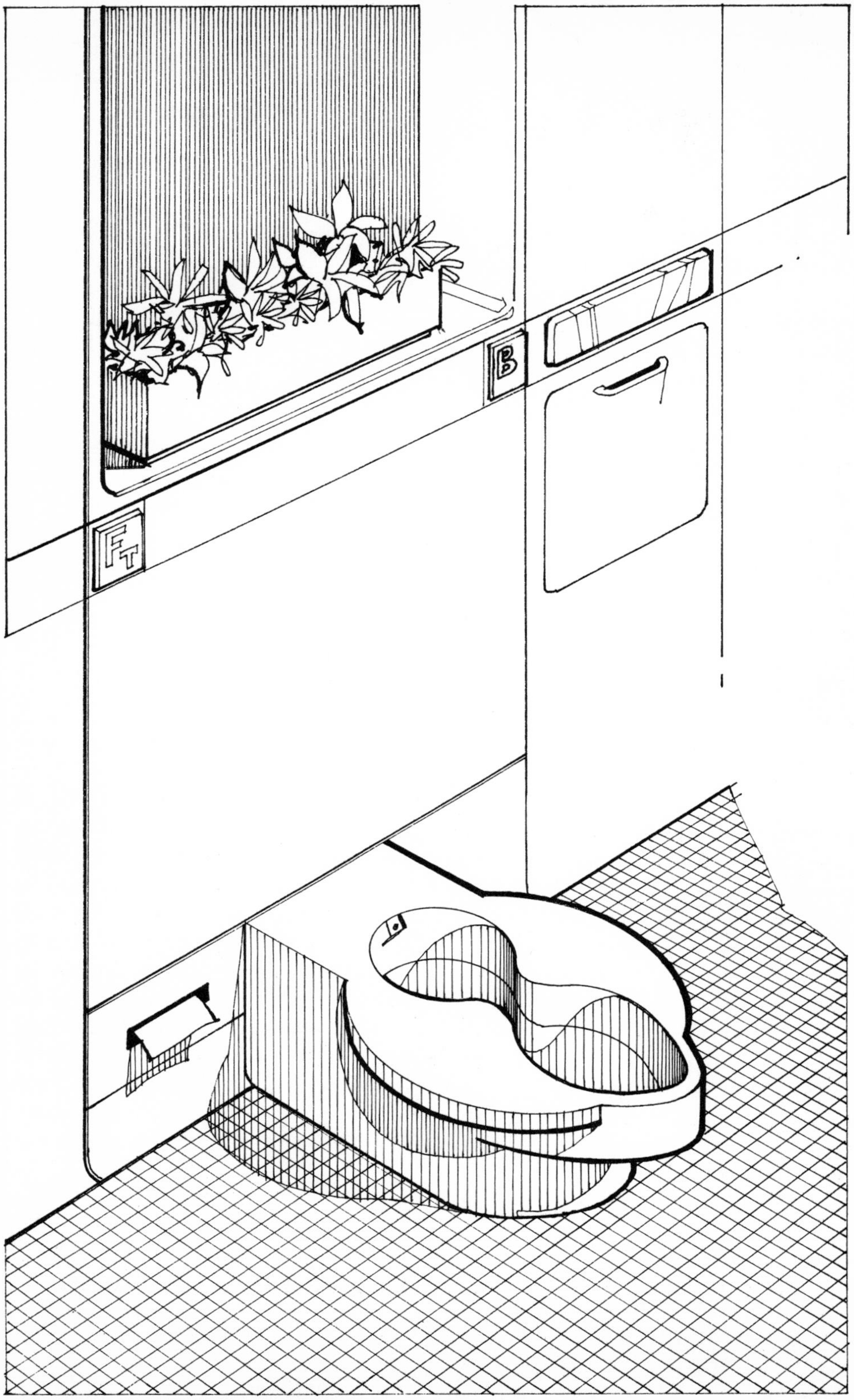
B
FT

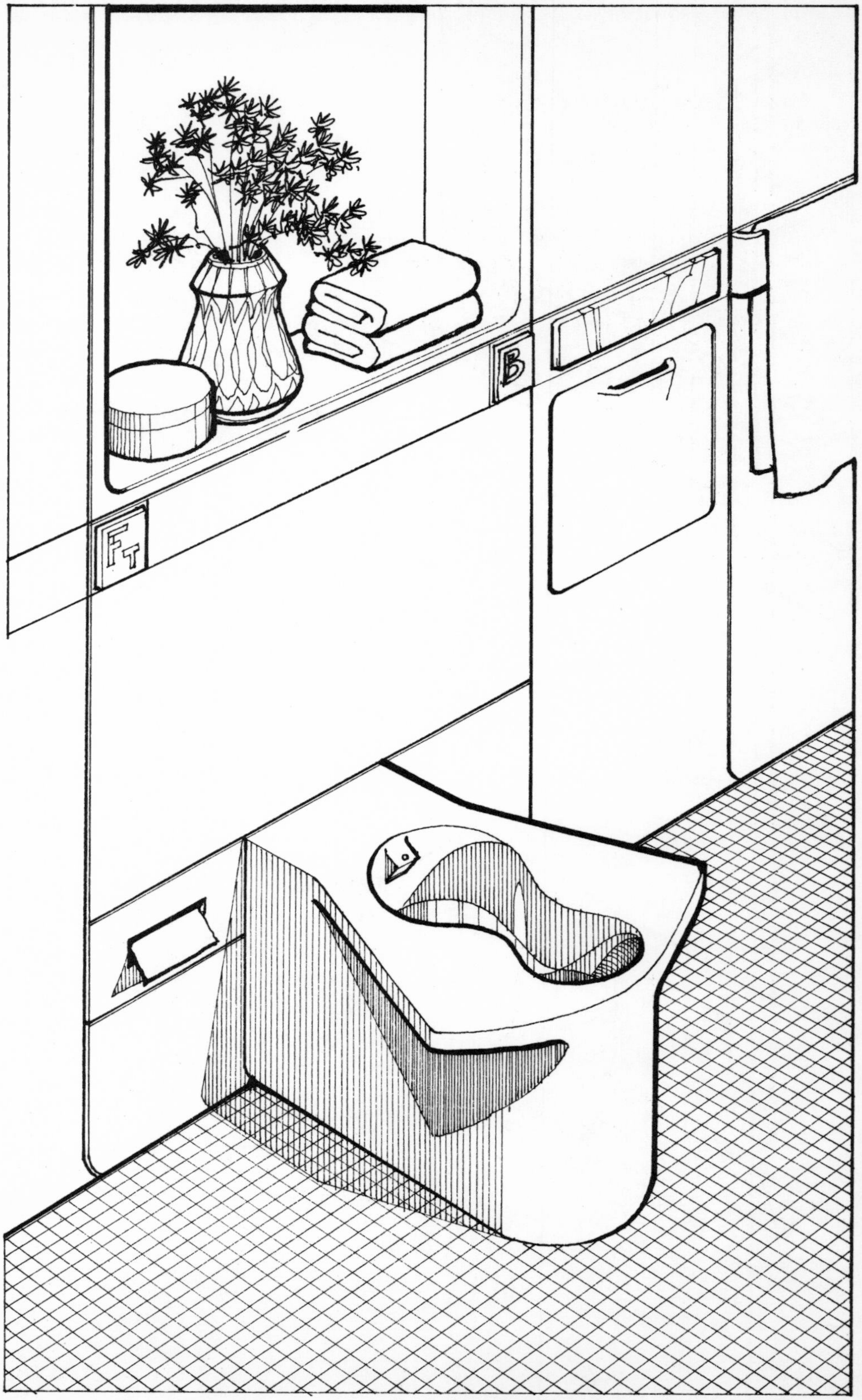

be argued that cleanability is also a function and, in the minds of many housewives, is equally important.

Similar difficulties are also commonly encountered with toilet seats and lids, particularly with the hinging and mounting mechanisms, which are often complex and provided with clearances so small that many parts are essentially unreachable. While there are many approaches to simplifying these mechanisms, the most foolproof is, of course, to eliminate the seat entirely.

51 / POSSIBLE APPROACH TO A HIGH-RISE WATER CLOSET

Summary — Design Considerations From a functional viewpoint, any fixture designed to accommodate defecation should observe the following criteria: encourage and permit the comfortable assumption of a squat-like posture; provide appropriate and adequate support; have an opening adequate to permit hand access to the anogenital region; incorporate provisions for anogenital cleansing; have functional, easily accessible controls from both a seated and standing position; minimize soiling problems and permit ready cleaning; and be conceived of as a part of a comprehensive modular system of personal hygiene facilities.

(Several possible approaches described earlier are illustrated in Figures 50 and 51.)

ANATOMY AND PHYSIOLOGY OF URINATION

11

THE PROCESS OF URINATION

Urination, or micturition, is the process of excreting from the body the waste fluids produced by the kidneys. The kidney is a highly discriminating organ that processes the body's supply of blood and eliminates varying amounts of waste substances according to the body's needs. The urine, which is the final excretory product, is a composite not only of waste products that may have been in the blood but also of foreign substances and the excess products of the metabolic processes. Because the kidneys function to maintain the constancy of the body's internal environment, the composition of urine may vary considerably from one discharge to another. The quantity of urine produced over a 24-hour period varies directly with the amount of fluid intake but generally averages between 1,000 and 1,400 cc. Normal urine has an amber color and a very faint odor unless allowed to stand at room temperature for any length of time. As the urine is produced, it is carried through the ureters, or ducts, to the bladder, where it accumulates until discharged from the body through the urethral openings.

Inasmuch as body posture has an effect on blood circulation, it can also affect urine composition and volume. The effect is not, however, significant unless there is considerable change or considerable stress from one posture, and there is no evidence to suggest that posture has any appreciable bearing on the act of urination itself, either in terms of comfort or of facilitating or hindering the process as in the case of defecation.[1]

Although the process of toilet training with respect to urination does not appear to be as complex and fraught with psychological overtones as defecation, it does, nevertheless, demand a similar period of training and require a similar degree of neuromuscular differentiation and control. The development of voluntary bladder control is generally not achieved until the age of 18 to 30 months. Usually nighttime control takes longer. Full control and the ability to void without any assistance is usually not achieved until well into the third or fourth year. Because of the differences in the positioning of the bladder, males generally have a greater difficulty in developing proper control since the anal and urethral sphincters are so close together as to require a particularly fine neuromuscular differentiation.[2] In the female the two sphincters are separated by the vagina, and while this simplifies the problem of learning to control each of the sphincters separately, the relation of the vagina to the bladder and the urethral sphincter often results in a sympathetic stimulation leading to a desire to urinate. This is particularly true during the later months of pregnancy when the ever-increasing pressure on the bladder results in more and more frequent urges to urinate. It may also be caused by vaginal stimulation prior to, or during, intercourse, especially if the bladder is at all full.

The urge to urinate frequently is also very common among the aged. Largely this is due to an atrophying of the kidneys and bladder and a weakening of the sphincter muscles. Another fairly common problem among the aged is incontinence, particularly among patients with prostate problems. This gradual degeneration of body functions may be regarded in some respects as a reversal of the initial developmental processes as, for example, in the loss of neuromuscular controls, which in many instances causes old men to be as inept in urination as small boys.

ANATOMICAL DIFFERENCES

Anatomical differences between the male and female result in differences between the sexes in certain aspects of the urination process. Aside from the problem of developing controls, the most significant and obvious difference is in the location and nature of the actual urethral openings from which the urine is discharged. In the female, the urethra is located just in front of the vagina, within the labial folds, and well inside the body envelope. As a consequence, for all practical purposes, she has little control over the direction of the urine stream in the customarily assumed sitting posture. In a standing position, however, a fair degree of control is possible by projecting the pelvis forward or backward (see Figure 52). In an erect standing posture the stream falls only slightly forward of the vertical axis, approximately 75 to 100 mm (3 to 4 inches), still within the body envelope. In the common "hovering" posture, the pelvis is tilted so that the axis of the urethra is projected backward and, depending on the fullness of the bladder and the tilt of the pelvis, the stream can be projected as much as 610 mm (24 inches) to the rear of the vertical axis. Similarly, by leaning backwards (in the sort of posture assumed when one is dancing the "limbo") the pelvis is tilted forward, and it is possible to project the stream considerable distances, particularly if the labial folds are held apart.[3] The labia restrict and diffuse the urine stream so that, in the extreme, it can assume an erratic, flat sheet-like or fan shape, particularly in females who have had considerable sexual experience and who have borne children, since this tends to result in a coarsening and distortion of the labial tissues. This is especially true in cases of difficult childbirth or when an episiotomy, or surgical enlargement of the vulva, has been performed prior to or during childbirth. One test of virginity in the past rested on the ability of a virgin to produce a narrow, clearly defined stream similar to a male's.

> When I began to run with the boys, I could piss through a fine gold ring.
> But now if you give me a washtub, I scarce can hit the doggone thing.[4]

As we observed earlier, this little remarked aspect of female urination formed the basis for the urinating contests among schoolgirls.

Further unpredictable distortions of the urine stream can be caused by temporary dermal adhesions of the labia resulting from vaginal secretions, semen, and so on. In both sexes, predictability and accuracy are equally difficult to achieve, if for no other reason than the tendency to attempt to empty the bladder deliberately and forcefully near the end. Each such voluntary explusive movement

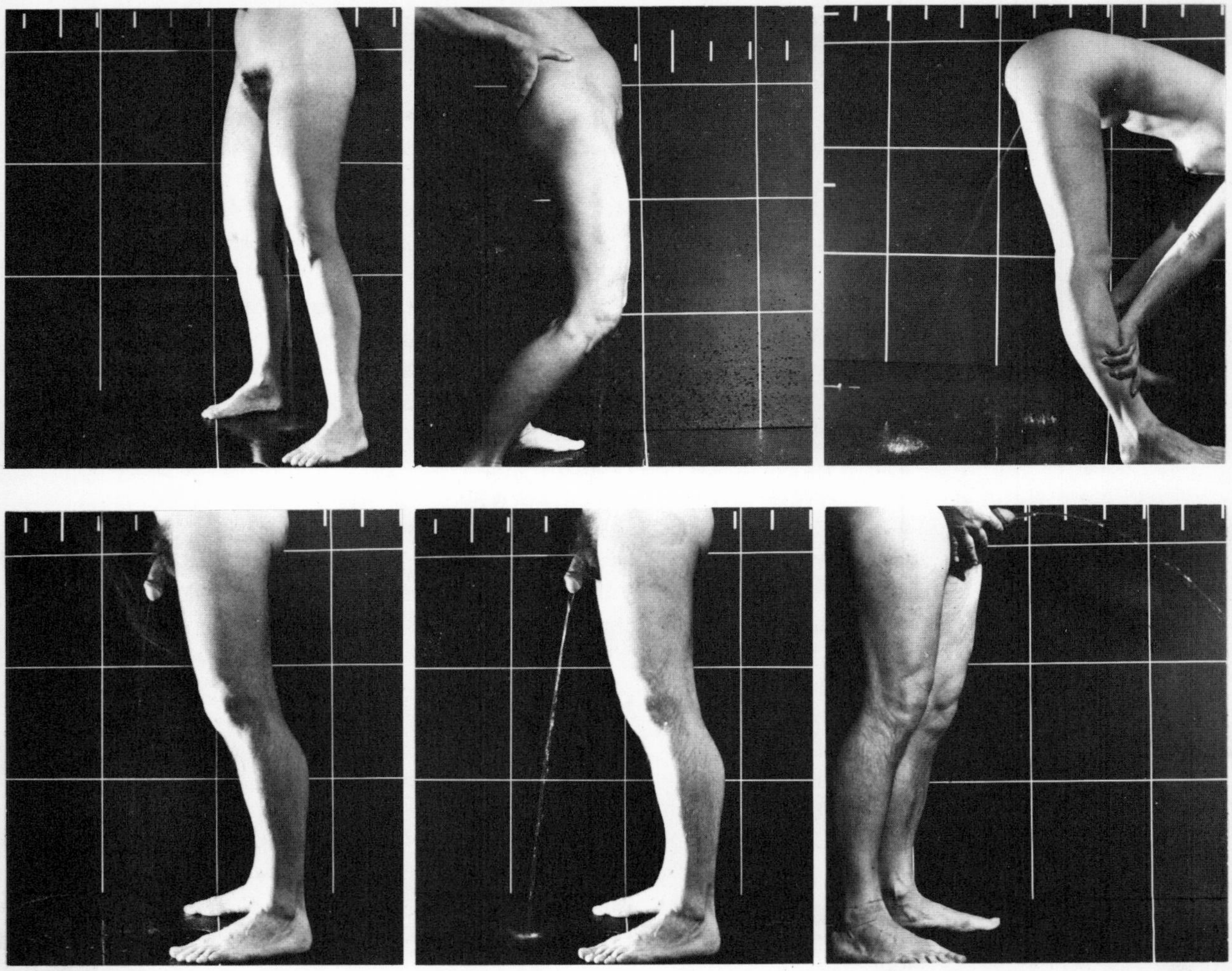

52 / COMPARATIVE MALE AND FEMALE URINATION POSTURES

results in short bursts of urine that are unpredictable as to distance.

In the male, the urethral opening is located in the penis and thus lies outside the body envelope, permitting approximate control of the urine stream within the entire volume circumscribed by its possible trajectory. This control (and trajectory) is, however, achieved only by manual manipulation of the penis. In point of fact, as illustrated in Figure 52, a flaccid adult penis undirected or, more accurately, unheld will not project a stream any farther from the vertical axis of the point of origin than the distance achieved by a standing female. An erect penis will not readily permit urination, because the engorgement closes off the ureters. In small boys, however, the situation is different, for the penis of an infant assumes almost a horizontal attitude with the familiar and inevitable result that he pees straight out between the seat and the bowl when seated on a water closet or pees on the seat or lid when held up. Having been forced by the circumstances of their clothing, however, to handle the penis, men then most commonly continue to do so throughout the procedure. This facet of men's urinary behavior is by now so familiar that we overlook its significance with respect to the apparent differences in the behavior and capabilities of the sexes:

> A man and wife have a urination contest. They draw a line on the ground, and the husband prepares confidently to win. "Uh uh, dear," says the wife, shaking her head; "No hands!"[5]

DESIGN CRITERIA FOR URINATION

12

DESCRIPTION OF ACTIVITY

Female Urination While it is physiologically perfectly possible for females to urinate in a standing position, the nearly universal custom in Western societies is for them to do so from a sitting (or hovering) position. Furthermore, the standing position requires considerable effort if one is not to soil oneself, but perhaps the most important restriction is that posed by our clothing. Contemporary undergarments are problem enough with regard to a sitting position, but one would be forced to disrobe completely in order to urinate in a standing position. While in the not too distant past, girdles and so on were worn mostly by women who obviously needed them and, even then, usually only on special occasions, the pattern today is for some form of restrictive undergarment, or combination garment such as panty hose, to be worn almost universally, even by some teenagers.

Insofar as we are considering this activity in the context of the home, there appears to be little difficulty with the current practice and little reason to suggest any substantial changes. Public facilities and their attendant practices are another matter entirely and will be dealt with in the section on public facilities, for it is here that the age-old unsanitary conditions and the reluctance to sit pose major problems. Accordingly, the rest of this discussion will focus on male urination, which is almost overwhelmingly accomplished from a standing position, even in the home, and which poses substantial sanitary problems.

Male Urination While, from a purely physiological viewpoint, males can urinate equally well from either a standing or sitting position, the restrictive effects of clothing, not to mention the psychological problems involved, as well as the convenience, have caused men to favor the standing position almost universally. In general, men will urinate in a sitting/squatting position only when this activity takes place in conjunction with defecation and they have already assumed a sitting position.

Because of the male's anatomy and his early-learned ability to control the trajectory of the urine stream, there is, in some respects, relatively little problem with any substantial self-soiling in a standing position. The major exception, of course, is the problem: "no matter how you shake and dance, the last few drops go down your pants," or on the floor, walls, and elsewhere. The qualification depends upon the nature of the facilities available. That there are serious soiling problems associated with current home facilities may be attested to by any housewife or cleaning woman. The soiled fixtures and soiled, discolored, and rotted floors and walls, with which everyone is familiar, result from the male's use of the water closet, which is completely inadequate for this purpose, instead of a separate urinal. The key to these problems lies in understanding the particular characteristics of the male urine stream.

Urine passing through the slit-like urethral opening is emitted in the form of a thin sheet that twists and spirals for approximately 100 to 150 mm (4 to 6 inches) and then disintegrates into a centrifugal spray (see Figures 53 and 54). Both the point of disintegration and the maximum diameter of the spray are directly proportional to the velocity of the stream, that is, the bladder pressure. A low velocity produces an increment (each twist in the integrated phase of the stream) of approximately 9.5 mm (3/8 inch); an "extreme" velocity, an increment of almost 50 mm (2 inches). "Normal" velocity produces an increment of approximately 25 mm (1 inch). In every instance, however, the centrifugal action causes the stream to disintegrate and assume a roughly conical shape. This dispersion is responsible for a substantial share of the soiling both of the self and of the surroundings that inevitably occurs when one is urinating from a standing position—and when the receiving container is not as close as in a wall-hung urinal, which intercepts the stream before the point of dispersion.

Another aspect that must be considered is the inability of the male to predict or position accurately the initial point of impact of the urine stream. Although the degree of accuracy is reasonable in most instances, there are a sufficient number of "accidents," or gross distortions, attributable generally to temporary and unnoticed dermal adhesions of the urethral opening, that can result in an immediate and wildly erratic stream behavior such as missing the container entirely or urinating on one's shoes, and so forth. Once the activity has begun, however, most adult males can, by a process of successive corrective maneuvers, exercise fairly accurate control thereafter. The notable exceptions are the ill and intoxicated, the very young, or the very old and infirm.

The normal water closet presents, however, a relatively poor target, particularly because of the psychological resistances involved in its use. Because of the general taboos on the elimination processes and the particular aversions to being directly and actively aware of elimination's taking place, most men will try to avoid urinating into the standing pan water—the easiest and most natural target—in order to avoid the embarrassment of being heard, since the noise, particularly with a full bladder, can be considerable and easily identified. Some, however, hold that "Real Men" always urinate into the water for the maximum effect and maintain that only those men who are uncertain of making enough noise try to be as quiet as possible so as to hide their masculine shortcomings—all in all, a curious equation of bladder fullness with masculinity.

> Two drunken Russians are urinating out-of-doors one cold winter night. Petrov, swaying, says to his companion, "Tell me, Ivan Ivanovich, why is it that when I piss it is like the snow falling silently on the white breast of Mother Russia, while when you piss it sounds like the roar of our mighty river Volga?" "Because, Comrade Petrov, you are pissing on my fur coat."

Once the decision to avoid the water is made, the choice of target areas is limited to the sides and front and back walls of the bowl. In most water closets the bowl configurations are such that these areas are small and difficult to hit with any degree of accuracy. Because of the necessity to stand up close to the front of the bowl to catch the dribble at the end of the action, the possibilities are further limited to the sides and back. Since, however, the back wall in most cases is vertical or nearly vertical, the target area presented is small and is useful for only a brief period since the length of the stream trajectory continuously varies. This leaves only the side walls as a feasible elongated target. Since this area rarely exceeds 50 mm (2 inches) by 180 to 205 mm (7 to 8 inches), it becomes obvious that not only is the proper trial-and-error maneuvering difficult to accomplish successfully, but also half of the cone of the urine stream inevitably falls on or outside the bowl, no matter how careful and accurate one may be in the process of continuously repositioning the stream. Jiggling the penis after urination results, of course, in more urine droplets going astray—onto the rim, the seat, the floor, and one's clothing.

Still another problem that arises in the use of the water closet is the back splash resulting when the urine stream hits a hard surface. While this is a potential problem with any container, it poses particular difficulties with the water closet since this fixture has obviously been primarily designed to accommodate defecation, and urination has, as it were, been left to be a hit-or-miss affair. Any stream of relatively nonviscous liquid hitting a hard surface (including a body of liquid) will result in a considerable splash. The direction and extent of this rebound, or splash, is determined not only by the force with which the stream strikes the surface but also, and more importantly, by the configuration of the surface and the angle at which the stream hits it. Proper manipulation of this latter factor can appreciably reduce the quantity of splash and can control its direction. Perhaps the worst problem is posed by the use of the old-fashioned flat-pan wash-out closet so much in

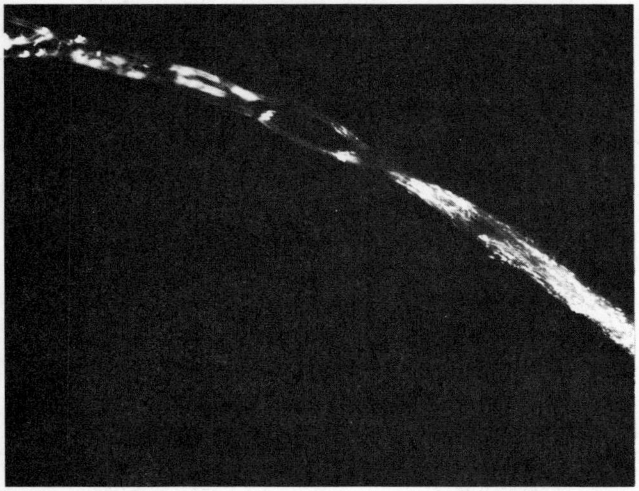

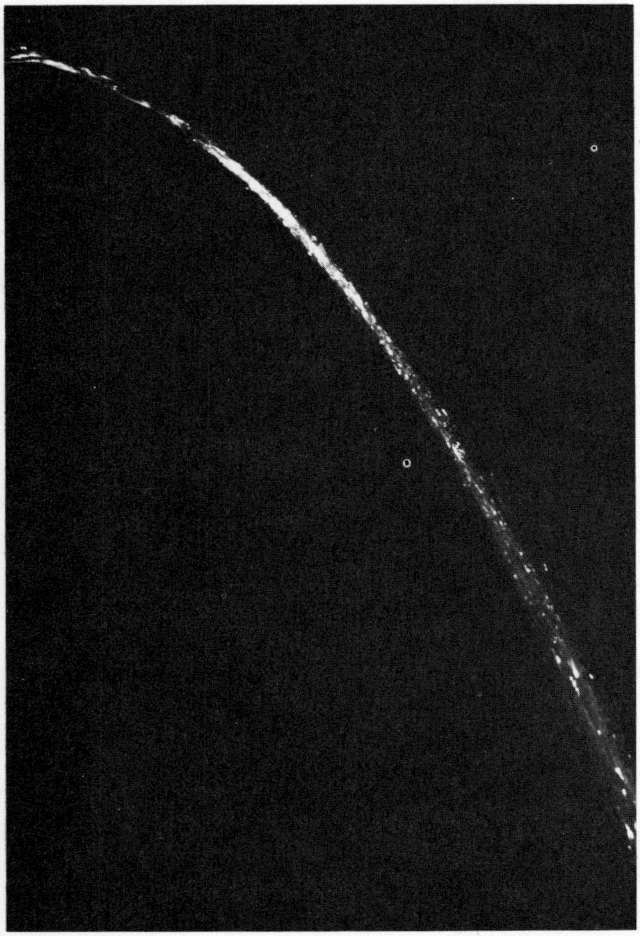

53 / STREAM DISPERSION
CHARACTERISTICS OF MALE URINE STREAM

favor still in many parts of Europe. Aside from its unhygienic aspects as far as defecation is concerned, it is undoubtedly the poorest urinal of any water closet still on the market. Because of its configuration (see Figure 47), the only comfortable or feasible target is the horizontal shelf, which generally holds 10 to 20 mm (⅜ to ¾ inch) of pan water. A urine stream striking this ledge results in the maximum possible back splash.

Table 2 and Figure 55 indicate the extent of back splash resulting from various combinations of stream velocity and intercepting surface angles. In every instance, the full extent of the spray could be measured within a 30-second period, the assumed average time of urination. Perhaps the most common duration is from 15 to 20 seconds, though the range can extend all the way from 10 seconds up to a minute and a half, or in extreme cases even longer, depending upon a given individual's bladder capacity and habituation. Graus cites 45 seconds as the average time in military situations.[1] This figure appears to be high and is undoubtedly due to the lack of opportunities for urination available in such circumstances. In the home situation a shorter duration tends to be more common. These dispersion figures are for a controlled steady-state simulated stream and can vary from one extreme to the other, depending on the particular circumstances.

Size and Shape of Container The particular combination of size and shape may vary over a considerable range so long as certain criteria are met.

When we consider that the stream assumes the form of a warped conical solid with a shifting base (see Figure 54), it is obvious that the size and shape of the necessary container or enclosure are directly related to its distance from the point of origin in order to contain the stream completely. The closer the container is to the point of origin the more compact it can be and the less danger of

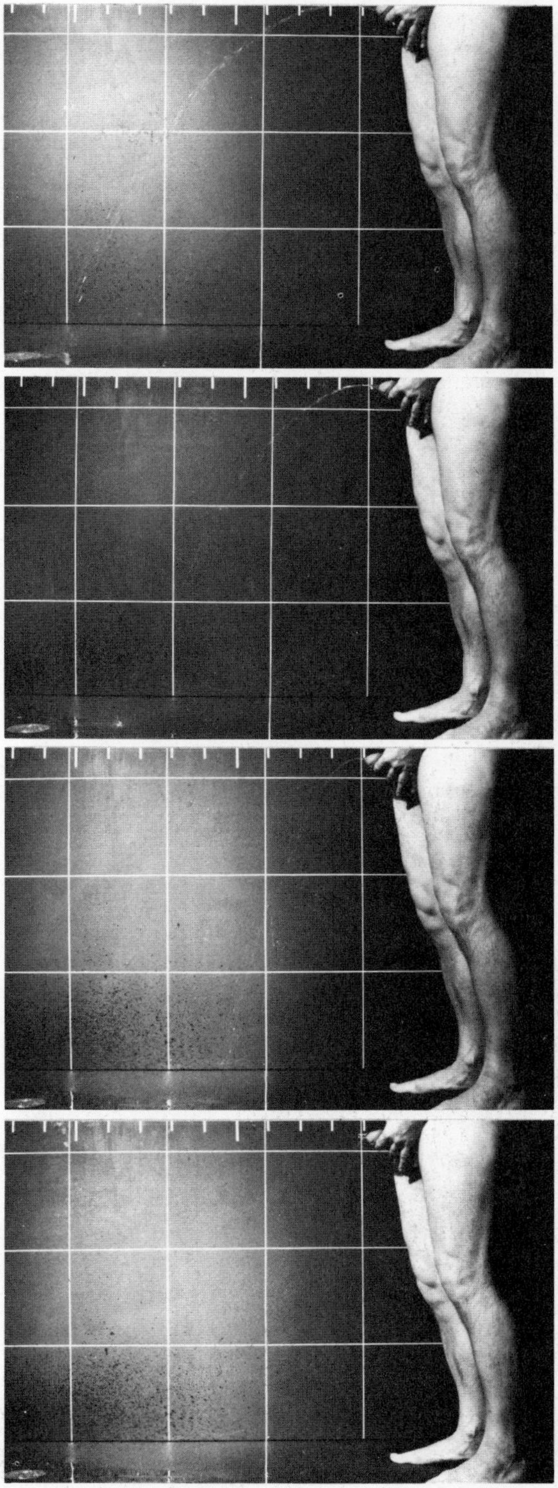

54 / CHARACTERISTICS OF MALE URINE STREAM

accidental soiling. In view of the range of heights of adult males, the front lip of the container should be set at a minimum height of 610 mm (24 inches) from the floor, the height at which regular wall-hung urinals are commonly set. At this height, the container needs to have a minimum opening dimension approximately 205 by 205 mm (8 by 8 inches).

The container must also be so shaped and positioned that it can be more or less straddled in order to catch the dribble and drip at the conclusion of urination, again in a fashion similar to existing wall-hung urinals.

In terms of shape, the most crucial point is that the contouring be such as to keep back splash to a minimum. To allow for variable bladder pressures or variable stream trajectories, the cross-section should be continuously variable so that a constant relationship can be maintained between the surface and the stream. As indicated in Figure 55, the smaller the angle between the stream and the impact surface the less the resulting splash. An angle of less than 30 degrees is desirable in both a lateral and a longitudinal direction. While a properly designed single-warped planar surface can keep splash within reasonable limits, it is preferable to warp both surfaces so as to approximate a dome or cone (see Figure 56). Such a form would result in a minimum of splash and would direct most of it forward. It is also critical that the axis of the container be set at an appropriate angle. In the course of normal urination the angle formed by a maximum trajectory rarely exceeds 60 degrees from the vertical (with the notable exception of small boys). Accordingly, the angle at which the container should be set lies in the 40- to 50-degree range. This is the "critical" range in the sense that maximum trajectory equals maximum pressure, which in turn equals maximum dispersion and splash. As the stream trajectory drops off into the 20- and 10-degree range, it begins to form a larger angle with surface, but the problems at this range are considerably less.

Experiments have also suggested that a single ridge placed in the longitudinal plane of the stream can assist in further reducing the problem of containment since it has the effect of dividing the stream and deflecting it laterally. As a result, it would be possible in some circumstances to provide a smaller container. A divider is likely to be

TABLE 2 / DISPERSION AND SPLASH CHARACTERISTICS OF A SIMULATED URINE STREAM AT VARIOUS PRESSURES

			Measurements at 229 mm		*Measurements at 406 mm*	
			Radius of:		Radius of:	
Length of Each Twist	Number of Twists	Total Length of Integrated Stream	Solid Spray	Furthest Spray	Solid Spray	Furthest Spray
10.2 mm	5	51 mm	13 mm	64 mm	13 mm	38 mm
15.2	5	76	13	83	19	44
20.3	5	102	13	89	13	51
25.4	5	127	19	95	19	64
30.5	5	152	19	102	25	64
38.1	4	152	19	102	32	76

Note: The point of origin was placed at a height of 735 mm (29 inches) to represent the average height for an adult male. The range, which includes 95 percent of the adult male population, is from 645 to 828 mm (25.4 to 32.6 inches).

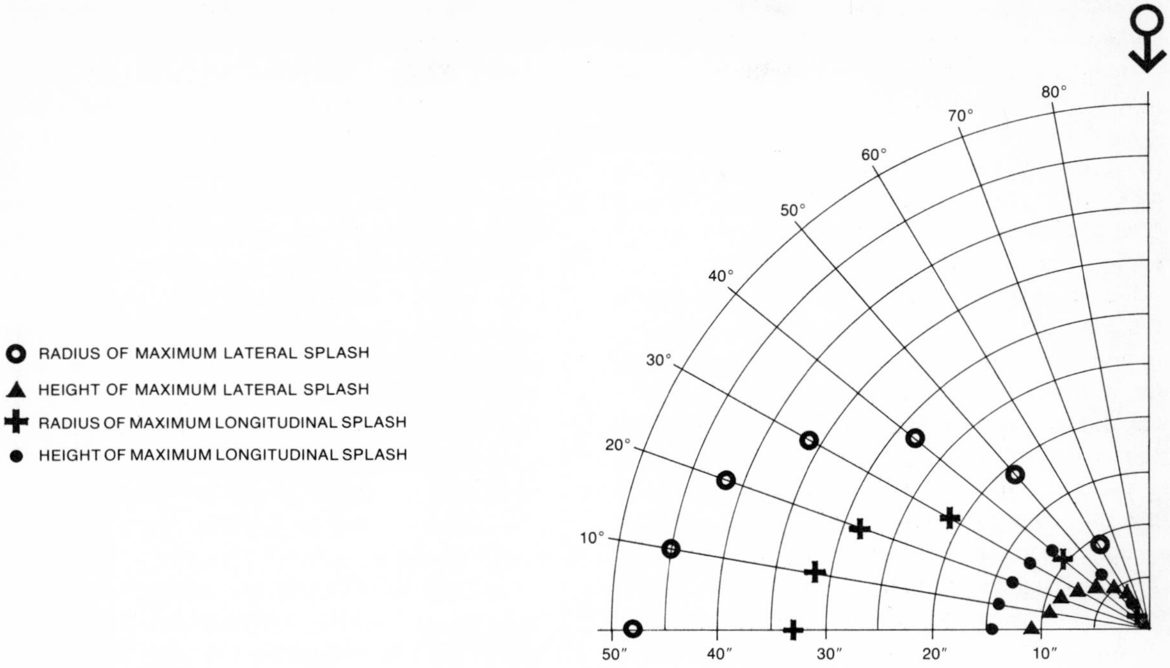

55 / VARIATIONS IN SPLASH EFFECTS ACCORDING TO ANGLES BETWEEN STREAM AND CONTACT SURFACE

56 / RELATIONSHIP BETWEEN STREAM AND CONTAINING SURFACES

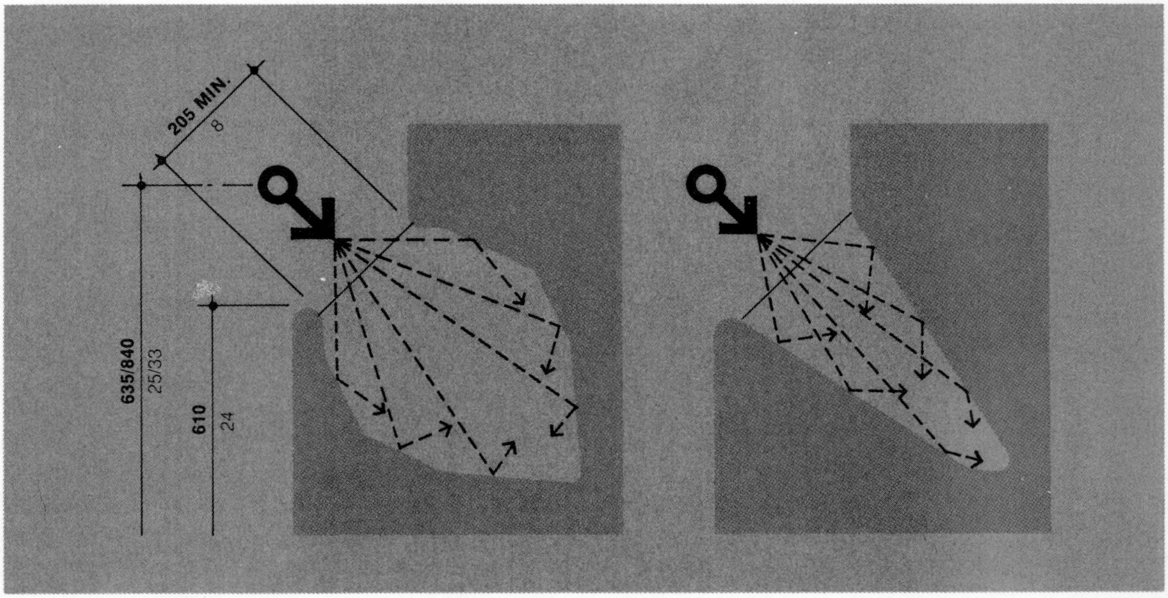

particularly useful in the area of greatest pressure impact. Many models of wall-hung urinals have, in fact, such a divider as a result of the trap's protruding into the bowl.

Another feature that may be desirable is something that would serve as a "target" in the critical area. This might conceivably be the ridge just described or possibly some very obvious marker set in the surface.

Insofar as the precise determination of a size for the container is concerned, this is again a function of both the shape of the container and its positioning and can be arrived at only after these other variables have been established within the limits set forth.

Avoidance of Noise The avoidance of a distinctive and clearly recognizable noise should be a major consideration in any design. Pan water such as exists in water closets is the most obvious thing to be avoided unless it is normally missed as in wall-hung urinals. It may well be that a dry container that is flushed is the best way to cope with this problem, since the noise of flushing, while it meets with some objections, is not nearly so embarrassing to most people as the direct noise of urination.[2] In the event that materials other than ceramics are used, attention should be paid to their denseness, or mass, in terms of "drumming" and generating sound.

Controls Since we are considering a fixture intended solely for stand-up use, the controls for flushing should be easily operated from a standing position. This can be accomplished by using a hand-operated control located 900 to 1,200 mm (approximately 36 to 48 inches) from the floor or by using a floor-recessed, foot-operated control similar to that suggested for the water closet. Or the flushing action might take place automatically as the urinal is closed and folded into the wall or by the use of a heat-sensing device that triggers the flushing action as soon as urination begins. A separate urinal with a separate flushing system could also save considerable water since the normal 20 liters (5 gallons) commonly used in flushing a water closet of solid wastes would not be necessary in this case.

Summary — Design Considerations In order to provide adequately for male urination in the home there are several possible approaches to be considered: provide a separate standard wall-hung urinal, design a new non-urinal-appearing urinal, modify the water closet so that it more adequately accommodates urination, and, finally, try to persuade men to sit when urinating.

From all practical and psychological viewpoints, this last possibility would seem to be totally unworkable. Aside from changing a natural and age-old habit, it is likely to meet with strong resistance, from the aspect of convenience, particularly since in recent years the male has become ever more accustomed to the speed and effortlessness of the urinal, which is now almost universal. The idea of having virtually to undress for an operation that is at present so simple would certainly meet with considerable opposition. There is also not much question but that it would encounter a great deal of psychological resistance since it would, in effect, deny the male the free use of his greatest glory ("the family jewels" in a particular American vernacular) and would "condemn" him to assume the position of a woman.

The first, and most obvious, approach of providing a standard wall-hung urinal would appear to solve most of the functional problems. Unfortunately, as we shall examine in detail in the section on public facilities, this is not always true, for there are many configurations of urinals currently in use that are equally as unfunctional from a sanitary viewpoint as the water closet. In any event, a standard urinal is not likely to meet with much acceptance because of the various psychological problems outlined earlier. In addition, it may be argued on practical grounds that such a fixture would entail too much extra space and expense even if the standard urinal were to be adapted for household tank-type operation. In view of these consid-

57 / POSSIBLE MODIFICATION OF HIGH-RISE WATER CLOSET TO ACCOMMODATE STANDING MALE URINATION

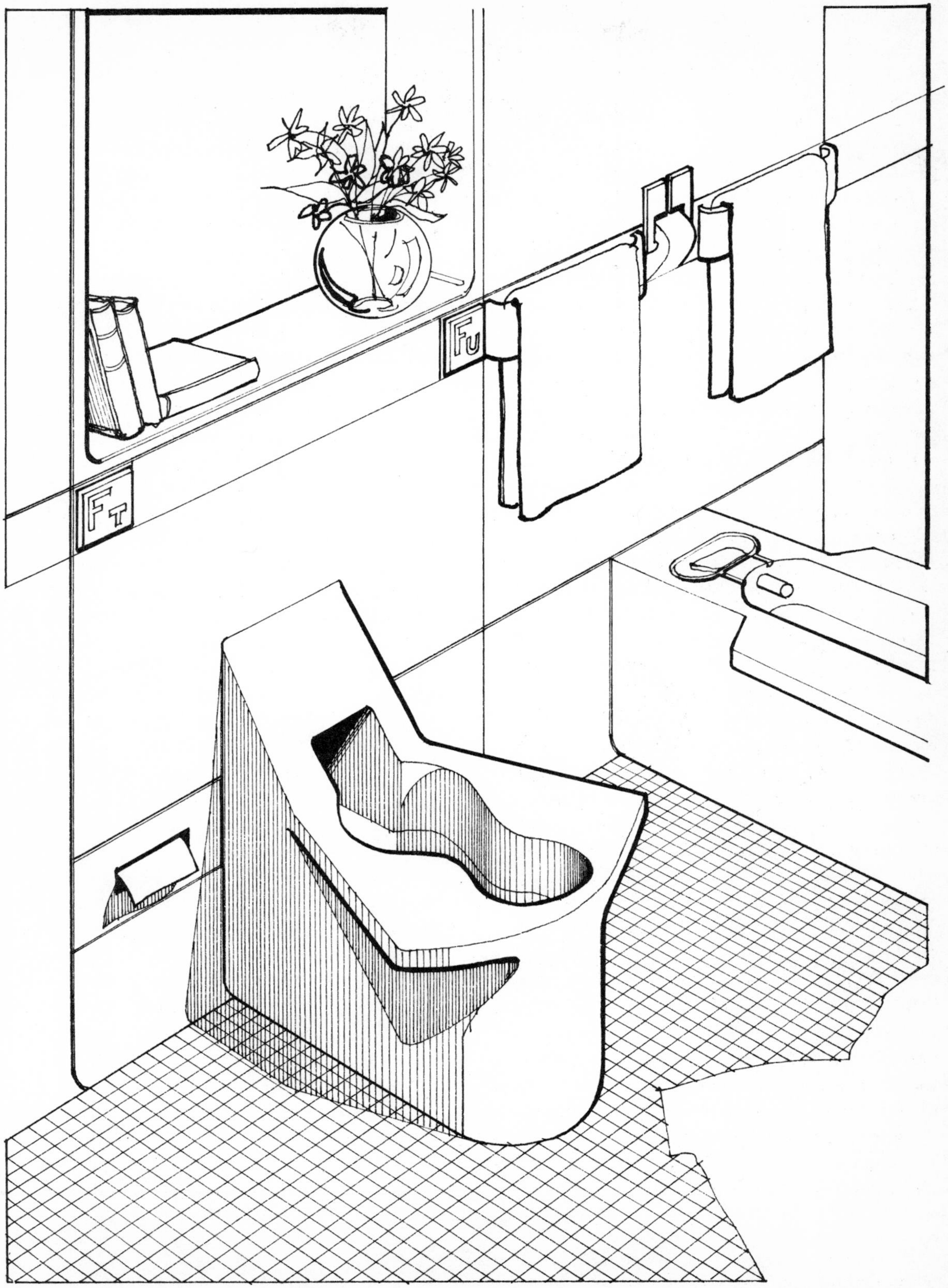
Fu
Ft

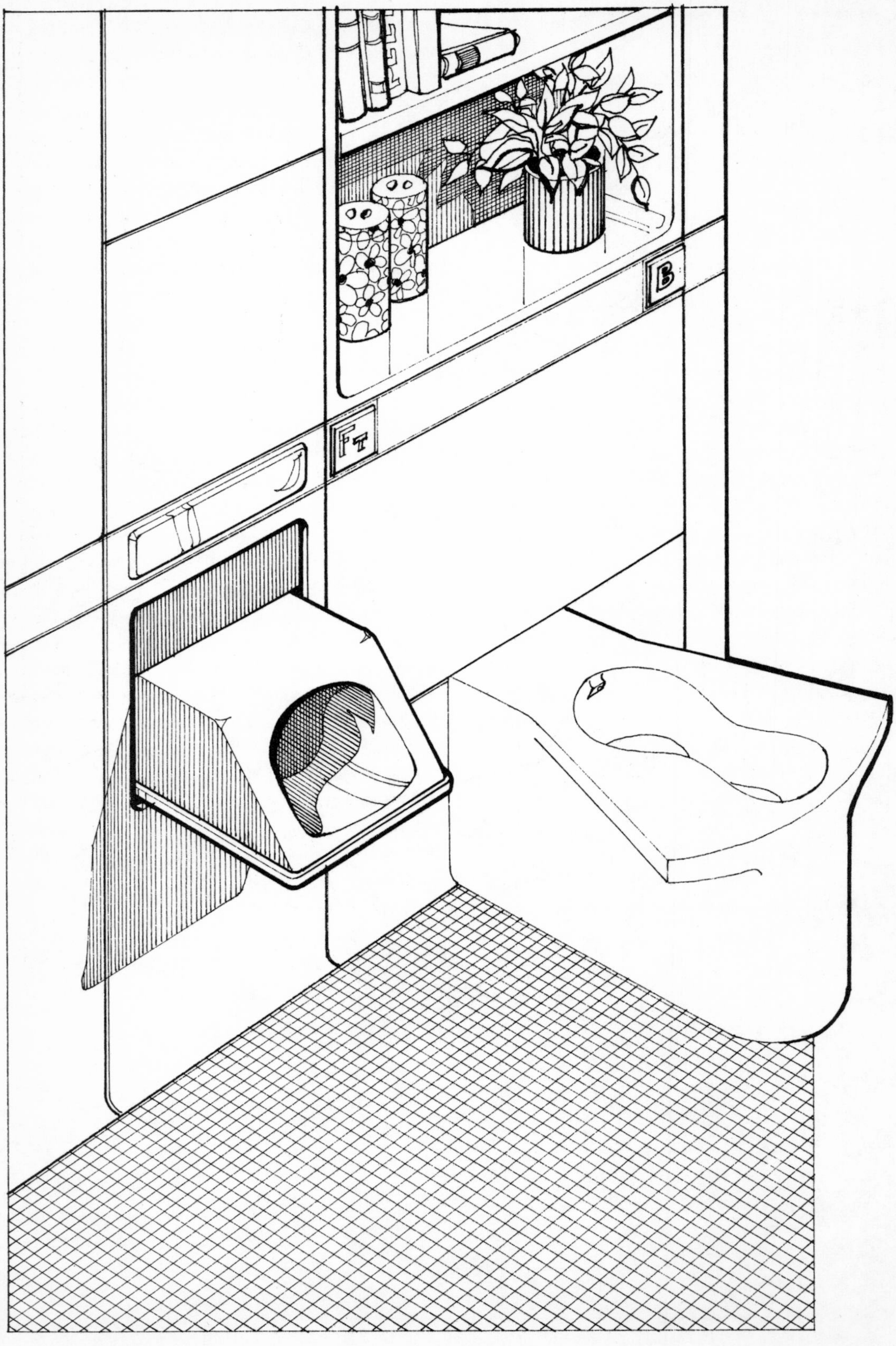
B
FT

erations, this remains a rather marginal possibility and solution to the problem.

Modification of a water closet offers the advantages of being familiar, relatively unobvious, and relatively inexpensive. The only such proposal that seems the least bit promising, however, is the modified conventional-height water closet described earlier (see Figure 51). By further modifying the contours of the back of the bowl, as illustrated in Figure 57, and by incorporating a valley on the center axis, it is possible to provide a natural and positive target area and a shape that serves better to contain the stream and minimize back splash. While not a perfect solution, it does, nevertheless, offer some significant improvements over any conventional closet in this respect. Raising the back even further improves its utility as a urinal, but the higher the back is raised the more difficulty it poses with respect to the arrangement of clothing, particularly in the case of seated females, who generally gather their outer garments up around their waist.

In this case it would also be preferable to eliminate the applied seat altogether in order to minimize cleaning problems or to use a minimal fixed seat pad. Our convention of using split open-front seats only on public water closets is completely backward. The biggest problem is in the home, where the water closet is *always* used for male urination and where, if the seat is not always raised—and it often is not—the front of the seat becomes soiled and rots. In public facilities, on the other hand, urinals are almost always provided, and the use of water closets for standing urination is far less common than it is in the home.

With the semi-squat water closet, described earlier, standing urination is wholly unsuitable and a separate urinal is necessary. Not only is the configuration unsuitable but also the distance from the point of origin to the container is even greater than with a conventional water closet, and this fact poses even more problems of proper containment.

In regard to the design of a home urinal, the most promising approach would appear to be one in which the fixture disappeared and was as innocuous as possible when not actually in use. As illustrated in Figure 58, this might be accomplished by a unit that folds up into a wall module. As conceived here, the urinal would be similar to the fold-up Pullman lavatories used many years ago in railway compartments. In a modular system such a unit could also be located over the water closet or the bidet or be treated as a separate unit.

An incidental but important safety feature is the provision of a night light, since the majority of people who get up in the middle of the night to urinate do not turn on the light, in order not to be fully wakened. According to the old story, of the people who get up in the middle of the night, 22 per cent raid the icebox for something to eat, 53 per cent get up to urinate, and the rest get up to go home.

58 / POSSIBLE APPROACH
TO A FOLD-UP URINAL

OTHER BATHROOM ACTIVITIES

13

Although the design of the bathroom and its equipment must be based primarily on the requirements posed by the major personal hygiene activities, that is, body cleansing and elimination, the solutions must also take into account the wide range of other activities commonly performed in the bathroom. Some of these, such as grooming and oral hygiene, are directly related to, and often performed in conjunction with, the basic hygiene activities and may be regarded as legitimately belonging here. Some, such as exercising and using a sun lamp, are a matter of personal preference. Conversely, there is a vast array of truly miscellaneous activities—activities having nothing to do with personal hygiene—that frequently, if not invariably, occur in the bathroom, primarily because of the facilities and opportunities available here. Activities such as keeping pets in the bathroom and using the bathroom as a photographic darkroom, for example, are based on the availability of water, mar-proof finishes, and other features. By the same token, the bathroom generally serves as the "first aid station" and the "sickroom," where one goes if ill or injured for specialized elimination, cleansing, and treatment. The "off-limits" character of the bathroom causes it, moreover, to be used for a variety of purely personal and psychological needs—masturbation, reading, and crying.

Whereas the bathroom and its facilities have been adopted for such extraneous uses, it does not mean that they should all necessarily be encouraged, but it does suggest that they should at least be recognized and, in the broader context of the home environment, accommodated somewhere.

MISCELLANEOUS HYGIENE AND GROOMING ACTIVITIES

All of these activities are concerned with the care of the body and have common requirements for privacy, for nudity of varying degrees, and for facilities such as a mirror, a source of water, storage space, and a means of disposing of wastes. While these requirements are not nearly as stringent as they are for the basic activities, they do present a variety of minor problems that must receive consideration in terms of overall design and location of facilities.

These activities may be loosely grouped in two categories: 1 / Personal hygiene and quasi-medical activities and 2 / grooming and body care.

Other personal hygiene and quasi-medical activities that may generally be considered to belong in this category are:

Oral hygiene
brushing teeth
rinsing mouth
gargling
expectorating
cleaning and soaking dentures
massaging gums
using water-pick or dental floss

Miscellaneous hygiene
vomiting
using sanitary supplies
treating skin blemishes
cleaning nose
cleaning ears

Quasi-medical
washing wounds
soaking limbs or other body parts
applying bandages
applying medications
taking medicine internally
inhaling steam
applying contraceptive devices
taking enema
douching
cleaning and inserting contact lenses

This list is by no means complete nor are the categories absolute, but it does suggest the range of other common hygiene activities needing various kinds of accommodation.

Oral Hygiene Of these activities, oral hygiene is probably the least demanding in terms of privacy of any of the personal hygiene activities, with the exception of certain of the grooming activities. In fact, on the contrary, many people seem almost proud to have it known that they are brushing their teeth—an interesting commentary on our early childhood training.

The essential requirements for equipment can be met with a lavatory providing clean running water and a place to spit. In recent years, however, with the widespread use of electric toothbrushes and water-picks, the requirements have grown more complex in terms of electrical outlets and, in particular, of storage space. This rapid proliferation of personal-care appliances is not, of course, limited to oral hygiene. It is especially strong with respect to the various grooming activities and suggests, even more strongly than before, that an integrated approach is necessary if all the appliances are to be accommodated in any orderly way. One industry survey estimates the personal-care appliance market for 1974 at 460 million dollars in the United States alone. Roughly half of this is accounted for by the vast array of hair dryers, stylers, setters, combs, and untanglers; another 30 per cent by electric razors; and the balance by sun lamps, toothbrushes, water-picks, massagers, vibrators, make-up mirrors, hot lather dispensers, and so forth.[1] Certainly the lavatory module, which is the focus of most such activity, will need to have much of this equipment built in.

As to the lavatory itself, the activity imposes no new requirements. It is, however, a particularly messy activity in terms of splattering both the fixture and its immediate surroundings. Toothpaste and spittle have a tendency to adhere tenaciously to a dry surface and require deliberate cleaning, or a continuously washed surface, such as might be provided by some form of self-rinsing lavatory. Such self-rinsing may obviously be accomplished in a variety of ways, from installing a rim flush to contouring the container in such a way that a swirling action of water is set up to cover most of the container.

In addition, the mirror is often essential for certain of the activities as well as for examining one's mouth, coping with dentures, and so on.

Miscellaneous Activities The second category of miscellaneous activities may be generally accommodated by the facilities normally available. In the case of vomiting, for which the water closet is most generally used, consideration should be given to providing some nearby support since a person in this condition is often weak and dizzy. In addition, some thought must be given in the design of the fixture to the unique soiling problems posed both by vomiting and by diarrhea, since the extent of this soiling is far greater than that normally encountered and that for which the fixture was basically intended. In the case of the elimination facility proposed in the preceding discussion, the pull-down urinal would seem to offer a more logical choice of fixture to use since its height and shape would be more nearly suitable.

The use of sanitary supplies, which is generally accomplished while one is seated on the water closet, presents a problem in the suitable disposal of the used supplies. This disposal problem is in many ways similar to that of disposing of other body wastes (feces and urine): the activity (menstruation) is usually regarded as a very private matter; the used supplies are generally highly disagreeable in appearance and odor; and one wants to handle the items as little as possible. Commonly, and perhaps logically, they are disposed of in the water closet.

In most cases, this is an adequate solution to the problem, but occasionally there are difficulties with sanitary napkins. Although most fixtures are manufactured to comply with various codes that require, for example, that the closet successfully and repeatedly pass two large crossed dry napkins, nonetheless there are innumerable instances where for one reason or another such attempts at disposal have caused stoppages in the system and resulted in overflows, particularly in septic tanks and tile fields. It has been suggested over the years, and it may well be worth serious consideration, that since the water closet is regarded by many people as the universal dispose-all, a mechanical grinder should be incorporated. Another approach to this disposal problem, which has been used for years in some public facilities, is to use a separate small electric incinerator. On the other hand, as the use of tampons grows, these disposal problems become relatively minor and in the case of some of the newer devices and techniques (retaining cups, self-induced menstrual flow) disappear altogether.[2]

The remaining items in this category—treating blemishes and cleaning the nose and ears—appear to call only for a mirror, a means of disposing of the wastes, and privacy.

Quasi-Medical The activities in this third group are performed relatively infrequently and require little beyond what should normally be available in the bathroom. The notable exceptions deserve, however, special attention whenever possible—that is, elderly persons or those with some chronic medical condition that requires regular and prolonged treatment. In such situations it would be desirable to make whatever provisions are necessary, since the activity would be a regular and not an exceptional one as, for example, in the case of an elderly person who needs to wear corrective contact lenses. In such a case, there would be a need for more than an ordinary amount of counter and storage space as well as additional electric outlets, a magnifying mirror, and adjustable lighting, in order to accommodate the lens washer and other necessary equipment. Furthermore, as we all generally and increasingly tend to take more drugs and vitamins, the space necessary for storage grows constantly. Special precautions also need to be taken with respect to the security of storage in households with small children, for the obvious drugs and medicines and also for cleaning supplies, and so on.

Grooming and Body Care Activities Grooming and body care encompass a wide and diverse range of activities that have been growing in importance in recent years, particularly since it has become respectable in most quarters, and necessary in some, that men groom themselves with as much attention as females have done heretofore. While this has not yet added any new practices to the list, the numbers of persons engaging in such activities have grown enormously, as have the requirements for space—storage, counter, and exercise space.

A general summary of these activities is:

Shaving and treating face—male

Shaving legs, underarms, etc.—female

Treating and arranging hair
cutting
waving, curling, setting, styling
coloring, tinting, tipping
combing and brushing
applying tonics, lotions, sprays, etc.
care of wigs and hair pieces

Grooming face
applying and removing makeup
applying and removing beauty aids, e.g., false eyelashes, etc.

Grooming body
applying powders, creams, lotions, etc.

Manicuring hands
trimming nails, cuticles
applying polish, false nails, etc.

Pedicuring feet
trimming nails
applying polish
removing calluses

Weighing body

Exercising

Using sun lamp

Of the activities listed, shaving, both male and female, is the only one that is more or less completely associated with the other basic hygiene activities and with bathroom facilities. It requires water and possibly an electrical outlet and is associated with other activities as part of a daily routine. Male shaving, for example, tends overwhelmingly to take place in the bathroom, even when electric razors are used, primarily because of its close association with other cleansing and grooming activities.[3] Although the use of battery-powered shavers and special whisker-softening agents has become more prevalent and has thus lessened the necessary association with the bathroom, shaving still remains tied to other hygiene activities from a practical standpoint and probably from a psychological one as well. The accommodations necessary for male shaving can generally be met by the normal facilities of a lavatory; a properly placed, well-lighted mirror; electrical outlets; and ample storage and counter space for all the toiletries, hot lather dispensers, hot combs, etc. Privacy is rarely a requirement.

In contrast, female shaving of the legs and underarms, when practiced, is generally part of the body-cleansing ritual, requiring more or less nudity, and is generally a bathroom activity. Even though female shaving is not a daily activity, the fact that it tends to take place largely in conjunction with bathing or showering poses a number of problems when a safety razor is used, as it most commonly is. The chief one is safety. Some provision must be made for a safe place to keep the implements in or near the fixture and for a safe posture, particularly in the shower. In this respect, shaving the legs is very similar to washing the legs and poses the same postural requirements—either a place to sit down or put a leg up on or something secure to hold on to—in addition to adequate lighting.

The remainder of the grooming activities listed present a unique situation, primarily in terms of overall planning rather than bathroom design, since they all can be, and frequently are, performed both in the bathroom and in other areas of the house, depending on a particular combination of circumstances. Cutting and styling hair, for example, may take place in the kitchen if this is where hair is commonly washed. With some portable hair dryers, hair drying may take place virtually anywhere, even while one is polishing floors or dusting. Makeup may be applied in the bathroom or in the bedroom at the "vanity" or dressing table. Removing makeup, on the other hand, generally requires water and is therefore usually a bathroom activity.[4]

Manicuring and pedicuring are generally regarded as relatively disagreeable and private and tend to be restricted to the bedroom, or bathroom, though polishing fingernails is commonly done publicly—even in the living room.

The determinants of where such activities take place are, first, a matter of a given individual's feelings about the body and his or her sense of privacy, modesty, and appropriateness and, second, the degree to which the bathroom is available in a given household. In situations, for example, where there is only one bathroom that must be shared among several family members, the tendency is for certain "nonessential" functions to be shunted to other areas of the house and so relieve the use-load on the bathroom. Furthermore, the increased use of various electric appliances in the different grooming processes has in many cases necessitated a shift to other areas simply because of a lack of adequate counter and storage space and of electrical outlets in existing bathrooms.

Aside from the normal provisions of a lavatory, a mirror or mirrors, and adequate lighting, the principal requirements posed by contemporary grooming practices are the provision of sufficient storage and counter space as well as electrical outlets to accommodate the range of personal-care appliances and products commonly found today, at least in the United States. In some instances, it may not be too extreme to suggest that a fourth "grooming center" be added to the bathroom's three traditional functions. Indeed, a number of well-to-do women have built-in professional hair dryers, massage tables, and other items in their personal bathrooms, which for completeness rival any health spa or beauty parlor.

The category of body care may, in some instances, encompass nothing more than a scale for daily weighing or, at the other extreme, include facilities for sunbathing, exercise equipment, a sauna, and so on. In the latter situation, obviously a great deal more space is necessary than is commonly provided in what we regard as a normal bathroom. The bathroom scale, in contrast, is a simple, small item that often poses, however, a storage and safety problem. As is true of most things that must be left out because no space has been provided for it, the scale has become a "high-fashion" item. Scales left out on the floor present, however, a hazard, especially at night. In an integrated approach, scales could be incorporated in a fold-up wall unit or possibly could pull out like a drawer. An even more sophisticated approach might be to develop a bath mat that incorporated pressure sensors and that would also function as a scale.

PERSONAL NON-HYGIENE ACTIVITIES

This category comprises those personal and individual activities essentially unrelated to hygiene activities but often engaged in incidentally while one is in the bathroom for other purposes, such as smoking, eating, drinking, reading, watching television, listening to the radio, telephoning, playing, masturbating, and so forth. The distinction between what is a primary and what is a secondary activity is sometimes blurred by motivations. In the case of a mother with several small children who takes her favorite magazine with her to read while taking a bath, it cannot be said with any certainty what is primary. Both may be of equal importance to the individual who, in many such instances, is using bathing simply as a vehicle to satisfy other personal needs.

From a design standpoint these activities pose little problem with respect to fixtures and equipment, but they need to be considered in the overall framework of the role the bathroom plays, both in a given individual's life and in the context of the rest of the house. While in many cases special accommodations may be necessary, these can, for all practical purposes, be considered personal rather than universal situations. Individuals planning a new or remodelled bathroom should, however, examine their habits (and dreams) to see which luxuries or degrees of luxury might be possible above and beyond the stereotyped universal bathroom.

Smoking, eating, and drinking are fairly common incidental activities while one is grooming and bathing and pose questions of safe places to lay things down, particularly when in the tub. In some instances, however, even a coffeepot and a small refrigerator are necessary since some individuals insit on their cup of coffee while shaving and watching the morning news.

Reading is common as a diversionary activity while one is defecating. In the survey, roughly 40 per cent of the respondents reported reading while using the toilet.[5] To a lesser extent, reading is also a secondary activity while one is bathing or relaxing in a tub. Reading in this instance is obviously something done for its own sake, as is an indeterminate amount of the toilet reading. In most instances no special provisions are necessary, though many individuals have a library in the bathroom or, in a few exceptional cases, a bathroom in the library.

Listening to the radio or watching television while one is engaged in personal hygiene and grooming activities or exercising may again be regarded as another species of highly personal activity that makes specific but personal demands.

Having a telephone in the bathroom is, for some individuals, a convenience and for a few a virtual necessity. In most cases, however, there is reason to suspect that a telephone in the bathroom is merely a status ploy and a matter of "one-upping" one's friends and business acquaintances:

> One investor, during the early Sixties, hit upon a telephone in the john as a status symbol. He would continuously make calls from his john, transacting business, and in case there was any doubt where he was, he would flush the toilet. Within a short time, the phone company was swamped with orders from real-estate investors for john telephones. After a while, the telephones were replaced by fancier models with hold buttons. The next step was logical but it never developed: Having secretaries answer the john phones.[6]

Although a convenience in some respects, a telephone in the bathroom can also present a possible safety hazard. The nearness and availability of the telephone could cause persons to interrupt their primary activity in order to answer the phone, which they might not bother to do if it were in another room. Such interruption during showering or bathing could be particularly hazardous. On the other hand, it has been suggested that a telephone in the bathroom could prove to be a safety feature, in that parents would not need to leave infants unattended while they answer the phone. Clearly, there is no one answer to this question—just as there is no substitute for judgment.

In some instances the bathroom is used as a "telephone booth" to gain privacy from other household members or guests when privacy is otherwise unobtainable.

Children's play in the bathroom also indicates that the bathroom is probably the most overworked multipurpose room in today's house—at least when such play stems from keeping the children "out from underfoot." Small children playing in the tub with water toys, while bathing or not, is a common and age-old practice, but use of the bathroom simply as a play space is a somewhat different matter and raises many questions of safety, suggesting that serious attention must be paid to this aspect of safety in the bathroom, particularly to general residential planning, since the primary reason for such play is obviously that the bathroom offers facilities not available elsewhere, such as water and relatively mar-proof surfaces.[7] This raises a number of issues that need further exploration: to what extent should such play be encouraged by the provision of facilities such as storage space for water toys and to what extent should it be discouraged. It would seem that discouragement is unreasonable, for unless specific provisions were made elsewhere for it, it would simply shift the problem to another area of the house even less equipped to handle it.

MISCELLANEOUS ACTIVITIES

The third major category of uses to which the bathroom is often put centers around the relatively unique facilities available here. These include shining shoes, storing wet umbrellas, keeping and washing pets, and using the bathroom as a photographic dark room. It is obvious that these uses have found their way into the bathroom primarily because the bathroom provides facilities not readily available elsewhere in the house. This again points to significant inadequacies in terms of overall house design and to the need for the bathroom to be properly designed as a multipurpose room when there is only one bathroom in the house.

Perhaps the commonest such activity, and one that has given rise to a considerable body of humor as well as annoyance, is the practice of using the bathroom for washing and drying hand laundry. Unfortunately, perhaps, the bathroom is by far the most logical place to do hand laundry since almost all the clothing items to be laundered originate in the bathroom or nearby bedrooms. In addition to providing the necessary facilities for washing and drying, albeit makeshift, the bathroom also provides in many instances a measure of privacy as far as "unmentionables" are concerned. For many persons, female undergarments, which make up the bulk of hand laundry, are private and a source of embarrassment when left in public view.[8]

The extent to which hand laundry is done in the bathroom varies considerably, depending on factors such as type of dwelling unit, availability of a washer and dryer, household composition, and family size, among others. Similarly, larger hand-laundry items, such as men's wash-and-wear suits, are often done in the kitchen but frequently hung to dry over the tub. Also related to laundering is the drying of swimsuits and the steaming of clothes, though both of these are relatively minor activities compared with hand laundry.

The principal problem to date has been providing for drying in such a fashion that it does not interfere with the basic use of the facilities. The solution may, however, lie in the provision of special laundry facilities directly connected with the bathroom itself—a notion that has been advanced many times in the past. It is equally as logical and efficient, for example, to take care of all laundering in a space adjoining the bathroom since, in fact, virtually all of a family's laundry originates in the bedroom–bathroom complex and ultimately ends up being stored there. In many instances, however, laundering, at least the hand variety, must be accommodated in the bathroom, and some drying arrangement must be designed that does not interfere with the basic uses of the facilities. In this respect, a separate, heated drying cabinet of the kind commonly found in Scandinavia may be preferable to an arrangement that occupies the space over basic fixtures and necessitates shifting about so the equipment can be used.

Another, somewhat specialized laundering activity that commonly takes place in the bathroom is diaper care. Although diapers are rarely laundered in the bathroom, they are frequently stored there and sometimes left to soak in some of the fixtures—the lavatory, the bowl of the water closet, and, in some instances, the tank of the water closet. Aside from the inconvenience this causes, these practices are to be deplored on sanitary grounds: first, urine can, over a period of time, destroy the finish on porcelain enamel and lead to infections from the bacteria present; second, the urine and feces on the diaper can pollute the cold-water supply when the diapers are stored in the water closet tank. In other circumstances, when a commercial diaper service is used, one has the problem of adequate temporary storage. The rapid growth and popularity of disposable diapers is easy to understand.

Cleaning A final activity that must be considered in the design of hygiene facilities is that of cleaning—of the fixtures and of the space. In a sense, cleaning might be regarded as a personal hygiene activity in that a person's level of hygiene is, to some extent at least, dependent on the level of sanitation of the facilities he uses—if not literally, at least psychologically.

In the home, the principal problem is generally not the level of sanitation but rather the ease of cleaning and the rate of soiling. Nonetheless, it is still the level of hygiene, either necessary or desired, that ultimately determines a given individual's felt degree of difficulty in any cleaning task: shall it be cursory and visual or thoroughly sanitary. This becomes a highly relative and personal matter.

The ultimate cleaning difficulties may be the result of either rapid soiling or difficult cleaning, or both. A cleaning task may be difficult by virtue of the nature of the substance to be removed or by virtue of the inaccessibility of the place to be cleaned.[9]

So far as the actual soiling agents and waste products are concerned there is little that can be done to alter their characteristics or improve their cleanability. If we accept the premise that a certain amount of cleaning of the facilities is inevitable and that some of it will be more or less distasteful, the question becomes one of minimizing the amount of cleaning necessary. Proper design could do much to eliminate many of the present common sources of irritation, such as the splattered urine, the hair and face powder in the lavatory, and the ring left in the tub. To a large extent, this could be accomplished, first, by designing the equipment so as to contain as much of the soiling as possible and have it disposed of by the built-in cleansing action of the fixture itself and, second, by arranging the installation of the equipment in such a way as to avoid unreachable, tight, and awkward spaces such as are commonly found around water closets and free-standing lavatories. It might also be desirable that manufacturers establish minimal clearances for each fixture from the viewpoint of both the basic use of the fixture and its ability to be cleaned.

In addition, attention must also be paid to the design and placement of fittings, which are often complex, cramped, and difficult to clean, and to the various surfacing materials used for walls, floors, and cabinet work.

The apparent degree of difficulty of a cleaning task is also a function of the frequency and promptness of cleaning and, in some instances, a function of whether or not the soiling is one's own or someone else's. The psychological problems associated with many of the cleaning tasks would appear to arise primarily when one is cleaning a mess left behind by someone else, so that, even though proper design can lessen the mess, it obviously cannot totally solve the problem of personal irresponsibility.

14

SOCIAL AND PSYCHOLOGICAL ASPECTS OF BATHROOM DESIGN

Whereas all of us need to perform the same basic bodily functions and all of us have more or less similar needs for personal hygiene facilities, the ultimate makeup and distribution of these facilities is obviously variable beyond a certain point and is dependent on a great number of factors, psychological as well as purely functional—family size, family life cycle, household composition, socioeconomic status, personal values, attitudes, privacy requirements, and so on. While the most obvious determinant of need might appear to be simply number, that is, family size and composition, this rarely is more than a multiplier, except in the most extreme cases.

The primary determinant of the kind and extent of our hygiene facilities is psychological, in terms of our various attitudes toward the body, elimination activities, sex, privacy, and modesty. Our responses to the body and bodily functions, which range from disgust and a desire to have as little to do with the bathroom as possible to enjoyment of the body in all its dimensions and a desire for facilities that can be enjoyed, determine the character of the bathroom and the way it is used. These basic body attitudes may also reflect themselves in requirements for privacy. Persons, for example, who have generally negative or apprehensive feelings inevitably demand the greatest degree of privacy for those "disgusting" activities. In addition we seek privacy in the bathroom for a variety of other essentially unrelated motivations ranging from aesthetic considerations, to a simple desire to be alone and private, to practical considerations of schedule, to questions involving the value structure of a given society, which dictates that certain behavior patterns be observed.

DEGREES OF PRIVACY

Privacy demands emerge as the major determinant of bathroom usage and numbers since it is these demands, irrespective of the particular motivation, that cause us to insist on individual time/space use of the facilities. If it were not for these privacy demands, the average household could probably manage reasonably comfortably with only one simultaneously shared bathroom, albeit a more spacious one than is customary. Instead, we settle, in most cases, for the sequential use of what is generally a one-person facility—hence the expression, "piss or get off the pot." When circumstances permit, we often insist on personal bathrooms for each member of the household. A major consequence of this sequential-use pattern is that it imposes a fairly rigid discipline upon us that must be scrupulously observed if we are to avoid chaos. This is true not only in countries where several families still share common hygiene facilities but also within a family situation, particularly where there are school-age children whose schedules coincide with those of working parents.

> The fact that the middle-class family rises almost together, and has few bathrooms, has resulted in a problem for it, which has been resolved by a very narrowly prescribed ritual for many of them—a bathroom ritual. They have developed set rules and regulations which define who goes first (according to who must leave the house first), how long one may stay in, what are the penalties for overtime, and under what conditions there may be a certain overlapping of personnel.[1]

The state or condition of privacy is relative, and there are a number of degrees of it that are obtainable or may be desired. Specifically, it is possible to establish three major categories: 1 / privacy of being heard but not seen, 2 / privacy of not being seen or heard, and 3 / privacy of not being seen, heard, or sensed—in other words, other people should not even be aware of one's whereabouts or actions. It is probably fair to say, however, that these categories generally represent degrees of tolerable privacy rather than degrees of desired privacy, in the sense that, given a choice, most people would, for these purposes, tend to pick maximum privacy. The degree of tolerable privacy obviously varies enormously, depending on the activity and the particular individual.

The degree of privacy we insist on, or tolerate, influences the various ways in which we physically create the state of privacy: the location of the bathroom relative to other areas of the house, the specific location of the entrance, the acoustical treatment of the space, the location and size of the bathroom windows, the extent to which facilities are intended to be for the sole use of one person, and the extent to which facilities may be shared—with or without compartmentalization of some sort.

Compartmentalization is often regarded as a means of securing greater privacy. This may or may not be true, however, depending on a variety of factors, including the location of the entrance to the compartment, whether the partitions are floor to ceiling, and whether there is a full door. In terms of the kind of partial compartmentalization commonly found today, it offers privacy *only* in those circumstances where none was had before, in other words, a single, minimal bath that was shared in use. If a bathroom was not shared, then a greater degree of privacy was available before—unless the compartmentalization is so thorough as to amount to a separate facility—because such compartmentalization assumes that the bathroom previously unshared may now be shared. The usefulness of this device obviously depends on the degree of privacy one is concerned about, and it is important, therefore, that this be clearly established at the outset.

In some instances, however, compartmentalization is also desired in order to satisfy personal feelings about space and security. Through habituation or feelings of insecurity some people have come to think that certain activities are appropriately or comfortably performed only in certain settings. This appears to be particularly true for activities involving total or partial nudity: bathing, elimination, and sex. This occurs, for example, in the case of persons who are acutely uncomfortable about engaging in sexual activities with the lights on or anywhere but in bed and also accounts for the unease that some have experienced in using the enormous bathrooms occasionally found in old, palatial hotels. One survey respondent, for example, commented that she much preferred the shower to the tub because pulling the curtain gave her a greater sense of "privacy." (Did she really mean security?) By the same token, a great many people will at least close, if not actually lock, the bathroom door, even when they are alone in the house and know that there is no real danger of anyone's walking in on them or of anyone's being aware of their activities. A snug space may operate as a clothing substitute in some of these instances. Professor Descamps at the Sorbonne distinguishes between persons who can broadly be classified as "nudists," at least in some circumstances, and persons he terms "textiles," those who cannot be nudists under any circumstances. In a large space one often "feels too out in the open and naked." In some such instances, this response may be a form of kenophobia, or fear of large spaces, as in the case of persons who are acutely uncomfortable when alone in a huge house.

Degrees of privacy, either desired or possible, are also a function of socioeconomic status and family values. In the lowest socioeconomic group, for example, where crowded living conditions force a lack of privacy—and where privacy has, in all likelihood, never even been experienced—privacy norms are much less severe than they are in situations where they are a realistic societal requirement.

> Upper-class girls, most of whom had their own individual bathrooms, reacted with interest when told of middle-class procedures (bathroom scheduling) in this respect. The lower-class girls were amazed that such a thing was necessary. Probably privacy, which they had never had, and overfastidiousness were not family values which made such arrangements important.[2]

At the upper end of the socioeconomic scale one often finds that privacy demands are carried to what may well be their ultimate conclusion—a total privacy that can then be manipulated for a variety of social and psychological purposes. There are situations, for example, where all the facets of daily living are treated as an art and where only the most carefully contrived and carefully controlled images are permitted to obtain, in other words, what some of us are prone to regard as the ultimate in good breeding and civilized behavior. Here, role and format are everything, leading to separate bedrooms, bathrooms, and sitting rooms, where people come together only when fully prepared and "on stage." This applies equally to speech, display of emotions, manner of dress, and to privacy demands, particularly with respect to the necessary intimate details of one's life. In these situations, the privacy demand may also be regarded as being based on aesthetics. In the Cornell survey, for example, the highest socioeconomic groups indicated the greatest desire for compartmented baths, even though they, by virtue of having several baths, presumably had least need for it from any pure privacy viewpoint.[3] Presumably a high degree of sensibility and fastidiousness is operable here, which reflects the notion that art and connoisseurship come into being only from a sufficiency of wealth and leisure. Conversely, it is argued that this degree of privacy is an extravagance that simply reflects the decadence and superaffluence of contemporary society and at the same time the neuroses and insecurities of a society preoccupied with illusion rather than reality. Obviously, here, as in all other such matters, what is right is whatever one believes.

PRIVACY AND THE INDIVIDUAL

Since the dawn of time, man has searched in various ways to answer the question, "Who am I?" This quest for a personal sense of identity seems to be a fundamental aspect of man's nature and is certainly a fundamental tenet of modern psychology, which is becoming increasingly concerned with this question. Until recently, Western culture has also laid great stress on the importance of the individual and upon self-expression. Basic, however, to the development and maintenance of a strong personal identity is privacy, both in a conceptual as well as an operational sense. In its simplest form it involves "aloneness," or freedom from the presence and demands of others. It also involves, however, the concept of possession—a "mineness"—of time, space, and property, each of which serves as a measure of our uniqueness and our self-expression.

> . . . through habituation and teaching, the mother reproduces in the child her own needs, in this case the need for privacy which inevitably brings with it related needs. Now the child grows up needing time to himself, a room of his own, freedom of choice, freedom to plan his own time, and his own life. He will brook no interference and no encroachment. He will spend his wealth installing private bathrooms in his house, buying a private car, a private yacht, private woods and a private beach, which he will then people with his privately chosen society.[4]

There are strong societal counterpressures for conformity and togetherness that exist side by side with our tendency toward individuality and that, it is suggested, are the cause of much of the personal conflict in contemporary society. Therefore, while we tend to buy the same clothes, car, and house as everyone else in our peer group, they must still be "ours" in a personal and private sense. To varying degrees we tend to measure our sense of identity by the number and quality of things we can call ours, things by which others can identify us.

Privacy and privateness sustain, therefore, our sense of individual identity to a degree that their removal has demonstrable effects on the personality that in some cases may be serious. This direct relationship between privacy and privateness and the opportunity for self-expression, individuality, and personal identity has long been recognized by a variety of institutions that have deliberately set about to remove privacy and privateness in order to minimize individual identity, so as to foster or force a strong group identity. Examples of this behavior may be found among those institutions that are highly structured and authoritarian: the military, prisons, and some educational and religious institutions. Each of these focuses its deprivatory attentions on certain common targets, those aspects that most of us normally use to give evidence of our individuality—clothing, the arrangement of the hair, possessions, and privacy in certain activities. The G. I. haircut, the nun's habit, the schoolboy's cap all serve the same function, as do the wearing of a *uni*form (the very word itself is significant) and the substitution of a number or "brother" or "sister" for one's own name. Similarly, the prohibition of personal possessions and the common sleeping, eating, and hygiene facilities all reinforce the relative unimportance and anonymity of the individual.

That the technique is more or less effective is beyond doubt, though it may be questioned whether it is always desirable. The military latrines and medical inspections have long been infamous for their effects, either humorous or tragic, on individuals who found it exceedingly painful to make the necessary adjustments. In many cases, the adjustments can also result in more or less severe psychopathologies. This seems to be particularly true of sudden and enforced privacy deprivation, which commonly occurs during catastrophies or war, when people are forced into a prolonged and unaccustomed intimacy. This is also true of many institutional settings such as schools, prisons, or hospitals. Privacy deprivation is not, however, a phenomenon limited to institutions; it is a common feature and a major problem in most of the slum housing around the world. Even the average American house today offers examples. The open planning and multipurpose rooms combined with small size—all intended to encourage family unity and cohesiveness—have in many instances produced only irritation and a variety of antisocial behaviors. F. S. Chapin observes:

> The sentiment of self-respect, the respect for self as an individual with status, can hardly thrive when the person is continuously open to pressures of the presence of many others in the household. Privacy is needed for thinking, reflection, reading and study, and for aesthetic enjoyment and contemplation. Intrusions on the fulfillment of personal desires need to be shut off in order to avoid the internal tensions that

are built up from the frustrations, resentments, and irritations of continual multiple contacts with others.[5]

"OFF-BOUNDS"

Because there is a strong social sanction for obtaining privacy from others for personal hygiene activities, the bathroom has gradually assumed a special, privileged, "off-bounds" character. In the majority of homes today the bathroom is, moreover, the only such space in the house. This is partly the result of present house-planning practices and partly the result of changes in child-rearing, which is considerably more permissive than it used to be. Children, by and large, may now be heard as well as seen and are not required to knock or ask permission to visit their parents' room or to maintain a respectful silence if the parents are busy. The result is that, by extension or usurpation, the privileged character of the bathroom is used to obtain privacy for a variety of emotional purposes that have nothing to do with personal hygiene: sulking, crying, daydreaming, or simply being alone. F. S. Chapin and a number of other commentators have noted that:

> . . . there is often need to escape from the compulsions of one's social role, to be able to retire from the role of parent, spouse, relative or child, as the case may be. A window may be closed against outside noise; a door may be shut to block demands of others for advice, consolation, help, or gossip; the radio or television set may be turned off to eliminate distracting claims on attention. . . .[6]

This off-bounds character is also exploited for a variety of other activities that have nothing to do with hygiene, such as masturbation and reading. Because of this guaranteed freedom from interruption or questioning, the bathroom is also a common location for the commission of suicide and, as we shall see later, a favored location for the commission of criminal activities in public facilities.

We also seek privacy from others in an operational sense so that we may be spared embarrassment or shame—with respect to personal hygiene functions. Shame or embarrassment can be defined as an outer-directed response: a fear of what we know or imagine others think or feel, with respect to a variety of circumstances. We may also experience shame or embarrassment when we fail publicly to live up to our own image or the image others hold of us. Thus, we are embarrassed when the wrong person walks into the bathroom by mistake, or when our body/beauty image is faulty (flat-chested, pimply, etc.), or when we are caught picking our nose. In this respect, adolescents have a strong need for privacy, since it is during this period that bodily changes create an acute body awareness and often result in self-consciousness. Endless experiments with grooming and the time thus spent also contribute to their privacy needs.

We also exhibit modest behavior out of deference to the unknown reactions of other persons. For example, we may take great pains and resort to all sorts of stratagems to avoid being heard in the bathroom simply because we don't know whether or not we might otherwise embarrass other people. In actual practice, however, it becomes extremely difficult to sort out the basic motivations that lead us to seek privacy in a particular situation or that cause us to be uncomfortable if deprived of it. It is likely too that the basic motivation is often a compound of deference to others' sensibilities, to social norms, to our own self-image, and to our own self-esteem.

PRIVACY AND SOCIETY

In addition to its purely personal and internalized aspects, privacy is also a value in a cultural and socioeconomic sense and to a large extent is a learned response to particular social situations. Privacy in these terms becomes a necessary condition for acceptable social behavior; in other words, we must have privacy in certain instances so that we do not violate cultural norms specifying that certain things be done in private. These cultural norms can vary widely, both from culture to culture and from age to age or from one segment to another within a given culture.

Perhaps the most obvious social components of privacy are those of role and relationship. This is particularly applicable to the preceding discussion of embarrassment since in many cases embarrassment is not caused by the presence of just any person but rather by the presence of specific culturally prohibited categories of people. What is an acceptable behavior and privacy relationship between a child and a child may not be between that child and a parent, or between children of different sexes. With respect to personal hygiene functions the obvious breaks come along the lines of sex, age, and relationship.[7] There are, however, a great many other possible differentiating points depending upon the particular matter in question, for example: rank, status, and occupation. There are a number of "privileged" roles in our society—those of the physician, the nurse, the masseur, the dressmaker, hairdresser, the washroom attendant, valet, and maid, each of whom is exempted from the general social rules with respect to privacy of the body. On the other hand, such exemption also carries with it certain obligations with respect to the manner in which this knowledge is obtained and how much of it, if any, may be transmitted to others. Actually, the only really "privileged" roles in the strict sense are those of social equals such as one's lawyer or physician. Virtually all other persons who attend one are, by a particular psychological logic, usually regarded as nonpersons in this respect. Servants and salespeople are often privy to matters that virtually no one else is, but it is generally not a cause for concern because they are simply not considered as mattering. Thus, the situation of the physician, for example, is different from that of a foundation saleswoman, and each in turn is different from that of the husband or wife. In other areas similar situations obtain, for example, with respect to the clergy, the lawyer, and the accountant, each of whom enjoys a particular functional privilege with respect to privacy in a given area.[8]

PRIVACY AND ACTIVITIES

Privacy requirements may also vary according to the specific activities involved. Since the strictest requirements for privacy generally apply to elimination functions, a husband and wife who are intimate with respect to virtually all other matters involving the body may often draw a line here. This is a convention that even nudists appear to observe. On the other hand, the variations in what is deemed to be acceptable behavior are enormous—even within contemporary Western culture. A great many Europeans, for example, are repelled by the standard American bathroom in which the water closet and washing facilities are all together in the same space, as contrasted to European custom where the water closet is generally in a separate room—evidence of the clear difference in attitude toward bathing activities versus elimination activities. As some observers have argued, this is not so much a reflection on European problems with elimination as it is on the general American preoccupation with compulsive "cleanliness," devoid of any enjoyment, which results in our minimal "functional" bathrooms. The Europeans and the Japanese at least enjoy bathing, which presumably is more than many Americans do. In many parts of the world bathing is viewed and practiced as a shared, pleasurable activity—a scarcely possible feat in the average American five-by-seven-foot bathroom, even if this desire were present.

Before exploring these attitudinal implications for space any further, we should also note that privacy requirements tend to parallel general bodily attitudes quite closely in terms of degree of negativism and the desired degree of privacy. As we move along the continuum from elimination we come next to the other body wastes and their associated activities: use of sanitary supplies and related feminine hygiene activities, use of contraceptives, trimming nails, cleaning ears, squeezing pimples, and so forth. Many marriage counselors deplore the view, commonly held in the United States, that the deployment of contraceptive devices, both male and female, is a "bathroom activity," that is, disgusting and private. In many other parts of the world, the deployment of such devices is regarded as a vital part of the foreplay of sexual activity and as an enjoyable mutual activity.

Of all the body wastes, male shaving is probably the only "elimination" activity with a positive image. Interestingly, this is not true of female shaving of legs or underarms, which is very much regarded as a private activity. Again, even this is a controversial subject. Many Americans, both male and female, have voiced their disgust at the body hair of some European women and wondered, even in the advice columns of the newspapers, why these women don't shave and whether it would be proper to speak to them about it. Other cultural values aside, at least one reason is that in some societies the only women who are traditionally so beautifully clean-shaven are the prostitutes! By the same token, there are strong opposing viewpoints on the beauty and morality of female pubic hair versus a shaved pubis.

Of all the personal hygiene activities, the ones that are, if not positive, at least neutral, and that generally require the least privacy are what we might term last-stage grooming, or grooming touch-up. Hair combing and putting on fresh lipstick, while still not regarded as polite and proper in some circles when done in public, are everyday occurrences and are performed in public. What we might term "basic grooming"—the use of cleansing creams and hair curlers, for example—is generally regarded as a semi-private activity, though obviously not by everyone. Indeed, in some instances, their violation is regarded as akin to farting before one's spouse as a sign that "the honeymoon is over" and, of course, raises all the basic philosophical arguments about the relative merits of illusion versus reality, and honesty versus fraud.

ATTITUDES AND AESTHETICS

When all the subtleties and variations of motivation and attitudes have been laid aside, the practical issues for design purposes can be reduced simply to acceptance or rejection of the human body and its functions and products.[9] The polarity of feelings in this regard is perhaps best illustrated by the following two quotations, both from the writings of prominent architects:

> The proper character of bath rooms, like all the other rooms in the house, must be a function of the peculiar combination of activities which the client elects to combine in its space. Obviously the sybaritic atmosphere, designed for pleasure in warmth, steam, nudity, sex, flowers and alcohol, cannot appropriately combine with the bathinette, the toidy seat, and the diaper pail. On the other hand, the well-designed family bath, large, commodious, practical, somewhat ascetic, can be a magnificent thing, not only in terms of utility, but also in terms of its expressive message. Ideally perhaps, every family should have one of each. But where for practical reasons this is impossible, a little of each, a compromise, is certainly possible, and a great challenge to the designer.[10]

> The most frequent mistake, to take a more modest but more specific example, is the luxurious bathroom. A bathroom is a bathroom, and its equipment is still its equipment even if as beautiful as that of the Italian firm, Ideal-Standard. What takes place there is not an adventure or a luxury but a necessity. The real refinement of the bathroom consists in its not being too refined. Everything in it must be functionally perfect, orderly, sanitary, and easily maintained. This much is in good taste and nothing more.[11]

Obviously, our views of the bathroom are passionately held and expressed and not likely to come together in the near future. Persons, for example, who view the bathroom as a positive and sensual, if not erotic place, and who wish to exercise and sunbathe in the bathroom and have TV and telephones are obviously going to make different demands in every respect from those persons who are repelled by the notion of spending any more time in the bathroom than absolutely necessary for the performance of essential hygiene functions. What is so unfortunate about Western, certainly many Anglo-Saxon, attitudes is the endless extreme swings from Puritanism to licentiousness. We seem never to be able to come to grips with the human body and human sexuality as a neutral fact of human existence. Witness, for example, the uproar that ensued in 1972 over the sending of a plaque depicting nude male and female figures into outer space on the Pioneer 10 spacecraft. Not only did the space agency receive thousands of outraged letters, but even the newspapers exercised editorial discretion:

> The Chicago Sun-Times published the drawing in an early edition—with the man's testicles erased. Then, in a later edition, all traces of the man's genitals had disappeared. The Philadelphia Inquirer was even more decisive. The drawing it carried showed the male with no genitals and the female with no nipples on her breasts.[12]

In recent years, there have been some indications that the situation may be changing somewhat. Certainly, there has come to be a much greater acceptance, at least in some quarters, of the body, nudity, and sex. It is no longer as likely, as it was in the recent past, for a woman to proclaim, with some pride, that she has never seen a man naked, even though she has been married for fifty years, and that no man has ever seen her naked. Society generally, and the young in particular, appear to have become much more relaxed in these respects. While we may be speaking of the tip of the iceberg, certainly the mixed living experiences of college students and the widespread interest in body awareness would suggest that at least a greater proportion of the population than heretofore is willing and able to come to grips with these aspects of life. We are also experiencing at present a great interest in, and awareness of, health and bodily fitness that is also encouraging. On the other hand, our early conditioning and training appear to place some limits on the degree to which such relaxation of taboos actually occurs. One college official has observed that the reaction to sharing a bathroom seems to depend to a large extent on a combination of family structure and social class. "If the students are upper class and have brothers or sisters they're not so uptight. If she's a single daughter, she's more uptight. If the student is lower class, he can be very uptight." Another Dean suggests that many students are having second thoughts about shared bathrooms. "It was a cool thing at first to have shared bathrooms as an experiment, but the next year the students wanted the dorm restructured in separate suites, to allow separate bathrooms."[13]

The author's own experience bears this out and suggests further that these taboos are particularly strong, as we might expect, with respect to elimination processes. At a professional conference held during the summer at a university campus, the conferees, most of whom were young male college faculty members, were housed in a high-rise women's dormitory wherever there happened to be empty rooms. As one might expect, there was the usual amount of ogling and lively interest in the students, on the campus, in the cafeteria, and in the lobby. It developed, however, that, so far as could be determined in an informal survey, all the conferees took special care not to meet any of the girls in the shared bathrooms, and one or two even admitted that if they were caught in a toilet stall when a girl walked into the room they simply sat there and waited till she left before emerging.

Attitudes aside, the bathroom is, from a purely factual and functional standpoint, one of the *most* important rooms in the home. It is the one space with which we have the most intimate bodily contact. It is the one space in which we are nude for prolonged periods of time. It is the first place we use upon awakening in the morning and the last one we use before going to bed at night. An agreeable or disagreeable experience there can set the tone for the day or the night. It is the place we invariably use when we are ill. It is also the one facility in the home that every one of us uses every single day of our lives and the one facility most of us would be unwilling to do without.

In many instances, the bathroom is emerging as a positive rather than a negative environment oriented toward health, exercise, relaxation, and the enjoyment of bodily rejuvenation. Obviously, such bathrooms need to be considerably larger than is customary in order to accommodate the additional equipment and space necessary for one to enjoy it as a "live-in bathroom."[14] The biggest problem here is with architects and builders who persist in ignoring the bathroom and who continue to treat it as one of the least important spaces in the home. In contrast, clients who build or remodel almost invariably tend to opt for larger and more personalized bathrooms.

Although we generally tend to think of large multipurpose bathrooms as "master bathrooms," as they most often are, in some instances they are also conceived of as "family rooms," as in the case of the German *Wohnbäd* illustrated in Figure 59. The "living bath" is here conceived as a space and an activity to be shared by the entire family as a natural part of daily living, a concept similar to the Scandinavian sauna and the Japanese bath. This concept has had a long history, though it has rarely been acknowledged during the last several centuries. In what some might regard as an even more extreme form, the living bathroom also assumes the role of simply another space in the home where one might even entertain friends when appropriate. Again, there is considerable historical precedent for this. Elsie DeWolfe, for example, entertained her friends in the bathroom on occasion, and Yves St. Laurent is reported to do his best designing in his bathroom, which he has outfitted as a studio. Indeed, there is virtually no limit to the aesthetic, philosophical, or functional approaches that can be taken toward the bathroom once one frees oneself from the shackles of stereotyped thinking. One can find examples today of bathrooms that are treated as family rooms, private sitting rooms, libraries, offices, formal drawing rooms, art galleries, garden rooms, beauty parlors, gymnasiums, and so on. This new interest in bathrooms is also evidenced by the recent appearance of two splendid picture books by David Hicks and Mary Gilliatt, which illustrate a number of these more imaginative approaches.[15] The mere existence of these books is also evidence that, at least in some quarters, the bathroom has even become fashionable. During the past year or two a number of sanitaryware manufacturers, both in Europe and the United States, have brought out bathtubs large enough for two and also twin washbasins (see Figure 60). Purely sanitary considerations aside, there is no question that this represents a major step forward from the not-too-distant past when, for example, ladies would take a bath in a linen shroud so as not to see themselves naked and thereby experience all manner of distressing feelings.

What we might regard as the body/sex liberation of the past several years is also producing some changes not only in our attitudes toward the bathroom but also in its character. One of the most persistent and curious myths of the modern Western world has been that good taste with respect to home furnishings is somehow the natural birthright and exclusive prerogative of the female sex—most particularly with respect to the bedroom and bathroom. Nothing could be further from the truth, but the result has been a nearly complete feminine domination of these areas until very recently. In an industry speech, fashion designer Bill Blass argued for at least a more classic, if not masculine, character for the bathroom and noted that for years a full half of the population has been totally ignored in this matter.[16]

This new interest in bathrooms is also apparent in the rapid growth, particularly in the United States, of a sizeable bath products industry supplying every conceivable kind of decorative bathroom accessory. In addition, many plumbing contractors are opening associated "bath boutiques" to be able to supply the consumer with a completely furnished bathroom package. While this represents a major advance in many respects, there is still vast progress to be made. Unfortunately, a substantial portion of accessory items sold can only be charitably described as "decorative shlock," and one cannot help but wonder whether the bathroom has really become more acceptable or whether more people have simply

59 / APPROACHES TO A "LIVING BATH"

"WÖHNBAD" OR "LIVING BATH": RÖHM, DARMSTADT, WEST GERMANY

"WÖHNBAD" OR "LIVING BATH": RÖHM, DARMSTADT, WEST GERMANY

"GOTHIC POOL" BATHTUB, 1830 MM BY 1370 MM (6 BY 4½ FEET):
AMERICAN STANDARD, NEW BRUNSWICK, NEW JERSEY, U.S.A.

60 / CURRENT APPROACHES
TO LUXURY BATHTUBS

"THE BATH" BATHTUB, 2135 MM BY 1675 MM (7 BY 5½ FEET):
KOHLER, KOHLER, WISCONSIN, U.S.A.

discovered, with some relief, that they could make something "pretty" out of that awful, ugly room. Furthermore, in a great many instances, decoration is not only making something more attractive in the mind of the householder but also disguising the item or function so that it virtually disappears. In this respect, the bathroom is nearly unique in the average home. Of all the rooms or items of equipment it is perhaps most subject to this kind of "decorating"—in the fairly obvious hope that the water closet, for example, will somehow not be so nasty if we hide it in a "chaise percée" or if we appliqué a golden eagle to its seat cover. Soap is, of course, disguised as a lemon or a tomato or a rosebud. The toilet paper is hidden in a filigree caddy and patterned with flowers. The faucet handles are swans or fish. The towel bars are ornate and gilded finialed brass rods. The washbasin may have a crinoline skirt around its base hiding all those ugly pipes. The tub may be built in and fitted with a lid so that it disappears when not in use. Recently some plastic tub units have been introduced with walls that are textured and paneled with moldings to resemble. . .what? We might also question some of the various design approaches taken toward the bathroom in which the bathroom finally emerges as anything but a bathroom. This, of course, begs the unanswerable question: What is a suitable character for a bathroom? One can only wonder what our kitchens would be like if eating and food preparation were tabooed in our society, as they are in some, instead of the body and its functions.

STATUS

Decoration is also, of course, in many cases a matter of status-motivated display. Fixtures carved out of blocks of semiprecious stones and equipped with gold-plated fittings are not necessarily a simple matter of "having the best." The "best," and real luxury, could also be something that functions superbly instead of something ordinary fashioned from pretty and costly materials. A tub made of lapis lazuli in a conventional configuration is no more comfortable or usable than the standard version.

Even the choice of items to be included is in many instances determined by status considerations. There is reason to suspect, for example, that many of the bidets found in the United States and in England are essentially status symbols attesting to the worldliness of their owners.

In this respect the bathroom plays a special role, for it permits a rather subtle form of possession display owing to its more or less private character as contrasted with the obviously public areas of the home. It allows for a kind of behind-the-scenes throwaway chic, which can have great impact since it is ostensibly not really meant to be seen, except possibly by intimates. In addition, depending on one's point of view, the bathroom also offers for some individuals the ultimate opportunity for ostentatious display and the extravagant gesture—"Imagine spending all that money on *that*!"

Whereas we tend to think of the bathroom as a private place where our most intimate items are kept, it can also be one of the most public spaces in the home, since guests can lock themselves in and peek and probe to their hearts' content if they are of a mind to. Indeed, some status-conscious individuals who are sensitive to this possibility have been known to take great care to patronize the "right" physician and the "right" pharmacy so that their pill bottles and prescription labels would be consistent with the rest of their carefully cultivated image. As every spy or actor (or any other person concerned with projecting and maintaining a particular image) well knows, such attention to subtle detail is all-important to one's success. In similar fashion, though generally at a somewhat different level, one rediscovers the marked hotel towels and bars of soap that signify one's sophistication or competitiveness in one-upping one's friends.

The "powder room," or guest bathroom, presents, for some people, a somewhat different opportunity, or problem, because it is, by definition, a public space. Here a conscious design statement is called for, and one finds that all too often it ends up as a self-conscious statement, revealing in its cuteness and coyness—as indeed many public bathrooms are, curiously and most particularly those in restaurants. It is here that one tends to find most of the disguised necessities that the "considerate hostess" hopes will not "offend" her guests. Or one finds the racy prints or mottoes that are presumably intended to put the guests at ease by demonstrating that their hosts are "just folks" too.

DESIGN CRITERIA FOR COMPLETE HYGIENE FACILITIES

15

As we have just discovered, a bathroom can be different things to different people and can vary enormously in its character and makeup. At the same time, however, there are certain common aspects that must be considered: supporting accommodations such as storage that are necessary to all activities; environmental requirements for heat, light, ventilation, and noise; the grouping and location of the various functional units relative to the rest of the living space; and finally, the optimum combination of these to form an integrated and complete facility for personal hygiene.

PLANNING CONSIDERATIONS

Several basic questions need to be answered in the preliminary stages of planning for facilities. Perhaps the first and most important of these is the amount of money that one is able and willing to spend. Certainly, in many parts of the world, available resources are the primary determinant of what can be provided, regardless of need in terms of family size. The provision of hygiene facilities follows the familiar pattern: beginning with communal facilities and ending with highly individualized personal facilities, depending on the society's and the individual's affluence. Even in the United States, according to the 1970 Census, some 7 per cent of the dwelling units still lacked complete bathrooms. As recently as 1950, a third of the dwelling units in the United States lacked complete bathrooms.

The second most important question is often the amount of space available, especially when one is remodeling existing dwellings or, as is the case in many of the world's urban areas, when one is attempting to add individual hygiene facilities to existing multiple-family dwellings. In a great many instances in Europe, for example, the basic problem is not so much cost as it is available space. In some cases highly specialized solutions such as minimal prefabricated components are often the only answer. In other cases, particular attention and ingenuity need to be paid to strategies for squeezing the greatest amount of usable space out of what is available. A great deal can be gained by avoiding traditional free-standing fixtures and by taking maximum advantage, for example, of possible counter space over the top of water closet tanks and possible storage space under lavatories. Ultimately, the greatest efficiency is to be found in an integrated modular approach similar to that in contemporary kitchens, where a fair degree of sophistication in design and engineering and production can provide facilities hard to match by an individual homeowner or builder.

The third basic planning consideration is, of course, need—in terms of family or household size and composition and the stage in the family life cycle. Obviously a young couple with one four-month-old infant has a different problem and different needs from, say, a family with five children of both sexes ranging in age from three to fifteen years. Similarly, the requirements of an elderly single person are considerably different again.

Variations in family size and composition also affect the need for hygiene facilities in a qualitative as well as quantitative way. This is, of course, true not only for hygiene facilities but also for the entire house. Simple addition or multiplication of stock units is only a partial answer and does not account for all the variations in attitude and personal approach just discussed. Each facility should ideally be designed and located in terms of the user's life style as well as in terms of the layout of the particular house in question.

The detailed analysis of the composition and distribution of facilities can begin from either end of the problem: given "X" facilities, what should they be and how should they be arranged for maximum effectiveness or, given certain family circumstances, what would be an ideal overall solution? The outline that follows illustrates some of the more common variations according to the requirements of each of the major categories of users.

Adults—single	
Facilities	Full range of fixtures: toilet/urinal/bidet, lavatory, tub/shower
	Counter space with mirror
	Full-length mirror
	Complete storage including private storage
	Drying cabinet for hand laundry
Location	Probably central, if this is the only facility, but closest relationship to sleeping area.
Adults—family heads (2) (With children and additional facilities)	
Facilities	Full range of fixtures: toilet/urinal/bidet, tub/shower, 2 lavatories
	Extended counter space
	Full-length mirror
	Selective storage but including private storage
Location	Private, related to master bedroom, or may also need to relate to living areas for guest use
Also	Assumes separate, nearby laundry and drying facilities
	May also have relation to dressing area plus space for exercising, etc.
Children, under age 10 (With separate facilities)	
a. Facilities	Full range of fixtures—probably shared
	Counter space with mirror
	Limited storage
Location	Off children's bedrooms but accessible from hall, related to laundry and to kitchen
b. Facilities	Toilet and lavatory
	Minimum storage
Location	Off kitchen and/or back door (This assumes heavy use by children, including some from outside the household, and the need for supervision. Also useful for adults in connection with yard work and so on. This facility is sometimes referred to as a "mud room.")
Children—teenage (With separate facilities)	
Facilities	Full range of fixtures: toilet/urinal and tub/shower, probably shared, individual lavatory
	Counter space with mirror
	Selected storage
Location	Private to bedrooms, close to laundry area
Guests and Visitors—adult	
Facilities	Toilet/urinal, lavatory
	Minimum counter space with mirror
	Minimum selected storage
Location	Related to public areas, easily located but still private

When this outline of requirements is matched against the number of facility-units available, two things are obvious. First, if there is only one "family" bathroom, it will of necessity be a multipurpose room needing careful subdivision and considerably greater space than the 1,500 by 2,100 mm (5 by 7 feet) usually allotted. Second, the greater the number of units available, the more nearly unique, private, and highly specialized in function each can be. It could, in fact, be argued that a single bathroom is obsolete and uneconomical if it is intended for use by more than two individuals. In such circumstances, the ideal single bathroom would need to increase in size, number of fixtures, and storage space, to the point where it could be replaced by two partial facilities offering considerably greater convenience and privacy.

The various logical possibilities for combinations and specializations might be categorized as follows:

1	"Family" Bathroom
1½	"Family" Bathroom + "Mud Room"
1½	"Family" Bathroom + Guest Lavatory
1½	"Family" Bathroom + Teenage Lavatory
2	"Master" Bathroom + Children's Bath
2½	"Master" Bathroom + Children's Bath + "Mud Room"
2½	"Master" Bathroom + Children's Bath + Guest Lavatory
2½	"Master" Bathroom + Teenage Bath + Teenage Lavatory
3	"Master" Bathroom + Teenage Bath + Teenage Lavatory + Guest Lavatory
3	"Master" Bathroom + Teenage Bath + Teenage Lavatory + "Mud Room"

Of these specialized facility-units, the one that is perhaps most nearly unique and in greatest demand in suburban and country locations, though rarely found, is what has been termed a "mud room." As suggested in the previous outline, it would basically serve the children who come trooping in and out of the house a thousand times a day often bringing along what appears to be all the children on the street. In addition to elimination and handwashing functions, it could also serve as a place to deal with winter clothing. The intent is obviously to keep the inevitable mess young children make out of the rest of the house and also to keep the children's frequently curious friends out of other, more private bathrooms. This facility could also be equipped with a shower and be used by the parents as a place to clean up after yard work or as a more convenient facility to use for elimination. The particular design of such a space depends on the range of uses intended, but it obviously calls for a significantly different treatment in all respects from either the "family" or the "master" bath. It is largely a public facility and one intended for hard use and relatively rough treatment. Obviously, it must be so designed as to be easily cleaned, possibly even by hosing down.

The other relatively specialized and nearly unique facility that should be considered in some circumstances is the arrangement outlined for older children, that is, a bathing and elimination unit that is shared and connects two bedrooms, with a separate and private lavatory/grooming/storage unit located in each bedroom. In essence, this is a return to a very old-fashioned arrangement, but it is one that, in certain circumstances, is highly logical in that it offers privacy and unlimited access to a functional unit by an age group that needs it most. It would also make water available for other purposes and might in some cases be considered for use by younger children as well.

The other units outlined are fairly standard in their composition but still need to be carefully considered and re-examined, in light of the various aspects and criteria in terms of the degree of privacy desired, one's attitudes toward the body and hygiene, notions about aesthetics, available resources, space, and the like. Similarly, decisions about the specific fixtures and equipment to be selected need to be carefully weighed in the light of these same considerations. The only general advice that can be given is that the higher the price the greater the selection one has in terms of color, style, size, and special features. In addition, careful consideration should be given in each case to the optimum location for a facility in relation to the areas it is to serve. Master bathrooms, for example, should be carefully related to the bedroom/dressing area and to possible exercising and outdoor areas, etc.[1]

GENERAL FACILITIES NEEDED

In terms of overall facilities, proper storage is an item of major concern and represents probably the single greatest shortcoming in present-day bathrooms. With the exception of expensive or custom-designed houses, bathrooms generally have only a "medicine" cabinet, which itself is usually inadequate for medicines, and occasionally a nearby linen closet. In actual fact a tremendous number and variety of items are necessary for personal hygiene and are logically stored in the bathroom. In addition, each of the several categories of items has particular sets of requirements for storage that must be considered. The following list outlines the various distinct categories of items for which storage accommodations should be available:

Enclosed Storage

Limited Access:

Prescription medicines and contraceptive devices

Patent medicines and drugs

Sick room supplies (bed pan, vaporizer, fountain syringe, ice bag, hot water bottle, heating pad, and sanitary supplies and devices)

Free Access:

Daily use items (water glass, toothbrush and other dental equipment and supplies, shaving equipment, deodorants, makeup, brush and comb, tissues)

Grooming aids (hair dryer, hot comb, curlers, hair clippers, scissors, nail clippers, sun lamps)

Scales

Linens (including bathmats, extra shower curtains)

General supplies (soap, toilet paper, tissues)

Cleaning equipment and supplies (brushes, mops, sponges, cleaning agents)

Soiled laundry

Children's equipment (potty seat, diaper pail)

Children's water toys

Active Open Storage and Work Spaces

Daily use items (same as above but while in actual use)

Soap, wet washcloths, sponges

In-use towels

Robes

Clothing worn in or brought in (in connection with bathing)

Obviously, not every category outlined here is necessarily applicable to every situation, but the outline does indicate the range of accommodations necessary for most families and the extent of the storage problem.

Probably the most difficult situation to solve is that of providing limited-access storage for items that are either dangerous or that one wishes to keep private, particularly in households with young children. Although families with young children have overwhelmingly indicated a desire for such locked or limited-access storage for safety reasons, almost half of the survey respondents in purely adult households also indicated a desire for it, largely, presumably, for privacy from guests. While the bathroom tends to be regarded as a private space, where private items may be kept, it is in actual fact one of the most public spaces in the house and is the only space where guests can lock themselves in and be undisturbed.

The simplest solution would seem to be to provide storage space that could be locked, but this has serious drawbacks in terms of misplacing keys or forgetting combinations, particularly during an emergency or at night. A more useful direction, taken recently, is to design latches requiring several steps to open that are too complex for young children to cope with. To some extent this problem is also being solved by the new safety requirements set up for the packaging itself, which specify that the actual bottles be similarly designed.

The typical "medicine" cabinet also presents a safety hazard simply by virtue of its design, and it can also be questioned whether it offers very efficient or sensible storage of the items commonly kept there. The storing of tightly packed glass bottles on glass shelves set over a lavatory has often resulted in broken glass and cut hands. As a general rule it may be said that the smaller the medicine cabinet the more crowded it will be, the more difficult items will be to reach, and the greater will be the resulting risk of accidents. This problem is further magnified by the common practice of employing a mirrored door, which means that the cabinet is set at the height dictated by the mirror rather than set at the height that might be preferable simply from an accessibility standpoint. While large cabinets obviate these problems to some extent, it may still be questioned whether most of the items commonly kept there might not be more advantageously stored in shallow divided drawers that offer easy accessibility and permit proper organization.

The requirements for the second category of items outlined—those with free access—are relatively simpler. Although sheer space is the basic requirement and may be provided in any number of ways, from shelves to drawers, flexibility is necessary in order to accommodate the various sizes and quantities involved. Because of the great diversity of the items in this category, it should be obvious that simply providing one large "catch-all" closet does not really solve the problem. Some items are clean; some are messy; some are used daily; some are used a few times a year; some are small and fragile; some are bulky.

Ideally, each of these various kinds of storage spaces would be located at the point where it is most apt to be used. Although many of these items have no absolutely clear-cut relationship to individual areas, there are, nevertheless, locations that are more or less appropriate and are more logical and convenient than storing some of these items all over the house, wherever there is room, as is so often the case. Laundry, for example, is often poorly managed because of the persistence of traditional assumptions. Although soiled laundry has commonly been stored in the bathroom, it is generally taken elsewhere for washing and ironing. Traditionally, laundry facilities were placed in the basement, or garage, or back hall, which perhaps was suitable in the days when laundering was a service function performed by others. More recently, these facilities have been related to the kitchen, since laundering is now most commonly performed by the homemaker, and in child-centered households the presumption has been that she structures her day around the kitchen, supervising children and so forth. In many instances, however, a better location might be in the bedroom/bathroom region of the house, where the bulk of the soiled laundry originates and where it returns for storage once clean. Since plumbing facilities already exist there, it is in many ways easier to handle laundry where it is rather than carry it all over the house. It may also be questioned whether certain items of underwear are not more appropriately stored in the bathroom than in the bedroom. If soiled garments are stored in the bathroom and clean ones carried in when bathing, then it might be just as appropriate to store the clean clothing there in the first place.

The last category outlined consists of items in use on a daily basis, for which some form of readily accessible storage is necessary. For the bulk of the daily use items, horizontal surfaces—larger and safer than lavatory rims—are probably sufficient. Since most of these items are used in conjunction with the washbasin and a mirror, the greatest need for such space is there. The other principal location is in connection with bathing or showering facilities. In all cases, the storage area or shelf should be so located as to be convenient without being hazardous. The total amount of such space that is necessary is likely, however, to be less than one might assume, *if* adequate enclosed storage is provided. At present, a great many items are left out simply because there is no other place to put them when not in use. Conversely, many things are left out purely for decorative and display purposes: perfume bottles, hair brushes, jars of bath salts, and the like. Indeed, most grooming preparations have, in recent years, been deliberately packaged so as to look reasonably attractive because they have to be left out in the open. The vast increase in grooming practices by both men and women in recent years and the proliferation of grooming appliances have magnified this problem considerably.

After inadequate storage, the next most common complaint has, for years, been inadequate space for hanging towels. This is, of course, so simply remedied by providing an adequate number of lineal feet of rod that one can only wonder how anyone can think that a single ordinary 760-mm (30-inch) rod is adequate for any more than one person. Yet for years, one such towel rod was all that was provided. For families with children this has posed particular problems, especially in circumstances where additional rods could not be added easily, as in the case of tile wainscoting, for example. A minimum of 610 mm (2 lineal feet) per person should be provided at the very least in order to permit proper drying of the towels. Rods that permit the towels to be spread out to dry are far preferable to the various "decorator" devices and novelties such as rings, hooks, and clips, which take up less room but which keep the towels bunched up. Towels even at their best, when frequently changed and properly dried after each use, are strictly speaking a relatively unsanitary way of coping with the drying problem compared with disposable substitutes, and every effort should, therefore, be made to make their use as sanitary as possible. Adequate hanging space is also important as a deterrent to the highly unsanitary practice of towel sharing that often results from inadequate space.

The remaining major category of items to be accommodated is that of clothing removed, principally for bathing and showering. This may be outer clothing, undergarments, or robes, and it may be clothing worn in or clothing brought in to be used after bathing.[2] To a large degree, however, it is likely that the extent of this practice, and of the consequent problem, is based on the combination of the number of bathrooms, number of persons in the household, and the location of the bathroom. One would assume that the reason a person does not pass to and from the bathroom in a robe is that he has strong feelings about personal modesty. In the case of a master bathroom directly accessible from a bedroom, provision of robe hooks should be sufficient. In the case of a multipurpose bathroom serving a family of five, provisions must also be made for hanging up outer clothing, laying down undergarments, and sitting down to dress.

Disposal Although personal hygiene in all of its basic aspects may properly be regarded as a process of disposing of body wastes of one sort or another and although fixtures may be regarded as disposal units for such wastes, there still remain other categories of waste products to be taken care of. These other waste products, which are generated directly or indirectly as a result of hygiene activities, may be categorized as follows:

Clean, dry trash (wrappings, bottles, tubes)
Razor blades (used)
Soiled, wet trash (used cleansing or facial tissues, sanitary supplies, contraceptives, bandages)

The first category is relatively simple and may be dealt with by the normal technique of temporary storage in some form of receptacle that is periodically emptied. Similarly, used razor blades can be dealt with by depositing them in a sealed receptacle, for example, the wall slot frequently found in medicine cabinets.

The third group is considerably more difficult to solve since additional requirements of visual and olfactory privacy and aesthetic sensibility are involved. Simply depositing these items in a receptacle, even a closed one, is often less than satisfactory. The most common solution is, of course, to dispose of some such items in the water closet, though this often results in mechanical problems and is not feasible for some items. Other possibilities are the inclusion of a grinder in the water closet or the provision of a small electric incinerator. Another approach is to use air-tight disposal bags that can be sealed and either incinerated or disposed of with the rest of the trash. This is particularly important when the items to be disposed of are in any way contaminated. Even when only a common cold is involved, it would be desirable to isolate or dispose of materials such as used tissues immediately rather than allow them to sit for any length of time in an uncovered container.

Mirrors One item that must be universally provided in some form or other is a mirror. Although generally provided in minimal form, consideration should be given to specialized forms of mirrors. For almost all grooming purposes, adjustable and magnifying mirrors, properly lighted, are extremely useful. Full-length mirrors are useful, and desired, for inspecting the results of one's dressing and grooming, particularly where exercising and similar facilities are provided. They can also be used decoratively and, in some instances, have been used to surface the bathroom completely. The extent to which we can each tolerate or enjoy the extensive use of mirrors is intimately related to our body image and our happiness with that image.[3]

The principal complaints concerning mirrors are "steaming up" and the need for frequent cleaning. The first can be resolved by proper ventilation, which should be provided in any event. The second point, although obviously a source of annoyance to some homemakers, could in fact be regarded as desirable since the problem is not that mirrors necessarily get dirtier than other facilities, but just that they show up dirt more easily—presumably a virtue in a room intended to be sanitary.

Special Features In addition to the basic accommodations, there are a variety of special items of equipment to be considered. These range from the convenient to the luxurious, though one person's luxury is another's necessity. Among such items we might consider: built-in hair dryers, sun lamps, exercise equipment and space, a sauna, a whirlpool bath, a couch for napping or massages, a refrigerator, drying cabinet for hand laundry, heated towel racks, a television set, and a telephone.

The more features one includes in the bathroom the more carefully one needs to plan for adequate and properly located electrical outlets. Even in a minimal bathroom today, it is necessary to provide more than the one outlet commonly found—simply to accommodate all the personal-care appliances.

MATERIALS AND ENVIRONMENTAL CONSIDERATIONS

Materials The materials used in a bathroom, whether for fixtures or for the basic space enclosure, are obviously an important consideration in the overall design. Because of the particular conditions of use to which they are subjected they must fulfill a variety of fairly stringent criteria. This is especially true of the materials from which fixtures are made. Although the particular combination of criteria to be met, and the degree of each, will vary somewhat, depending on the item and its intended use, the list of pertinent criteria includes a number of items: structural soundness, dimensional stability, chemical stability and inertness, abrasion resistance, stain resistance, nonabsorption, freedom from odor retention, and visual and bactericidal cleanability. With a wide variety of totally new man-made materials appearing on the market it is particularly important that their performance characteristics be properly evaluated.[4] It is also important to note and follow the manufacturer's directions with respect to proper cleaning procedures. All too often, fixtures of every description are damaged, imperceptibly but irrevocably, by the improper use of abrasive cleansing agents.

The materials used on the surfaces of the space itself should be nonabsorbent and capable of being easily cleaned. Although traditionally this has meant the use of hard-surfaced or glazed materials, this may change in the future, as in the case of the "soft bathroom" cited earlier. The question of what is an appropriate material is very much a function of the kind of bathroom in question and its size. The conditions of use in a powder room can be quite different from the conditions of use in an average-size family bathroom and different again if we are dealing with a large and sumptuous master bathroom. What may be permissible in one instance may be totally inappropriate in another. Particular attention must be paid to flooring materials, which should be nonabsorbent, nonslip, and easily cleaned. If carpeting is used, it should be capable of being taken up and cleaned frequently. From the standpoint of sanitation, it would also be desirable if the colors and patterns used were such as to show up dirt rather than hide it.

Acoustics One largely unresolved problem, and one of considerable concern and embarrassment to people, is the matter of noise. Bathroom sounds, whether of human or hydromechanical origin, tend to be pronounced, easily identifiable, and hence a cause of intense embarrassment for many people—both the originator of the noise and any listeners.[5] The sound of a flushing water closet is considered objectionable, both because of modesty and because, particularly at night, it is simply a loud noise. Attention also needs to be paid to cutting down on sound transmission. One useful device is to insulate the walls, floor, and ceiling so as to dampen the direct transmission. One thing that tends to aggravate the problem is the hard-surface materials commonly employed in order to meet the criteria for cleanability, waterproofness, and so on, and here sound-absorbing and moisture-resistant ceilings and carpeted floors can contribute enormously.

Another common practice that tends to aggravate the noise problem is the extensive undercutting of the door to allow for ventilation. Ironically, ventilation supplied in this way is poor. A proper mechanical exhaust system would not only permit a tighter door fit but could also contribute an additional anonymous masking noise of its own.

From the standpoint of pure noise and annoyance, without reference to embarrassment, the biggest single problem is caused by piping systems that are improperly sized and that are in no way isolated from the fixtures or the enclosing structure. Although outside the scope of this study, this a problem deserving considerably more attention than it has received to date.

Heat and Ventilation The bathroom, like the kitchen, is one of the two principal spaces in the home that have special ventilation requirements. The activities that take place generate odors and a high degree of humidity, both of which are disagreeable. The common simple device of opening a window is often unsatisfactory because of the nudity involved. First, there is often a marked loss of privacy and, second, there is the danger of cold drafts. In order to avoid these secondary problems and provide adequate ventilation under all circumstances, a mechanical system is generally preferable.

Because of nudity and the temperature differential involved in stepping out of a hot bath, for example, it is also desirable to provide a supplementary source of quick-acting heat in addition to the normal heating unit. This can be provided in the form of an electric heating element or ceiling-mounted heat lamps. Proper heating and ventilation can also obviate the condensation problems that were common in the days of poorly insulated and heated spaces.

Lighting In addition to general room illumination, supplementary lighting is necessary for several special applications. The most important one is in connection with shaving and grooming. Care must be taken with the type and placement of such lighting sources so as to avoid glare, strong shadows, or source reflections in the mirror.[6] Care must also be taken with the choice of bulbs so that colors, of makeup, for example, are not distorted.

Supplementary lighting may also be necessary in a bathing facility if it is so enclosed or located that it receives insufficient light from the general room illumination source. (Inadequate lighting in shower stalls was a recurring complaint of survey respondents.) Obviously, in any situation where there is extensive compartmentalization of fixtures, a number of light sources may be required.

A specialized form of supplementary lighting that, from a safety standpoint, ought to be included in every bathroom is night lighting. At the very least this should take the form of a phosphorescent switch located immediately by the door. It would also be desirable to provide a low-wattage night light that would provide some measure of safety. This might well be incorporated in the water closet or urinal since these are the facilities primarily used.

Although windows are a primary light source, they sometimes have the same disadvantages as were listed previously under ventilation—chiefly lack of privacy. Nevertheless, many of the survey respondents indicated a desire for considerably larger windows than those commonly found in bathrooms—ostensibly to provide better light and also ventilation. It is significant, however, that a secondary but still important consideration was the fact that larger, that is, normal-sized windows could not be identified from the outside as belonging to the bathroom. This represents perhaps the ultimate denial of personal hygiene as a fact of life.

One of the relatively unexploited aspects of windows in bathrooms is the possibility of sometimes having spectacular views to enjoy. Unfortunately, all too often, our prejudices and apprehensions prevent us from taking advantage of these opportunities. One observer, for example, writes with some bitterness about the public facility on the highest level of the Eiffel Tower that "has frosted glass in its square porthole of a window; and therefore no view at all."[7] Apparently one of the most spectacular viewing opportunities was available on transatlantic flights at the end of World War II when the Liberator bombers used had their tail-turrets converted to toilet facilities. Although one does not ordinarily have such spectacular opportunities available, the possibility of even limited views—of an enclosed garden, for example—should not be overlooked.

APPROACHES TO A TOTAL FACILITY

We have thus far been concerned with the determination of the accommodations necessary for personal hygiene based on functional, social, and psychological considerations. In this context, a bathroom fixture—that is, a container to hold water and equipped with supply and drain fittings—does not constitute adequate accommodation of any given personal hygiene function. It represents only one component part of a full facility and represents only one step up the evolutionary ladder from a container without supply and drain fittings. In each instance, a number of other items of equipment are necessary. These are generally what are referred to in the trade as "accessory" items. This view—that they are somehow frivolous—may have had some validity in the distant past, but it can scarcely be maintained today that these are anything less than necessary and integral functional parts of a given facility. This position arises, of course, from a marketing rather than a functional user-oriented point of view and is deplorably common in a number of other industries, such as the automotive. Not only must such items be provided but they also need to be provided in logical and functionally determinable ways. A "facility" can, therefore, be defined as encompassing all those fixtures, "accessory" items, storage spaces, and other areas necessary to accommodate fully a given personal hygiene activity. In a sense, this is analogous to the "work-center" concept used for years with respect to kitchen design. Similarly, a "total facility," equivalent to a partial or full bathroom, can be defined as encompassing all those unit facilities necessary to accommodate fully the normal range of personal hygiene activities integrated with the environmental aspects of the space enclosure, namely storage, disposal, lighting, acoustics, heat, ventilation, and materials. The important point is that a total facility needs to be conceived of as an entity and be provided as a completely integrated system.

Judged on the basis of these criteria, the average bathroom is hopelessly antiquated and inadequate. In the vast majority of cases it still consists of a miscellaneous assortment of oddly sized, unrelated, and minimally equipped fixtures with inadequate storage, counter space, lighting, and ventilation. In many respects, the bathroom is in about the same stage of development as the kitchen was forty or fifty years ago when a stove, sink, and icebox sat in splendid isolation against opposite walls of a room and storage was accounted for by some unreachable fixed shelves in the next room. This is a startling contrast to most contemporary kitchens, which are totally designed integrated facilities with full utilization of space and with individual items carefully related to one another for convenience.

In part at least, this state of affairs is a result of the way in which the plumbing industry developed. Historically, ceramics works simply added china sanitary fixtures to their existing production of dinnerware, tiles, and other ceramic products. Metal fabricators produced fittings and certain accessory items, and foundries turned out cast iron tubs. In time, certain of these firms merged and undertook to produce and market a more nearly comprehensive range of products, but no one as yet offers a truly comprehensive bathroom *system*. In fact, throughout much of the world, the original materials-processing pattern still holds true, the majority of the manufacturers thinking of themselves as being in the ceramics business or the metal-fabricating business instead of as being in the bathroom business. To a degree this is understandable since the production of such a complete system would entail a wide variety of products, materials, and engineering and production capabilities and would represent a substantial transformation for most of industry. Such a transformation is, however, essential if we are ever to have properly designed and fully equipped hygiene facilities that are comprehensive and coherent in function and design. While most of the necessary individual items are available in one form or another from some manufacturer, finding them is a major task and trying to integrate them into a design is next to impossible. At the very least, a degree of standardization and coordination is necessary so that the various pieces, even though made by different manufacturers, would be compatible with one another. Even that is far short of a satisfactory solution so long as builders persist in their minimum-first-cost approach to equipping a bathroom. One obvious answer is to have the prime manufacturer provide an integrated functional unit incorporating all the necessary features.

Obviously, the notion of a fully designed integrated facility implies prefabrication in order that the necessary control and coordination be achieved. Prefabrication is implied because it is, by definition, the opposite of field fabrication, or custom building, which is the current practice. Nevertheless, prefabrication per se is not an answer—as, in fact, we have seen any number of times in the past. A prefabricated motley assortment of ill-designed fixtures and hardware is little better than a field-assembled collection. Prefabrication basically allows for coordination; however, this coordination must be exercised, and it must also be exercised as a step in a total design process. When we speak of prefabrication we must keep in mind that it is only a technique of mass production, albeit one that permits careful control of quality and coordination of parts.

The key question is, first, what precisely is it that one wishes to prefabricate and, second, what degree of fabrication is the most suitable for any given application? When, for example, we speak of prefabrication with respect to the bathroom, we must bear in mind that prefabrication already exists in the bathroom to a degree. All pipe, for example, is prefabricated, as well as all connections. All fixtures and fittings are prefabricated. Should there be a greater degree of prefabrication involving larger components or possibly involving the entire bathroom as a single entity?

Prefabrication in the bathroom dates back at least to the 1920s and, interestingly, every prefabrication concept, from plumbing trees to component systems and from one-piece combined units to complete bathroom packages, can be found. Some were built in prototype and a few even reached the point of being marketed. Whereas, with few exceptions, most of them failed to gain any significant public acceptance, the basic reasons for the failure have little to do with the concept of prefabrication. In the majority of cases, the prefabrication was carried to the ultimate extreme of a complete room that was hauled into place and connected to the utilities. This understandably met with strong opposition from the labor unions and local vested interests as well as from the

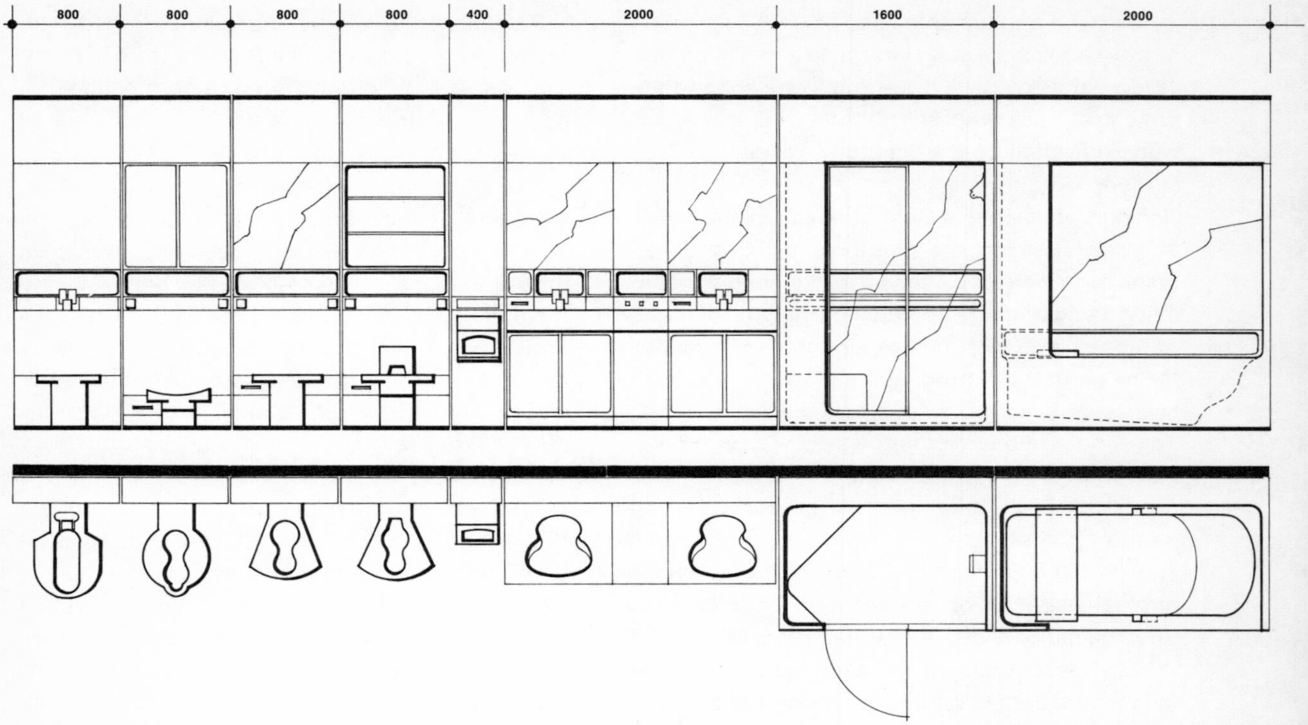

consumers who were offered no choice of package. Moreover, prefabrication could not have been expected to solve much more than the economic problem, since no basic functional studies of personal hygiene activities have been made before this present one. They all did, however, exploit the one great advantage in the prefabrication concept: the possibility of incorporating all the items necessary to make up a total facility.

Present-day systems are somewhat more sophisticated in terms of available materials and fabrication techniques, permitting greater cost savings and the formation of larger and more complex pieces. Conceptually, however, little has changed. The basic impulses that have led to prefabrication have essentially been concerned with cost and space saving. The latter is particularly true of European efforts.

When we examine the basic design approaches, they tend to break down into four major categories: (1) plumbing cores, plumbing walls, and plumbing trees; (2) multiple function fixture units; (3) component systems; (4) complete one-piece bathrooms.[8] In all these approaches one of the major problems is that the unit needs to be designed and built with enormous care. Otherwise, a given mistake will be repeated thousands of times and often in circumstances that, by the very nature of the design, do not permit later correction. This is apparent, for example, in some of the plumbing walls that have been designed with all the fixture positions predetermined and with connections fixed in place. Many of these unfortunately continue to repeat the same antiquated and minimal standards and effectively lock in a poor design forever, since alteration of such a prefabricated wall assembly is usually difficult and often impossible. This holds true for many of the combination units and the one-piece complete bathroom packages as well.

Although such one-piece units unquestionably have application in certain specialized circumstances, they cannot be viewed as a universal solution. First, they fix the design forever and permit no alteration and, second, they pose a major potential problem if some subassembly should

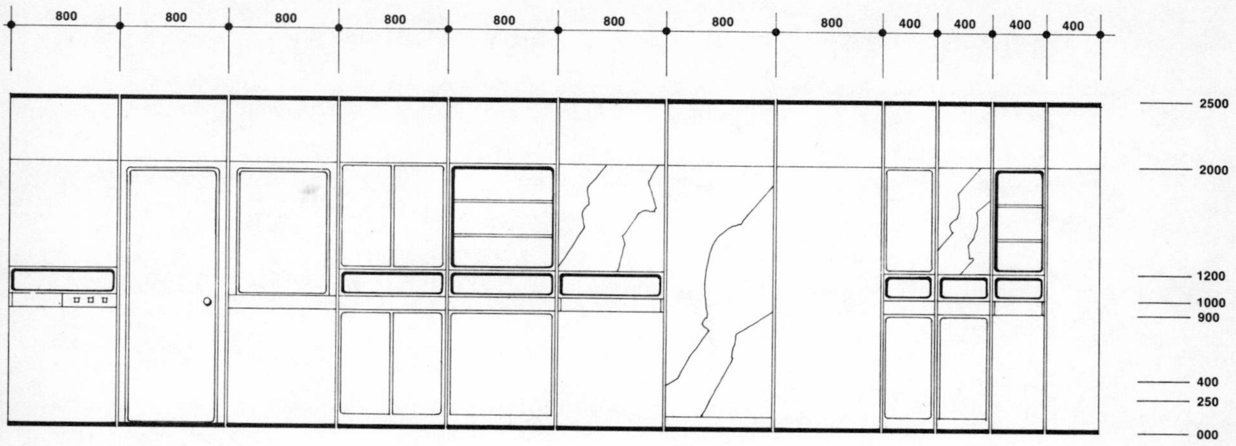

61 / POSSIBLE APPROACH TO A MODULAR BATHROOM SYSTEM

fail. This is particularly true in the case of the complete one-piece bathroom packages, which have to be installed before the building itself is completed and which for all practical purposes can never be removed or altered if it should become necessary. One can only wonder what would happen if some manufacturer had to "recall" several thousand bathroom units to correct some hidden flaw that had subsequently been discovered. Although there are service problems now, plumbers are competent professionals who are to be found in virtually every local community, but if we shifted to a large-scale mass production system whereby complete bathrooms were turned out on assembly lines, there is reason to suspect that the repair and maintenance problems could present some major difficulties.

We must also bear in mind that, in most of the Western world, the consumer has become accustomed to an enormous range of choices. A system that offers little choice and no alteration to suit changing needs or tastes is likely to have a relatively limited appeal in the marketplace.

The modular component system, in contrast, while still offering all the advantages of the others, has the enormous advantage of being flexible and of permitting both alteration and maintenance. It is also, of course, more widely useful and will always find a bigger market, simply by virtue of the fact that a given system will be capable of solving many more problems of many more kinds of bathrooms than any of the other approaches. A component system would permit one to build as large or as small, or as minimal or as elaborate, a bathroom as desired, and would allow it to be modified as necessary. A component system also offers long-term advantages with respect to maintenance costs since, in the event of failure, it will be possible and perhaps desirable simply to remove and dispose of a bad component. In the space, electronics, and automobile industries this is rapidly becoming a standard practice because labor costs have reached the point where it is cheaper to replace an article than to attempt to repair it in the field. One possible such approach to a modular component system is suggested in Figure 61.

PART TWO

PUBLIC HYGIENE FACILITIES

In this section, we shall consider the special problems of a variety of public hygiene facilities, as distinguished from the problems of hygiene for the individual in the home situation. Although people's basic hygiene needs remain essentially the same, there are obviously significant differences in how we commonly satisfy these needs in public facilities, not only in terms of the equipment design itself but also in terms of what equipment is provided and how such equipment is arranged. There are a variety of social and psychological factors at work that cause us to respond differently in public situations, and there are also substantive differences in the situation itself that necessitate different approaches. Perhaps the most important are considerations of sanitation, maintenance, vandalism, and physical safety—none of which are major problems in the home.

While public facilities as a group have certain problems in common, there are still vast differences between, for example, the restroom of a deluxe hotel, the restroom of the corner bar, the restroom of a highway gas station. These differences are as important as the differences from one's home bathroom.

HISTORICAL ASPECTS OF PUBLIC FACILITIES

16

The history of public facilities for personal hygiene is directly related to the history of urbanization and to our awareness of public health and its relationship to sanitation. The phenomenon of urbanization with its concomitant features—numbers of people, density, and travel—determines the problem and the need. Our awareness of, and sensitivity to, public health and sanitation determine the degree and kind of response we make. Throughout history, this awareness has varied enormously both between cultures and periods and produced widely disparate responses in spite of virtually identical needs.

A public facility may be defined as one that is provided in the interest of public convenience, sanitation, and health in a communal location by, or on behalf of, a communal agency for use by anyone with need. Need, in this situation, may arise from one of two circumstances. The first is being *away* from one's own facilities—being "caught short" as the expression has it. The second is not having facilities of one's own at all. Underlying all of this, of course, is the assumption that "facilities" are necessary at all, an assumption that essentially derives its validity from the conditions of an urban situation. In either a nomadic or an agrarian situation the circumstances are sufficiently different in both kind and degree not to pose the same kinds of problems. The nomad, the herder, or the farmer is first of all rarely "away from home," and an alfresco solution in any case is almost always possible and indeed sometimes desirable. From time immemorial, the farmer has used the excrement of his family as well as of his animals to fertilize his fields. And nomadic peoples simply pack up and move to another site. Among the nomadic Tartars, apparently a favored curse was, "I would thou mightest tarry so long in one place that thou mightest smell thine own dung as the Christians do!"[1] Water for drinking, cooking, bathing, and so on is again, by definition, always available in such circumstances because it is the availability of water that determines the site for temporary or permanent settlement in the first place.

As a settlement becomes permanent and increasingly urbanized, sheer numbers and density of population tend to preclude alfresco elimination from the perspective of public sanitation and health. In many parts of the world, even today, however, this has not yet become an operable constraint, with consequences that are all too familiar and unfortunate. An urban environment is, by definition, an environment of specialists, of persons who commonly go away from home to a particular work place, and it is also a market center, which means it involves substantial numbers of people traveling to and from—or, for our purposes, people who are away from home. Water, while perhaps available in sufficient quantity in total, is often not available in the place it is needed because of the expense of constructing transport systems; again, this problem haunts us even today, with the consequence that many people the world over lack, at the very least, adequate bathing facilities. A current technological concomitant is that they also probably lack elimination facilities. The need for public facilities, in summary, stems from two factors, both directly related to urbanization: lack of any facilities and the needs of "travelers" who are beyond the reach of their facilities. As a consequence of these two somewhat different kinds of need, the public facilities that have evolved throughout our history have tended to meet one need or the other. The primary need, and the one that is still very much with us today, is the need for public facilities for elimination. The secondary need, which in most circumstances has diminished in importance, is for public bathing facilities—with the major and obvious exception, of course, of facilities for the traveler, such as the hotel and motel. In the discussion that follows we will examine each category separately.

The simplest, most primitive, and still very common answer to the problem of elimination in public is simply no solution except to heed the call of nature whenever and wherever one happens to be. In some instances a modicum of discretion is sought by using an alleyway, for example; in other instances it is still a common sight in some parts of the world to find people urinating or defecating wherever they happen to be. The only thing that seems to be altering this practice today in fact is the hazard posed by increased automobile traffic.

At some point in our history there appeared on the scene an itinerant vendor of public convenience, of a sort. Passing through the streets with a bucket and a large cloak, the vendor, for a suitable fee, would set his bucket down for your use and shield you from public view with his cloak. It is probable also that he provided the additional service of protecting the temporarily defenseless patron from mischief makers and thieves. Dr. Johnson describes such a service in Scotland in the eighteenth century, and other sources suggest that such a service was commonplace in many of the small towns in eastern Europe and Asia Minor as recently as the 1920s.

The first evidence of actual physical facilities for public use is to be found at Knossos, dating back to approximately 1700 B.C. These facilities are startlingly sophisticated in their form and technology and in many respects are little different from our facilities today. Most of the great cities of the ancient world were similarly advanced and provided hygiene facilities both for the local populace and for the traveler. By and large, however, this was primarily a matter of providing communal facilities on a broad scale in lieu of private facilities. The epitome of this approach was of course Rome and its stupendous baths. The pattern is one that is typical of the development of most of our services and technologies. They are provided initially on a communal basis because of the costs involved, but as a society becomes wealthy enough there begins a gradual shift toward individual facilities and services.

Rome also provides us with our first real example of the public facility for the man in the street—the public urinal, or "pissoir," or "Vespasienne." In the first century A.D., the Emperor Vespasian undertook, as part of his rebuilding of Rome, the erection of numerous street urinals as a public convenience and also apparently as a means of increasing his treasury, for the urine was collected in great cisterns and sold to cloth dyers.[2]

For the next thousand years or so, public facilities would appear to have suffered the same general decline as did the rest of our hygiene facilities and practices in most of the Western world. The facilities ranged from none, to designated dung heaps, to privies, to "carriage pots" for the wealthy traveling by carriage. At the time of Louis XIV a lady of the court writes that

> . . . at Fontainebleau one must wait for darkness to use the open spaces. This grieved Her Grace, who preferred privacy and something to sit on. She found the streets of Fontainebleau full of reminders of a human frailty she deplored, and especially of souvenirs of the Swiss Guards, of which she wrote with astonishment.[3]

Similarly, Charles II and his court, who spent the summer of 1665 in Oxford, were berated in a contemporary account:

> Though they were neat and gay in their apparrell, yet they were very nasty and beastly, leaving at their departure their excrements in every corner, in chimneys, studies, coleholes, cellars.[4]

Some hundred and fifty years later Lord Byron is reported to have been barred from a London hotel for "deeming the hall to be a less inclement place than an uncovered yard" one cold and wet night One is surprised that the lord would have chosen so mean a lodging that no chamber pot was provided, but be that as it may. It is fascinating to note that Leonardo da Vinci in describing his proposals for building new towns makes the point that all stairways in the "public housing" blocks should be made spiral stairs so as to prevent the sanitary misuse of stair landings. Yet, in the 1970s in the United States, we find that a common problem of many public housing projects and other slum tenements is the very same.

It is not until well into the nineteenth century that we again find evidence of any major concern with, and awareness of, the problems of public convenience and public sanitation in the major cities of the world. It isn't until the 1840s that the public street urinal makes its reappearance, this time in Paris. By the 1860s Paris also boasted *pavillons pour dames* which were, however, fully enclosed kiosks in contrast to the typically open or only partially shielded male urinals. In the eighties the *chalet de necessité* had become bisexual and incorporated water closets as well. In many respects these anticipate our current public facilities and, in some instances at least, these are still our current facilities. The eighties also saw the return of the itinerant vendor albeit in the more sophisticated form of *les Water-Closets ambulants,* which were horsedrawn carriages with several toilet compartments that cruised the main thoroughfares.[5]

In England, the spread of "sanitary conveniences" was, in part, encouraged by the great Crystal Palace Exhibition of 1851, where there were unprecedented numbers of people to be accommodated and where the facilities provided clearly had to reflect the quality and aspirations of the exhibition itself. According to the official report some 800,000 visitors paid to avail themselves of the facilities.

Another consequence of the great London exhibition and the others that followed was to stimulate rail travel all across Europe and the building of terminals, complete with sanitary facilities, often of several classes according to the class of carriage. In many respects, this represents the real beginning of the availability of public facilities on any sizeable scale. Yet a few years later, George Jennings, who was responsible for the installation of the facilities at the Crystal Palace, was turned down by the authorities when he proposed building underground "halting stations" at strategic locations around London complete with all conveniences and respectable attendants for the charge of a small fee. His offer

> . . . was declined by Gentlemen (influenced by English delicacy of feeling) who preferred that the daughters and wives of Englishmen should encounter at every corner, sights so disgusting to every sense, and the general public suffer pain and often permanent injury rather than permit the construction of that shelter and pri-

vacy now common in every other city in the world.[6]

During the later years of the century, however, the struggle had largely been won and public facilities became widely available in more major cities. Perhaps unfortunately, many still survive with little modernizing. In many places, the facilities that have survived and are still fit for use are no longer as accessible as they once were. Most were designed for pedestrian use and, with a nice beaux arts feeling for symmetry and grand planning, were located on traffic circles or roadway dividing malls. The need for public facilities serving the urban pedestrian has, however, diminished considerably, particularly since so many retail and commercial establishments are now required to provide facilities for the public. Indeed, because of the condition of many municipal street facilities many people tend to avoid them anyway, a matter we shall discuss in more detail later on.

In this century, the development of public facilities has been largely related to the evolution of transportation modes and the accommodation of the traveling public: railway and rapid transit systems, air terminals, and travel by automobile. The once simple outhouse, behind the general store that also sold petrol, has now evolved to the point where all the major oil companies advertise "clean restrooms" at their stations in recognition of the fact that a substantial number of their customers stop primarily to use the toilet facilities and only secondarily to service their vehicles. In many places today the average person is a vehicular person, not a pedestrian one. With the advent of limited-access superhighways without normal roadside services it soon became apparent that it was still necessary to provide sanitary facilities. In the beginning, the planners only provided for pull-offs or lay-bys where a weary driver could stop, stretch, and walk about a bit. The "rest stop" invited, however, other collateral and inevitable uses, and the areas were soon fouled with excrement and littered with picnic refuse. Often at considerable cost, these stopping places have now been provided with sanitary facilities and picnic tables. In 1968, when the program of providing "comfort stations" along the interstate highway system began in New York State, the average cost per facility was in the neighborhood of a quarter of a million dollars, or about $40,000 a seat. Approximately $40,000 is for the building (with seven seats) complete with plumbing, heating, and lighting. Another $40,000 is necessary for a sewage treatment plant; $8,000 to find and drill for water; $20,000 for landscaping and picnic tables, and the balance of some $160,000 for drainage, sidewalks, parking areas, curbing, acceleration and deceleration lanes. In addition to these capital costs, it takes a staff of four to operate and maintain the facility on a 24-hour basis, plus heating and lighting costs.[7]

Urbanization is now forcing the large-scale development of public facilities in wilderness areas and national parks as well. The obvious reason for this development is the worldwide explosive popularity of camping, which has led to ever more sophisticated and nearly complete facilities' being provided at campgrounds. Not yet so obvious, but an increasing problem, is the change this brings to what we still tend to think of as the pure wilderness. The suggestion has been made, only half in jest, that we need to build a "privy" on the peak of Mount Rainier and apparently most other mountain peaks as well. While public attention has been focused on the growth of camping, little attention has been paid to other wilderness activities such as mountain climbing. It has been estimated that at present the number of climbers in the United States alone runs to somewhere between 250,000 and a million. Whatever the figure, it has become apparent that many climbing trails and mountain peaks are literally covered with the refuse and excrement of hundreds of climbing expeditions and grow worse daily. What seemed like an inconsequential problem once upon a time is today assuming major proportions with the growth of population and the vastly increased usage of the areas. While this may scarcely seem to be a problem, it has to be remembered that though a mountain may be vast, the number of possible campsites and climbing trails is severely limited. On one recent occasion, there were some 250 people camping at Camp Muir at the 10,000-foot level of Mount Rainier and waiting in long lines to use the two toilets, the contents of which are regularly flown out by helicopter. Similar problems are reported at Mount Whitney where the Forest Service has reluctantly concluded that it must restrict the number of hikers who can climb the mountain at any one time. Ironically, Forest Service officials ordered the removal of a fiber glass toilet because "it failed to blend with the environment as required by the Wilderness Act of 1964." The Swiss News Agency commenting on the lack of facilities on the Matterhorn has observed that "The latrine-like smell spreading all over does not contribute greatly to our slogans praising the Alpine air."

When we examine the development of public bathing facilities, we find essentially the same basic patterns of need and impetus as before—convenience for the traveler and sanitation for the local population who do not possess their own facilities. Our earliest evidence of public bathing facilities of both types dates back again to Crete, Rome, and the other early Mediterranean civilizations. Bathing is obviously, however, an altogether different activity from elimination and, almost inevitably, public bathing places developed an important social component above and beyond their fundamental hygienic purposes. In time, all the early baths, like the medieval stews that followed, came to be important institutions in the community as places to meet and socialize, a function that is still very much alive today in the *sento,* the public bath of Japan, and in the saunas of Finland.

In many instances, however, this social aspect came in time to dominate the public bath scene in a somewhat distorted way, so that finally the words *bagnio* and *stew* came to be synonymous with brothel. Indeed, during many periods in our history the public bath could scarcely be considered a hygienic facility at all; its raison d'être was social, and its waters were more often a vehicle for spreading disease than for cleansing. Interestingly, it appears that we are witnessing a contemporary revival of this with many of the so-called "Turkish baths" and "saunas" found in large cities around the world today, which generally cater to a strictly male clientele and among whose many advertised services bathing must rank as purely incidental.

It wasn't until the nineteenth century that the revived interest in public health and sanitation, coupled with the rapid growth and crowding of the cities, led again to the development of public baths on any scale, both in Europe and in the United States. For the most part, however, these baths were essentially hygienic and utilitarian and were intended "for the amelioration of the condition of the labouring classes." Some were built by municipal authorities, others by charitable groups. Largely they were located in working-class neighborhoods in the industrial towns or were part of the mill or mine properties itself and never became more than purely hygienic facilities. At present, most of these baths in Europe and the United States have been supplanted by the availability of individual facilities as a consequence of improved housing standards and a higher standard of living. In other parts of the world, however, the public bath where it exists still fulfills a major function. Japan, for example, despite the enormous strides it has made in most areas, still has a major housing problem that it has just begun to tackle. It has been estimated, for instance, that approximately 80 per cent of the urban population does not have private bathing or toilet facilities available to it. In this situation, the public bath plays a crucial hygienic as well as social role. The situation in many other parts of the world is obviously as difficult, if not worse, particularly as more of the population flocks to urban areas unequipped to accommodate them. Lest the reader feel too smug, it must also be remembered that even in most of the wealthy industrial nations a substantial portion of the population, even in the major world capitals, lives in what we in the United States, for example, would term substandard housing, where hygiene facilities are shared and are down the hall, or in the yard, or in some other inaccessible or semi-public place.

Another category of "public bath" we must consider is that based on the provision of a specialized service that by its nature tends to be feasible only on a communal basis. The most obvious example of this is the spa, which largely owes its existence to the real or imagined curative properties of particular waters or springs. Although, strictly speaking, these should not be considered sanitary facilities, they do represent another important facet—water therapy. Interestingly, many such spas have been in more or less continuous operation since Roman times or earlier, while bathing defined as body cleansing, public or private, has suffered numerous setbacks and declines throughout our history. Most of the spas and hot springs in Europe, which were fashionable a hundred years ago, are every bit as popular today for "taking the waters."

The sauna, or steam bath, still found throughout Scandinavia and many other parts of northern Europe, has similarly enjoyed an uninterrupted history of popularity dating back before recorded history. Although regarded by many as basically therapeutic and an adjunct to bathing, it is in actuality one of the finest body-cleansing techniques known, while its therapeutic benefits are incidental. Today the steam bath most commonly exists as a public, or more properly commercial, facility, particularly in urban areas, because of the cost and space problems of having a private one. Prefabricated saunas are, however, becoming more widely available and may in time become standard equipment for those who desire them. In a somewhat similar fashion, the Japanese public bath, which is partly therapeutic and partly hygienic, may also have its days numbered as more families are able to afford their own soaking tubs and private bathrooms.

When we examine facilities provided for the traveler, the early historical pattern has in general been fairly similar to that of facilities for elimination: the wealthy traveled with their own portable or folding tubs or used the facilities provided by the inn. The one interesting variation, which appeared in the medieval period and which survived until almost the turn of this century, was for a bathing facility to be part of a barber-surgeon's establishment, where one could have a total bodily rejuvenation—bath, shave, haircut, and manicure. Some similar establishments still exist in the form of health or athletic clubs and, in a few instances, as part of the services of major rail and airport facilities in Europe. It is somewhat surprising, and a pity, that more such establishments don't exist in major airports and in the business sections of major cities, where many people who stay in the city for the evening might find such services extremely pleasant and useful. Only in a few Italian cities are such *alberghi diurna* still to be found where one can have a bath, a nap, a haircut or permanent, a shave, or a manicure or pedicure; or can have one's clothes pressed or shoes repaired and shined; or can buy theater tickets.

As Bernard Rudofsky observes in his brilliant book on streets:

> Most of these conveniences are unavailable in the United States except on taking up residence at a hotel. The foreigner searching the street for what is called, coyly and deceitfully, a rest room, is directed to a subway station which may be half a mile out of his way. There, upon paying the fare for a trip he has no intention of undertaking, he comes upon a latrine that may bring on vesical nightmares in a person unfamiliar with local hygiene.[8]

The conventional hotel bedroom/bathroom that we accept, or demand, as standard today dates only to 1908, when Ellsworth Statler built a hotel in Buffalo, New York, and advertised "A Room and a Bath for a Dollar and a Half." Although some hotels had provided lavatories or bathtubs in the rooms prior to that, his was apparently the first to include a complete bathroom. For all practical purposes this was also the prototype for the universal 5-by-7-foot bathroom that has survived to this day, both for residential as well as hotel use. Unfortunately, most people in their own homes require far more space than when traveling.

The fortunes of public facilities are very much dependent on the economic feasibility of providing private facilities versus public and on the needs of travelers. Early railway cars, for example, provided bathing facilities in their first-class accommodations, but as travel times shortened, these were largely abandoned in favor of terminal facilities. It may well be that as supersonic transports cut travel time even further, the need for terminal facilities will decrease accordingly. We may similarly speculate that as our communications technology becomes even more widespread and sophisticated and as people are able to "work" at home, the need for most forms of public facilities will disappear, just as sidewalks have in our suburbs.

17 SOCIAL AND PSYCHOLOGICAL ASPECTS OF PUBLIC FACILITIES

Most of the verbalized reactions to public facilities concern their physical condition and level of cleanliness and maintenance. These essentially negative reactions stem, however, from more than simply a sense of refinement or aesthetics and find their roots in our feelings about territoriality and privacy. In addition, our general unverbalized or unconscious attitudes toward public facilities are substantially more negative than they are toward the home bathroom or toward the idea of the bathroom in general terms. Similarly, most of our feelings about the body, sex, elimination, privacy, and cleanliness are magnified in this context of "publicness," for the fact of publicness, with its inevitable territorial violations and loss of privacy, increases our apprehensions. In addition we are concerned for the most part with elimination functions, which generally appear to raise the most psychological difficulties. Aside from hotels, most of us, with the exception of the Japanese and Scandinavians, have little experience with public bathing facilities so that in the main this discussion will focus on the more common denominator of the public toilet.

We also find that our negative reactions extend to equipment, materials, and fittings. Some persons harbor strong feelings against having anything in the home, for example, that is commonly found in a public facility. If a water closet is unmentionable, then a public water closet, or public type of water closet, is utterly unspeakable. While undoubtedly some of this could legitimately be considered a matter of aesthetics, some people's feelings on the matter are more vehement and spring from other motivations. Indeed, it is particularly striking since in so many other areas of the home, the kitchen particularly, it is commonly a status symbol to have an item of commercial or professional equipment. Consider, for example, a recent court case in Australia wherein a woman refused to pay for a new water closet installed in her house because "it resembled a public lavatory and had a man's seat!" (an elongated bowl with an open-front seat). The woman went on to tell the court that "she was so disgusted that she could not bring herself to use it."

Not only are open-front seats an anathema for many people, but so are black seats, since these are most commonly used in public facilities. Similarly, all "home" seats must have a cover, again one suspects more for psychological reasons than practical ones. The urinal is similarly unacceptable to many people. Indeed, until fairly recently many older people were strongly opposed to showers in the home because they were "unsuitable."

PUBLICNESS

The concept of "publicness" is a compound of several factors: the degree of strangeness of other users from oneself, the extent of usage of a facility, and perhaps most important ultimately, the level of cleanliness and maintenance, which, in turn, relates to our concerns regarding territoriality and privacy.

Let us first examine the problem of "strangeness." On one hand, we still tend to have the primitive apprehension about the stranger in terms of simple fear and of privacy violations, as well as concerns about role and status.[1] Violations of privacy are measurable by the relationship between the involved parties. In this context, however, we are dealing not with obvious and defined family relationships as in the home but rather with a set of loosely implied or felt affinities based largely on perceived social differences.

Thus, a hotel bathroom, for example, while "public" in a strict sense, is generally regarded much as one would regard one's own home bathroom, largely since it literally and psychologically is one's temporary home, on the assumption, of course, that it is the kind of hotel that one would normally frequent. In this situation, cleanliness and maintenance is rarely a factor, nor, of course, is simultaneous use or lack of privacy.

As we move along the continuum, the facilities at one's place of work, or one's club or bowling alley, for instance, tend to be viewed fairly neutrally because one, after all, does know many of the people there and has a certain affinity with them. (The exception, to be examined later, is the "executive washroom.") As we move further afield, however, our attitudes begin to change. Our attitudes toward the facilities at our favorite restaurant or department store are fairly neutral, but they begin to get more negative and apprehensive as we move to establishments that we wouldn't ordinarily frequent. This "class"-based feeling reaches its peak in the case of what we tend to regard as really public facilities—such as those in airports, railway stations, athletic stadiums, and highway rest stops, "where goodness knows who may have used or touched something before us." While such fears and reservations are all too often amply justified by the physical evidence around us, a major portion is attributable to our various religious, ethnic, and racial prejudices and apprehensions about the "stranger." In the extreme, this leads to the institution of separate facilities—for blacks and whites and for the "untouchables."

Central to this question of publicness are also our feelings about elimination. While our own personal excretory processes and products may be more or less disagreeable, those of strangers tend, in general, to be viewed even more negatively—generally, as before, in direct relationship to the degree of strangeness of the stranger in question, viewed in peer group terms. In this sense the level of cleanliness and maintenance becomes a critical factor in our reactions, for it is a major determinant of territory/privacy violations. Our privacy, or "territories of the self" in Erving Goffman's terminology, is based on a sense of possession, of "mineness."[2] Thus, in a relatively spotless public bathroom, with no one "passing wind," or whatever, it is perfectly possible for us to pretend that we are in a private situation—in a bathroom, or booth, that is "mine." This illusion is quickly and rudely shattered if we should happen to find fecal matter in or on the bowl or see the floor awash in urine. In this situation it becomes impossible to deny that someone else has rudely violated "our," albeit temporary, territory. In some respects, this circumstance is akin to the practice of some burglars who defecate on the premises before leaving and thereby demonstrate symbolically and incontrovertibly that they have successfully violated the victim's territory and privacy.[3] Hence, the more spotless the facilities, the less overt and tangible evidence there is to remind us of the fact that it is indeed a public facility that we are sharing with others, either simultaneously or sequentially. The less the tangible evidence (the better the cleanliness and maintenance) the fewer the apprehensions and negative reactions. Thus, when we complain about the cleanliness of a public facility, we are in reality giving voice to a whole constellation of complaints ranging from aesthetics to simple disgust, to privacy violations, to symbolic defilement.

Such territorial violations can also, however, be visual, auditory, olfactory, or even tactile as well as physical, as in the case of the "warm seat" phenomenon. Many people, for example, feel uncomfortable sitting down somewhere and finding that the seat is still warm from the previous occupant. The seat may be perfectly clean, but the uneasiness and discomfort exists, nonetheless, particularly in the case of water closet seats. This is not only someone else's body heat but also someone else's bare-body heat and is more sharing than many people feel comfortable with. This phenomenon occurs in many different contexts, for example, "hot-bunking" on submarines or the still-warm and rumpled bed in the hotel or whorehouse. Ultimately this leads back to the sense of personal ownership, the sense of "mineness" that lies behind many of our privacy demands.

The territory/privacy violations just described are operable essentially because of our general societal taboos against discussing, watching, or acknowledging elimination functions or against intruding on the privacy of others by paying attention to such activities. We mutually screen out and ignore one another, therefore, even though they are there and we know "what they are doing." Our responses are much more geared to the tangible evidence of other people than to the obvious fact of other people's possibly being actually present. This is, of course, a central factor with respect to our hygiene/privacy behavior and one we shall examine in more detail again.

"PRIVACY-FROM"

A central concept in our responses to public facilities is that of "privacy-from" others, one component of which we just examined. Our modesty/privacy demands are complex with respect to matters of personal hygiene. In the home situation, our privacy demands range along the continuum of not being seen or heard to not having someone else even be aware of our activities and are predicated on a certain set of fairly clearly established relationships among the parties involved. Essentially our concern in the home is with "privacy-for" the individual. In the public situation, however, we have an equal concern with "privacy-from" other persons and their activities. This is a critical concept because the two forms can operate independently of one another. Having one form does not necessarily guarantee having the other.

In an operative sense, privacy-from can be considered to begin with the provision of exclusive or limited-access facilities. Perhaps the best example is the "executive washroom," which has as its principal function the protection of the selected users from the presence of other persons. Granted the validity of the standard arguments for the exclusive facility—for example, saving valuable executive time—the fact remains that the status/privacy aspect is paramount.

This aspect is based on the generally unverbalized recognition that the elimination processes are human and universal and, in a sense, the great leveler of all mankind. King, prime minister, football star, corporation president, or stock boy—all have identical biological needs, and all are *equal* before the imperious demands of nature—to wit:

> Presumptuous pisse-pot, how did'st thou offend?
> Compelling females on their hams to bend?
> To Kings and Queens we humbly bend the knee,
> But Queens themselves are forced to stoop to thee.[4]

It has been remarked that the only known exceptions to this otherwise inviolable natural law are American movie and television performers, who never have to go to the bathroom, or at least so it would seem. For the rest of us poor mortals the situation is perhaps best summed up by the old European expression: *"aller ou le roi va a pied,"* or "I'm going where even the King must go on foot."

This equality, which is implicit in the act of elimination, has occasionally also been exploited in a positive fashion, as we noted earlier with regard to "the French courtesy." The invitation to join the King or ambassador in defecation and share a few moments of informal private conversation must certainly have ranked as a substantial gesture of honor and personal favor. On the other hand, obviously not everyone shares such sentiments. It has been reported, for example, that one Brahmin member of President Johnson's Cabinet left because of Johnson's penchant for coarseness and his insistence that he be accompanied into the bathroom to continue conversations.[5] "The French Courtesy" may also have been the origin of the "man-to-man" talk.

In most cases, however, we tend to insist that the "great" have absolute privacy in such circumstances; hence, we have the institution of the "executive washroom" and the provision of the private washroom for the board chairman. Similarly, in military situations, the first preparations made for a visiting field marshal are to erect a private facility so that he does not have to share the normal communal and semi-public accommodations. Involved are the preservation of the image and in some situations maintaining the security of the personage and guaranteeing his freedom from importunities by the less exalted. A recent newspaper article reported on the private dressing room, complete with private bathroom, being provided for TV talk show host Jack Paar. Mr. Paar noted that some years earlier at another network he had to use the public facilities and one night met an aspiring young writer—Dick Cavett—whom he hired and who subsequently replaced him. He went on to say that if he had had a private bathroom at NBC at the time, there wouldn't be a Dick Cavett around today.[6]

This notion of preserving the image is in fact quite common and accounts, at least in part, for the status attached to the relative privacy, or sole use, of hygiene facilities. We find instances of this in any number of situations: in the number of bathrooms a house has; in the "star's" dressing room, which must have a private bath; in the fact that privacy is also a salable commodity, as in the "first-class" European hotel; and in first-class air travel, which has one facility for every six or seven passengers instead of one for every twenty or thirty passengers as in tourist class.

In addition to status or role preservation, privacy-from is also, particularly in our puritan Anglo-Saxon culture, very much concerned with segregation by sexes and becomes an issue when one is dealing with another cultural pattern. The range of attitudes concerning personal hygiene that we find if we examine the situation from a worldwide perspective is enormous. We find, for instance, a pattern common to Japan, Italy, and France, among others, where many public facilities are not segregated by sex and where alfresco elimination in public in the absence of convenient facilities is fairly common. Indeed, it is apparently still legal for a taxi driver in England "to water the wheel" of his vehicle when necessary without its being considered the committing of a public nuisance. In contrast, in the United States particularly, we have quite the reverse situation where privacy demands and sex segregation are strictly enforced by both legal and social sanctions and where casual public elimination can lead to swift arrest.

It is this lack of sex segregation and privacy-from, for example, that causes so many Americans and British anguish when traveling abroad. A woman entering a public facility will ultimately have visual privacy for herself when she reaches the sanctuary of her stall, but meanwhile she has been forced to pass a bank of unshielded in-use male urinals on the way. She has no privacy from urinating males. Similarly, a man has to urinate in full view of passing females or, in other circumstances, in full view of the female attendant. In either case, the traveler (cultural outsider) has suffered a major violation of privacy norms. In the 1972 Munich Olympics, for example, some United States athletes were reportedly a bit disconcerted by the mixed-occupancy locker room and hygiene facilities.

These psychological hazards of tourism operate, of course, in all sorts of different directions. On the one hand, we find a recent work like *Johns in Europe—Toilet Training for Tourists,* which tries by words and photographs to condition the American traveler to some of the "horrors" that await him abroad. On the other hand, Thai guidebooks warn the Thai traveler against climbing upon and squatting over one of those abominable and noisy Western-style water closets. Similarly, while we point out that when visiting in Japan one must never, never wash in the bathtub, the Japanese in turn are cautioning their travelers never to wash outside the bathtub as at home but in the tub like the Westerners, dirty and unpleasant though it may be.[7]

Although not as strongly perhaps, we also feel a similar reaction to public bathing facilities where the mores and habits of one culture are viewed with unease by others, at the very least. Admittedly, it rarely becomes a problem of the same dimensions simply because most Americans, for example, don't go to a public Japanese bathhouse or to a Finnish sauna except by deliberate choice. In so doing, they are presumably prepared for the experience of mixed bathing and of bath attendants who may be of the opposite sex, not to mention the vastly different physical experiences to be encountered.

Privacy-from, if it is to be achieved at all in such circumstances, is had through the device of what Goffman calls "civil inattention." This device of scrupulously observed avoidance behavior is widely employed in many cultures and situations and demands that we avoid observing other people's behavior and in particular, with a notable exception to be discussed later, that we avoid making eye contact. Insofar as possible, we tend generally to try to ignore the presence of other persons while at the same time acknowledging them by being careful not to intrude on their privacy. A clear illustration of this device in operation may be seen in patron behavior in Soviet restaurants, which have the disconcerting habit, for us, of filling every empty seat with unrelated diners. A party of two seated at a table for four can preserve their privacy only by buying two more meals or by mutually practicing civil inattention or avoidance behavior with the inevitable two other diners.

This particular situation is also illustrative of certain spatial and territorial problems. In point of fact, with a rectangular table that permits two pairs of diners to sit opposite one another, or side by side, the closeness is no greater than that normally encountered in banquette seating arrangements anywhere in the world—a situation that also calls for civil inattention with respect to one's neighbors. In the case of a square or round table for four, however, the problems of clearly defining and maintaining territory, pairing-bonds, and privacy all become acute and, in the case of many visitors, extremely irritating.

Civil inattention is perhaps the one situation in which most of us are as "polite" in our behavior relative to others as the British or the Japanese are most of the time. We seem instinctively to realize that the delicate behavioral devices that guarantee our privacy and that of our neighbors is a mutually dependent exercise. Privacy-from in this case also becomes privacy-for.

When we observe behavior patterns, for example, in any sizeable men's room, we find that almost invariably a man entering to use a urinal will look first for a vacant one *that is not adjacent to one in use* if possible and then for a clean one. Only in a crowded situation is the intimacy imposed by tight fixture spacing tolerable or permissible.[8] A violation of this pattern is at once suspect and cause for concern, aggression, or whatever. To a somewhat lesser degree the same rule applies to the use of water closets and washbasins. The unstated assumption is that one will observe, whenever possible, not only a visual but also a physical avoidance behavior. While such behavior is perhaps most pronounced in public hygiene facilities, a similar pattern obtains in almost all public situations, such as buses, subways, and park benches.

There are, on occasion, however, some interesting and significant reversals of this general behavior, most notably in the deliberate and enforced intimacy imposed in military and school environments when a particular coping camaraderie appears to operate. Speaking of his experiences in World War II, one observer has written that:

> Toilet taboos were suspended for the duration. Fifty of us shared one latrine and took turns cleaning it, in a symphony of grunts and smells and flushing noises. There were no doors on the booths, nor privacy at the urinal. Answering nature's call meant subjecting yourself to loud and detailed criticism—perceptive and merciless descriptions of your sex organs, ranging from ridicule to glowing admiration; brilliant critiques of your style of defecation, with learned footnotes on gas-passing. Expert discussions gave new meaning to your technique of urination—which hand, or how many, or no hands at all—or how nonchalant you managed to look. We soon learned to flaunt our genitals and brag about our toilet mannerisms. Anyone who was modest about these was immediately and forever labelled a homosexual.[9]

"PRIVACY-FOR"

Privacy-for in the strict sense is achieved by many of the same devices we employ in the home situation. These include: a discreet location; discreet identification; the use of visual barriers or compartments; the use of masking sounds, most commonly piped-in music; ventilation; plus a variety of behavioral devices.

In some public situations, however, these devices are sometimes carried too far, particularly as far as discretion of location is concerned. Many public facilities are so discreet in their location or signing as to be virtually nonexistent for the passerby or the uninitiated. Several years ago, a British survey of public facilities commented:

> Not everyone knows that the surest way to a public convenience in Hull is to ask for the nearest royal statue.[10]

Or, as another commentator has observed:

> How do you find it? Architects should remember that this is a particular problem in the case of a lady, since she may not ask. Yet the solution is not to make it so obvious that you cannot miss it, even when not searching. For in that case, a true lady will not use it. I feel that in the game of hunting-the-toilet, a lady with a professional education in architecture and city planning has a distinct advantage over her sisters. For there are certain laws, which, consciously or unconsciously, designers follow.[11]

And, indeed, as was further asked, how explicit and unambiguous are the terms *convenience* or *lounge* or *comfort station* to a stranger?

Cultural relativism also crops up with respect to the perceived appropriate degree of shielding or closure provided by water closet compartments. Many European countries, for example, insist on complete floor-to-ceiling enclosures and doors—in effect, complete rooms. In the United States, on the contrary, we most commonly provide partitions that begin about 300 mm (12 inches) above the floor and end at about 1,700 mm (5½ feet), generally with a lockable door—an arrangement much deplored by many Europeans. In still other places, one can find open banks of water closets, particularly in military installations, schools, and some factories. This is, of course, a deliberate elimination of privacy for particular psychological and institutional objectives.

Perhaps our principal behavioral device for achieving privacy, both "from" and "for," is our mutual agreement to ignore one another and our activities. There are exceptions to this covenant, of course, particularly in the case of small children, who often compete and compare the results of their excretory powers. In some instances, this carries over to adulthood, most generally in circumstances of drunken camaraderie. In most normal circumstances, however, this covenant is something we almost universally rely upon.

A measure of privacy is also achieved in some public situations by the apparent paradox of group activity. Most commonly this is employed by ladies who are part of a mixed party at a restaurant, for example. As if on cue, one finds all the ladies excusing themselves to go off to the "rest room." While this pattern undoubtedly has other elements involved such as comparing notes about their respective dates or their luncheon partners, plans for the evening, and so on, it is also a fairly effective privacy device, used by women of all ages in all circumstances. It operates by obscuring the identity of any particular individual and removes the burden of being the one who had to go do you know what.

Ladies, of course, also typically employ the device of grooming to obscure their basic activities. A woman will invariably return from the ladies' room with her hair and makeup touched up and in perfect order and with fresh perfume—so who is to suspect she really didn't excuse herself to "go powder her nose"? Although men, of course, also invariably groom themselves, the device is not nearly as effective because the results are rarely as strikingly obvious.

Perhaps the most extreme device, though a very common one, for achieving privacy for one's elimination needs in public is simply not to go at all. While this is not a matter of privacy in an operable sense, it is a question of motivation for privacy, coupled, of course, with problems of sanitation, which we will examine in more detail later on, and problems of coping with undergarments. Because of this and early training the majority of women, in the United States at least, have come to practice restraint when out in public, ultimately much to their discomfort and the detriment of their health. Bladder and urinary tract infections are far more common in women than men, and a great deal of this is apparently attributable to women's practice of "holding it" as long as possible so as not to go in public places. This brings to mind the old question about the difference between a camel and a lady, to wit: The camel can go all day without drinking; the lady can drink all day without going. Several recent studies have indicated that more than 60 per cent of the women with urinary tract infections had distended bladders resulting from infrequent urination—perhaps too high a price to pay for one's sense of modesty.

Another attempt at achieving a kind of privacy is, of course, through the use of euphemisms, both for our destination and our activity. Although this is almost never a successful ploy insofar as actual disguise is concerned, it nevertheless fills an important social function for many people who cannot bring themselves to use the honorable Anglo-Saxon words like "piss" and "fart" or who are concerned about offending their companions. Aside from sometimes being too cute, it is generally a harmless enough charade that most people acquiesce in for the sake of observing social conventions. In many respects it is much like the convention of not looking—what we refuse to see, and what we refuse to speak of, obviously doesn't exist. Like the famous rhetorical question "What do you say to a naked lady?", what do you say to a dinner guest who says, "Excuse me, but I need to shit"?

Lack of privacy, or more particularly, lack of privacy to the degree demanded by any given individual, can have unfortunate consequences. The most serious—uneasiness and indignation aside—is usually its inhibiting effect on elimination functions, most often male urination. Some persons have difficulty performing in the presence of members of the opposite sex, some in the presence of strangers of either sex, some simply in strange surroundings. Although it may strike some as surprising that this is still a problem in this generally more relaxed and permissive era, the advice columns of the newspapers carry letters asking about these problems with great regularity.

"OFF-BOUNDS"

One of the significant aspects, or functions, of the bathroom from a social viewpoint is its "off-bounds" character, which stems directly from our feelings about privacy and our general avoidance of the subject of elimination. Just as we confer an off-bounds character upon our home bathrooms, so do we upon public facilities. Unfortunately, this privileged aspect has recently made the public rest room more and more attractive for a variety of increasingly antisocial and criminal activities. Whereas in the past the bathroom might be used to sneak an illegal cigarette, or to masturbate, or to engage in homosexual activities, today we are also finding the public bathroom used for narcotics dealings, muggings, and finally, bombings. In some circumstances this off-bounds aspect has been institutionalized as a kind of informal social center. The off-bounds character works here in two ways: first, with respect to the privacy accorded to a person actually, or ostensibly, engaged in elimination in a stall; and second, with respect to the more general privacy accorded to stratified facilities as, for example, in schools and in some factories. In the absence of other off-bounds facilities the bathroom becomes the only available safe place where one can engage in forbidden activities like horseplay, reading comic books, smoking, and shooting craps. In recent years, the bathroom has evolved as the favorite, and perhaps inevitable, place for bombs to be left in public buildings. It offers, as it does in the home, an anonymity and a freedom from questioning and observation not easily found elsewhere. It is one of the few places in a public building where a stranger or non-employee can go without challenge—an unlocked public toilet being assumed—and where a parcel can be left unobserved, and where a person can remain virtually indefinitely without challenge. The rules of social conduct further ensure that no one will pay very close attention, either to one's person or one's activities. This also facilitates a variety of activities such as altering one's appearance, contacting other persons, making exchanges, destroying evidence, leaving messages, and taking narcotics. Many security-conscious institutions are, of course, sensitive to this aspect, and visitors to certain classified areas of Atomic Energy Commission installations and those of various defense contractors must be accompanied to the bathroom by a security guard.[12]

Perhaps one of the best illustrations of the susceptibility of public facilities to abuse because of their privileged character is provided by the "shit-in" planned for Chicago's O'Hare Airport a few years ago by Saul Alinsky as a civil-rights tactic intended to embarrass Mayor Richard Daley. As Mr. Alinsky described his plan,

> For the sit-down toilets, our people would just put in their dimes and prepare to wait it out; we arranged for them to bring box lunches and reading materials along to help pass the time. What were desperate passengers going to do—knock the cubicle door down and demand evidence of legitimate occupancy? This meant that the ladies' lavatories could be completely occupied; in the men's, we'd take care of the pay toilets and then have floating groups moving from one urinal to another, positioning themselves four or five deep and standing there for five minutes before being relieved by a co-conspirator, at which time they would pass on to another rest room. Once again, what's some poor sap at the end of the line going to say: "Hey, pal, you're taking too long to piss"?[13]

From both a strategic and sociological viewpoint, this scheme is interesting, for it takes advantage of two phenomena—first, the necessary ready availability of public facilities and, second, the implicit stricture against examination or discussion of other people's elimination behavior. As Mr. Alinsky so correctly observes, who indeed is going to say, "You're taking too long to piss"?

A somewhat different kind of "shit-in," as described in the *Decameron*, depends for its exquisite agony not only on the ultimate physical discomfort involved but principally on the psychological discomfort. In the story, a certain nobleman, tired of endlessly hosting traveling parties of nobles, decides to put a stop to it once and for all and so arranges a sumptuous feast in his great hall for his distinguished and elegant guests; course after course, wine after wine—and then, just before the end, he orders the hall locked for the night.

The public rest room has also become a natural locus for violent crimes against persons, for muggings and robberies, and has become a serious problem in many of our larger cities. Just one rather tragic recent example was contained in a letter to one of the newspaper advice columnists from a distraught mother who complained bitterly because her two elementary school children had developed severe constipation and experienced acute discomfort because they were too terrified to use the bathrooms at the school because of the muggings and beatings commonly taking place![14] The reasons for this choice of location are not hard to find; they again stem directly from our attitudes and mores toward elimination and hygiene facilities. First of all, the location is often relatively isolated and deliberately secluded so as to afford the maximum privacy. In many such instances, few people are ever around. The ideal physical arrangement for public elimination is also the ideal physical arrangement for committing a crime. In addition, of course, such intentions are further facilitated by the relative helplessness and immobility of a person engaged in elimination activities; that is, one may be literally "caught with one's pants down." A somewhat bizarre instance of such exploitation is to be found in the "marriage by capture" ritual of the Ik of Uganda.

> The time was invariably the evening, to give the cover of darkness. The opportunity offered itself when the girl to be captured left the outer stockade, after dark, for a final defecation. At this rather delicate moment she was seized and made off with.[15]

This example also points up another interesting contrast in behaviors, for it would be a highly unlikely action for many of us, particularly those of us with Anglo-Saxon backgrounds. While we do, on the one hand, tend to associate the organs of sex and of elimination, we also tend, on the other, to make clear distinctions between the activities. While attracted by the one we tend generally to be repelled by the other—sufficiently so that in such circumstances of potential opportunity we pass it by as, for example, most of our military experience suggests. While females might be avidly pursued in all other circumstances, catching one engaged in elimination was generally an embarrassment and felt to be out of bounds. Even in the case of many married couples in our society the acts of elimination are regarded as repugnant and highly private affairs with few if any sexual overtones. On the other hand, we must remember that this has not been true historically. In the days when out-of-doors elimination was the rule, we may be fairly certain that such scruples were not always observed when desire and opportunity converged. And, of course, for many persons with rather fully developed sexual appetites such distinctions disappear entirely, as, for example, in the practice of analingus.

In short, we have tended to place the public rest room off-bounds not only in a social operational sense but also often physically, by locating it beyond the boundaries of our normal social area in a quite literal way.

HOMOSEXUAL ACTIVITY

In a somewhat different vein, the public rest room has also long served as a natural locus for the homosexual world, for making contacts, soliciting, and engaging in sexual activity. Complaints about this sort of "public nuisance" were common in France a hundred years ago and have not abated since. The vice squads of every police force in the world are familiar with the phenomenon, and, indeed, some of their more rigorous apprehension or entrapment tactics have recently provoked a flurry of protests and court actions. Without delving into the legal or ethical questions involved in procedures such as the use of hidden cameras, we should note that the procedures violate completely our otherwise socially approved off-bounds privileges as well as the basic privacy of the persons involved. In 1973, the California Supreme Court ruled that police officers may no longer hide in public rest rooms watching for illegal sexual activity and went on to observe that, in the absence of a reasonable belief that a crime is being committed, such indiscriminate spying constitutes an illegal exploratory search and violates the common right of personal privacy.[16]

A somewhat different but nonetheless fascinating example is reported in a recent book about the C.I.A. In order to judge the state of King Farouk's health, the agency purportedly tapped into the drain lines of two urinals in a public rest room in order to obtain a sample of Farouk's urine. An agent stationed inside signaled which urinal the King was using.[17]

The basic attractiveness of the public rest room for such purposes stems partly from the figurative and literal off-bounds character just discussed and partly from the natural and ostensibly acceptable opportunities for the semi-public display of the genitals in using the urinal, for example, and in the myriad of opportunities for suggestive maneuvers involving grooming, adjusting one's clothing, use of the mirror, and so on. All these activities are perfectly normal in the setting and can be challenged only when they become too overt or when some other person violates the avoidance rule by paying deliberate attention. Then, if eye contact is established, one has presumably reached the figurative and literal moment of truth. In this respect, the normal eye avoidance rule becomes very important because it helps the homosexual to do his searching quickly, for if everyone normally looked at other people and their activities, it would be far more difficult and time consuming to establish contact with the right person.

GRAFFITI

The off-bounds character of the public rest room also facilitates its use as a vehicle for personal expression. It offers freedom from interruption and detection, and it also guarantees us an audience for our witticisms, or our hostilities, as the case may be. The fullest realization, and exploitation, of the potential of a captive audience has finally come about in the United States, where it has been proposed to sell commercial advertising space on the inside of the water closet compartments in commercial buildings. While, on the surface, this appears very much like the practice of selling advertising space in public transit vehicles or on the street urinals in France, it will be interesting to see the public's reaction. One suspects that many people may find it a gross invasion of their privacy and territoriality in a way that graffiti would never provoke, since graffiti have about them an element of "us" or of "brotherhood" and conspiracy whereas advertising is much more "other" or "institution." It may provoke a violently negative reaction similar to the introduction of taped music and advertising messages in the public transit system in Washington, D.C., some years ago. One could ignore the advertising cards if one chose to, but one could not ignore the music or messages. Similarly, here, it is doubtful that in the confined space of a water closet compartment one could successfully ignore a four-color, full-door advertisement directly in front of one's face.

Although the practice of writing graffiti knows no bounds in location, the public rest room is a favorite place for such expression and is often likely used by persons who would not otherwise indulge themselves in this manner. It takes a fair amount of passion and dedication to get hold of a can of spray paint and surreptitiously paint obscenities, political slogans, or one's name on some public building or subway car, but it takes no more than reaching into one's pocket to mark one's sentiments on a toilet stall wall, especially if one is faced with the temptation of an on-going dialogue to contribute one's witticisms to, or to challenge.

Graffiti have sometimes been referred to as folk art, but perhaps a more accurate description might be social outlet since certainly one important role would seem to be to provide an emotional safety valve for people—at least insofar as we are concerned with graffiti that express a particular hostility or frustration. Not all graffiti, of course, are consciously hostile; some are merely obscene or pornographic and some are truly witty and erudite if irreverent.[18] While graffiti offer the Walter Mittys their secret life, as it were, they also offer the satisfaction of a relatively safe method of getting one's revenge for real or imagined wrongs. And last but not least, the activity offers in some instances an outlet for otherwise repressed creativity.[19]

The former is interestingly attested to by the experience of institutions that have decided to "join them if they couldn't lick them" by installing blackboards and chalk. Although this tactic hasn't stopped the graffiti, it appears not to encourage the activity either; however, it does in many cases rather subtly change the kind of expressions given vent to since the institution has now co-opted the graffitor and removed one of the important psychological motivations, which might be most simply stated as giving annoyance. If the object of your feelings now says, "I don't mind and I shall indulge you in your childish games and here is your coloring book," it becomes both insulting and not nearly as satisfactory a pastime as before. In this respect, the situation is a bit like the use of "suggestion boxes." Acknowledgment and apparent permissiveness tend to defuse, at a certain level, overt expressions of hostility since they reassert the superior position of the parent/institution in a particularly devastating way.

Co-opting also alters the character of the situation rather substantially by altering the character of the opportunity. The essence of co-opting is to present a fleeting and ephemeral opportunity, whereas the graffitor seeks both literally and figuratively to "make his mark on the world." "What is the point of composing a poem for a men's room blackboard, if it is going to be erased in an hour? If one writes directly on the wall it may be several days or weeks before the janitor washes it off."[20] Indeed, much of the current graffiti, committed by the young particularly, are of the identity-seeking kind; hence, the need for semi-permanency is a critical factor in the choice of spray paints and subway cars, for example, as is the age-old practice of carving one's initials in school desk tops and tree trunks.

At the other extreme, graffiti that are essentially hostile can also be motivated by the desire simply to defile and deface and in this respect are a milder form of vandalism. "Since 'dirt' is supposed to be deposited in the clean white receptacles found in bathrooms, what more flagrant act of rebellion than to place symbolic dirt on the very walls surrounding the receptacles!"[21] Psychologists have long suggested that such behavior is a surrogate form of an infantile "smearing impulse" involving playing with one's feces. In this case, the repressed hostility is expressed against the parent/institution rather than the actual parent.[22]

Bathroom graffiti also appear to serve, in many instances, as a convenient way to break our verbal taboos against "talking dirty." Many of the admonitions concerning one's proper, or improper, elimination behavior and many of the "philosophical" verses one finds deal with themes and words that most of us do not verbalize in ordinary circumstances, for example:

Here I set broken-hearted,
Tried to shit and only farted.

Don't throw you butts in the urinal—
it makes them soggy and hard to light.

It is interesting that managements themselves are often the ones who post such notices, albeit in institutionalized form—framed, behind glass.

Perhaps the one category of wall-writing that is nearly unique to public toilets (the other location being public telephone booths) is the sexual advertisement, most commonly homosexual:

"For a good blow job, call———."

"I'm big, 9″ long, 3″ around, and hot!"

The public bathroom, in summary, serves, for better or worse, many functions in our society other than simply the obvious one of accommodating our hygiene needs.

Although this is true of the home bathroom to a limited degree also, the principal difference is that most of the social functions in the public situation are in fact seriously antisocial. Altering this situation will not be simple, since the attitudes we cherish with respect to our personal hygiene practices are the very ones that permit and encourage the use of the bathroom for these other roles. The answer will, of necessity, have to come from a rearrangement of our social attitudes so as to permit closer supervision in some form or other. Perhaps the least objectionable way would be through the increased use of attendants, combined, where feasible, with the inclusion of other personal-care services as is sometimes found—shoe shine stand, barber shop, and others—all of which help to generate more traffic and to ensure that people will be present at all times.

SOILING AND CLEANLINESS

Earlier, we examined cleanliness and maintenance from the viewpoint of territorial violations and privacy. Cleanliness, or more specifically, soiling, can also be examined from several other viewpoints. Whereas some soiling may be more or less consciously and deliberately antagonistic and directed toward a specific individual or institution or toward the world in general, a great deal arises simply out of the physical circumstances of poor design and poor maintenance. Soil begets soiling, in the sense that we each in turn tend to exercise less care the dirtier the facility we find. This is first of all, of course, a function of our wholly negative attitudes toward cleaning up after anybody else, most especially the body wastes of strangers. Second is the fact that a soiled fixture is for most people "unusable" in the ordinary way. A soiled fixture presents us with the choice of either cleaning it ourselves, which is out of the question, or using it in an awkward and unnatural way, which results invariably in our further soiling the fixture or its surroundings. Another solution is, of course, to seek out another fixture that may be cleaner. This is often done in large multiple-fixture installations where there is that choice. The difficulty arises from the fact that, much of the time, a person seeking out a facility is doing so from urgent need and has little option but to use whatever he finds. He cannot often shop around until he finds one that suits him better. The situation is particularly difficult for females since they cannot tell the condition of the facility they have selected until after they have paid their coin and unlocked the compartment. Selectivity thus becomes expensive at best and is often not possible at all if one does not have more exact change.

Perhaps the most dramatic illustration of a situation that brings all these various aspects into play is that of female urination. Here we have a case of a negative attitude reinforced and invariably justified by physical circumstances. Folklore appears to have firmly established in the mind of every Western female that she must never sit down on a public toilet if at all possible lest she acquire some unmentionable social disease; besides, the seat is likely to be soiled and disagreeable. So, in the morning, the first female in does not sit but hovers over the water closet and thereby inevitably splashes or dribbles some urine on the seat or the floor. Each succeeding female in turn is of course increasingly justified in following suit until by the end of the day the floor is awash in urine. If it were possible to do away with the myths about catching social diseases and if women could be persuaded to sit properly, as they do at home, they wouldn't each of them in turn contribute to the problem they all deplore with such vehemence and justification.

> In January, 1910, *The British Medical Journal* published an editorial note advocating the provision at railway stations for urinals for women . . . and numerous doctors supported this proposal, while 'A Doctor's Wife' wrote that "We all stand."[23]

This cumulative effect also applies to the washbasin in a somewhat similar fashion. Here the soiling agents are hair, face powder, soap curd, and stains, but again each successive user feels justified in being less and less careful as the day wears on. The same is true of male urination as well. Once the floor is wet, one wishes to avoid stepping into the puddle and so stands back and, of course, adds more to the mess. Hence arise all the familiar formal and informal admonitions to "stand closer," "improve your aim," and the like.

Armed with foresight, and the proper guidebooks, however, the discriminating international traveler may indeed be able to choose the appropriate place of solace. One Jonathan Routh has published a series of guidebooks to the public facilities of New York, London, and Paris. These carefully researched and wholly admirable little guides provide locations, hours, prices, and a brief listing of the particular personal and cultural amenities available at each.[24]

Searching for Mr. Routh's books provided still

another fascinating cross-cultural glimpse at our attitudes toward such matters. The author acquired the New York guide first in a large New York bookshop—in the humor section. Some months later in Europe he asked for the other guides at one of London's largest booksellers and was told with rather a smirk to look for them in the "humor" section. Naturally, where else would one look? He found neither and when he protested to the clerk that they were travel guides and might they not be there, he received an "Indeed?" Later, in Paris, he found the two missing volumes—in the "humor" section, of course. Admittedly the books have some rather delightful and whimsical illustrations but this would hardly appear to justify their being catalogued under humor, unless quite obviously there is no other polite way to deal with such a subject. The original paperback edition of this book, incidentally, was most often to be found buried among the sex novels.

IMAGE OF THE HOST

At another level, the extent and quality of the facilities provided, most particularly in terms of maintenance and sanitation, leave with the public guest an image of his host. This is an aspect that has perhaps been most clearly recognized by the oil companies and perhaps least recognized by the restaurant industry. There are, of course, sound reasons for both circumstances, and it raises an interesting and often overlooked point. This is the extent to which hygiene facilities are either a major or minor aspect of the organization's services.

In the case of the gas station it is clear that in many instances the basic reason for a customer's stopping is to satisfy a basic personal need. While there he may also buy some gas or have his vehicle tended to in some other way, but fundamentally the stop is made for reasons that have nothing to do with the presumed basic service for vehicles. This fact is not lost on the major oil companies, many of whom prominently display large signs proclaiming "Clean Rest Rooms." One British company has even gone so far as to set up a "key club" where for a small yearly fee one is given a key to specially equipped and maintained rest rooms at its stations. Obviously, if, as some consumer groups maintain, there is virtually no difference between the automotive products of one company and another, then service to the traveling public becomes the critical selling point. This is scarcely, of course, a consideration for the station so situated as to be "the last one for three hundred miles." Yet, interestingly, in spite of this recognition, the American Automobile Association's biennial survey of motorists' complaints continues to rank dirty rest rooms as the second most frequent complaint. (Poor directional signing ranks first.)

In general, we find that hygiene facilities tend to be most important in organizations that deal with the traveling public. In addition to the gas stations, which are perhaps the most clear-cut example, this applies to air terminals, bus terminals, and to the municipal facilities in towns and parks, which cater to the pedestrian traveler. Not surprisingly, we find that the quality of the facilities provided tends to have a direct relationship to the degree of responsibility that can be attributed to a given facility. In this respect municipal facilities tend generally to be the poorest and most neglected. In terms of image significance the correlation is as noted with quality and competition. In the United States, for example, dirty and broken-down hygiene facilities are common in the few railroad stations that still exist, but then this is consistent with the general level of all their facilities. Airline facilities, in contrast, tend to be excellent, at least in terms of cleanliness, and tell us once again that going by air is the only way to travel.

At the other end of the scale are public facilities provided by institutions in which the facility is clearly only a convenience and, one sometimes suspects, provided only because the law demands it. In particular, this situation appears to be the case with restaurants and bars the world over. There are, of course, notable exceptions, principally establishments where decor is an important ingredient in the overall scheme. For example, the various Restaurant Associates establishments in New York City, including the Four Seasons and the former Fonda del Sol, fall notably into this category where the rest rooms are so distinguished and handsome that people come especially to see and use them:

> The atmosphere of the men's room is impossible to describe to anyone who has never found himself in a truly holy toilet. The walls glow with softly illuminated religious paintings. One stands there quite transported, urinating into an enormous, nine-foot revolving waterwheel. Uplifting devotional music mingles with babbling-brook sounds. Gone is all sense of shame or puritan self-revulsion; it's impossible to feel such ignoble feelings while pissing to Handel's "Messiah."
>
> The Madonna Inn men's room was a miracle of micturition; a deification of defecation. One entered not to void one's bladder, but rather to fulfill one's soul, on a sacred pilgrimage, the next best thing to Lourdes.
>
> Only in America.[25]

What is perhaps more surprising is the number of establishments, notable or otherwise, that provide unbelievably minimal, cramped, and filthy facilities, more often than not in the basement next to the stockrooms, where they are also used by the kitchen help. The principal answer for this seems to be that rest rooms are nonproductive in terms of space utilization and investment, and as one owner succinctly put it, "My customers come here to eat, not shit." Perhaps, but almost all customers use the rest rooms for urination and grooming and one can only guess at how many evenings out have been rendered less than fully pleasurable by one's experiences with the rest rooms. On the other hand, one must also concede the business logic since that part of the host's image is, in these instances, clearly minor in the public mind. One explanation for this phenomenon may well be our general reluctance to complain about our experiences—particularly with guests during dinner.

PAY FACILITIES

Just as in the example of the key clubs mentioned earlier, the institution of executive washrooms and pay toilets (the "Johnny Cash" of the "Polish Joke") arises both from the sanitation problems encountered the world over with public facilities and the attitudes engendered by them and from our respective prejudices and apprehensions. Unquestionably, pay toilets at one time enabled the "gentlefolk" to have available to them facilities not likely to be used by undesirables:

> A man doesn't often have to classify himself socially, but in the men's room of the Grand Central the issue comes squarely up: choosing between the free room, the five-cent section, and the ten-cent section, according to one's station in life. That decision, which one makes privately and almost unconsciously, is curiously revealing. Middle-class ourself, we invariably elect the five-cent section. The free room seems squalid to us, and the dime room ostentatious.[26]

At current prices, however, this distinction is largely illusory and outdated, though it still remains true that, in facilities where both pay and free toilets are provided, the free toilets are invariably in the worst condition. The charges are, however, an important source of revenue for many public agencies in helping to offset the cost of maintaining the facilities. One estimate places the revenue from pay toilets in the United States at upwards of 30 million dollars annually.[27]

Perhaps the most important consequence today of charging a fee for the use of public facilities is that it discriminates against women in a particularly invidious way. Males are almost invariably provided with free urinals, but women are rarely served with such nice distinction and generally have little choice. (Although female urinals exist, these are not very widely used, for a variety of reasons that will be discussed later.) When one considers the substantially greater frequency of urination during the day compared with that of defecation, there is no question that the ladies have ample reason to feel put upon, and many do.

In the past several years this has, once again, become a significant social issue for a variety of groups ranging from the women's liberation movement to the Committee to End Pay Toilets in America, which have had a fair degree of success in making this an election issue in a number of instances and in persuading several legislatures to outlaw charges, at least in public buildings. "In the new *Handbook,* scouts are warned never to leave the house on some urgent community project without taking along what it calls 'emergency change'—for use in pay toilets."[28]

The controversy is, of course, much older. In 1934, for example, a lady wrote to *The New Statesman* arguing for the abolition of the fee and urged her sisters to "use the gutter and go to jail if necessary for our convictions."

In all fairness, however, it should also be observed that a great many young women, like Holly Golightly, have managed quite comfortably on the "change to powder their noses" that they cadged from their evening's escort. A gentleman, anxious to impress, could hardly be less than generous in the face of such a request; and besides, the young lady had to have enough to tip the attendant in the style to which she would like to become accustomed.

The matter of sexual discrimination in toilet facilities is also likely to grow in significance in the near future because of our changing employment practices. There have already been complaints in some public school systems, for instance, that there were not enough toilets for the male teachers who have only recently entered the elementary and secondary school systems in substantial numbers. Similarly, female members of the British Parliament have requested additional facilities in what was traditionally an almost exclusively male institution. And most recently, the United States Navy has authorized the service of women on shipboard. These instances and hundreds more call into question not only our traditional assumptions about the numbers and disposition of facilities for each of the sexes but also our more basic assumptions about separate facilities. California has already taken a step in this direction in its new camping facilities in the state's parks by eliminating the male urinals to make unisex facilities, arguing that the public has accepted this system on the airlines. The practical and sanitary difficulty with this approach is, of course, that water closets make poor urinals, for men or women. It is likely that we may need to explore more fully the possibility of shared facilities as is the case in Japan and in many parts of Europe.

Equality of the sexes or classes aside, it is obvious that a fee in itself does relatively little today to improve the situation from a sanitary standpoint. What does seem to make a substantial difference is regular cleaning and maintenance. In this respect, the general European pattern of both charging a fee, albeit often for paper, soap, and towels as well as for the use of the facilities, and providing a full-time attendant has much to recommend it. Unfortunately, it is perhaps questionable whether any but the largest establishments will be able to afford such service in the future, even in Europe, in the face of an expanding economy.

Our attitudes toward elimination, as well as toward personal service, also become a factor here. In the United States a washroom attendant's position is probably regarded as one of the more demeaning, much like the position of the untouchables, the sweepers of India. In part this may be due to the confusion of an attendant's job with that of the janitorial crew that actually does the major cleaning, but the more likely explanation is our general antipathy toward most forms of personal service. Yet a British "lavatory attendant" can boastfully, and I am sure with some irony, refer to himself as a "gentlemen's gentleman" and claim by extension some association with that long and honorable profession. In the Emil Jannings film *The General,* Jannings is reduced from his prerevolutionary position as a czarist general to that of a lavatory attendant, thus powerfully symbolizing the extent and humiliation of his condition.

Certainly the position cannot be ranked among the finest employments, but then many other industrial as well as personal-service jobs are equally disagreeable in one respect or another, and all are becoming harder and more expensive to fill. This distastefulness of "latrine duty" goes a long way to explain the deplorably filthy condition of many public facilities in small establishments all over the world—nobody wants to clean them, and unless someone is specifically hired to do it, no one does clean them, at least with any regularity. Offenses to the eyes and nose aside, this is an area where public health becomes a concern and where more attention needs to be directed in terms of design and possible automation of cleaning operations. A survey in New York City in 1972 revealed that of some 500 public facilities inspected, in subways, parks, bars, and restaurants, 368 "were without paper, soap, running water, or had broken fittings on commodes," and further that 90 per cent of the rest rooms in the city's subway system were closed down completely.

While it is commonly argued that the cost of attendants is prohibitive, it may be time for equal attention to be paid to the physical costs of vandalism, not to mention the social costs of crime. It may develop that attendants are not so costly after all.

18

PLANNING AND DESIGN CRITERIA FOR PUBLIC FACILITIES

The general category of "public facilities" encompasses a broad range of facility types, as well as a broad range of behaviors and methods of performing certain hygiene activities. These differences rest not only on the degree of publicness or privateness of a given facility but also on the context within which a given facility is provided, for example, an airport concourse versus an executive washroom or a hotel room versus a roadside filling station. Some facilities, for example, are highly public, while some are virtually private; some involve simultaneous use, some sequential; some are carefully controlled for access and use, some are not; some are provided by a highly visible and responsible management, some are not. In addition, each of these types is often further differentiated with respect to character and equipment because of our general insistence on segregation of the sexes and the fact that the sexual differences in the performance of certain hygiene activities tend to be magnified in the public context. In spite of these vast differences, however, all share certain common problems such as location, identification, maintenance, supervision, and vandalism.

For purposes of discussion, we can group this diverse assortment of public facility types into several broad contextual categories along the continuum from most public to most private, as follows:

Transient Facilities (totally public)
Streets, parks, fairgrounds
Campgrounds
Filling stations, highway rest stops
Transportation terminals
Alberghi Diurni

Temporary Facilities (totally public)
Festivals, public demonstrations, sports events
Construction sites

Institutional Facilities (totally public)
Prisons, hospitals, dormitories, industrial plants

Work and Retail Facilities (semipublic)
Bars, restaurants
Offices, public buildings, retail shops
Mobile Facilities (semipublic)
Airplanes, trains, buses
Lodging Facilities (semiprivate)
Hotels, motels, ship's staterooms

In examining each of these groupings, we shall deal primarily with their salient characteristics and their differences from one another. The specific criteria for particular activities and their accommodation are essentially similar to those already outlined and can be adapted to suit the particular circumstances.

TRANSIENT FACILITIES

The facilities in this group can be broadly categorized as those provided for the convenience of the traveling public, most commonly by some public agency or other remote "host." Although the facilities can vary in size, they are often large and involve simultaneous usage by widely diverse groups of people. Most commonly, only elimination functions are accommodated and the pattern of use is characterized by speed and carelessness. There is generally, moreover, little repetitive use and often no supervision. In general, this category can be regarded as the most public and the one posing the most severe problems of security, maintenance, and sanitation.[1]

Street and Park At the most basic level are the street urinals that still exist in many parts of the world. Commonly, these accommodate standing male urination only, with no provisions for washing. They primarily offer a locus for what would otherwise be indiscriminate urination, and a modicum of privacy. Interestingly, for such facilities to be of any use at all, they must be located in busy and obvious locations. While this offends the sensibilities of some, it has the virtue of offering reasonable security with respect to the safety of one's person when so engaged. Although rarely constructed any longer, and often in fact removed, they do still serve a useful function in many circumstances, particularly in the rapidly urbanizing areas of the developing nations.

Park facilities are commonly more nearly complete, as are some street facilities, and accommodate both sexes—sometimes segregated, sometimes not. Such facilities are generally provided by some public agency as a basic convenience and accommodate elimination functions and hand washing only. Often these are somewhat discreetly placed in relatively isolated locations and pose major problems with respect to sanitation, vandalism, and safety.

One approach to these problems is to provide larger and more centrally located facilities. This would not only offer the inherent protection of larger numbers but would also be more efficient, permitting the employment of an attendant and allowing for more frequent cleaning and maintenance and a broader range of facilities—for example, for the handicapped and for small children. Fewer and larger facilities not only offer economies of scale with regard to construction and operating costs but also tend to provide a better level of sanitation and maintenance than is generally possible with small, scattered facilities. Rapid turnover and large volume suggest the need for more frequent, if not almost continuous, cleaning, which is vastly preferable to the once-a-day cleaning possible otherwise.

Since such facilities are public in the fullest sense of the term and intended for a limited range of activities and a rapid turnover, the equipment should reflect this and should be of the public variety described in the next chapter.

Campgrounds While the facilities commonly provided at campgrounds share many of the attributes of park facilities, this subgroup is unique in that there is a need to accommodate virtually the full range of hygiene activities in one form or another. In particular, bathing facilities are necessary and, most logically, are provided in the form of showers. Because such facilities are often used by families for periods lasting several weeks, there is also a regular and repetitive usage, which suggests that such facilities need not always be totally public. To a large extent the character and patterns of use, and user attitudes, can be determined by the nature of the facilities provided. If, for example, only gang showers, basins, and the like are provided so as to require simultaneous use, then the facility is totally public. If, however, a part of the facilities were provided in the form of complete individual bathrooms, one would establish a somewhat more private sequential pattern of use that might be appreciated by families traveling with young children. In any event, the equipment provided should reflect the criteria developed for public use.

Filling Stations and Highway Rest Stops In this category, we are again dealing primarily with the accommodation of elimination functions in the highly public context of little repeat usage, generally simultaneous use, rapid turnover, and no group affinity. Whereas the filling station would appear to offer the inherent advantages of supervision and a highly public location as far as vandalism and personal safety are concerned, virtually all filling stations, in the United States at any rate, provide for sequential use by one individual or group at a time with key-controlled access. This is, of course, a reflection of the fact that during a busy period there is no supervision, so that maintenance and sanitation are perennial problems, primarily because no one individual is responsible for it on any regularly scheduled basis. These problems are in large measure a function of size.

When we examine the large superhighway rest stops, whether publicly or privately provided, which include restaurant facilities as well as automotive facilities, the level of sanitation and maintenance is generally considerably better. Large facilities can also offer more services and amenities such as special facilities for the handicapped and for small children, and even showers, as in some European rest stops. This subcategory receives perhaps the most intensive usage of any of the groups. Although the primary accommodation is for elimination functions, patrons in these circumstances (while they may be hurried and desperate with respect to elimination needs) often spend considerable time in washing, grooming, and the adjustment of their clothing, particularly during the summer months. When restaurant facilities exist, the hygiene facilities are commonly used twice—upon arrival and again upon departure.

If we interpret "rest stop" more broadly than is common, more consideration should perhaps be given to the provision of amenities such as showers and some complete bathroom units similar to those provided at many of the international airports, where parents could cope more easily when traveling with small children. Such facilities should include a washbasin, shower, water closet/urinal, overcounter and full-length mirrors, ample counter space, a seat, clothes hooks, and provisions for the supply and disposal of towels and sanitary supplies. Obviously, such amenities would have to be rented for a particular time period, as they commonly are now, when available. The fixtures and equipment should be of the public variety throughout.

Transportation Terminals This group, while sharing many of the common attributes outlined earlier, can be further broken down into two subgroups—one serving commuters and the other serving long-distance travelers, though the distinctions are sometimes blurred.

In the first category, the principal concern is almost exclusively with the accommodation of elimination functions. Because such facilities generally serve a local commuting population, however, they tend to be subject to all the problems of sanitation, vandalism, and criminal activity that characterize similar relatively isolated, low-use facilities. This is a particular problem with rapid-transit and subway systems. One approach being tried in the new San Francisco Bay Area rapid-transit system is to provide individual locked pay facilities that, it is hoped, will reduce these problems somewhat. The fixtures provided in such circumstances may well have to be the minimal vandal-proof, prison variety.

Major transportation terminals, on the contrary, generally afford some of the most nearly complete facilities to be found anywhere, though there can be considerable variation between the facilities provided in the main terminal building of an airport, for example, and those provided along the various gateway fingers. These differences in both size and facilities needed are proportional to the volume of traffic and also reflect the differences in use patterns between the two locations. Facilities located along gateway fingers are conveniences to accommodate only the elimination needs of hurrying passengers and employees. The turnover of users can be extremely rapid and large, depending on circumstances, and the character totally public. In particular, such facilities tend to be most heavily used by deplaning passengers, which often results in bunching and extreme temporary crowding. The general pattern is to enter, urinate, rinse hands, dry, and exit. The total elapsed time is often less than two minutes, particularly since a large proportion of the users do not bother to wash. In such circumstances, particular attention needs to be paid to the clearest and most efficient layout of the facilities and to patterns of traffic flow. Most users are likely, moreover, to be carrying something—briefcases, parcels, or luggage—and wider-than-normal doorways and passages are necessary. In this connection, the elimination of entry and exit doors can sometimes be useful so long as appropriate visual and auditory barriers are provided. In many such busy facilities, the doors are, for all practical purposes, open almost constantly anyway. In the majority of cases, the facilities are arranged in an essentially sequential, circular pattern, that is, urinals first, then water closets, washbasins, and finally towels or driers, opposite the urinals on the way out. Often, however, this results in congestion at the common entry/exit point, and consideration should be given to sequential linear arrangements that would permit a separation of entry and exit points.[2] Because of the patterns of use just outlined, the fixtures and equipment provided should be of the public variety and incorporate every automatic and self-cleaning feature.

The hygiene facilities located in the main terminal area, whether of an airport or train station, must provide additional facilities and amenities, for they serve, in part at least, somewhat different users—persons who often have considerable time on their hands, and additional needs, because of the layover between connections, weather difficulties, or simply early arrival. Such facilities, in addition to serving purely elimination needs, should also provide facilities for bathing. Often, particularly at major international terminals, it is desirable to include adjunct personal-care services such as a shoe shine stand, barber/hairdresser, nursery, and dry cleaner/presser. While, for the most part, these facilities can be of the public/simultaneous-use kind, a portion needs to be provided as complete bathroom units with showers, dressing area, and so on. These units must recognize the kind of two-person, or even three-person use that might be involved and provide sufficient hooks and hangers for street clothing, space for hand luggage, and the like. The fixtures and equipment in these facilities should be designed for public use, but obviously any number of other amenities can be welcome additions to the basic provisions for hygiene, since in many respects the users' needs in such circumstances are for a total personal-care facility.

Alberghi Diurni Literally translated as "day hotels," facilities of this sort, which closely resemble the terminal facilities just discussed, are unfortunately seldom found, except in a handful of Italian cities. While these are not, strictly speaking, public hygiene facilities, they must be considered here under the broader definition of personal-care facilities—just as bathrooms in the home have evolved into more than a minimal personal-hygiene facility. Just as the highway rest stop serves the automobile traveler and the terminal facility provides the air or rail traveler with a full range of accommodations, the day hotel serves the transient urban population. Situated in critical major downtown locations, these facilities can provide a wide range of personal-care services to persons who are temporarily beyond the reach of their own facilities, for example, commuters who remain in the city after work to go to the theatre. In Milan, for example, such a facility is located at the edge of the main cathedral square in the center of town, just steps away from the Galleria and the principal shopping streets and one block from La Scala.

The range of potential services can be considerable: normal personal hygiene facilities plus bathing facilities; rooms for taking a nap; barber and hairdresser; manicure and pedicure; shoe repairs; clothes cleaning and laundering; florist's shop; theatre tickets; candy shop; as well as a retail shop selling sundries such as stockings, combs, perfume, contraceptives, and deodorants. Obviously, such establishments are privately run and need to observe high standards of sanitation and security. While these services are generally individually available in most major cities, they are seldom available at all hours nor are they all available in one convenient location, except in special circumstances such as private clubs.

TEMPORARY FACILITIES

This category comprises those minimal conveniences temporarily provided in quantity to accommodate unusual circumstances such as large irregular gatherings: rock music festivals, political demonstrations, some sports events, and the like. Generally, only the most essential accommodations for elimination are called for, since in most instances the size of the gatherings, their short duration, and their usually informal organization obviate the need for, or indeed the possibility of, any more elaborate provisions. Most commonly, such accommodations have been provided in the form of individual portable chemical units ("Porta-Johns"), which serve for the necessary period and are then removed, emptied, and cleaned. While such facilities may be sequential in use rather than simultaneous, they are, nevertheless, by their very nature, totally public, relative to their location, privacy, cleanliness, and frequency of use. In such circumstances, the level of sanitation is very much a function of the number of units provided and the attitude and behavior of the particular group in question since interim cleaning and maintenance are generally out of the question.

An alternative approach to such situations, most commonly found in Europe, is to provide mobile hygiene facilities that are fitted into vans or trailers. These can accommodate about six persons at a time and also provide washing facilities as well as elimination facilities, mechanical ventilation, and a far greater waste-holding capacity. These mobile units generally have an attendant assigned to supervise the operation and can provide a much higher level of sanitation and convenience, in spite of simultaneous usage. Similar and even more nearly complete units of this sort have been developed for use by the military and include showers, incinerator closets, heating, and ventilation.

The other major category of temporary hygiene facilities is to be found in the construction industry, where again, commonly, portable chemical closet units are provided by a rental agency for the use of the workers. The only difference in this situation is the longer term, repeated usage of the facilities, which might lead to a greater degree of care in use. On the other hand, the ultimate sanitary quality of these units is largely determined by the frequency with which they are cleaned or replaced. Although in recent years their quality has improved considerably, because they have been molded in one piece of fiber glass, they remain minimal as accommodations, especially when one considers that they may be in service for several years on large construction projects. In at least one instance, in Ontario, Canada, workers have protested the inadequacies of the "bacteria boxes," as they termed them, by leaving one on the steps of the provincial legislature. When we consider that these facilities are only relatively temporary—in use for months or years instead of just hours or days—it would seem that somewhat more elaborate units that offer a minimal level of sanitation and ventilation as well as hot water for washing might appropriately be provided.

INSTITUTIONAL FACILITIES

This category is unique in that we are dealing with the full range of personal-hygiene activities: elimination, body cleaning, shaving, and grooming, but in a severely public context. In some instances, this is a function of the large size of the group to be accommodated at a given time and in others it is the result of a deliberate policy of stripping away every vestige of privacy for particular institutional goals. Historically, this was common in prisons, military establishments, and schools, where the individual had no rights and was expected to conform to institutional demands regarding behavior and attitudes. In these circumstances, the open ganged water closets and showers were one way of enforcing these demands and reminding the individual of his status. These dehumanizing devices have, in many instances, not only been extremely difficult for some individuals to cope with but have also, in the case of prisons in particular, provided an opportunity for the most vicious forms of personal assaults. "The single sound-proofed cell with shower would be one of the greatest improvements in prison design . . . the shower in each cell would eliminate assaults, rapes, and murders of inmates, which now occur in larger shower rooms."[3] Although today most schools and even the military have moved away from such totally public arrangements in favor of more conventional sequential-use arrangements, the open ganged scheme is still common in prisons and in many industrial plants where large numbers must be accommodated at one time.

Today we almost universally provide privacy at the water closet but use large open ganged showers when large groups are involved. This is obviously a satisfactory arrangement in some circumstances such as country club locker rooms, but it may be a questionable approach in other circumstances where one could reasonably expect to find little group cohesion. The common practice in many school dormitories of providing individual washbasins in every room with communal bathing and elimination facilities down the hall (as is also common in many older hotels, incidentally) is to be deplored on hygiene grounds since such washbasins are invariably used as emergency urinals, at least by males. This, incidentally, is why many fixtures such as wash-basins and bathtubs are listed as having "acid-resistant enamel." People have questioned this and asked who pours acid into such fixtures: the answer is nobody, but in certain circumstances both are employed as emergency urinals. It may also be noted in this connection that the greater height proposed for lavatory installations would tend to alleviate this problem to a large extent.

Certainly there is no one clear answer in regard to which particular arrangement is best, since the context and the characteristics of the user group can substantially affect the suitability of any given scheme, though the general tendency is to move in the direction of greater privacy for each of the hygiene functions. In most instances, however, costs will suggest that bathing facilities, which are the least intensively used, will continue to remain at least sequentially if not simultaneously used. This is, for example, the common pattern in most hospitals and health-care facilities, where individual rooms are provided with water closets and washbasins but bathing facilities are shared. Similarly, the specific requirements for equipment, storage, and counter space are very much a function of the programmatic assumptions and the general arrangement of facilities. No matter what the arrangement, however, the fixtures should reflect the criteria developed for public facilities since sanitation and maintenance will remain as major concerns. Only when complete individual facilities are provided might this change, since the context would then become a semi-private one as in a hotel room.

WORK AND RETAIL FACILITIES

This category is somewhat loose in its organization and includes both facilities provided for employees and those provided for customers, though this distinction is not always observed in practice. We are, however, concerned almost exclusively with the accommodation of elimination functions in a semi-public context. In general, the distinction between employee and customer facilities is made only in elegant, or large, retail and food-service establishments, primarily because of the volume of customers to be served. In most office buildings and small retail shops, however, the facilities are provided essentially for the convenience of the employees, and the few visitors who request to use them are accommodated as a matter of courtesy rather than right. Indeed, in many office buildings the facilities are locked to discourage casual use by visitors to the building. In this respect, most office and small retail facilities can be considered as semi-public since the volume of use is relatively small and repetitive and the users are generally known to one another. Even here, however, a distinction can be made in terms of the private executive washroom available only to the privileged few or to the privileged individual.

In the case of bars and restaurants, however, the facilities may equally have to serve the customers and the employees and can generally be regarded as semi-public, though the more elegant the establishment the greater likelihood that separate facilities will be provided for each. In these circumstances, the customer facilities may be quite elegant and non-public, as befits an establishment trying to suggest to its customers that it is their home away from home. Obviously, the question of appropriate layout and selection of equipment is very much a function of the kind of establishment in question.

MOBILE FACILITIES

This group comprises those semi-public elimination facilities provided as a necessity for passengers using long-distance modes of transportation. Because of the generally low volume of sequential use and the relative frequency of cleaning, these are commonly among the most satisfactory of public facilities and offer virtually complete privacy. Commonly, there are also differences in the facilities provided for each class of travel or, at the very least, differences in the number of facilities provided per number of passengers. The success of these compact and relatively sophisticated facilities relies heavily, however, on the level of regular cleaning and maintenance. While the criteria for equipment choice need to be observed in this context, as in others, certain details will be different because of the limited space configurations possible.

LODGING FACILITIES

This last category comprises those hygiene facilities provided in conjunction with temporary lodgings in hotels, motels, ship's staterooms, and so forth, which are, for all practical purposes, private, at least during any given period of occupancy. In most circumstances these are comparable to a person's own home facilities and are so regarded and used. In point of fact, with the daily cleaning that these facilities generally receive, they are probably cleaner than most home facilities. As a consequence, in most instances, the equipment, furnishings, and design can approximate that provided in the home and can vary considerably in character, decor, and lavishness, as may seem appropriate. Certain criteria, however, are obviously somewhat different from those needed in the home—for example, the need for storage space, towel storage, simultaneous occupancy, and so forth.

In summary, public facilities vary enormously in their character, usage, and population served, and each must be examined in the light of the particular circumstances surrounding any given installation. The common threads tying them together are the more or less public condition of use and the problem of maintenance.

DESIGN CRITERIA FOR PUBLIC FACILITY EQUIPMENT

19

Just as there are some important differences in our attitudes toward personal hygiene in private versus public circumstances, there are also some important differences in our requirements for equipment and facilities. While obviously our basic physiological needs and capabilities remain constant, our method of performing these activities is often different, as are the circumstances surrounding their performance. Often, we are in a greater hurry than at home; we may have more articles of clothing to contend with as well as purses, packages, briefcases, and luggage; and we generally engage in a comparatively limited range of activities. The use of a washbasin in public situations, for example, is most commonly limited to perfunctory hand rinsing and to grooming activities, and female urination is performed differently in public situations than in the home.

Public facilities, depending upon the particular variety, also receive considerably harder usage than is common in the home and have to deal with major problems of sanitation and maintenance, not to mention unique problems of vandalism. There are also substantial differences between the various categories of what we consider to be public facilities and the specific kinds of equipment and accessories that may be necessary or appropriate in each situation. For the purposes of this discussion, we shall restrict ourselves to an examination of the demands posed by the most extreme case of transient facilities.

HAND WASHING AND GROOMING

In public facilities, the use of the washbasin is, for the most part, limited to a perfunctory rinsing of the hands following elimination and to other incidental activities such as using water to comb one's hair, remove makeup, and so on. Even this perfunctory rinsing is often, however, not performed. In one survey of a large public men's room, only 60 per cent of the patrons bothered to wash their hands after elimination.[1] The principal exception is in the case of work places where there is often inescapable reason to wash one's hands thoroughly. When we consider that the average total time spent by men, between entering and exiting, is less than two minutes and that this time period encompasses urination (40 to 50 seconds), adjusting one's clothing, rinsing the hands, drying the hands, disposing of the towel, and checking one's appearance or grooming, it is obvious that, in general, the washing activity is minimal indeed. The pattern for women is very much the same, though in some circumstances the total time spent is considerably greater because of grooming activities.

As described in Chapter 4, the basic washing process remains essentially unchanged from that practiced in the home, except that soap is not always used—and, indeed, not always provided. As before, the activity is performed with a running stream of water. In this instance, there is also an even greater tendency to hold the body erect, so as to avoid touching the fixture with one's outer clothing or wetting one's necktie. (Several current approaches to purely public hand-rinsing basins are illustrated in Figure 62.)

The basic criteria for dimensions and configuration remain essentially the same: with a working height for the hands set at approximately 965 mm (38 inches), the basin height can be set at 915 mm (36 inches); the front-to-back dimension can be set in the range of 380 to 430 mm (15 to 17 inches), with a minimum clearance from the water source to the back of 100 to 125 mm (4 to 5 inches); the minimum side-to-side dimension need be no more than 305 to 380 mm (12 to 15 inches). Whereas this basin width may be satisfactory from the viewpoint of accommodating the hand-washing activity, it is not an adequate side-to-side width with respect to the overall dimensions necessary to accommodate the user. In public facilities there is a commonly understood, and observed, assumption that, in situations where a choice exists, one does not use any facility immediately adjacent to one already in use. Although this privacy/territory behavior is most clearly marked with respect to the use of urinals, it holds almost as strongly for washbasins as well and suggests that it would be desirable to provide more nearly adequate space for each user. In this case, a minimum dimension of approximately 815 mm (32 inches) is necessary in order to provide the requisite clearance for loosened outer garments, articles tucked under one's arm, and so on (see figure 66). This may be taken care of simply in the spacing of the fixtures or, perhaps ideally, by incorporating this spacing into the design of the fixture itself, together with privacy barriers between each fixture in order to establish clearly the demarcation between each.

With respect to configuration perhaps the most important criterion is that the fixture be as nearly self-cleaning as possible. This may be at least partially accomplished by contouring the basin and by locating the drain elsewhere than directly under the stream so that the runoff automatically rinses the basin. It would also be desirable to provide oversize and easily cleaned drain screens that could perhaps be formed integrally with the body of the basin. There seems little reason to provide for the stoppering of the basin in most public situations.

The water source should provide tempered water from a single source and be of the fountain type, so as both to provide free and quick hand access and minimize the possibilities of actual contact with the fitting and the consequent problems of sanitation. It is necessary, of course, that a pressure-regulating valve be used so as to contain the stream within the basin. In this situation, however, there may be reason to consider several other possibilities as well, for example: the provision of only fixed-temperature water at approximately 43° C (110° F) and the actual delivery of the water as a splash-free spray rather than simply as an aerated stream. Experience with both of these devices suggests that they are perfectly satisfactory approaches in most public situations and that they can appreciably save on water consumption and on the energy necessary to provide hot water.[2] In the vast majority of instances, the user wants tempered water and only rarely, purely hot or purely cold water.

A major problem with almost all public installations is the kinds of water controls commonly provided. The use of standard wheel or lever controls is unsanitary and permits the possibility of the water's not being turned off by the user in a hurry. The spring-loaded pressure valves commonly found may be a little more sanitary insofar as only the heel of the hand makes contact with the fitting, but it is less than satisfactory in that the water commonly shuts off as soon as the hand is removed, and this necessitates rinsing of one hand at a time. Proper washing, using soap and both hands together, is virtually impossible in these circumstances. Other devices such as hospital-type foot pedals, though rarely found, are little more satisfactory because of their awkward mode of operation.

Ideally, water controls should either be self-activating or require minimal contact by the user and should automatically shut off after a predetermined interval of approximately 45 to 60 seconds. This might be accomplished, first, by any of a number of automatic control devices, such as proximity sensors or photoelectric cells (see Figure 9), and second, by either electronic or pressure-operated timing valves. On-and-off touch controls, while they may be satisfactory in some situations, cannot be recommended for most public facilities because of the danger of their being left in the "on" mode by hurried or unfamiliar users. Needless to say, the method of operation should either be totally automatic or absolutely obvious to any user. The placement of controls in this situation depends very much on the kind of control device selected.

Another major shortcoming in many public installations concerns the provision, or lack of

62 / CURRENT APPROACHES TO HANDBASINS FOR PUBLIC FACILITIES

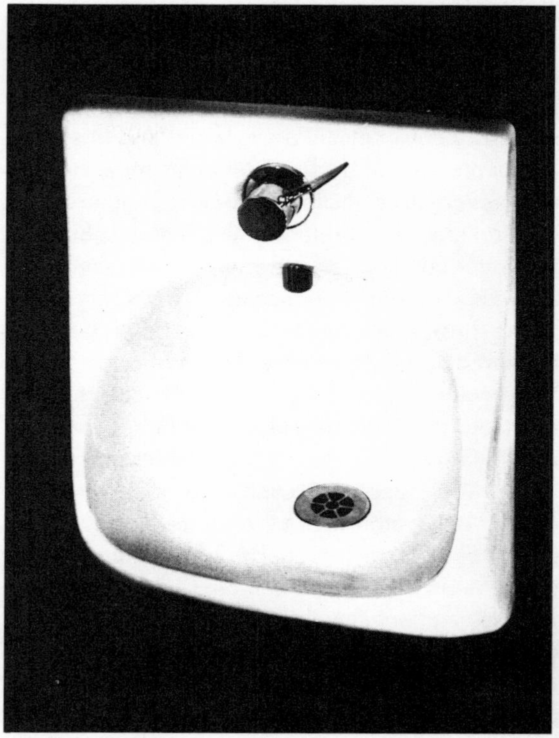

"HANDEX" BUILT-IN HANDBASIN:
ARMITAGE SHANKS, STAFFORDSHIRE, ENGLAND

"RONDEL" HANDBASIN:
ADAMSEZ, LTD., NEWCASTLE-UPON-TYNE, ENGLAND

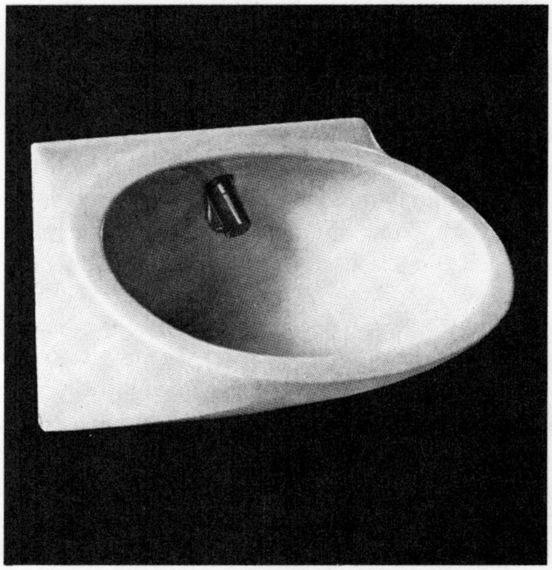

provision, for soap. In most categories of truly public facilities, it is desirable that soap be provided—but in some dispenser form, either liquid or powdered, rather than in bar form. Bar soap is, in most instances, unsanitary at worst and unsightly and unpleasant at best, except in the most elegant and fastidious establishments with a regular attendant on duty. The preferred dispensers should be located directly over the basin bowl itself and operate with a minimum of user contact.

The provisions for drying in public facilities have traditionally taken one of three forms: warm air blowers, paper towels, or cloth roller towels. Probably the least satisfactory solution, particularly in large public installations, is the cloth roller towel. The supply of such towels is relatively quickly exhausted and, as often as not, the user does not observe the courtesy of pulling a fresh portion into position for the next user. As a solution, it is often unsightly and unpleasant if not actually unsanitary and its use is fairly effectively limited to drying the hands, precluding other occasional and necessary uses. Nonetheless, it does solve the disposal problem, which can be considerable and which arises with paper towels. From a user viewpoint, however, cloth roller towels are probably best limited to semipublic facilities that receive relatively light use.

Warm air blowers also obviate the disposal problem and are relatively sanitary in use; they are, however, extremely time consuming, limited in their usefulness, and loathed with a passion by many. Indeed, it is not at all uncommon to find people using toilet tissue or their handkerchiefs in preference to using the blowers. In large and busy facilities, there is also often an insufficient number of blowers for the volume of traffic, and this results in a bottleneck in the rapid and efficient processing of users.

In general, it may be safe to say that disposable paper towels are vastly preferred by the majority of users but not necesarily by the host institutions. Paper towels are sanitary, quick, and easy to use for a variety of purposes and also permit an extremely rapid processing of users. They can, however, pose a maintenance problem if the disposal receptacles are not emptied frequently enough or if the receptacles are not designed with rapid and careless use in mind.

A problem common to all techniques is that there are generally far fewer drying facilities provided than washing facilities and that these are commonly located some distance from the washbasins. Because the user is forced to walk from one to the other with wet hands, the floor can quickly get to be a mess. Not infrequently, this situation also poses a problem for the user who may have a purse or briefcase, which one is either forced to leave behind at the basin or to carry with wet hands over to the towels or drier. One preferable, albeit more costly, solution might be to treat each washbasin as a self-contained center and provide both towels and disposal at each, as well as the other necessary amenities.

In this connection, a shelf for temporary storage is a necessity at each washbasin, for putting down one's parcels, purse, or briefcase. At the very least such a shelf should be 205 mm (8 inches) wide and should not interfere with the free use of the basin nor be so arranged as to pose any danger of the shelf's being wet. In ladies' rooms in particular, this shelf is commonly used to lay down one's coat as well as purse.

Grooming requirements represent another often unresolved problem area in public facilities, particularly in the case of women's facilities, where grooming activities tend to be fairly extensive and time consuming. An increasingly common approach is to provide a separate grooming area away from the washing area. In more elegant establishments, the grooming facilities are often provided in another room altogether and may include a sit-down counter with a mirror, special lighting, tissues, and receptacles for disposal. This separation is necessary in order to free the basins for other users who may simply wish to wash. Another common argument used in this connec-

63 / POSSIBLE APPROACH TO A PUBLIC HANDBASIN

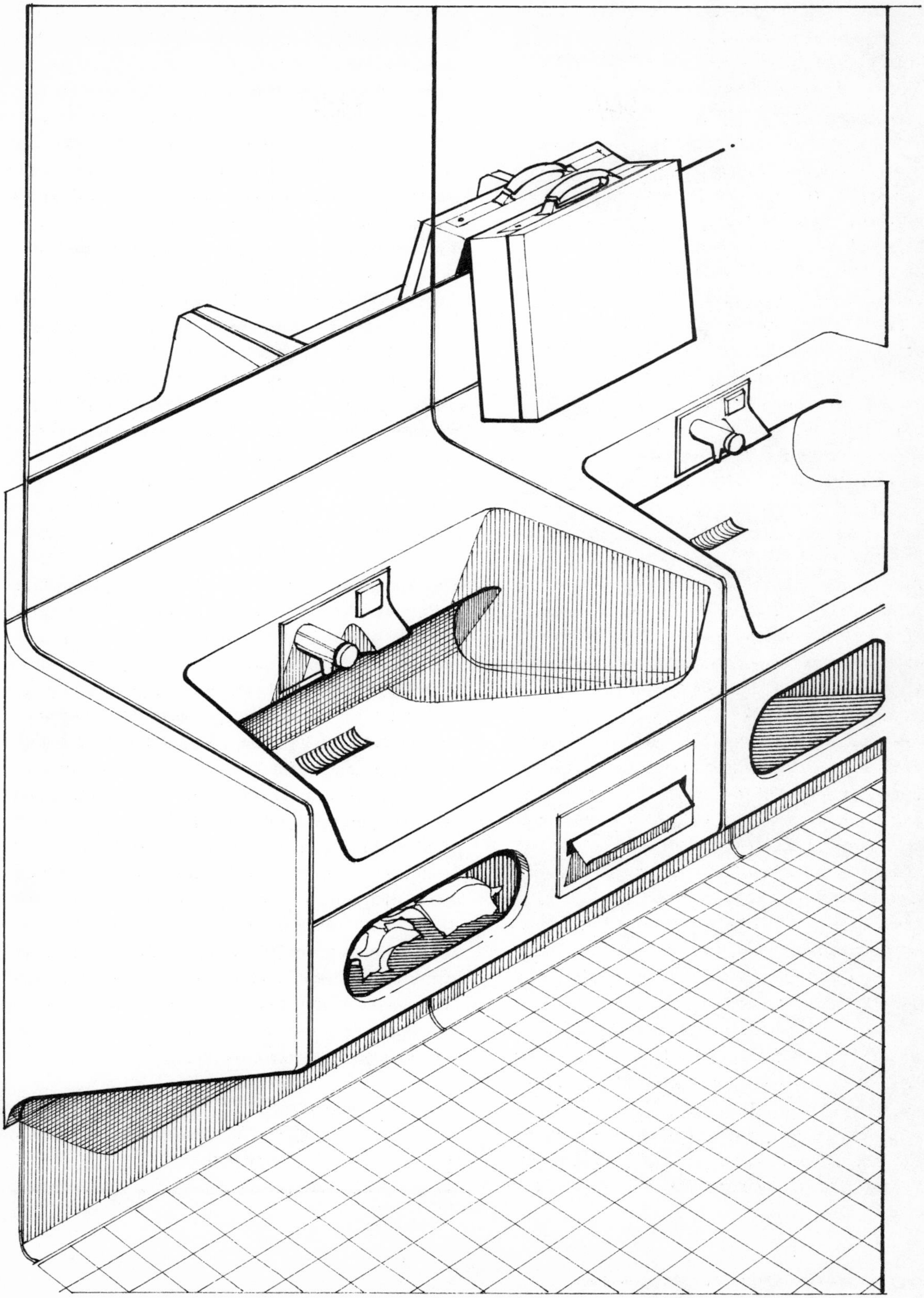

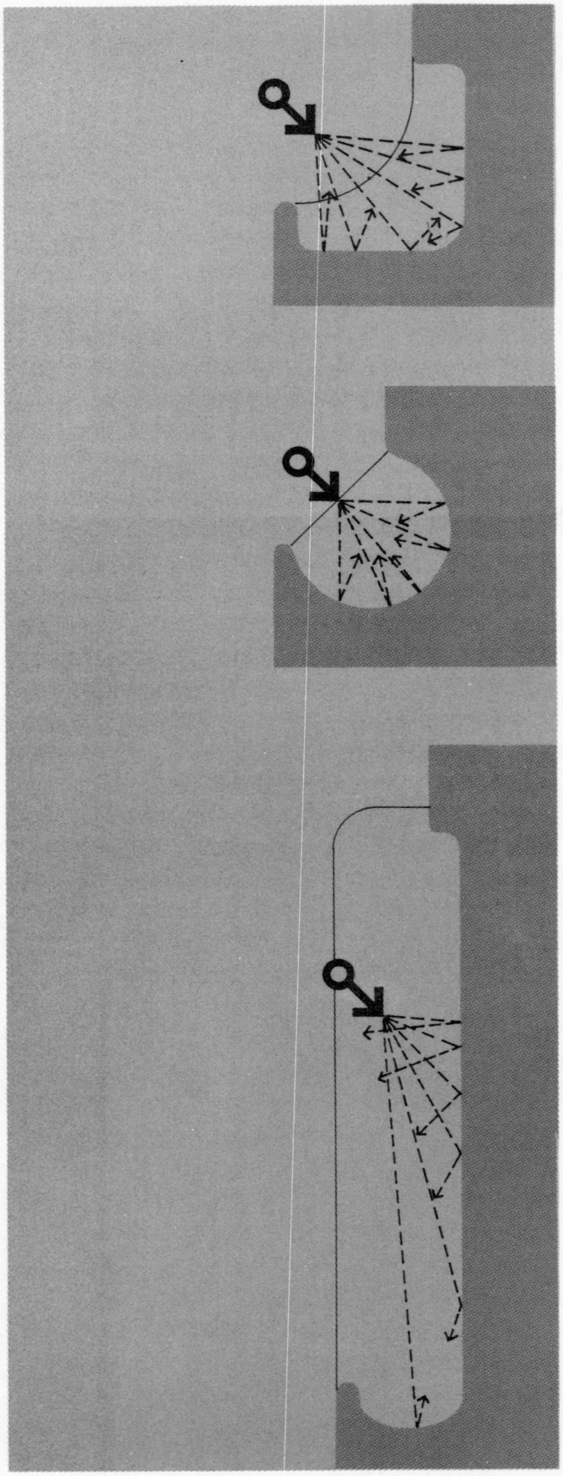

tion is that grooming activities make an unsightly mess of hair and face powder in the basins, but transferring this activity to another location only partially solves the problem, essentially by providing more comfortable and convenient facilities.

In men's facilities, the provision of a mirror suffices, since the grooming commonly consists simply of hair combing and tie straightening. Even in this case, however, there are often traffic problems created by the general separation of washbasin and towels or driers. One is forced either to perform one's grooming activities before washing one's hands or to wash, move away from the basin to dry one's hands, and then move back again for grooming. The provision of a comprehensive integrated facility would do much to alleviate these problems. (One possible approach to such a facility is illustrated in Figure 63.)

MALE URINATION

The basic criteria for accommodating standing male urination, developed in Chapter 12, also apply to public facilities. There are, however, several important exceptions in this instance; noise avoidance is generally not a consideration nor is the matter of disguised appearance of concern. On the contrary, a public urinal should be obvious about its intended function and should be immediately available. To a degree, the conditions of use are also somewhat different: the frequency of use of a given fixture is vastly greater than in the home; the user frequently comes with a greater sense of urgency; and commonly he is far more casual with respect to being careful about his actions. In addition, in many public places such as airports, bars, and restaurants, he is likely to have been drinking and hence is able to perform with less accuracy than normally.

Not only are water closets poor urinals but so

64 / URINE BACK SPLASH
WITH TYPICAL CONVENTIONAL
URINAL CONFIGURATIONS

are many existing urinals, particularly in terms of containing back splash. While use of the water closet results primarily in soiling of the fixture and floor because of inadequate containment, the use of some urinals results in substantial soiling of oneself because of the back splash and the nearness of the reflecting surface to the user, as suggested in Figure 64, and in Figure 65, which clearly shows the rusting of an adjoining metal water closet stall partition. One is seldom aware of this problem, however, because clothing keeps one from sensing the back splash.

If we refer back to Figures 52 and 54, we can see that the angle of delivery of the urine stream can vary considerably. In part, this is an inherent characteristic of the stream, and in part it is due to the way in which a particular individual may manually manipulate the penis while urinating. In order to accommodate this variation in the stream properly, it is necessary, as before, to provide a receiving configuration that has a continuously variable receding surface so that the stream, as it changes angle, can maintain a more or less constant shallow angle with the receiving surface. Many existing urinals, however, particularly of the wall-hung type, do just the opposite and are, in effect, reflecting saucers. The configuration in such cases is critical because of the close distances involved between the user and the fixture. In many public installations, where the privacy barriers between adjoining fixtures are minimal or nonexistent, there is a pronounced tendency for the user to stand as close as possible in order to maintain the privacy of his person, and he thus magnifies the soiling problem. Furthermore, when one is using a wall-hung urinal, which is mounted relatively high, the tendency is to position the penis in a more or less horizontal attitude, which results in the greatest amount of back splash possible. With a floor-mounted or pedestal-type urinal, the problem is not quite as severe, since it is possible to aim the stream lower so as to maintain a shallow angle of interception with the surface. Again, there is considerable variation in existing configurations, some of which are worse than others, as, for example, when the receiving surface slants forward

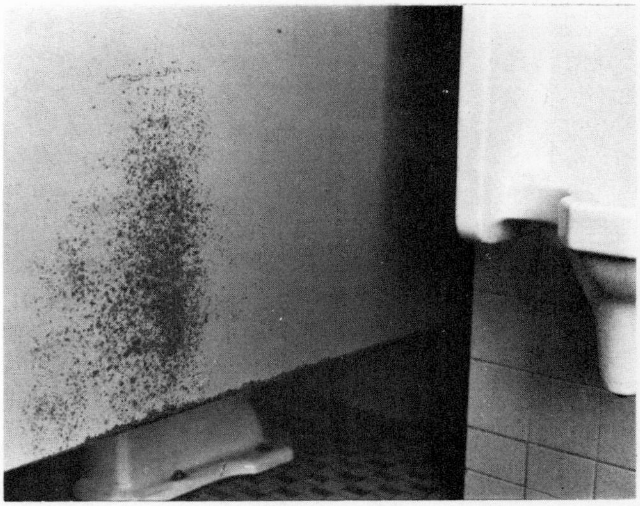

65 / BACK SPLASH FROM CONVENTIONAL URINAL

instead of away from the user. Perhaps the epitome of confused design thinking is provided by an installation the author discovered in a recently built European hotel where the floor-mounted urinals were fitted with heavy glass splash plates across the bottom so as to keep one's shoes clean. The manufacturer of these fixtures obviously recognized the existence of the problem, but one can only wonder why he did not try to cure it instead of applying a "bandage" to it.

There is no one ideal configuration; both wall-hung and floor-mounted types can function satisfactorily if the basic criteria are observed. Wall-hung units essentially need to have a greater back-to-front dimension than is customary and a more or less conical configuration set at a 40- to 50-degree angle, as indicated in Figure 56. With floor-mounted units the back receiving surface must slope or curve away from the user so as to provide the shallowest possible angle of interception.

Although the dimensions of any given fixture will, to a large extent, be dependent on the particular configuration, mention must be made of the side-to-side dimension necessary for a single user. This dimension may be reflected in the actual

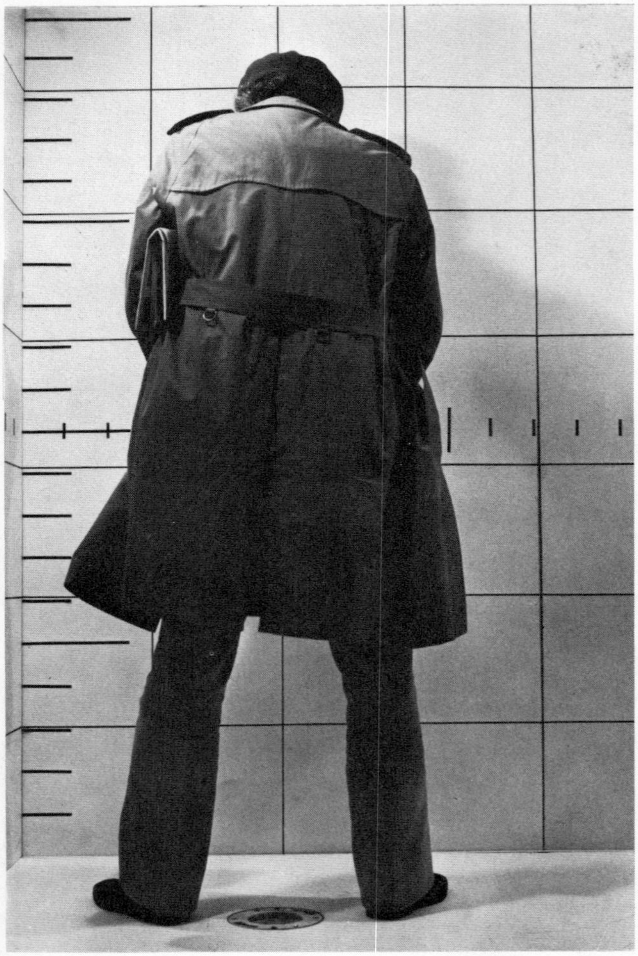

66 / TYPICAL STANCE OF A URINATING MALE, ILLUSTRATING NECESSARY FIXTURE SPACING

width of the fixture itself, or it may simply be accounted for in the spacing of fixtures and privacy shields, if any. Although not commonly done, except in some floor-mounted installations, it is in many ways preferable to set the width with the fixture itself so as to guarantee adequate spacing.

Most commonly, the width allotted is 610 mm (24 inches), and in some instances as little as 535 mm (21 inches). While these dimensions might be adequate in single-fixture installations, they are generally inadequate insofar as large multiple-fixture installations are concerned. When we examine the most extreme though common case of a standing male at a urinal with his feet spread, his overcoat and jacket opened and pulled back, and a paper or briefcase tucked under one arm in a typical stance (see Figure 66), the necessary clear width is more nearly 915 mm (36 inches). At the customary 610-mm (24-inch) spacing, adjacent individuals would literally be standing shoulder to shoulder, with no sensory clearance and no room for their garments. The common pattern of leaving at least one unoccupied fixture between oneself and the next user whenever possible is likely as much a function of our tight fixture spacing as of privacy considerations. When no dividers or privacy shields are provided between fixtures, a clear spacing of approximately 900 mm (35½ inches) is indicated. With dividers, this spacing could be reduced to approximately 800 mm (31½ inches).

From the standpoint of privacy and of clearly defining the "territory" of each urinal, it would be desirable if dividers were incorporated between fixtures. These dividers should extend a minimum of 205 mm (8 inches) beyond the fixture and start no higher than 510 mm (20 inches) from the floor and should extend up to a minimum height of 1,000 mm (40 inches) in order to shield the user from view by others.

In a public facility, flushing controls assume far greater importance than normally and also offer a clear instance of the common conflict of interest between the user population and the host institution. From a user viewpoint, automatic flushing devices that need no handling are far preferable to the common flushing valve in terms of sanitation and ease of performing the activity. A great number of sophisticated devices are available and

67 / POSSIBLE APPROACH TO A PUBLIC MALE URINAL

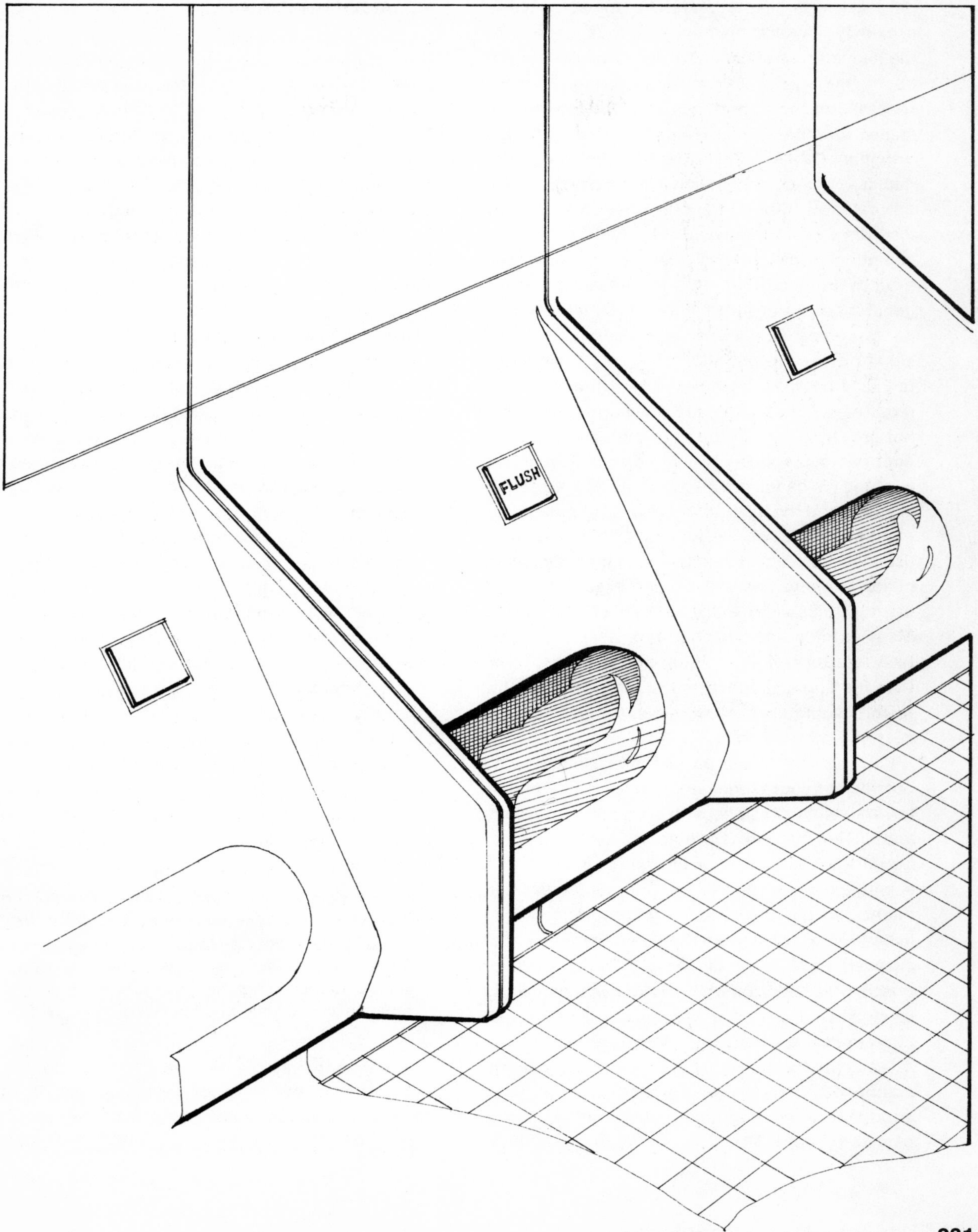
FLUSH

have been for many years: photoelectric cells, proximity sensors, heat sensors that respond to the temperature of the urine, floor treadles activated by the user's weight, and flushing buttons recessed in the floor. T. Crapper & Company installed automatic treadle-flushed urinals in Sandringham Castle in the 1880s.[4] Continual or automatically timed flushing can also be considered in this category, though these are viewed with some disfavor today because of their high water consumption. Unfortunately, few such automatic devices are to be found, primarily because of the general apathy toward hygiene facilities, the tendency of most agencies to base their design decisions on the lowest initial cost, and their reluctance to provide anything beyond the minimum required by law. Automatic flushing is important not only from the viewpoint of the user who does not have to handle the flushing mechanism before washing his hands but also from that of the general public and the institution, in terms of guaranteeing that the fixtures are, in fact, flushed after each use. Since cleaning and maintenance represent major ongoing costs, it can be argued that the more self-cleaning a fixture can be the better. Many of the automatic control devices are essentially less accessible and hence more vandal-proof than the conventional devices, and therefore this feature would also help to offset the higher initial cost of the installation.

With respect to the problems of cleaning, the outside configuration should be as simple and as accessible as possible, with a minimum of joints and hidden surfaces. Dividers, for example, might be an integral part of each fixture instead of a separate piece as at present. Another feature that might be considered is the incorporation of an ashtray so as to alleviate the perennial problem of cigarette butts' being disposed of in the urinal, or possibly the redesign of the fixture so that it could safely accept and flush them away. For the ultimate in user amenities, Mr. Routh reports that in one elegant Parisian establishment, the urinals are equipped with red velvet armrests.[5] (One possible approach to an integrated modular urinal is suggested in Figure 67.)

FEMALE URINATION

Unquestionably, one of the most serious unresolved problems of public facilities concerns the lack of satisfactory provision for female urination. This has been a major concern for at least the century that public facilities have existed in any substantial numbers and has been the topic of bitter complaints and letters to the editors of public journals. The basic problem lies in the fact that, for a variety of justified and unjustified reasons, the vast majority of women do not sit on a water closet in a public facility as they do at home. In one survey conducted in Great Britain, almost 96 per cent of the women interviewed indicated that they never sit on a water closet in a public facility.[6] Instead, they hover over the water closet, as illustrated in Figure 68, in order to avoid any contact with the fixture. Such a posture is, however, awkward and difficult to maintain and more often than not, especially when one is in a hurry, results in urine's being dribbled on the seat, the bowl, and the floor. Obviously, each successive user feels, in turn, even more justified in avoiding contact with the soiled fixture and puddle on the floor and so tends to assume an increasingly extreme posture with the inevitable result that her performance is, in turn, increasingly poor. Women's deplorable tendency to postpone urination as long as possible, particularly when out in public, contributes to this problem since urgency and a bladder full to the point of bursting can result only in somewhat hasty and careless urination. In addition, in some circumstances at least, the carelessness may be deliberate:

> Sometimes . . . one finds a whole lot of pee on the edge of the seat and run down on the floor in a pool. I suppose a woman has done it on the edge of the seat on purpose. I have often felt I should enjoy doing that; or just stand up and hold up my clothes and do it straight down on the floor.[7]

The incontrovertible argument for this practice of hovering is, of course, the virtual inevitability of the fixture's being soiled, though this is one of those circular, self-fulfilling situations wherein if

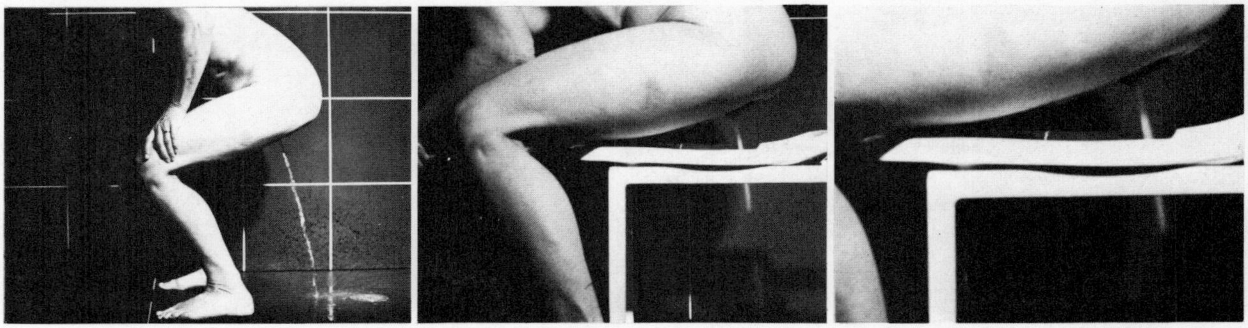

68 / TYPICAL FEMALE HOVERING URINATION POSTURE

everyone sat as she does at home the problems of soiling would be virtually nonexistent. The initial impulse leading to this practice is, however, the fear of catching some venereal disease through direct bodily contact with the seat. This fear is at least partially justified in certain circumstances but not in all. A number of studies have indicated that the agent in question is *Trichomonas vaginalis,* a common, annoying, and persistent infection of the vagina primarily transmitted via sexual intercourse but also via extragenital contact; in perhaps as many as one-third of the cases, it is transmitted via towels, water closet seats, or sauna benches, for example—anywhere where there is direct vulvar contact with a contaminated surface.[8]

Ironically, the open-front seat, which many women find objectionable on aesthetic or psychological grounds, is, in point of fact, highly desirable as a means of reducing the risk of such infection, though in and of itself it is not totally foolproof. A great deal of the difficulty lies in the manner in which women actually sit or hover on, or over, a seat, that is, whether she sits fully back on the seat initially so that no part of the vulva touches the seat or rim or whether she sits forward and then slides back. In some instances, with old-fashioned round or egg-shaped water closets, where the front-to-back dimension of the opening is small, there is the same danger of the woman's touching the front of the seat with the vulva as with men's touching the front with the penis—in either case, a totally unnecessary and inexcusable situation. The open-front seat mitigates this problem to some extent, but it can still remain a problem if the fixture itself is not of adequate size.

In certain circumstances, however, even hovering is not totally risk-free, since *Trichomonas vaginalis* can also be transmitted via aerosols and back splash from contaminated pan water.[9] This can present a particular hazard in extremely heavily used facilities where the closet may not have been flushed by the last user or in old facilities, particularly in Europe, where a tank flushing device is used instead of a pressure valve and where the interval between flushings may not be short enough to keep pace with the volume of users. In this respect, women should try to use a clean and flushed closet whenever possible and, incidentally, should always wipe from back to front so as not to contaminate the vulvar region.

Recognition of these problems has, over the years, prompted several manufacturers to offer various female urinals, or "urinettes," designed to be used in a hovering or standing/straddling position. The original intent was not only to obviate the problems of physical contact but also to offer women the same speed and convenience that urinals offer to men by being placed in open banks

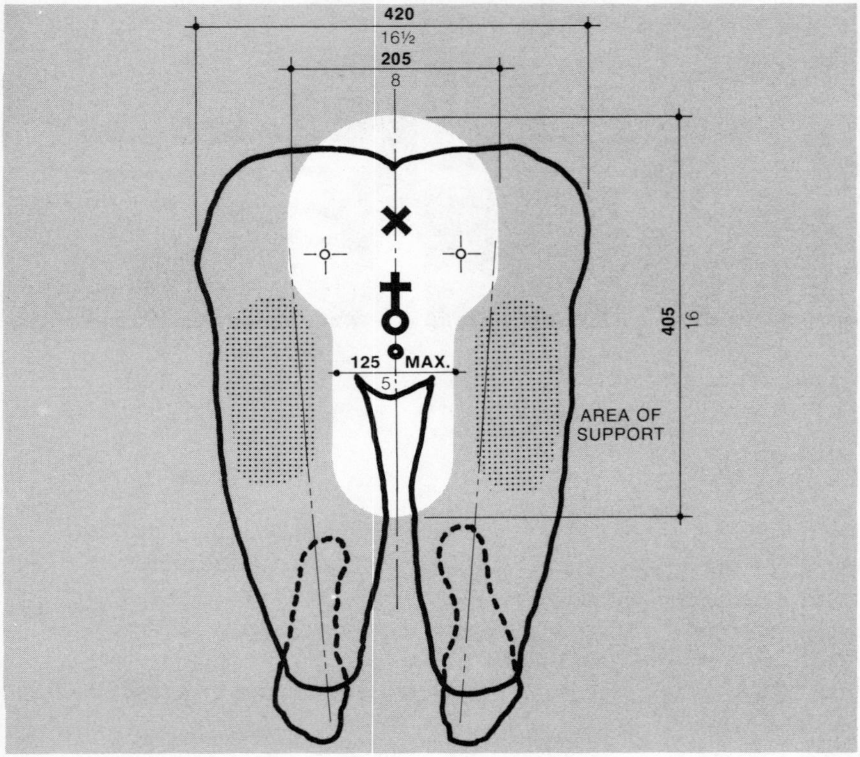

69 / PLAN VIEW OF NECESSARY DIMENSIONS AND CLEARANCES FOR A FEMALE PEDESTAL WATER CLOSET/URINAL

along a wall. Unfortunately, this approach did not take into account the privacy needs most women feel in this respect nor the management problems posed by clothing. In most instances today, a woman has to disrobe substantially in order to urinate in any manner, and this poses major problems of exposure, privacy, and of what to do with one's outer garments, purse, and so on. In addition, fixtures that must be straddled pose the problem of how to cope with the variety of undergarments found today. Women can, of course, urinate while assuming a variety of postures (see Figure 52), but these possibilities have little to do, in most circumstances, with the limitations posed by clothing.

Perhaps the first assumption to be made is that the facilities for urination should be accorded the same privacy and accommodation as water closets and be placed in a stall, for certainly the postures assumed and the necessary degree of undress are virtually identical whether we are dealing with defecation or urination. It might also be more desirable, as well as more economical, to consider the development of a combination fixture rather than a separate urinal to be placed in a separate stall.

In terms of posture, the hovering or semi-sitting position illustrated in Figure 68 is more susceptible of general use than a standing/straddling posture because of the problems posed by clothing. A hovering posture, is, however, awkward and difficult to maintain. One way to approach this is to provide support that involves a minimum of bodily contact while one is maintaining the hovering posture. This is desirable from the standpoint of coping with clothing and would also tend to force the user to remain in the proper position. Thigh support set at an average height of 510 mm (20

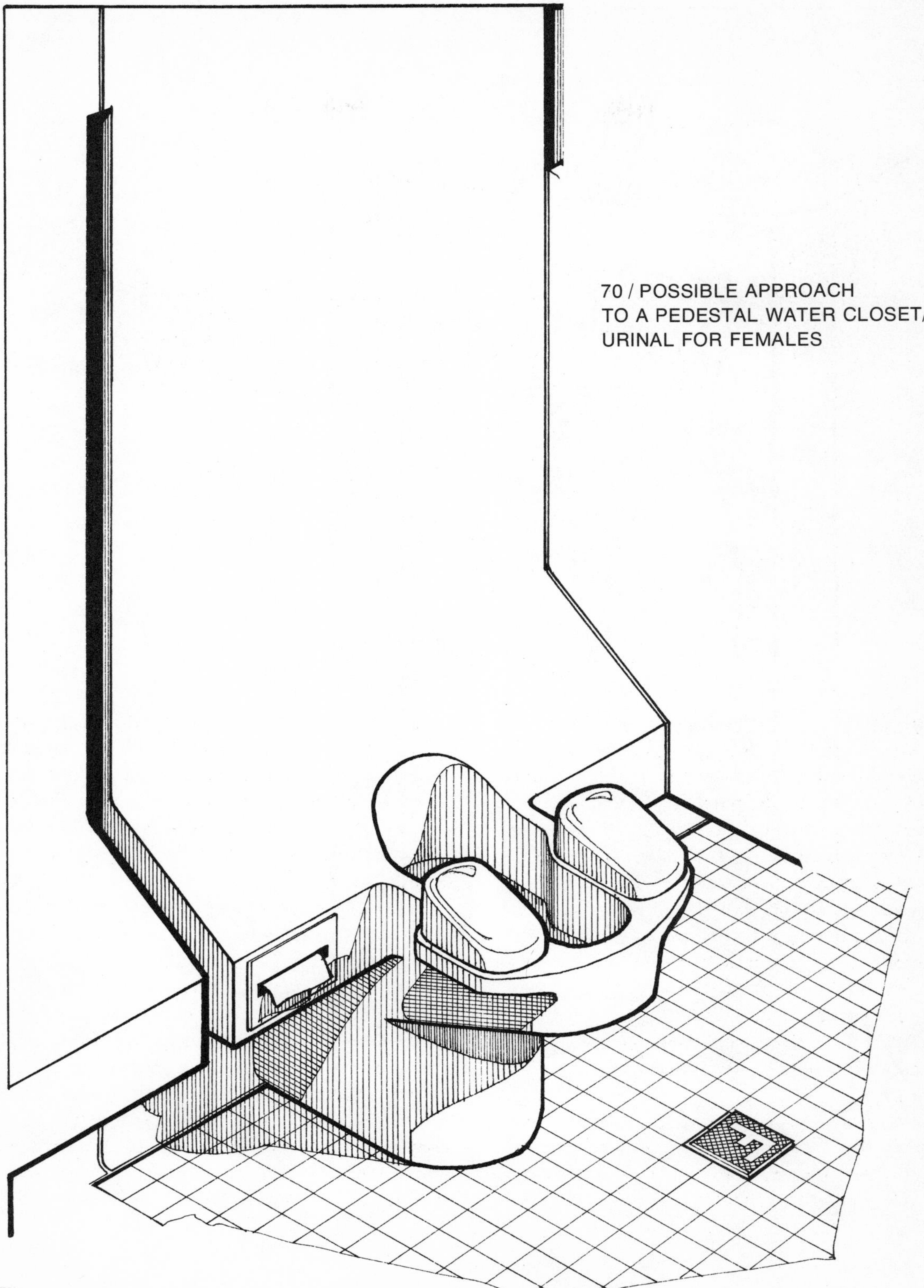

70 / POSSIBLE APPROACH
TO A PEDESTAL WATER CLOSET/
URINAL FOR FEMALES

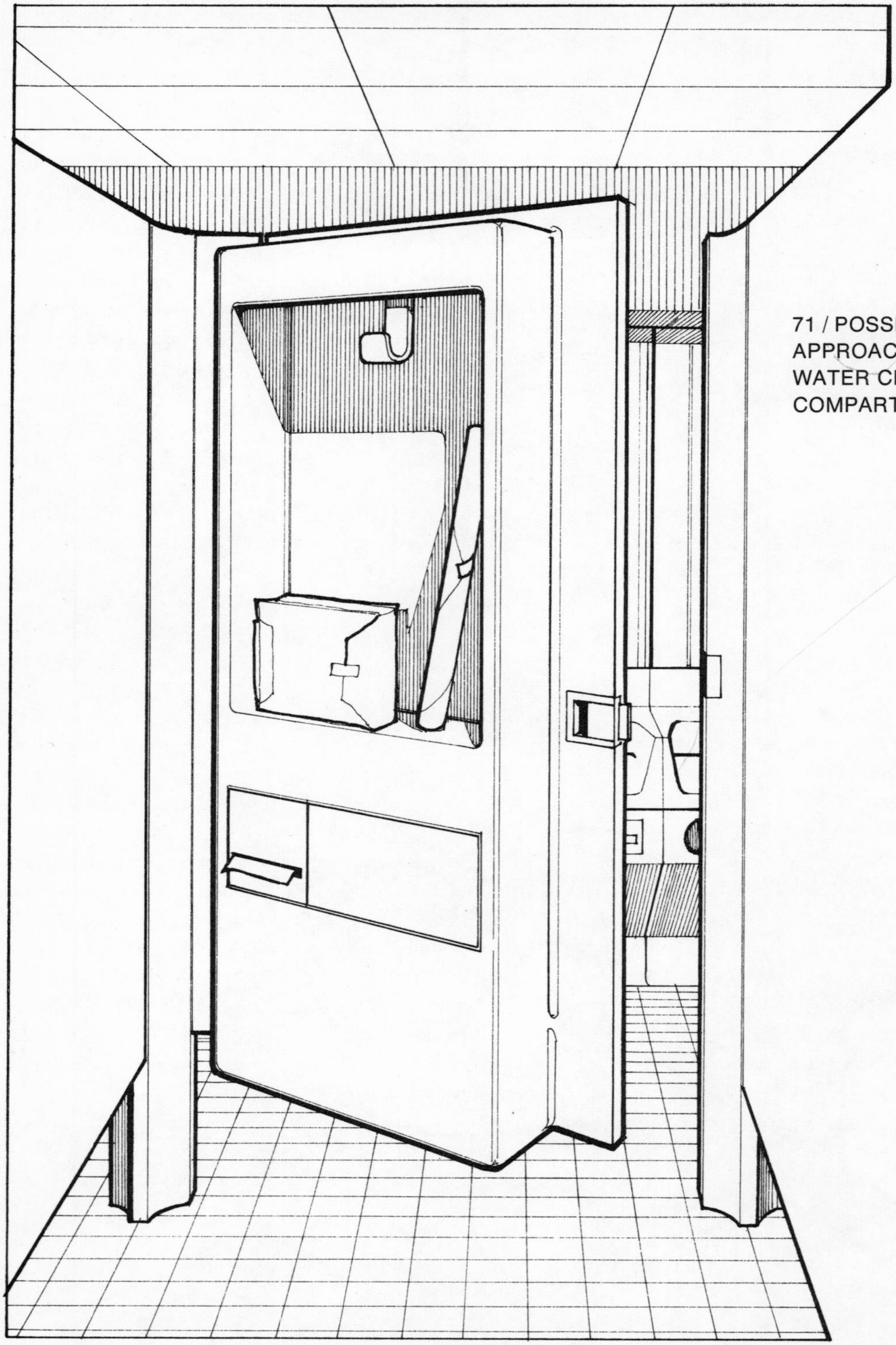

71 / POSSIBLE APPROACH TO A WATER CLOSET COMPARTMENT DOOR

inches) and sloped forward at an angle of approximately 15 degrees would permit the user to lean in comfort but not really sit or shift position. Such a posture would be equally suitable for defecation and would resemble that assumed on the proposed high-rise closet.

As illustrated in Figure 69, the dimensions of the opening should be considerably larger than normal so as to obviate any possibility of touching the fixture and to provide sufficient length for the proper containment of the rearward directed urine stream. A front-to-back clear opening of approximately 405 mm (16 inches) is indicated. The width of the opening at the back is 205 mm (8 inches) and 125 mm (5 inches) at the front. This clear width in front is necessary to permit hand access for blotting and also to permit the legs to remain more or less together, since they generally are restricted by undergarments.

With respect to configuration, perhaps the most important criterion is that the front lip of the fixture be a minimum of 75 mm (3 inches) below the level of the thigh supports so that there is no possibility of inadvertent body contact while one is assuming position. For ease of cleaning it would perhaps be desirable if the thigh support pads were integral with the body of the fixture.

Another major problem area in most public facilities is the flushing control lever, which is generally located on the wall behind the user and at an ambiguous height. It is typically awkward to use from either a sitting or standing position. (In men's facilities this is most commonly resolved by kicking it with one's foot.) Ideally, the flushing control should be easily visible and accessible and not require handling; for example, a floor-recessed button to be foot-operated.

One possible approach to a pedestal water closet/urinal for females is illustrated in Figure 70. In this instance the fixture is again assumed to be modular and to determine the width of the stall and also to be simple and easy to maintain.

Water closet stalls themselves often pose problems of temporary storage, especially in women's facilities. In addition to being of adequate size, to accommodate taking off and putting on one's coat (a minimum of 915 mm [36 inches] by 1,420 mm [56 inches]) and affording the user adequate visual privacy, the stall must also provide certain other facilities such as a toilet paper dispenser, sanitary napkin disposal, coat hooks, and a safe place for one's purse and other packages. Regrettably, it has become increasingly common in some large public facilities for purse snatchers to swoop in and grab purses off the floor of the stalls or even to fish them off the coat hooks over the top of the stall doors. This is made possible, and even easy, because in most public facilities no provision has been made for the articles one may be carrying, so that one has little choice except to leave articles on the floor—which can be not only dangerous but also unpleasant if the floor is wet—or sometimes to hang them on the coat hook or try to balance them on top of the paper dispenser. While this may be a forgivable oversight in men's facilities, it is inexcusable in women's facilities, where virtually every user is likely to be carrying at least a purse. One possible approach to these problems is to mold a storage shelf plus paper dispenser into the stall door itself, as illustrated in Figure 71. This has the advantages not only of convenience but also of having all one's possessions in one location and in view at all times so that they cannot be forgotten as one leaves. As in all the other circumstances examined earlier, it should be apparent that it is necessary to view each activity in its entirety and to take a comprehensive and integrated approach to the solutions.

PART THREE

FACILITIES FOR THE AGED AND DISABLED

Thus far in our examination of personal hygiene attitudes, practices, and accommodations, we have been dealing with these issues in the context of what we might generally consider to be the normal range of body functioning and of physical capabilities found among the majority of the population. There is also, however, a fairly sizeable segment of the total population that suffers from a variety of functional impairments or disabilities that, in many instances, also limit their ability to cope with their personal hygiene needs in the normal fashion while using normal accommodations. For these persons, it is not merely a question of safety, comfort, and convenience but also one of whether or not they can even perform some of the necessary activities by themselves without assistance. In some instances, they could manage simply with the additional safeguards and design refinements already proposed for everyone; in other, more extreme instances, special accommodations need to be made.

In this section, we shall examine the general problems posed by functional impairment with respect to personal hygiene. Since the variety and degree of severity of these impairments is enormous, we can only attempt to review the overall situation rather than be prescriptive.

SOCIAL AND PSYCHOLOGICAL ASPECTS OF DISABILITY

20

THE DISABLED POPULATION

For the purposes of this discussion, the population in question can be loosely defined as consisting of all persons suffering from some significant, chronic activity limitation that directly affects their ability to cope with their personal hygiene needs. This group is vast and highly diverse in its overall composition and in the nature and degree of impairments involved. It encompasses young and old alike as well as persons confined to wheelchairs and those who are fully ambulatory. Whereas it is difficult, if not impossible, to identify this population precisely or estimate its size accurately, an indication of its magnitude can be had from the fact that over the last decade, in the United States alone, an estimated 85 million persons (approximately 45 per cent of the population) reported having one or more chronic disease or impairment. Of this group, some 23 million persons indicated that they were limited in their activities and approximately 4 million indicated that they were unable to carry on with their major activity, defined in this instance as the ability to work, keep house, or engage in school or preschool activities.[1] While obviously not all of these persons can be presumed necessarily to have difficulties with personal hygiene, the proportion is likely to be substantial.

Viewed from another perspective, it has been estimated that there are some 12 million persons in the United States who suffer from arthritis and rheumatism, some 2 million hemiplegia (stroke) victims, 500,000 who suffer from Parkinson's disease, 100,000 paraplegics and quadriplegics, 200,000 who suffer from muscular dystrophy, 500,000 with multiple sclerosis, and 500,000 victims of cerebral palsy.[2] In a substantial number of instances, these are the persons likely to suffer the most severe impairment of their locomotor activities—and hence their ability to manage with conventional hygiene accommodations. On a worldwide basis, it is likely that the proportion of any given population so afflicted is even higher, partly because of the inadequacies of medical care and partly because of the higher incidence of both disabling diseases and disabling accidents.

In addition, we must consider that there are some 20 million persons over the age of 65 in the United States at the present time. People who reach this age, however good their general health, inevitably develop impairments of sight, hearing, touch, and movement, owing to general arteriosclerosis and degeneration of the central nervous system. Their sense of balance deteriorates; they are unsteady on their feet and unstable when standing for any length of time; and they have difficulty bending over. These changes, not necessarily associated with any special disease process, must find accommodation within the physical environment itself if these people are to continue to function with any degree of normalcy or independence. In addition to these generalized functional impairments, a substantial proportion of this group also suffers from one or more of the specific and localized disabling conditions we have just noted.

COSTS OF DISABILITY

The monetary and psychological costs of this impairment and disability are enormous, both to society and to the individual involved. In addition to the direct initial medical costs, which can be substantial enough in themselves, there are sometimes additional costs for rehabilitation and special training and the formidable continuing costs of assistance and special care—all compounded, in many instances, by the long-term loss of productive employment. As the longevity of the population continues to increase, we may also expect that the incidence of chronic degenerative diseases will rise, at least for the immediate future, and add to the problems facing society. While some significant progress has been made in recent years with respect to various insurance and assistance programs designed to alleviate some of these financial hardships, the problems remain substantial.

One important and sadly underutilized strategy for dealing with at least part of these problems is the extensive use of rehabilitative training and the provision of a home environment that would permit a disabled individual the maximum degree of independent self-care and some semblance of a normal productive life. In purely economic terms, it has been estimated that, while the cost of rehabilitative training for a paraplegic, for example, might run to $10,000 or more, the costs of lifetime custodial care might well exceed $100,000.[3] In human terms, the difference in costs is incalculable, as is the difference in purely physical terms:

> The impressive evidence clearly indicates that bed sores, contractures, frozen joints, certain types of incontinence and atrophy, emotional and intellectual aberrations, as well as social and economic disorganization, commonly observed in impaired or disabled patients, are attributable generally to injudicious, overlong immobilization, or to the deprivation of adequate stimuli. Indeed, disability may be regarded as a chronic condition frequently induced by man through ignorance, indifference, and inertia.[4]

Tragically, it has been estimated that in the United States no more than 10 to 20 per cent of the seriously disabled population has had the benefit of any rehabilitative training and fewer still have the benefit of a supportive physical home environment. On a worldwide basis, the situation varies greatly. In some countries virtually no services or assistance are available at all; in others, such as Sweden, even special housing is provided.

IMPORTANCE OF HYGIENE FACILITIES

Clearly, personal hygiene facilities that enable a handicapped individual to operate either independently or with a minimum of assistance can play an important role in easing the problems. This is equally as true of institutional- and custodial-care facilities as of home facilities. Personal hygiene is a significantly and potentially difficult activity that is an integral and inescapable fact of one's daily life. The activities themselves are relatively strenuous and the facilities often hazardous, even for young and able-bodied persons.

Although peoples' bodily needs and functions may be said to remain fairly much the same, regardless of the aging process, or of diseases, their functional ability to move and self-perform various activities is in many cases severely limited and quite different. This becomes obvious, for example, with respect to defecation. Although the squat water closet proposed earlier may be ideal for the general population from the viewpoint of physiology and comfort, it is clearly unsuitable for the elderly and the handicapped. The situation is somewhat ironic and complicated since many of these persons have severe constipation problems brought about by poor diet, loss of muscle tone, and lack of exercise and presumably could benefit from a water closet compatible with and aiding the natural defecation process. Many cardiac patients, for instance, who are otherwise relatively freely mobile, experience difficulty with defecation because the Valsalva maneuver (the contraction of the chest, abdomen, and diaphragm during "straining") stresses the heart. In contrast, some disabled persons who use wheelchairs may be normal in all respects except for the special difficulties they have with moving from one piece of equipment to another. Similar difficulties can be found with respect to virtually all personal hygiene functions.

In the case of physically disabled persons, for example, the criteria for self-care used to evaluate an individual's degree of independence include management of personal hygiene needs as one of the four or five major indicators in determining whether the individual is ready to leave an institutional environment.

PSYCHOLOGICAL ASPECTS

Inability to manage one's own personal hygiene needs is not simply a physical problem. It frequently also poses formidable psychological problems that can have far-reaching effects. For many aged persons, for example, the point when assistance is needed in the bathroom is critical and often represents a turning point in the person's outlook. It serves as the last bitter reminder that one has regressed back to a helpless infantile level and can no longer cope by oneself. As one observer has noted,

> One of the things we had come to realize in the clinic study was the profound effect which the change in normal bathing habits has on people. It seemed not to matter whether "normal" was a daily bath, a bath twice a week, or a Saturday night climb into a tenement kitchen tub. When it was no longer possible for a patient to continue what for him or her had been standard practice in bathing, the patient who had managed to cope effectively with many other tough problems of chronic illness and aging seemed to give up altogether. His self-image changed as radically as it would have changed by having mutilating surgery. It was observed that this was often accompanied by a markedly diminished effort to cope, which prior to this had been remarkable. The need to make radical changes in his bathing pattern seemingly was perceived by the patient as a major landmark of failure.[5]

Although bathing is the activity at which assistance is most commonly needed, this can be equally true of other hygiene activities such as washing and setting hair and wiping after defecation.

When we consider the damage done to one's ego by helplessness of any sort, let alone helplessness in such a basic and private facet of one's daily life as personal hygiene, the significance of the event should not be surprising. For many elderly persons who have gradually and painfully watched their other outer-directed capabilities wither away, this is at least one activity and one self-sufficiency that they can psychologically cling to. With that loss, there is also a loss of dignity, both in a body-related sense and in the sense of having, once again, to ask for, or require, assistance.

Personal hygiene and grooming levels are also directly related to a person's self-image and sense of worth. Willful abandonment of one's normal levels of body care, for example, can also signify willful abandonment of one's role and image and, in some instances, be intended as a subtle form of punishment directed at a presumably neglectful society or family, that is: "No one cares how I look anymore anyway, so why should I bother?"

Insofar as personal hygiene is concerned, these problems are magnified by our general societal attitudes toward hygiene activities and toward child-rearing and the initial achievement of self-sufficiency in these matters. In many instances, these problems are still further compounded by the attitudes and responses of other family members who are required to provide the necessary assistance. While few find it enjoyable to assist another person, even a loved one, with his personal hygiene needs, it is fairly well tolerated with infants, but somehow an aged or disabled relative, no matter how well loved, does not elicit the same response as a baby and, in fact, is often resented. Possibly this is because one can only look forward to the situation's worsening instead of improving with the passage of time. Often too, the aged or disabled person finds it difficult to appear grateful in such circumstances and can only express frustration and bitterness at the whole situation, and this response, in turn, tends to provoke a similar one in the person helping. Needless to say, the loss of personal privacy involved in such circumstances violates some strongly ingrained values and is also a source of discomfort and embarrassment for many individuals. In these instances, we have violated both modalities: privacy-for and privacy-from.

Even in situations where dependence/assistance is not the issue, many persons in this group suffer unease and embarrassment over real or imagined, or possible, violations of our taboos concerning the privacy of elimination functions because of incontinence. One of the most common and most difficult problems encountered with certain chronic and disabling conditions is the loss of positive bowel and bladder control. While many persons with these problems can be trained to cope more or less successfully, mainly through absolute adherence to a set schedule, there is always an underlying fear of accidents and the fear of not being in a suitable situation at the necessary time. In addition, the techniques and devices necessary to cope with incontinence are, to many, distasteful in the extreme, given our normal practices and attitudes with respect to elimination. The use of indwelling urinary catheters, or condom catheters, hooked up to urine bags taped to the leg, or the digital massage of the anal sphincter to induce defecation, or the wearing of diapers are all unpleasant, in a psychological as well as a physical sense, and require the development of a whole new set of attitudes and skills. In addition, both elimination activities are enormously time consuming in their management. Defecation, for example, can easily take an hour to complete, which is a far cry from our normal practice whereby elimination activities are purely reflexive, rather than premeditated, and fast. Persons who have undergone colostomies or ileostomies have the added burden of worrying about tell-tale odors and about whether they may be offensive to others.

Interestingly and ironically, the only parallel situation is to be found in the elimination techniques used in space flights, though this was even more difficult from a psychological viewpoint because of the research need to bring fecal samples back to earth for biomedical study. After the fecal bolus was collected in a plastic bag, it was necessary to insert a colored biochemical preserving agent that then had to be uniformly distributed throughout the sample by kneading. The management of personal hygiene in these circumstances was a price the flight crews paid, but not happily.

All these problems facing the disabled or handicapped person are also exacerbated by the general societal attitudes toward age, disability, and disease. Whereas society has, in general, progressed considerably since the days when having a disease meant that one had sinned against God and therefore should be flogged or at the very least ostracized, and when poverty was a crime, and when slop was standard hospital and poor home fare, and when "cripples" were objects of open ridicule, harassment, and scorn, we have not, in actual fact, progressed all that far. Our attitudes may be said simply to have gone underground. We may behave more civilly and graciously toward those "less fortunate" than ourselves, but it is open to question whether the basic attitudes have changed all that much. We appear always to have harbored feelings of fear, suspicion, and embarrassment with respect to persons who were "different" and, in particular, who were obviously diseased, disfigured, or disabled—persons who were "incomplete" or "imperfect."[6] In our contemporary urban societies we have also added age to the list of undesirable states of being. The aged have come to be regarded as a burden, and our constant emphasis on youth and beauty reinforce even more strongly our innate fear of rejection and of death.

One of the unfortunate consequences of these attitudes is that they frequently inhibit people from taking preventive measures and using safety devices because this would represent an admission of age and a tacit admission of diminishing capabilities. Often it seems that it is necessary to fall and break a hip before one is willing to face up to the inevitable facts of life and install a grab bar and a safety mat. As with the bidet, a common rejoinder is "Oh, I don't need that," "that" being any proffered modification or item of equipment that might make personal hygiene activities safer or more convenient. While such determination to continue one's habits without modification may be understandable and even admirable, it can also be foolhardy.

In summary, the psychological, as well as the physical, problems associated with personal hygiene are vastly more complex and difficult for persons with disabilities and handicaps than for others, and it needs to be recognized that they are as difficult for the person directly involved as for persons associated with them.

DESIGN CRITERIA FOR PERSONAL HYGIENE FACILITIES FOR THE AGED AND DISABLED

21

DISABILITIES

The disabled segment of the population is a highly diverse group, in terms both of age and of the severity and nature of the disabling condition or conditions involved. Before examining the impact of these disabling conditions on a person's ability to manage his personal hygiene activities, we must examine the nature of the disabling condition itself in order to have some understanding of why it presents a problem and, perhaps most importantly, of how a solution might be effected. All too often we "solve" problems by altering a situation so that the obvious symptom disappears, but we have not really solved anything, because we have failed to see or deal with the underlying condition that produced the problem.

In broad terms, one of the possible ways we can examine disabilities is with respect to the impairment of specific functional abilities, namely:

visual and auditory impairment
sensory and tactile loss
loss of equilibrium and balance
impairment of judgment and reflexive responses to stimuli
circulatory impairment
loss of manipulative ability
loss of locomotor ability

In each instance, there is a considerable variation in the degree of impairment involved that must be recognized. With respect to the loss of locomotor abilities, for example, one of the most significant forms of impairment as far as we are concerned, we need to distinguish between persons who have suffered virtually complete loss of their locomotor abilities and who are, for all practical purposes, bedridden; persons who are confined to a wheelchair but have no upper-extremity function and who must be assisted in the use of the chair; persons who are confined to a wheelchair who can propel themselves and manage their own transfers to and from other equipment; persons who can walk with leg braces or with "walkers"; persons who can walk unaided but have difficulty with steps, rough pavements, and so on; and finally, persons who can walk unaided but who must do so slowly and with care. Obviously, in each instance the practical consequences for everyday living are considerably different.

Often, particularly when severe impairment is involved, a given individual is more than likely to suffer to some extent from several different chronic impairments at the same time. A person with spinal cord damage, for example, may suffer not only locomotor impairment but also loss of bladder and bowel control and loss of tactile sensation. Satisfactory management of one's own personal hygiene needs in such circumstances is time consuming and complex, not only with respect to the individual's activities but also with respect to the particular physical accommodations necessary in each case.

While the potential causes of chronic disability are many, it may be useful to examine briefly some of the more common causes, particularly since they also tend to result in multiple impairments.

Spinal Cord Injury (Paraplegia, Quadriplegia) may be caused by an injury or a disease such as poliomyelitis. The common results of such damage are loss of limb function, loss of sensation in the affected parts of the body, loss of bladder and bowel control, and muscular spasticity. In effect, the person loses all control over the part of the body that is below the level of the damage to the spinal cord. Thus, the severity of the functional impairment is largely a question of the specific location of the injury. A high-level injury in the region of the neck, for example, generally results in an almost complete paralysis of the body and in loss of upper-extremity as well as lower-extremity function, as in quadriplegia. In such circumstances the person must be assisted in virtually all activities. An injury in the region of the lower back, in contrast, generally involves the loss of lower body functions only, i.e., paraplegia. Depending upon a variety of individual factors such as age, these persons can frequently manage their own wheelchairs, their own transfers to and from other furniture and equipment, and their own personal hygiene needs. One complication is, however, that while, in many instances, a person may have the use of the arms, there may also be a loss of the trunk control, which means the person can simply fall over unless restrained in some way. This can seriously complicate transfers and movements while seated on the water closet, for example.

Hemiplegia damage to brain tissue that may be caused by interruption of the blood supply (as in stroke or blood clot) or by tumors or head injury. The most common results are a loss of all muscle function (paralysis) of one side of the body—the side opposite the site of the brain damage; lack of sensation in the involved side; edema (swelling) of the involved hand and foot; difficulty maintaining balance in a sitting or standing position; and impaired visual perception, judgment, comprehension and, frequently, ability to speak. This situation is further complicated by the fact that "handedness" is involved and that the majority of the persons who suffer from hemiplegia are elderly and have diminished muscular capability in their unaffected side. While incontinence is only sometimes a problem, one's ability to move and perform basic activities is generally seriously impaired.

Arthritis a painful inflammation of the joints that may result from a variety of diseases. The two common causes are osteoarthritis, or degenerative arthritis, which is generally related to the aging process, and rheumatoid arthritis, a progressive disease that destroys the tissue and structure of the joints and is generally unrelated to age. The most common primary result is intense pain in the joints, particularly when moved. In turn, this tends to lead to lessened activity and ultimately to atrophy of the related musculature owing to disuse, the fixation of joints in deformed positions, and a general inability to move, manipulate, or grasp. In serious cases, a wheelchair or a walker is often necessary. Gross movements, such as are involved in bathing, dressing, and using the water closet, become extremely difficult and hazardous because even grab bars are often difficult for an individual to use effectively.

Parkinsonism a progressive degenerative disease of the central nervous system that affects basic motor functions. The common symptoms are a gradual stiffness and slowness of movement; a tense, bent-over posture; uncontrollable muscle spasticity; a fast shuffling gait; and finally, a deterioration of mental processes. This is primarily an affliction of the elderly and, while it may not present any major direct problems such as in the previous instances, it does nevertheless affect an individual's ability to perform all activities safely and effectively. In severe cases, the person's difficulties with walking may result in confinement to a wheelchair.

Multiple Sclerosis a chronic degenerative disease that destroys nerve tissue in apparently random areas of the brain and the spinal cord. Because the disease has no specific pattern, the resulting impairments can vary from individual to individual and can also build up over a period of time. These can include impairments of vision and speech, a loss of memory and impaired judgment, a loss of sensation in the extremities, impaired motor functioning and spasticity, difficulty with balance, and bladder incontinence. This is primarily a disease of young adults that tends to become progressively worse with time.

Muscular Dystrophy a chronic progressive disease that wastes and weakens the body's voluntary musculature. This is most common in young children and results in difficulties with keeping one's balance, walking, and so on. In its last stages, it affects all muscles, and death frequently results from respiratory failure.

Cerebral Palsy a condition of injury to the motor centers of the brain. Although this appears most frequently as an injury suffered during birth, it may also occur in adult life as a result of head injuries, blood clots, and a variety of severe diseases such as encephalitis. Depending on the particular area of the brain damaged, the functional impairments can vary considerably from complete or partial paralysis to simple tremors, lack of balance and coordination, involuntary and awkward movements, speech impediments, visual impairments, and diminished mental abilities.

Aging In addition to the major causal agents just discussed, varying degrees of dysfunction and disability can also result simply from the aging process itself, with no discernable disease or injury involvement. While there are always individual exceptions, certain physical and mental deteriorations can generally be considered to be a natural and inevitable part of the aging process. These include visual, auditory, olfactory, and sensory deterioration; slower reflexes; problems with balance, coordination, and manipulative skills; increased fragility of the skeletal structure; and increased liability to dizziness and faintness brought on by sudden movements or by bending over.

Aging also brings about certain other changes that, while they cannot be classed as disabilities, have a direct bearing on personal hygiene. The aging process produces some marked changes in the skin, for example, a lessened elasticity owing to a decrease in the subcutaneous fat deposit and a dryness owing to diminished production of sebum. Commonly, this results in a dry, flaky, and itchy skin and calls for less frequent bathing, the use of superfatted soaps, and sometimes even oil baths. Sedentary living habits, changes in diet, and diminished muscle strength frequently result in constipation—first functional constipation, and then self-induced constipation brought on through the overuse of laxatives. In turn, this can lead to complications with hemorrhoids, colon spasticity, and so forth.

BODY CLEANSING

Cleansing Hands and Face Persons who are partially ambulatory, that is, who use a walker or braces, have minor problems of access. Although they may use a countertop lavatory, there should not be other storage or cabinetwork below it that may interfere with their standing as close as possible. Since many of the aged and disabled have serious balance problems and suffer attacks of dizziness when bending over, it is essential that the height of the lavatory be in the 865- to 915-mm (34- to 36-inch) range suggested earlier.

Persons using wheelchairs, in contrast, have major problems of access that are further compounded by the lack of standardization in wheelchair dimensions. In order for a wheelchair user to use a lavatory, he must be able to position the chair in the same relationship to the lavatory as to a desk or table. Depending upon the design of the particular wheelchair, this may present a major or a minor problem. If the side armrests extend fully to the front of the seat, then the bottom of the lavatory must be set at a height that will allow the chair to be fully positioned under it. Partial armrests permit positioning the chair in front of the lavatory and allow a lower lavatory height, which is generally desirable from a comfort standpoint. Because of variations in wheelchair dimensions, not to mention body sizes, it is difficult to specify heights that will fit all persons. This is especially a problem in institutional and public installations where different users must be accommodated. One approach, taken in a proprietary European device, is to provide an adjustable-height lavatory.

In order to keep the height of the working surface—the top of the lavatory and its related counter space—in a more or less normal relationship to the user's arms, it is necessary that the lavatory be no more than 100 mm (4 inches) deep. Several wall-hung lavatories of approximately this dimension, designed especially for this purpose, are commercially available. For the preferable countertop installation, it is possible to make do with commercially available stainless steel, special purpose, institutional sinks that have both the necessary minimum depth and an adequate horizontal dimension.

The underside of such a lavatory must be smooth and free of obstructions. Because the arms are even more widely spread in the seated than in the standing posture, the side-to-side dimension must be a minimum of 610 mm (24 inches) and could reasonably be as much as 760 mm (30 inches). The front-to-back dimension of the lavatory basin can be set in the same 455- to 560-mm (18- to 22-inch) range as before. The most critical dimension, however, is the distance from the front of the lavatory to the back wall, which must accommodate the user's feet. With the vast majority of wheelchairs, the footrests are fixed in a forward sloping position so that the horizontal distance from the knees to the tip of the toes can easily be as much as 455 mm (18 inches). In order, therefore, for the person to be as close to the lavatory as possible, the dimension from the front edge of the fixture to the back wall must be a minimum of 760 mm (30 inches).

It is necessary that drains, traps, and water supply lines be as far back and as high as possible in order not to present either an obstruction or a hazard. In conventional installations, a common hazard is burns received from hot water supply lines. It must be remembered that many wheelchair users have no sensation in their legs and so can receive serious burns without being aware of it at the time. In some instances, it may be desirable to insulate the piping as well. This, incidentally, is a caution that should also be observed with room-heating devices such as baseboard radiators and electric heaters.

Because of the relative immobility of the wheelchair user it is also important that the water source be properly positioned and easily available. The fountain type of water supply suggested earlier would prove ideal, particularly for face washing. It would also be extremely useful for washing the various special items of equipment, rubber gloves and so on, that are commonly a necessary part of the personal hygiene ritual.

Controls present special difficulties for wheelchair users and also for persons suffering from arthritis. The conventional "decorator" wheel controls are particularly difficult to grasp and use. Lever handle types, particularly the wrist-operated controls commonly used with surgical basins, are vastly preferable, but perhaps ideally the controls should be of the electronic push-button variety for maximum ease of use. It is likely, however, that the size of the touch button must be such that it can be safely activated by the fist or ball of the hand rather than by a finger, that is, 50 mm (2 inches) square rather than 20 mm (¾ inch). The positioning of such controls must be within the comfortable minimum range of reach when one is either seated or standing. Because in many cases there is also a loss of tactile sensation, it would be desirable to provide the water supply with a temperature-regulating device.

Adequate counter space is important in any circumstance. In the case of disabled persons it becomes critical in order to minimize the amount of movement necessary to reach essential grooming and hygiene equipment and supplies. For a wheelchair user, everything must be available within the approximate 1,830-by-915-mm (72-by-36-inch) reach of the arms while seated. In this respect, conventional medicine cabinets and mirrors are useless insofar as placement is concerned. For a wheelchair user, the mirror (and lighting) must be positioned for use from a sitting position, and if other persons are to use the same facility, then it must be arranged to accommodate both. Disabled and elderly people also frequently have a need to store more medicines and special supplies than is otherwise the case, so that the problem is not only one of proper location but also of adequate space. In the case of wheelchair users, for example, one approach might be to provide drawer units below the lavatory counter on either side of a 915-mm (36-inch) chair well, an 1,830-mm (72-inch) overall width for the lavatory/grooming center being assumed.

Whenever possible, the designer must also pay attention to subtle details such as what kind of pulls or handles are to be used, whether ball bearing drawer glides are essential, and what particular problems of "handedness" are posed by a hemiplegic.

Cleansing Hair This is an activity that can present major problems for almost all disabled and aged persons because of common problems such as access, possible reaches, excessive bending and loss of balance. In most instances, it is probably best performed in the shower or with the assistance of another person. In the case of arthritics, who simply cannot raise their arms, there is little other choice.

Cleansing Body—Bath One of the most strenuous, difficult, and hazardous activities for disabled and elderly persons is attempting to take a tub bath. There are massive problems with getting in and out and with getting up and down from a standing or sitting position to a flat sitting or reclining one. In addition, there are often substantial problems of simply reaching all the body parts—a task that is extremely difficult in the case of most seriously disabled persons. While from a purely physical viewpoint it can be argued that persons in such circumstances should not attempt to take tub baths, there are both psychological and physiological reasons why it will probably continue as an activity. For example, tub baths can be therapeutic, as in the case of whirlpool baths and oil baths.

If we assume that tub bathing will continue as a necessary activity, the first problem to be faced is that of access and the assumption of a seated bathing posture. In the simplest case, of an elderly fully ambulatory person, there is a need for a grab bar at the entry to hold on to while he is getting in and out and for bars at the side for assistance in getting up and down. Grab bars intended for the use of the disabled and aged should be of a larger diameter than normal, approximately 40 mm (1½ inches), so as to provide a better grip. A nonslip bottom surface is essential.

An alternate approach might be to use a normal depth tub mounted so that the rim is at a height of approximately 660 to 760 mm (26 to 30 inches). As illustrated in Figure 19, this would permit a seated instead of standing entry and exit, which would lessen the potential dangers of a fall. The most difficult and hazardous part of the sequence is the shift from a standing to a sitting or reclining position in the bottom of the tub and then the shift to standing again from such a position. Over the years there have been any number of patented and unpatented designs and proposals made for tubs with doors that would presumably ease the problems of entry and exit, that is, the problems, particularly for the arthritic, of stepping up and over the side of a conventional tub. While these problems may indeed be eased by such approaches, the bigger problem of getting up and down would remain unsolved. In part, this problem has been solved by some of the hydromechanical tub chairs that permit a person to sit and then be automatically lowered and raised. This is not, however, a fully satisfactory solution in some cases, because the legs must still be lifted over the side of the tub when one is turning into the tub and one's freedom of movement for washing is hampered by the chair.

Tubs to be used by disabled persons should not be fitted with conventional shower door assemblies, which, at best, can present a hazard and, at worst, prevent the person from being able to enter the tub at all.

For persons who are semi-ambulatory or who are confined to a wheelchair, the process of entry is considerably more difficult and complex and is commonly performed by transferring from a chair outside the tub to another chair set inside the tub and then, in some instances, by transferring again to the bottom of the tub or to a low stool. This is possible only for persons with well-developed upper torso muscular abilities. Many elderly persons can manage only the transfer to the tub and need assistance beyond that point. Obviously in such circumstances, one is not really taking a tub bath but merely a modified sponge bath using a hand shower. In extreme cases of immobility, the individual is placed in a mobile sling hoist and placed in the tub. Most commonly this technique is limited to institutional use. Another recent approach, designed for bedridden patients, employs an inflatable tub used directly on the bed.

When we examine the access problems, both of semi-ambulant persons and wheelchair users, the most basic issue is how to minimize the gross movements necessary in the assumption of a seated bathing posture. Since wheelchair users begin from a normal sitting position at an approximate 455-mm (18-inch) height and since semi-ambulatory persons can reasonably manage to sit at that height, it would be desirable to arrange the tub so that only one direct horizontal transfer or one assumption of a sitting position is all that is necessary. This could be accomplished by raising the floor of the tub to a height of 455 mm (18 inches) and providing a wide access door that would allow one either to transfer directly or sit and then pull one's legs in. Another possible approach is to provide a deep sit-down tub with a door in which one would remain in a normal upright seated position. The former approach has the additional important advantage of greatly easing the problems if another person has to help with the actual washing process, since that person would be operating at a more or less normal working height. The latter approach may have some advantages when balance is critical, since the person could be strapped in a normal upright position. Both approaches, incidentally, are essentially similar in their posture and their minimal requirements for movement to the sit-down shower. The basic difference is in the additional complexity of the fixture necessary to provide a pool of water.[1]

Because such tubs need to be entered when empty, it is essential that the tub be filled as quickly as possible, which suggests that more than one water supply may be necessary. Similarly, an oversized drain will be necessary for rapid emptying. Obviously, the water controls must be equipped with a temperature-regulating device and be simple and easy to operate. In contrast to earlier recommendations, the controls in this instance should be located and arranged for ease of use from the seated position while one is inside the tub. Grab bars will still be necessary for pulling oneself into the tub and for aid in sitting and standing up. Hand showers should be provided as well as appropriate shelf space for items used at the bath such as the long-handled scrub brush that is commonly needed in order for one to be able to reach the feet.

Cleansing Body—Shower Relative to using commonly available tubs, it is generally simpler, easier, and safer for aged and disabled persons to use the shower method for body cleansing, primarily because there are no problems of access and one can remain in a standing or sitting position. This assumes a shower unit designed as such and not a bathtub used as a shower receptor, which is almost as difficult and hazardous for showering as for bathing. The shower head can be fitted with a mixing reservoir so as to provide premixed soap, an oil bath, or whatever and thus become comparable with the unique characteristics sometimes claimed for the tub method.

For fully ambulatory persons and for many semi-ambulatory persons, the shower unit proposed earlier would be perfectly adequate (see Figure 26). The principal difference in use would likely be that this group would be more apt to use the shower from a sitting position and to rely more on the hand spray than on the primary shower head. A possible modification to accommodate them more fully might be to reposition the shower head so as to serve the seated user, or to provide a hook from which the hand shower could be hung. In addition, the seat height should be raised to 455 mm (18 inches) and the depth increased to 380 mm (15 inches). In some instances, it might also be desirable to provide a safety strap.

For wheelchair users, some major modifications would be necessary, primarily to facilitate access and transfers. With respect to the basic enclosures, the dimensions suggested earlier are also suitable here: 915 by 1,525 mm (36 by 60 inches). For maximum versatility, one of the long sides of the enclosures must be completely open, and the seat, 455 mm (18 inches) high and 380 mm (15 inches) deep, should extend fully across one end. The entrance curb must also be eliminated and drainage accommodated either by a recessed entrance drain or by recessing the entire floor of the enclosure and providing a slatted floor flush with the room floor. This will permit the individual to perform a transfer from either side. In one case, the transfer can be made from outside the enclosure; in the other, by wheeling backwards into the enclosure. In either case, grab bars are necessary in the area of the seat to facilitate the transfer.

Since the entire washing activity in this case takes place in a seated position, all the other facilities must be designed and positioned to accommodate this. The seat itself needs to be an open slatted or mesh type of construction to permit cleansing of the anal-genital and general buttocks region from below. This is most simply accomplished with the hand spray, but a washing device could also be incorporated into the seat. Provision must also be made for a safety strap, a storage shelf to hold necessary supplies and equipment, lighting, mechanical ventilation, and so on. The water source could be either a hand shower or a repositioned fixed shower head, or both, as suggested previously. Controls must be accessible from the seated position, be simple to grasp and operate, and be equipped with a temperature-regulating device. If the hand shower is used, particular attention must be paid to the provision of a suitable closure device at the entrance, possibly a bifold or accordion-fold door. If a curtain is used, a method of securing the edges must be employed. In either case, it suggests that a completely waterproof enclosure is desirable not only for the shower unit itself but also for the immediate surroundings.

Since drying after showering is also a major problem in terms of reaching all the body parts, it is also desirable to provide a fast-acting temporary source of heat such as a ceiling-mounted infrared heating unit. Such a shower unit would also permit an alternative mode of use sometimes employed, that is, a shower wheelchair that could be used in the open space without transferring to the seat. Since, however, one transfer is involved anyway, the basic method is just as suitable and saves the expense of a second chair.

Cleansing Body—Perineal Although a neglected region of the body generally, this is an aspect of personal hygiene that becomes critical for many aged and disabled persons. Hemorrhoids are a common problem among this group and require scrupulous cleanliness of the anal region. In addition, wheelchair users who experience difficulties with wiping after defecation and who are forced to sit constantly need to practice regular and frequent cleansing of the region simply for cleanliness and for their own comfort. In these circumstances, the bidet is even less of an answer than it is normally, and serious consideration needs to be given to the provision of a washing capability within the water closet itself. Many of these individuals suffer from incontinence and there is inevitably a need to cleanse oneself after an accidental discharge. As we shall see in a moment, such a functional capability for washing is essential in the case of persons who are unable to wipe themselves at all. The unpleasant alternative in such circumstances is to have another person perform the activity.

DEFECATION

In many instances this activity presents as many if not more difficulties than body cleansing, primarily in cases of incontinence where the difficulties are not only of transfers but also of one's own body functioning. Because it is a much more frequent and more personal activity, it is also one that most aged and disabled persons are more acutely aware of than bathing. In many instances there are problems of constipation and prolonged sitting that ultimately result in the legs' "falling asleep" from having the blood circulation impeded; there are problems with "straining"; and there are problems simply with sitting down and getting up.

For many ambulatory and semi-ambulatory persons, the first difficulty is with the sitting height. In many instances, even the normal 380- to 405-mm (15- to 16-inch) height is too low a seated posture to assume without the aid of grab bars. While an even lower height may be desirable from a purely physiological viewpoint, it is an unreasonable supposition in these circumstances. A fixture like the high-rise water closet described earlier (see Figures 45 and 51), equipped with a washing capability and grab bars, would be far more suitable, particularly if the individual assumed the appropriate doubled-over posture. It would be desirable whenever possible to position the water closet next to a wall so that support bars can be conveniently and securely mounted. In existing installations it would be helpful, at the very least, to install a proper posture seat as illustrated in Figure 43.

For wheelchair users the first problem is again one of access and transfers. In the ideal situation the water closet would be located so that there is room to wheel the chair directly alongside, so as to effect a direct horizontal transfer. Obviously the height of the water closet seat should match that of the wheelchair. In most circumstances, the high-rise water closet described earlier would satisfy this criterion. In this case the size of the opening is sufficient to allow hand access for anal sphincter stimulation and insertion of suppositories. In existing installations the common solution is to install a "seat extender," which is essentially an elevated replacement seat that fits over the water closet. One version of this employs a solid tube, which is perfectly adequate for aged persons who simply need a higher seat. Most disabled persons require, however, an open version that allows hand access. Because of the difficulties attendant upon wiping, the inclusion of a washing function is essential and a flushing and washing mechanism that could be simply operated by one's elbow would be of enormous benefit (see Figure 46). Fixtures similar to those described in Figures 46 and 51 could also provide the necessary trunk support for those individuals requiring it and be fitted with safety straps. In most instances it is also necessary to provide a storage area for items such as suppositories, rubber gloves, and ointments that is easily accessible from the seated position.

URINATION

This varies significantly from group to group in terms of the problems it presents. In the case of ambulatory aged males there are substantial problems of lack of steadiness, balance, and neuromuscular control that make the use of a conventional water closet even more problematic than normally. In these circumstances a stand-up urinal would be of great benefit, particularly if fitted with a grab bar for steadying oneself and a night light. In the case of females, the problems are principally those of sitting height.

For most wheelchair users and other severely disabled individuals urination is a serious problem but not one that directly involves water closet or urinal design. Because of incontinence, most such persons have to manage with indwelling or condom catheters, urine bags, and the like and face problems of emptying, changing, and cleansing rather than problems of urination.

GENERAL PLANNING CONSIDERATIONS

While we have thus far been dealing with specific and detailed problems of personal hygiene accommodation, there are also some general aspects of overall planning that must be recognized. Perhaps the most important of these is the so-called "architectural barriers" problem wherein, because of inadequate space, inadequate door openings, and so on, a person in a wheelchair cannot even get into the bathroom or, if once in, cannot maneuver the chair so as to manage comfortable and safe transfers to hygiene equipment. Unfortunately, in most existing circumstances, both private and public, this is the rule rather than the exception and applies equally to bathrooms used by the aged as well as the disabled.

Perhaps the first criterion to be observed is that the bathroom be located so as to have a direct relationship and a direct line of travel between it and the bedroom. While this may appear terribly elementary, more often than not one finds bedroom/bathroom/closet configurations that are anything but direct and obvious and hallway spaces that are too tight for comfortable maneuvering. Attention must also be paid to the arrangement of doors, door swings, and, most important, to the size of the doors, which must be wide enough to clear a wheelchair easily—a minimum of 915 mm (36 inches). The standard hinged door is difficult for wheelchair users to cope with because of its necessary extra width. Either a bifold door that requires only half the radius of movement or a sliding door is far easier to manage. This is true not only in terms of the movements required just to open the door but also in terms of the problems of closing it and maneuvering around the opened door in a tight space. Particular attention must also be paid to the elimination of sills and thresholds at door openings and to the maintenance of continuous floor surfaces, even when there may be changes in flooring materials. Door handles are far easier to use both by disabled and aged persons if they are of the lever rather than the wheel type. Lever handles can be more easily grasped and operated, particularly if one does not have full capability of the hand—in some instances simply by using the heel of the hand or even the whole forearm.

As to the bathroom itself, the basic criterion is that it be large enough to permit the individual to move from one piece of equipment to another with a minimum of effort and that the equipment be arranged so as to facilitate transfers in the easiest possible fashion. More than the normal amount of space is sometimes needed in relation to a given fixture, so that another person who may be providing necessary assistance can operate comfortably and safely. In general, the minimum amount of space necessary for a bathroom to accommodate a wheelchair user is approximately twice the space allotted in the standard minimum bathroom, i.e., 2,150 by 3,050 mm (7 by 10 feet). In an ideal situation, the particular arrangement and the minor variations in facilities provided must be determined on the basis of the unique requirements and capabilities of each user. This becomes especially important in the case of hemiplegics, for example, where "handedness" is an essential component of the overall problem.

Other general planning criteria include the provision of adequate and appropriately accessible storage for the needed variety of hygiene equipment and supplies; careful location of light switches, which ideally should be of the luminous variety; care in the selection and placement of space-heating elements; emergency signaling devices; and door locks that can be opened in an emergency from the outside.[2]

In summary, the ultimate irony is that most of the "special" requirements necessary for aged and disabled persons are really not that special. Basically they represent careful attention to human needs and in many cases would be equally as suitable and useful for the normal population. What is perhaps really "special" is that in the case of aged and disabled persons, we cannot permit ourselves the casual adaptation to an unresponsive environment that we normally tolerate.

NOTES

CHAPTER 1 / HISTORICAL ASPECTS OF PERSONAL HYGIENE FACILITIES

1 For a thorough historical summary of Western attitudes and practices, see: Reginald Reynolds, *Cleanliness and Godliness* (Garden City, New York: Doubleday and Co., Inc., 1946); Lawrence Wright, *Clean and Decent* (New York: The Viking Press, 1960); H. L. Miller, "A Social History of the American Bathroom," unpublished master's thesis, Cornell University, 1960; Wallace Reyburn, *Flushed with Pride* (London: Macdonald & Co., Ltd., 1969); Theodor Rosebury, *Life on Man* (New York: The Viking Press, 1969); Sigfried Giedion, *Mechanization Takes Command* (New York: Oxford University Press, 1948), pp. 628–712. All have extensive bibliographies that can direct the dedicated further.

2 Wright, op. cit., p. 102.

3 Ibid., p. 115.

4 Miller, op. cit., p. 17.

5 See David Hicks, *David Hicks on Bathrooms* (New York: World Publishing, 1970); Mary Gilliatt, *Bathrooms* (New York: The Viking Press, 1971).

CHAPTER 2 / SOCIAL AND PSYCHOLOGICAL ASPECTS OF BODY CLEANSING AND CARE

1 P. Schilder, *The Image and Appearance of the Human Body* (New York: International Universities Press, Inc., 1950).

2 See: "The Groomer," *Time,* September 4, 1972, p. 67; and R. Beard, "The British Management-Spotter's Guidebook," *The Manchester Guardian,* April 21, 1973, p. 17.

3 See: Bernard Rudofsky, *The Unfashionable Human Body* (New York: Doubleday and Co., Inc., 1971).

4 N. Allon, "The Stigma of Overweight in Everyday Life," a paper delivered before the National Conference on Obesity, Fogarty International Center for Advanced Study in Health Sciences, H.E.W., October 1973.

5 Havelock Ellis, *Studies in the Psychology of Sex* (New York: Random House, 1936), vol. 1, part 3, p. 33.

6 See: W. E. H. Lecky, *History of European Morals from Augustus to Charlemagne* (New York: D. Appleton, 1869), vol. 2, pp. 107–117.

7 Reynolds, op. cit., p. 96.

8 Thorsten Veblen, *The Theory of the Leisure Class* (New York: The Macmillan Co., 1912).

9 R. V. McCall, Jr., P. H. Gleye, and L. Singer, *The Men's Room* (Chicago: Institute of Design, I. I. T., September 1971, mimeographed, unpaged).

10 "West Germany: Dirty Linen," *Time,* May 18, 1970, p. 30.

11 J. A. Cameron. "A Particular Problem Concerning Personal Cleanliness," *Public Health,* vol. 76, March 1962, pp. 173–177.

12 J. A. Flugel, *The Psychology of Clothes* (London: The Hogarth Press, 1950).

13 A. Montague, *Touching: The Human Significance of the Skin* (New York: Columbia University Press, 1971).

14 See p. 202 for a discussion of other aspects of this phenomenon.

15 See: H. Zinsser, *Rats, Lice and History* (New York: Little, Brown & Co., 1934).

16 A. Leaf, "Getting Old," *Scientific American,* September 1973, p. 46.

17 J. O. Hendley, R. P. Wenzel, and J. M. Gwattney, "The Transmission of Rhinovirus Colds by Self-Inoculation," *The New England Journal of Medicine,* vol. 288, no. 26, June 28, 1973, p. 1361.

18 Alan Watts, "Do You Smell?" *Alan Watts Journal,* vol. 1, no. 12, October 1970.

19 R. G. Shafer, "Company Data on Soap and Detergent Ads Given to FTC is Thorough, Contradictory," *The Wall Street Journal,* August 20, 1973, p. 7; and "The Underarm Pitfall," *The Wall Street Journal,* August 22, 1973, p. 14.

20 P. Bart, "Advertising: Success for the Deodorants," *The New York Times,* Sunday, April 26, 1964, p. 14F. Also see: Rosebury, op. cit.

21 L. Barzini, "The Man, the Actor, the Reluctant Lover: Mastroianni," *Vogue,* October 15, 1965, p. 158.

22 See: Ellen Frankfort, "Health Forum: The Sweet Smell of Modess," *The Village Voice,* September 30, 1971, p. 30, for observations on the woman as a good piece of furniture—well sprayed, painted, and polished.

23 "Advertising: It's a Tough Life," *Time,* June 22, 1970, p. 78. Also see: W. B. Key, *Subliminal Seduction* (Englewood Cliffs: Prentice-Hall, Inc., 1973).

24 S. C. Brown, ed., "Of the Salubrity of Warm Bathing," *Collected Works of Count Rumford* (Cambridge: Harvard University Press, 1969) vol. 3, p. 407. The original work dates from approximately 1780.

25 C. Northcote Parkinson, *Mrs. Parkinson's Law* (Boston: Houghton-Mifflin Co., 1968), p. 73.

26 For two interesting points of view on this phenomenon of merging sexual identities, see: "Finale for Fashion," *Time,* January 26, 1970, p. 39; and "Killing a Culture," *Time,* October 12, 1970, p. 57.

27 Cameron, op. cit., pp. 173–177.

28 Tiny Tim, "The Perfect Mother," *Esquire,* December 1970, p. 144.

29 Philip Roth, *Portnoy's Complaint,* (New York: Bantam Books, 1970), p. 52.

30 Ian Fleming, *You Only Live Twice* (New York: The New American Library, 1964), pp. 69–70.

31 For a brief history of modern toilet tissue, see: Reyburn, op. cit., pp. 80–82.

32 Cameron, op. cit., pp. 173–177.

CHAPTER 3 / THE ANATOMY AND PHYSIOLOGY OF CLEANSING

1 A. J. Carlson, "Physiologic Changes of Normal Senescence," *Geriatric Medicine,* 3rd ed., E. J. Stieglitz, ed. (Philadelphia: J. B. Lippincott Co., 1954), p. 77.

2 Arthur Grollman, ed., *The Functional Pathology of Disease,* 2nd ed. (New York: McGraw-Hill Book Co., Inc, 1963), pp. 896–897.

3 J. H. Swartz, and M. G. Reilly, *Diagnosis and Treatment of Skin Diseases* (New York: The Macmillan Co., 1935), p. 4. There are a number of important exceptions to this that must, however, be noted, such as certain highly toxic pesticides that can be absorbed into the skin and any number of substances that can cause severe blistering and other reactions.

4 See: Rosebury, op. cit.

5 I. Martin-Scott, and A. G. Ramsay, "Soap and the Skin, with an Investigation into the Properties of a Neutral Soap," *British Medical Journal,* vol. 1, June 30, 1956, p. 1526.

6 See: P. Siegel, "Does Bath Water Enter the Vagina?" *Obstetrics and Gynecology,* vol. 15, no. 5, May 1960, pp. 660–661.

7 See: H. V. Viherjuuri, *Sauna: The Finnish Bath* (English edition, Helsinki: Otava, 1967); and S. C. Brown, ed., op. cit., pp. 387–431.

CHAPTER 4 / DESIGN CRITERIA FOR CLEANSING HANDS, FACE, AND HAIR

1 M. Langford, *Personal Hygiene Attitudes and Practices in 1,000 Middle-Class Households* (Ithaca: Cornell University Agricultural Experiment Station Memoir 393, 1965), p. 46.

2 See: D. S. Ellis, "Speed of Manipulative Performance as a Function of Work-Surface Height," Journal of Applied Psychology, vol. 35, 1951, pp. 289–296; also G. M. Morant, "Body Size and Work Spaces," and K. F. H. Murrell, "Equipment Layout" in *Symposium on Human Factors in Equipment Design,* W. F. Floyd, and A. T. Welford, eds. (London: H. K. Lewis and Co., Ltd., 1954), pp. 17–24 and 119–127 respectively.

3 Langford, op. cit., pp. 45, 46.

4 Ibid., pp. 47, 48.

5 J. Crisp and A. Sobolev, "Water and Fuel Economy—The Use of Spray Taps for Ablution in Buildings," *Royal Institute of British Architects Journal,* vol. 62, July 1956, pp. 386–388. See also: "Sanitation Standards," *Architectural Record,* vol. 81, January 1937, p. 43.

CHAPTER 5 / DESIGN CRITERIA FOR CLEANSING THE BODY—BATH

1 Unreported data, Cornell Survey on Personal Hygiene Attitudes and Practices in 1,000 Middle-Class Households. See also: Langford, op. cit., Appendix C, Tables 23, 28.

2 *NEISS News,* U.S. Department of Health, Education, and Welfare, Washington, D.C., March 1973.

3 See: "Softening Up the Bathroom with Plastic Foams," *Modern Plastics,* October 1971, pp. 60, 61; and "The Prototype of a Soft Bathroom," *Domus,* no. 493, December 1970, p. 36.

4 See: B. Akerblom, "Chairs and Sitting," *Symposium on Human Factors in Equipment Design,* op. cit.; C. A. Ridder, *Basic Design Measurements for Sitting,* Fayetteville: University of Arkansas, Agricultural Experiment Station Bulletin 616, October 1959; R. A. McFarland et al., *Human Body Size and Capabilities in the Design and Operation of Vehicular Equipment* (Boston: Harvard School of Public Health, 1953), pp. 129–141.

5 S. Carlsoo, "A Method for Studying Walking on Different Surfaces," *Ergonomics,* vol. 5, no. 1, January 1962, pp. 271–274.

6 H. T. E. Hertzberg, "Some Contributions of Applied Physical Anthropology to Human Engineering," *Annals of The New York Academy of Sciences,* vol. 63, art. 4, 1955, p. 622.

7 See: "1956 Women's Congress on Housing," as reported in *Domestic Engineering,* June 1956, p. 110.

CHAPTER 6 / DESIGN CRITERIA FOR CLEANSING THE BODY—SHOWER

1 Ogden Nash, *Verses from 1929 On* (Boston: Little, Brown, 1959), p. 168.

2 Langford, op. cit., Appendix C, Table 26.

CHAPTER 7 / PERINEAL CLEANSING

1 J. G. Bourke, *Scatalogical Rites of All Nations* (Washington, D.C.: W. H. Lowdermilk & Co., 1891), p. 141.

CHAPTER 8 / SOCIAL AND PSYCHOLOGICAL ASPECTS OF ELIMINATION

1 See: M. Douglas, *Purity and Danger* (New York: Praeger, 1966) for a thorough analysis of the problems of ritual pollution and defilement. This is also reflected in the fact that among drug users marijuana is referred to as either "pot" or "shit," a significant choice of terms. See: R. Blum et al., *Utopiates* (New York: Atherton Press, 1964), pp. 240, 241.

2 See: Alex Comfort, *The Anxiety Makers* (London: T. Nelson & Sons, Ltd., 1967), pp. 123–144, for an account of some of our more excessive preoccupations with literal and symbolic purges.

3 A. T. Jersild, *Child Psychology,* 4th ed. (Englewood Cliffs: Prentice-Hall, Inc, 1954), p. 138.

4 Franz Alexander, *Psychosomatic Medicine* (New York: W. W. Norton & Co., Inc, 1950), p. 117.

5 J. Gathorne-Hardy, *The Rise and Fall of the British Nanny* (London: Hodder and Stoughton, 1972), p. 264.

6 R. Fliess, *Erogeneity and Libido* (New York: International Universities Press, Inc., 1956), pp. 116–117.

7 Havelock Ellis, op. cit., vol. 2, p. 407.

8 G. C. Hill, "In Vegas, Glitter Gulch Finds Lunchbox Trade Beats High-Rollers," *The Wall Street Journal,* May 22, 1972, p. 1.

9 For a thorough cataloguing of mankind's attitudes toward, and uses of, excretory products, see: Rosebury, op. cit.; Bourke, op. cit.; Reynolds, op. cit.; Havelock Ellis, op. cit.

10 Readers seeking nostalgia or information are referred to: C. Sale, *The Specialist* (London: Putnam & Co., 1969); and W. R. Greer, *Gems of American Architecture* (St. Paul, Minnesota: Brown & Bigelow, 1935).

11 A. Dundes, "Here I Sit—A Study of American Latrinalia," *Kroeber Anthropological Society Papers,* no. 34, Spring 1966, p. 103. As Dundes further notes: in our culture, the emphasis is on "productivity" and a man "must *make* much more than feces. He must *make* something of himself and he must *make* a living." Largely, this rests on the hypothesis of male pregnancy-envy in which men substitute other "productions," i.e.: feces, "my brainchild," a pet project as "my baby," and so forth. In particular, see Bruno Bettelheim, *Symbolic Wounds* (New York: Collier, 1962).

12 For more illustrations of our society's attitudes and counterculture exploitations of them, see Jerry Rubin, *Do It!* (New York: Simon and Schuster, 1970).

13 For an amusing commentary on this subject, see Mark Twain, *1601, or Conversation As It Was by the Fireside in the Time of the Tudors* (New York: Golden Hind Press, 1933).

14 David Halberstam, *The Best and the Brightest* (New York: Random House, 1972), p. 434.

15 For a fascinating history of Mr. Crapper's work, see: Reyburn, op. cit. For many, many more examples of "dirty" words see: G. Jennings, *Personalities of Language* (New York: T. Y. Crowell Co., 1965); P. Fryer, *Mrs. Grundy—Studies in English Prudery* (New York: London House & Maxwell, 1964); A. Montague, *The Anatomy of Swearing* (New York: The Macmillan Co., 1967); E. Sagarin, *The Anatomy of Dirty Words* (New York: Lyle Stuart, 1962); M. Pei, *Words in Sheep's Clothing* (New York: Hawthorn, 1969); R. Hartogs, *Four-Letter Word Games* (New York: Dell, 1967); A. Barzman et al, *The Nice (and Naughty) Book* (New York: Bantam Books, 1965); and, of course, an unexpurgated edition of Rabelais' *Gargantua and Pantagruel* for really imaginative vocabulary.

16 J. Pudney, *The Smallest Room* (London: Michael Joseph, 1954), pp. 78, 79.

17 For both examples and a fascinating analysis see G. Legman, *Rationale of the Dirty Joke* (New York: Grove Press, 1968) and especially the forthcoming second volume, which will deal with scatological themes.

18 S. Walker, *Mrs. Astor's Horse* (New York: F. A. Stokes Co., 1935), pp. 165, 166.

19 See Art Buchwald, "No-Flush Law," *Los Angeles Times,* November 24, 1970.

20 J. A. Tannenbaum, "Some Nostalgic Alums Buy a Whole Lot More Than Old School Ties," *The Wall Street Journal,* December 6, 1972, p. 1. The article also closes with the observation that "You can sell a pile of horse manure if you put the name 'Notre Dame' on it."

21 *Time,* vol. 82, no. 9, August 30, 1963, p. 27.

22 Havelock Ellis, op. cit., pp. 392, 393.

23 Halberstam, op. cit., p. 532.

24 Fliess, op. cit., p. 170.

25 Albert Ellis, *The Folklore of Sex* (New York: Charles Boni, 1951), pp. 122–123.

26 Havelock Ellis, op. cit., vol. I, part 1, p. 52.

27 Langford, op. cit., pp. 72, 75, 76.

28 C. M. Turnbull, *The Mountain People* (New York: Simon and Schuster, 1972), p. 253.

29 See I. Buchen, ed., *The Perverse Imagination: Sexuality and Literary Culture* (New York: New York University Press, 1970).

30 Havelock Ellis, op. cit., vol. 1, part 1, p. 63.

31 Langford, op. cit., pp. 23–25.

32 H. Aaron, *Our Common Ailment* (New York: Dodge Publishing Co., 1938), p. 39.

33 For a more nearly complete discussion of this "off-bounds" aspect of the bathroom, see pp. 206–208 and also, of course, Roth, op. cit.

34 W. H. Parry, "Bottle Hunters Find New Mother Lode: The Outhouse," *National Observer,* February 26, 1972, p. 15.

35 *Infant Care,* U.S. Children's Bureau Publication No. 8, Washington, D.C.: U.S. Government Printing Office, 1926.

36 Gathorne-Hardy, op. cit., pp. 262, 263.

37 See: D. G. Prugh, "Childhood Experience and Colonic Disorder," *Annals of The New York Academy of Sciences,* vol. 58, art. 4, 1954, pp. 355–376; and W. H. Sewell, "Infant Training and the Personality of the Child," *The American Journal of Sociology,* vol. 58, no. 2, 1952, pp. 150–159.

38 Jersild, op. cit., pp. 140–141.

39 P. H. Mussen, and J. J. Conger, *Child Development and Personality* (New York: Harper and Bros., 1956), p. 198.

40 R. S. Stewart and A. D. Workman, *Children and Other People: Achieving Maturity Through Learning* (New York: The Dryden Press, 1956), p. 38.

41 T. P. Almy, "Physiological and Psychological Factors in the Production of Constipation," *Annals of The New York Academy of Sciences,* vol. 58, art. 4, 1954, p. 401.

42 Unpublished data, Cornell Survey of Personal Hygiene Attitudes and Practices in 1,000 Middle-Class Households.

43 Aaron, op. cit., p. 69.

44 See: Karl Abraham, "Contributions to the Theory of the Anal Character," in *Selected Papers of Karl Abraham* (London: The Hogarth Press, 1948), pp. 370–392; Otto Fenichel, "The Scoptophilic Instinct and Identification," in *The Collected Papers of Otto Fenichel: Series 1* (New York: W. W. Norton & Co., Inc., 1953), pp. 373–397; and Ernst Jones, "Anal-Erotic Character Traits," in *Papers on Psychoanalysis* (Boston: Beacon Press, 1961), pp. 413–427.

CHAPTER 9 / ANATOMY AND PHYSIOLOGY OF DEFECATION

1 H. L. Bockus, *Gastro-Enterology* (Philadelphia: W. B. Saunders Co., 1944), vol. 2, p. 469. See also: P. B. Hawk, B. L. Oser, and W. H. Summerson, *Practical Physiological Chemistry,* 13th ed. (New York: The Blakiston Co., Inc., 1954), p. 446.

2 Bockus, op. cit., p. 508.

3 *A Study of Health Practices and Opinions,* Report No. FDA-PA-72-01, Food and Drug Administration, U.S. Department of Health, Education, and Welfare, Washington, D.C., June 1972.

4 E. S. Nasset, "The Physiology of the Alimentary Tract: Colon," *Medical Physiology,* 11th ed., Philip Bard, ed. (St. Louis, Missouri: The C. V. Mosby Co., 1961), p. 446.

5 T. P. Almy, "Introduction to the Colon: Its Normal and Abnormal Physiology and Therapeutics," *Annals of The New York Academy of Sciences,* vol. 58, art. 4, 1954, p. 295.

6 In the 1966 Cornell Survey of Personal Hygiene Attitudes and Practices in 1,000 Middle-Class Households, 14 per cent of the respondents reported suffering from hemorrhoids, second only to arthritis, which was reported by 17 per cent.

7 J. G. Benton and H. A. Rusk, "The Patient with Cardiovascular Disease and Rehabilitation: The Third Phase of Medical Care," *Circulation,* vol. 8, 1953, pp. 417–426.

8 Bockus, op. cit., p. 511.

9 F. A. Hornibrook, *The Culture of the Abdomen* (Garden City, New York: Doubleday, Doran & Co., Inc., 1933), pp. 75–76.

10 J. R. Williams, *Personal Hygiene Applied,* 4th ed. (Philadelphia: W. B. Saunders Co., 1932), p. 374.

11 Aaron, op. cit., pp. 66–67.

12 See: G. W. Hewes, "World Distribution of Certain Postural Habits," *American Anthropologist,* vol. 57, 1955, pp. 231–244.

13 E. G. Wagner and J. H. Lanoix, *Excreta Disposal for Rural Areas and Small Communities* (Geneva: World Health Organization, 1958).

14 Bockus, op. cit., pp. 518, 521.

CHAPTER 10 / DESIGN CRITERIA FOR DEFECATION

1 H. T. E. Hertzberg, "Some Contributions of Applied Physical Anthropology to Human Engineering," *Annals of the New York Academy of Sciences,* vol. 63, art. 4, 1955, p. 629. See also: C. A. Dempsey et al., "The Human Factors of Long Range Flight," *Journal of Aviation Medicine,* vol. 27, February 1956, pp. 18–22.

2 B. Akerblom, "Chairs and Sitting," *Symposium on Human Factors in Equipment Design,* W. F. Floyd and A. T. Welford, eds. (London: H. K. Lewis & Co., Ltd., 1954), p. 30. See also: E. A. Hooton, *A Survey in Seating* (Gardner, Massachusetts: Heywood-Wakefield Co., 1945); W. E. Lay and L. C. Fisher, "Riding Comfort and Cushions," *S. A. E. Transactions,* vol. 35, 1940, pp. 482–496; S. Lippert, "Designing for Comfort in Aircraft Seats," *Aeronautical Engineering Review,* vol. 9, no. 2, 1950, pp. 39–41; R. A. McFarland et al, *Human Body Size and Capabilities in the Design and Operation of Vehicular Equipment* (Boston: Harvard School of Public Health, 1953), pp. 129–141; C. A. Ridder, *Basic Design Measurements for Sitting* (Fayetteville: University of Arkansas Agricultural Experiment Station Bulletin 616, October 1959).

3 I. L. McClelland, *The Ergonomics of W. C. Pans* (Loughborough, England: Institute for Consumer Ergonomics, Ltd., May 1973).

4 U.S. Patent No. 3,383,710; Stillwater Development Co., New York City.

5 Among the survey respondents, for example, 34 per cent flushed while seated and 66 per cent after standing up. Unpublished data, Cornell Survey of Personal Hygiene Attitudes and Practices in 1,000 Middle-Class Households.

6 Langford, op. cit., p. 59.

CHAPTER 11 / ANATOMY AND PHYSIOLOGY OF URINATION

1 Homer W. Smith, *The Kidney—Structure and Function in Health and Disease* (New York: Oxford University Press, 1951).

2 J. L. Despert, "Urinary Control and Enuresis," *Psychosomatic Medicine,* vol. 6, no. 4, 1944, p. 294.

3 Ellis reported a maximum distance of 915 mm (36 inches) achieved by leaning back and holding the labia apart. Havelock Ellis, "The Bladder as a Dynamometer," *American Journal of Dermatology and Genito-Urinary Diseases,* vol. 6, no. 3, May 1902, p. 91.

4 Legman, op. cit., p. 335.

5 Ibid., p. 336.

CHAPTER 12 / DESIGN CRITERIA FOR URINATION

1 H. Graus, "A Scientific Approach to Military Plumbing Fixture Requirements," *Air Conditioning, Heating and Ventilating,* February 1957, p. 96.

2 Langford, op. cit., pp. 29, 30.

CHAPTER 13 / OTHER BATHROOM ACTIVITIES

1 "Personal Care Power," *Housewares,* November 1973, p. 20.

2 See: Ellen Frankfort, "Health Forum: Vaginal Politics," *The Village Voice,* November 25, 1971, pp. 6, 74; and Boston Women's Health Book Collective, *Our Bodies, Ourselves* (New York: Simon and Schuster, 1973).

3 Langford, op. cit., pp. 51, 52.

4 Among the survey respondents, for example, approximately three-quarters used water for removing makeup and one-quarter used it for applying makeup. Ibid., p. 51. Also see: *Farmhouse Planning Guides* (Ithaca, New York: Cornell University Agricultural Experiment Station and New York State College of Home Economics in association with Cornell University Housing Research Center, 1959) for data on the extent of the performance of hygiene and grooming activities in the various parts of the house. See especially Part II.

5 Langford, op. cit., p. 63.

6 S. Braun, "Let's Make a Deal," *Playboy,* March 1973, p. 176.

7 Survey respondents indicated that approximately 40 per cent of their children played in the bathroom in one way or another. Langford, op. cit., pp. 55, 56.

8 Ibid., pp. 28, 29.

9 Ibid., pp. 50, 60.

CHAPTER 14 / SOCIAL AND PSYCHOLOGICAL ASPECTS OF BATHROOM DESIGN

1 J. H. S. Bossard and E. S. Boll, *Ritual in Family Living* (Philadelphia: University of Pennsylvania Press, 1950), pp. 113–114. In this connection, also see Langford, op. cit., pp. 23–25, for a discussion of the particulars of bathroom-sharing practices.

2 Bossard and Boll, op. cit., p. 114.

3 Langford, op. cit., pp. 78–80.

4 D. Lee, "Are Basic Needs Ultimate?", *Personality in Nature, Society and Culture,* 2nd ed., Clyde Kluckholn and H. A. Murray, eds. (New York: Alfred A. Knopf, 1956), p. 339.

5 F. S. Chapin, "Some Housing Factors Related to Mental Hygiene," *Journal of Social Issues,* vol. 7, nos. 1 and 2, 1951, p. 165.

6 Ibid.

7 Langford, op. cit., pp. 18–21.

8 See: Erving Goffman, *The Presentation of Self* (New York: Doubleday Anchor, 1959), pp. 107–140.

9 For a most amusing description of our foibles see Horace Miner's famous "Body Ritual Among the Nacirema," *American Anthropologist,* vol. 58, 1956, pp. 503–507; also the poems "The Geography of the House" and "Encomium Balnei," in W. H. Auden, *About the House* (New York: Random House, 1965).

10 R. W. Kennedy, *The House and the Art of Its Design* (New York: Reinhold Publishing Co., 1953), p. 258.

11 Gio Ponti, *In Praise of Architecture* (New

York: F. W. Dodge Corp., 1960), p. 143. Mr. Ponti was the designer of the beautiful equipment for Ideal-Standard that he refers to.

12 J. R. Adams, "Open Dorms and Co-ed Bathrooms," *The Wall Street Journal,* October 9, 1973, p. 26.

13 J. R. Bishop, "'Hey Look—It's a Bird!' 'It's a Plane!' 'No. It's . . . It's a Dirty Picture!' Plaque Meant to Show What Earthlings Look Like Upsets Some Real Earthlings," *The Wall Street Journal,* May 23, 1972, p. 1.

14 Alexander Kira, "The Case for the Live-in Bathroom," *House & Garden,* May 1972, p. 108.

15 Hicks, op. cit.; Gilliatt, op. cit.

16 Keynote address by Bill Blass at National Bath Products Show, New York City, May 1973.

CHAPTER 15 / DESIGN CRITERIA FOR COMPLETE HYGIENE FACILITIES

1 For specific planning assistance the reader has available a number of references: the books on bathroom design by Gilliatt and Hicks mentioned earlier; J. F. Schram, *Modern Bathrooms* (A Sunset Book) (Menlo Park, California: Lane Books, 1968); J. Manser, *Bathrooms* (London: Studio Vista, Ltd., 1969); G. Goulden, *Bathrooms* (London: Macdonald & Co., Ltd., 1966); *Badrum* (Stockholm: Forlags AB Hem i Sverige, 1970); W. Holzbach, *Das Moderne Bad in Alt-und Neubauten* (Munchen: Udo Pfriemer Verlag Gmbh, 1969); as well as numerous publications issued by various governmental agencies and universities.

2 Langford, op. cit., pp. 81–83.

3 See: W. H. Auden, "Mirror," *Vogue,* December 1962, pp. 116, 117, 180, 181, 182; A. Ogden, "The Praise of Mirrors," *Harper's Bazaar,* September 1961, pp. 279–281; Lewis Mumford, *Technics and Civilization* (New York: Harcourt Brace and Co., 1934), pp. 128–131.

4 See: *Performance Characteristics for Sanitary Plumbing Fixtures* (Washington, D.C.: Building Research Advisory Board, National Academy of Sciences–National Research Council, February 1968).

5 Langford, op. cit., pp. 29–30.

6 See: "Evaluation of Methods and Fixtures Used for Bathroom Mirror Lighting," *Illuminating Engineering,* vol. 42, December 1947, pp. 999–1024; "Lighting a Lavatory and Vanity Counter," *Illuminating Engineering,* vol. 49, July 1954, p. 360; "Lighting a Bathroom," *Illuminating Engineering,* vol. 49, August 1954, p. 401; "Lighting a Bath and Health Room," *Illuminating Engineering,* vol. 51, March 1956, p. 267.

7 J. Routh, *The Guide Porcelaine—The Loos of Paris* (London: Wolfe Publishing, Ltd., 1966), p. 14.

8 For an excellent summary of current examples of the application of prefabrication to the bathroom, see: C. A. Visser, *Kunststoftoepassingen voor Sanitair* (Rotterdam: Bouwcentrum, 1966).

CHAPTER 16 / HISTORICAL ASPECTS OF PUBLIC FACILITIES

1 Bourke, op. cit., p. 143.

2 See: pp. 95–96.

3 Reynolds, op. cit., p. 324.

4 Wright, op. cit., p. 76.

5 For a detailed and well-illustrated history see: Claude Gaillard, *les Vespasiennes de Paris ou les Pricieux Edicules* (Paris: Editions de la Jeune Parque, 1967).

6 Wright, op. cit., p. 201.

7 D. H. Beetle, "Comfort is Expensive," *The Ithaca Journal,* Ithaca, New York, September 16, 1968, p. 8.

8 Bernard Rudofsky, *Streets for People* (New York: Doubleday and Co., Inc., 1969), p. 301.

CHAPTER 17 / SOCIAL AND PSYCHOLOGICAL ASPECTS OF PUBLIC FACILITIES

1 See: R. G. Coss, "The Cut-Off Hypothesis: Its Relevance to the Design of Public Places," *Man-Environment Systems,* vol. 3, no. 6, November 1973.

2 Erving Goffman, *Relations in Public* (New York: Basic Books, 1971), pp. 28–61.

3 A. B. Friedman, "The Scatological Rites of Burglars," *Western Folklore,* vol. 27, July 1968, pp. 171–179. Also see Erving Goffman's analyses of modalities of violations and the territories of "use," "stall," and "turn," which are all involved in this situation.

4 Bourke, op. cit., p. 139.

5 Halberstam, op. cit., pp. 435–436.

6 "Jack Paar's Suite Cost $50,000," *The Ithaca Journal,* Ithaca, New York, December 8, 1972.

7 M. Kulley, *Johns in Europe—Toilet Training for Tourists* (Los Angeles: Coraco, 1970).

8 H. N. Brandeis, "The Psychology of Scatological Privacy," *Journal of Biological Psychology,* December, 1972, vol. 14, no. 2, pp. 30–35.

9 A. Sherman, *The Rape of the A. P. E.* (Chicago: Playboy Press, 1973), pp. 70, 71.

10 D. Crawford and A. Williams, "Public Inconveniences," *Design,* September 1966, no. 213, pp. 32–43.

11 D. S. Brown, "Planning the Powder Room," *AIA Journal,* April 1967, pp. 81–83.

12 R. Rapoport, "Electronic Alligators," *Saturday Review of the Sciences,* March 1973, p. 37.

13 "The Playboy Interview," *Playboy,* March 1972, p. 172.

14 Also see: L. Jones, "The Toilet" in *The Baptism and The Toilet* (New York: Grove Press, 1963). One approach to solving these problems recently taken by the San Francisco Bay Area Rapid Transit System is to provide a series of single-occupant bathrooms.

15 Turnbull, op. cit., p. 127.

16 See: "The Peephole Problem," *Time,* November 12, 1965, pp. 59–61; and P. Kyler, "Camera Surveillance of Sex Deviates," *Law and Order,* November 1963, p. 16.

17 See: P. McGarvey, *C. I. A.: The Myth and Madness* (New York: Saturday Review Press, 1972), p. 53.

18 See particularly: R. Reisner, *Graffiti: Two Thousand Years of Wall Writing* (New York: Cowles, 1971); and Dundes, op. cit., pp. 91–105.

19 See: R. Ricklefs, "Co-Co 144's Underground Art School," *The Wall Street Journal,* April 26, 1973, p. 24; and Norman Mailer, *The Faith of Graffiti* (New York: Praeger Publishers, Inc., 1974).

20 R. Sommer, *Design Awareness* (San Francisco: Rinehart Press, 1972), p. 58.

21 Dundes, op. cit., p. 101.

22 See: Jones, op. cit., pp. 413–437; and Sandor Ferenczi, "The Ontogenesis of the Interest in Money" in *Sex in Psychoanalysis* (New York: Dover, 1956), pp. 269–279.

23 Havelock Ellis, op. cit., p. 398.

24 J. Routh with S. Stewart. *The Better John Guide—Where to Go in New York* (New York: G. P. Putnam's Sons, 1966). J. Routh, *The Good Loo Guide—Where to Go in London* (London: Wolfe Publishing, Ltd., 1968 rev.); J. Routh, *The Guide Porcelaine—The Loos of Paris* (London: Wolfe Publishing, Ltd., 1966).

25 Sherman, op. cit., p. 31.

26 *The New Yorker,* vol. 10, no. 24, July 28, 1934, p. 9.

27 B. Calame, "Brother, Can You Spare a Dime? Group Assails Pay Toilets," *The Wall Street Journal,* April 23, 1973, p. 1.

28 "Be Prepared," *Playboy,* May 1973, p. 20.

CHAPTER 18 / PLANNING AND DESIGN CRITERIA FOR PUBLIC FACILITIES

1 See: Crawford and Williams, op. cit., pp. 32–43.

2 See: McCall et al., op. cit., for a more detailed examination of such a transient terminal facility.

3 "Letters—Prison Design," *American Institute of Architect's Journal,* January 1974, p. 63.

CHAPTER 19 / DESIGN CRITERIA FOR PUBLIC-FACILITY EQUIPMENT

1 McCall et al. op. cit.

2 J. Crisp and A. Sobolev, "Water and Fuel Economy—The Use of Spray Taps for Ablution in Buildings," *Royal Institute of British Architect's Journal,* vol. 62, July 1956, pp. 386–388. See also: "Sanitation Standards," *Architectural Record,* vol. 81, January 1937, p. 43.

3 McCall et al, op. cit.

4 Reyburn, op. cit., p. 37.

5 J. Routh, *The Guide Porcelaine—The Loos of Paris,* pp. 17–18.

6 Data, courtesy of Adamsez, Ltd.

7 Havelock Ellis, op. cit., pp. 469–470.

8 W. McK. H. McCullagh, "The Gap Seat," *The Lancet,* April 4, 1953, p. 698; and L. Laakso and K. Kunnas, "Trichomoniasis," *Annales Chirurgiae et Gynaecologiae Fenniae,* vol. 54, no. 3, 1965, pp. 351–354.

9 H. M. Darlow and W. R. Bale, "Infective Hazards of Water Closets," *The Lancet,* June 6, 1959, pp. 1196–1200; J. A. Burgess, "Trichomonas Vaginalis Infection from Splashing in Water Closets," *British Journal of Venereal Diseases,* vol.

39, no. 4, December 1963, pp. 248–250, and "Infection and the Water Closet," *British Medical Journal,* June 13, 1964, pp. 1523–1524.

CHAPTER 20 / SOCIAL AND PSYCHOLOGICAL ASPECTS OF DISABILITY

1 *Limitation of Activity Due to Chronic Conditions: United States, 1969 and 1970,* Series 10, No. 80; and *Current Estimates from the Health Interview Survey: United States—1972,* Series 10, No. 85, National Center for Health Statistics, U.S. Department of Health, Education, and Welfare, Washington, D.C.

2 *Facts on the Major Crippling and Killing Diseases in the United States Today* (New York: The National Health Education Committee, Inc., 1966).

3 N. Ulman, "Aiding the Injured: Insurers Rehabilitate Accident Cases, Allow Prepayment on Claims," *The Wall Street Journal,* January 13, 1967, p. 1.

4 B. D. Daitz, "The Challenge of Disability," *American Journal of Public Health,* vol. 55, no. 4, April 1965, p. 531. Also see: J. Mermey, "Denying the Handicapped: The Trap of 'Hospitalitis'," *The Village Voice,* January 19–25, 1973, p. 1.

5 D. Schwartz, "Problems of Self-Care and Travel Among Elderly Ambulatory Patients," *American Journal of Nursing,* vol. 66, no. 12, December 1966, p. 2680.

6 See: M. Douglas, *Purity and Danger* (New York: Praeger, 1966); B. Wright, *Physical Disability—A Psychological Approach* (New York: Harper and Row, 1960); and Erving Goffman, *Stigma: Notes on the Management of Spoiled Identity* (Englewood Cliffs, New Jersey: Prentice-Hall, Inc., 1963).

CHAPTER 21 / DESIGN CRITERIA FOR PERSONAL HYGIENE FACILITIES FOR THE AGED AND DISABLED

1 A tub based on the first approach is available from Safe-T-Bath, Inc., Tulsa, Oklahoma, U.S.A., and one based on the second from Medic-Bath, Ltd., Manchester, England.

2 For detailed space requirements, see: S. Goldsmith, *Designing for the Disabled,* 2nd ed. (New York: McGraw-Hill, 1967); and the national standards and codes of one's respective country that apply to facilities for aged and disabled persons.

INDEX